In the Night's Cool Air, Temptation Blooms . . .

Maggie heard Matthew making his way to her loft and closed her eyes, feigning sleep. For a long moment he simply knelt beside her bed, watching her. Maggie could hear him breathing, and her skin tingled knowing he was close enough for her to reach out and touch. She dared not open her eyes. She had to make him believe she slept, for she had no doubt as to the outcome of this night should he learn the truth.

Maggie almost jumped when Matthew's fingers gently brushed aside the heavy lock of her hair that had fallen and hid half her face from his view. She was amazed that he couldn't hear the thunder of her heart, for it grew in volume and strength with each lingering touch. And by the time his lone finger had touched upon the rapidly pounding pulse at her throat, she could deny no longer her need.

With a low growl, his warm mouth covered hers and Maggie gave up any pretense of sleep. With a soft cry her lips opened beneath his and her arms reached out hungrily to pull him to her . . .

Books by Patricia Pellicane

Charity's Pride
Desire's Rebel
Whispers in the Wind

Published by POCKET BOOKS

Desire's Rebel

Patricia Pellicane

PUBLISHED BY POCKET BOOKS NEW YORK

This novel is a work of historical fiction. Names, characters, places and incidents relating to non-historical figures are either the product of the author's imagination or are used fictitiously. Any resemblance of such non-historical incidents, places or figures to actual events or locales or persons, living or dead, is entirely coincidental.

Another *Original* publication of POCKET BOOKS

POCKET BOOKS, a division of Simon & Schuster, Inc.
1230 Avenue of the Americas, New York, N.Y. 10020

ISBN: 0-671-63092-X

First Pocket Books printing July 1987

10 9 8 7 6 5 4 3 2 1

POCKET and colophon are registered trademarks
of Simon & Schuster, Inc.

Printed in the U.S.A.

To Barbara Bretton
who gave me the most
precious of gifts—
her friendship

Preface

"I will tell you what I have done. My only brother I have sent to camp with my prayers. Had I twenty sons and brothers, they should go. I have retrenched every superfluous expense in my table and family; tea I have not drunk since last Christmas, nor bought a new cap or gown since your defeat at Lexington. I know this—that as free I can die but once; but as slave I shall not be worthy of life. These are the sentiments of all my sister Americans. . . . What must glow in the breasts of our husbands, brothers and sons! They are as with one heart determined to be free. What we fight for is this plain truth: That no man has a right to take our money without our consent. It is written with a sunbeam. . . . We shall be unworthy of the blessings of Heaven if we ever submit."

So wrote a woman of Revolutionary days. Her name is lost; her cause was not.

Encyclopaedia Britannica
Library Research Service

Desire's Rebel

═══ One ═══

"Yᴏᴜ ʙʟᴏᴏᴅʏ ʙᴀsᴛᴀʀᴅ!" Mᴀɢɢɪᴇ raged in breathless horror as she fought a desperate battle against the blackness that threatened to overtake her consciousness. Her slanted brandy-gold eyes narrowed with hatred and glowed like the yellow flame of a tallow light in the dimly lit parlor. Her soft pink lips thinned into a stiff white line as she snarled between clenched teeth, "I could kill you for this!"

Caleb laughed with gloating satisfaction as he watched his wife's body tremble with a rage that knew no bounds. Her hands clenched into fists and opened again. She wanted to smash something . . . anything! She wanted to scream out her fury and frustration, but most of all she wanted to tear his eyes out.

For one delicious moment he felt a surge of happiness unequaled. It seemed he was capable of stirring the bitch after all. He cared not about the extent of the hardships he had brought down on them. Her loss of composure alone was worth all they would suffer.

Maggie's mind raced, repeating again and again his carelessly spoken words, "I lost the farm, lost the farm, lost the farm," until its echoing song formed one continuous chant in the far recesses of her mind and she began to fear the mindless rage that took hold of her brain and caused a

1

cold trembling throughout her body. Her words were no idle threat. In her heart she knew she could easily kill him, and the knowledge brought stark terror to her gentle soul.

Maggie fought against the foreign tendency toward violence. A few moments later, after many deep, calming breaths, she finally managed to regain her composure.

Dear God, what was she to do? Her childhood home, the only home she had ever known, was gone. He had lost everything! All the years of endless chores and backbreaking work, the years of hope, of dreams, all lost forever.

Her thin shoulders slumped with sudden despair. She felt whipped and broken, hardly able to stand under the heaviest weight of weariness she had ever known.

God, what a disaster her life had become, and she could only imagine it growing worse. She wanted to cry out and beat her fists against his smug, sulky mouth. She couldn't start again. She couldn't! Even had she the will, she had not the strength, for her hands and back just weren't enough. Maggie could almost feel her soul shrivel and go dry like an autumn leaf, and for the first time in her twenty-eight years she felt incredibly old.

Tears of despair misted her eyes as dismal clouds of pain and fear settled themselves over her family's future like the darkness of a coming storm. *Get hold of yourself, Maggie. Think of Joseph. At the very least, the child deserves a roof over his head. Think! Where will you go? What will you do?*

Maggie closed her eyes, searching for an inner strength. Good God, did all the responsibility have to fall on her shoulders? What would become of them? How was she supposed to care for an invalid husband, a six-year-old son, an elderly aunt, and herself, and do it all without a home to call their own?

In an unguarded moment Maggie allowed her carefully secreted hatred for this useless excuse of a husband, the object of her torment for the last six years, to show. A sad smile touched the corners of her mouth as she remembered a time when she had thought this sneering man so handsome. Naively, she had believed she would always love him. But he had changed all that. Through years of abusing his family, he had managed to destroy every tender feeling she had ever known. And Maggie knew in her heart she had neither the power nor the will to ever love a man again.

For an instant she thought the dimness of the room was affecting her eyes, for she could have sworn his blue gaze danced with laughter. Maggie pushed aside the nonsensical thought and allowed the strength born of anger to suffuse her body. Her back stiffened with pride. She'd not allow this man to witness her defeat. She would see them through this or die in the attempt. What alternative was there? Beyond the staggering fear that raged through her mind an idea began to form. Perhaps there was a way. If she could go to the new owner and tell him of her family's plight. Would he listen? She'd damned well make sure he did. But would he care? She'd do anything to keep her family together. It didn't matter what was asked of her. She'd do it.

"Where is he? What is his name? I'm going to talk to him."

"Your efforts would be wasted, madam." Caleb sighed wearily, already sick of the subject. "He'll not listen to you, nor care of our woes. He cheated to get this farm. He'll never give it up."

Maggie stared, her mouth open in shock. "Can you not go to the authorities? Surely he cannot be allowed to get away with this."

Caleb shot her a look of contempt. "Indeed, you are a stupid woman, Maggie. I can prove nothing. The farm belongs to him."

"How long before he takes possession?" she asked dully, her mind already seeing to the packing of the few things she held dear.

"Immediately," Caleb responded almost happily. Maggie's eyes narrowed as she realized his unmistakable enjoyment of her suffering. So, he hated her so much he found enjoyment in this disaster. He seemed almost happy watching her misery. Her spine stiffened further yet, and she vowed silently, *We shall see, Caleb. We shall see which of us has the last laugh.*

Caleb Darrah watched from the keeping-room window as his wife of ten years mounted the despised animal's back in one effortless swoop. His face contorted with disgust for both horse and rider. It had been six years since that beast had tried to kill him. Six years since his hands and body had claimed the golden flesh of its traitorous rider. Six years of ever-growing hatred.

God in heaven, but he loathed her and that devil of a horse she had refused to destroy. He'd never forgive or forget her accusing look once he had regained consciousness. She had actually found him at fault. She had gone so far as to charge him with cruelty! Why, it was almost laughable. Just because he had taken a whip to the beast. For Christ's sake, he had brought untold numbers of horses to obedience. But that damned animal was just as obstinate as its mistress. He wished the two of them to hell.

Jesus Christ, where was Jack? He had to get out of there. He needed Peggy and her expertise, and he needed her now. Good God, but she was a toss that would send any man's piece to throbbing. When he was in her bed he didn't even notice the uselessness of his legs. He could feel himself growing hard just remembering their last time together. She had gotten so wild for him that it had taken his tender member almost a week to recover from the ecstasy her mouth had brought.

A mean smile brought his surly mouth into a tight line. Maggie—sweet, docile, vacant Maggie. She thought him incapable of pleasuring a woman. Just because he had refused her advances, she believed that part of his body as useless as his legs. Above all else, he longed to throw his visits to Peggy in her face, but he dared not. Maggie took much abuse from him, abuse deservedly bestowed, he reasoned, but he suspected she'd not ignore his infidelities. She might even go so far as to put him out.

Even though everything she owned had become his upon their marriage, what could he, a cripple, do to stop her if she chose to support him no longer?

A small smile of revenge touched the corners of his once handsome mouth. It was almost worth the loss of the farm just to be rid of that horse. To witness Maggie's torment at parting with her prized animal would be the ultimate reward.

"I've not yet done, Maggie, my girl," he promised as she and the horse mounted a distant hill and disappeared behind its gentle rise.

Maggie stepped into the cool, damp barn and breathed deeply of nature's scents: drying hay, horseflesh, and rich, moist earth. She did not cry. In six years she had never allowed herself the luxury. The years since Caleb's accident had hardened her heart. His vile curses left her empty. His slaps went unnoticed. She could stare through him and walk away, his words leaving her as dry and dead as kindling.

But now, as her gaze moved lovingly over the wooden stalls and she walked toward the dark red stallion that snickered its welcome, she gave in to the aching pain. Harsh, wracking sobs tore through her slender body. She buried her face in the warm, silky side of her best friend and choked out in a broken voice, "Oh God, Red, how am I to bear it?"

She wondered if a heart could break from sorrow, for the knifelike pain that gripped her chest in   breathless hold was unbearably intense. For an instant she thought of giving up, but the image of Joseph came to her mind, and she knew she had to go on.

After a time she managed to gain control of her emotions. Even though she was very much alone, since Elijah was nowhere to be seen, Maggie felt her cheeks color with embarrassment at her weak and tearful display. With new-found resolve that somehow all would work out, she attempted a smile and wiped away the last of her tears on the sleeve of her shirt. What she needed was to clear her mind and think. And she knew of no better way of doing that than to ride.

Maggie saddled Red and brought him outside. Her thoughts returned to the man who, no doubt, watched from inside the house. There was a time when she had loved him dearly. Later she had pitied him. Now she felt nothing but contempt. His hatred and cruelty had made their lives a living hell, and she had been powerless to prevent it.

She had not returned to their bedroom, not even to clean it, since the night some months after his injury when she had sought to bring him some measure of relief and had been labeled "slut" for her efforts. Each night she shared a pallet in the kitchen with Joseph and slept comfortably enough with her child snuggled in her arms. Maggie knew of Caleb's visits to Peggy, but she cared not. It was simply still more reason to find disgust in his person.

Despite her tormented state, Maggie's full, throaty laughter echoed sweetly over the swaying sea of tall meadow grass as she took the small hedge with the practiced ease of one long accustomed to the saddle. Fluffy, her constant companion since his birth, yapped in joyful exuberance as his small body squeezed through the thick foliage and continued after the racing horse.

Maggie's slender frame bent forward, and her long unbound hair slid from beneath her hat to become indistinguishable from the stallion's rich mahogany mane as the horse took yet another obstacle in its easy long-legged stride.

At a distance, but for the length of her hair, Maggie might have been taken for a young lad because she was dressed, as usual, in a white full-sleeved muslin shirt and man's trousers. Still, on closer inspection, such an error was laughable indeed, for her buff-colored trousers belted around a minuscule waist and hugged fully rounded and most decidedly feminine hips. Her breasts were full, so much so that they seemed at odds with the long leanness of her willowy body, and Maggie found herself self-conscious and often embarrassed when she was subjected to many a bold stare.

Maggie leaned low in the saddle and allowed the horse full rein. She felt the familiar and exciting surge of power as the animal's muscles bunched and stretched and its strong legs lunged forward with ever-increasing speed. The wind caught her hat and flung it behind her as it whistled through her hair, flinging the waist-length tresses into wild disarray. Her almond-shaped eyes half closed against the rush of air until she felt at last a lightening of the heaviness in her heart.

"Thank God for you, Red," she whispered close to her friend's ear. As always, a long ride on the animal's back could rid her of her sadness and wash away the disappointment of day-to-day life. And today, above all, she needed to forget what she would face on her return.

So engrossed was she in the pleasure of her ride that she never heard the heavy pounding of another horse's hooves as animal and rider strained to overtake her. Only when Maggie slowed as she approached a thicket of trees and underbrush did the trailing horse manage to come abreast.

Maggie was shocked into silence as a steely, viselike grip encircled her waist and lifted her effortlessly from her saddle. With a gasp, she found herself flying through the air and then landing with breath-stealing force on a heretofore unseen black horse. Mercifully, the horse was instantly brought to an abrupt halt, but no sooner had Maggie breathed a sigh of relief than she found herself tumbling to the ground amid a cloud of choking dust while emitting a most unladylike oath.

Her hair lay over her face, and in her stunned state she seemed unable to do more than simply watch as a pair of brown boots dismounted the raven horse and came to stand before her.

Fluffy, who had by this time caught up with his mistress, gave a series of warning growls aimed at the unseen stranger. But then, to Maggie's amazement and chagrin, Fluffy almost immediately sat beside his mistress and began the job of dislodging unwanted fleas from his thick fur.

Apparently, Fluffy sensed no danger, which was easy for him since huge brown hands were not reaching for his shoulders and lifting him to stand up on shaking legs. Maggie's shoulders were released, and those same hands proceeded to push aside the glorious tangle of curls that still covered her face.

Maggie's lips tightened over her straight teeth when she heard the amusement in his voice. "Are you all right?"

How dare he laugh when it was he who had caused her to fall in the first place? Angrily, Maggie shook off the fingers that had the audacity to touch her with such familiarity, and she snapped in an accusing tone, "I am, sir. And I insist you refrain from further interference."

Matthew Forrest grinned as he watched the woman he had just rescued from imminent death rudely push aside his offered comfort and take a step back.

In her efforts to be free of his insistent ministrations, Maggie took another step right into a small hole and once again landed on the softest part of her anatomy.

Matthew chuckled at her muttered "Damn" as he knelt at her side. Still unable to see her face because of the cloud of unruly curls that seemed forever in her eyes, he tried again to push aside the red mass. "Now I insist you accept my help."

"Help? Is that what you believe you have been offering? Sir," she growled through clenched teeth while pushing away his hand and taking a deep, calming breath— inadvertently pushing her breasts up against her shirt front—"I cannot remember the last time I fell. Today,

8

because of your *help*, it has happened twice. Please do me the honor of helping someone else."

At last, Maggie managed to push her disheveled locks aside. And as each saw for the first time the face of the other, they gave simultaneous gasps of astonishment, followed by a long moment of silence.

The sun shone warmly against their skin. A gentle breeze ruffled their hair and clothing. Birds flitted overhead, chirping merrily from branch to branch, and yet neither noticed the beautiful spring day as black eyes met gold with startling force.

Matthew's low words rumbled into a softly whispered caress as he leaned closer to study this vision of loveliness before him. "Are you telling me you had control of the horse?"

Maggie gave a soft gasp as the warmth of his clean breath teased her cheek and sent a wave of chills down her back. In her entire life she had never seen a man such as this. My God, he was big enough to block out all else from her vision and so striking she was helpless to do more than stare.

Maggie realized he had asked her a question. With nothing less than superhuman effort she managed to force aside the wild and ridiculous urge to lift her mouth toward his. Her voice was breathless and shaky as she asked, "What?"

Matthew grinned at her response and leaned closer still, his eyes never leaving the lushness of her parted lips. Lips that he somehow knew would be soft and yielding beneath his, the allure of which he had no intention of resisting. "Do you always ride so recklessly?"

"I take issue with your opinion, sir," Maggie managed while silently praying he'd take no notice of her trembling voice. "I often ride Red in such a manner and until today have suffered no ill effects."

Matthew only vaguely heard her softly spoken response. His whole body was attuned to her presence, and his mind registered little above his need of taking her here and now. God, but she was luscious. He wondered if she was as soft and sweet as the sound of her voice. He was dying to know who she was, but, more than that, he was dying to touch his lips to hers.

Maggie sat on the ground, her arms at her sides as if to brace herself against falling back, and watched in a trance-like state as his mouth came ever closer to her own. A voice warned in the back of her mind, *He is going to kiss you! Impossible!* another countered. Yet, no matter her denials, a man whose name she did not know was bringing his mouth toward hers, and she found herself helpless to stop it. More than that—she gasped as the truth made itself known—she found herself wanting to know the touch of him.

A tiny cry escaped her as his lips brushed lightly over hers. He had meant to test her reaction, but Matthew was mildly surprised to find it was he who was breathless with aching need, he who trembled with a desire that flared magically to life at her scent, and he who groaned with something close to pain as their lips parted only to join again with soft sighs.

It had been six years since she had known the touch of a man. Six long years without a gentle word or a lingering caress, but Maggie had thought her heart had hardened against these tender emotions and had gone so far as to convince herself that the absence was no loss. So she found herself astonished as the touch of his firm lips released a surge of longing she had no idea she had repressed.

Maggie's eyes opened wide with surprise. Her lips parted slightly in unconscious invitation, and her body was charged with new life and trembling with a yearning that knew not the meaning of propriety. She could no more have prevented her response to this man than she could have ordered herself to stop breathing.

She wanted him; of that neither had a doubt. Matthew groaned as he felt her tremble and knew her passion was as near to exploding as his. His arms reached around her waist and lifted her to her knees as he fused his mouth to hers.

For an instant Maggie stiffened with shock. Could this be happening? Could she be kneeling on the soft earth, allowing this stranger to hold her in his arms? To bring his mouth to hers? But her thoughts were fleeting at best, gone within the blink of an eye.

Her years of decent, proper behavior slipped into oblivion as if they had never been, and Maggie moaned a soft sigh of unexpected pleasure as his tongue parted her lips and slid along the smoothness of her teeth to tantalize the sensitive flesh just inside her lips. A tightness was forming across her abdomen, a tightness she had once known but had never found the means to appease.

She moaned again as his tongue slid further into her mouth to explore every warm crevice of that sweet, sensitive hollow. She had never known a man could kiss like this. How had she lived so long and never known?

Blood pulsed madly in her veins and caused a deafening roar in her ears. She was oblivious to her own whimpers of delight as her arms slid up his wide chest and her fingers closed around the back of his neck.

Maggie knew nothing but this moment and the deliciousness of this man's arms holding her body against his. Her mind, dazed with passion, realized only the wonder and the magic of his kiss and the clean, manly taste of his mouth. She never knew a mouth could hold such heat. She felt herself ignited, burning with a need she had never felt. She didn't care if she burst into flame; she had to have more.

A soft cry of loss slipped from her as he pulled his mouth away with a breathless gasp. His breathing was ragged as his lips moved gently over her cheek to her ear and down the golden column of her throat, sending thrills of wild excitement down her back. She never heard her desperate cry, "Oh God, please," as her body pressed mindlessly closer, begging for more.

From somewhere she heard a deep growl, and his lips were on hers again, this time almost punishing in his intense need for her total submission. Only she wasn't submitting. She was giving and responding and pleading for even more. Her fingers cupped his face and held his mouth to hers as her tongue quickly learned to answer his deep thrusts.

The boldness of her action caused him to crush her to him as he fought for what little control he had left. Maggie moaned as his hands loosened their hold and ran along the small of her back and up the sides of her slender midriff to cup the fullness of her yearning breasts.

She must be dreaming. Surely pleasure such as this did not exist on God's earth. It was fantasy beyond her wildest dreams.

Her shirt slid from her trousers and was flung carelessly aside. Dark eyes coveted the shadowed flesh that was not quite hidden beneath the thin fabric of her chemise, and Maggie felt her heart pound near to bursting as she watched him lift the material over her head and heard the tortured groan that seemed to catch in his throat.

"Oh God," he choked, his voice trembling with wonder and awe as his fingers cupped the lushness of her naked flesh. Unable to believe the loveliness of the woman before him, he wondered at his own sanity. Could this be real? Could he be imagining this? "You are so beautiful. Who are you? Where did you come from?" he asked as his mouth lowered to take the tip of her breast into its flaming heat.

Maggie gave a low cry, mindless of his words, as the sweetest tormenting sensations she had ever known spread fire to her toes and back up again, swelling the ache in her abdomen to a painful throb.

Gently he pressed her to the soft, damp grass, his mouth hovering over parted lips, still moist from his last kiss, while his fingers threaded through the thick mane of curls that haloed her face. "Can you be real?" he murmured against her mouth as his hand slid from her hair to her neck and shoulders to tease the tips of her aching sun-kissed breasts until they throbbed with terrible need. "Can this?" he continued as his mouth left hers, breathless and aching for more, to wander with raging heat to the object his fingers so lovingly caressed.

It took a long moment, but his softly murmured questions finally seeped into her dazed mind, and as her tilted world began to right itself, his rough fingers slid beneath the waistband of her trousers, to brush hungrily, possessively, over the core of her need. Suddenly her senses returned with startling clarity, and her body stiffened as she cried out, "No!"

My God, what was she doing? Her cheeks flamed as she realized what she had been about to do. How could she have allowed this? "Please. I'm sorry. Please!" she cried as she struggled to free herself from his embrace.

It was easy enough to slip from Matthew's arms as his mind was more than a little occupied at that exact moment. His look was one of pure amazement as he watched her scramble to her feet while clutching her chemise to her chest.

"What?" he asked, dazed by a passion so strong that her sudden absence left his mind dull and empty. Still, it took no more than a moment for his mind to understand, and he came quickly to his feet. "What the hell is the matter with you?"

"I'm sorry. I'm terribly sorry," she choked out as she turned her back to him and slid her chemise and shirt over her head.

She was tying the strings of her shirt into hopeless knots, knowing that in her entire lifetime she'd never again feel such shame, when he took her by the shoulders and gave her a hard shake. He growled, "Will you stop that and tell me what's wrong?"

Maggie gasped, suddenly afraid. Would he hurt her now that she had led him on and then refused him? Good God, she didn't even know this man. How could she have done this? He could murder her and it would be days before anyone found her body.

Matthew looked into the wide golden eyes of the beautiful woman before him. His lips thinned with anger as he watched her fear grow to terror. He spat out a vile curse and shook her yet again. In his anger, he lifted her clear off the ground and snarled, "Aye, you've every reason to fear me, madam. I could take you now, gentle or harsh, at the moment it matters little."

"No! Oh, please," Maggie cried, helpless to do more than push at his rock-hard shoulders.

Matthew released her so abruptly that she staggered and fell against him. In an instant his arms came to steady her and stayed to gently enfold her within their warmth. "I want many things from you, madam, but fear is not one of them."

Maggie buried her face in the warmth of his chest. She couldn't face him, not after what they had just done and almost done. It was so horribly mortifying. "You must forgive me," came the muffled sound as she pressed her face closer still.

"Will you not tell me what happened?" he asked as his finger tipped her chin so her eyes might meet his gaze.

"I cannot."

"Why?" he asked, his eyes beginning to crinkle with laughter.

"I know not what happened. I've never . . ."

"I sensed as much," he returned, fully aware of her innocence from their first kiss.

"I'm sorry."

"Stop saying that and tell me why," he whispered as his face lowered and his warm mouth nuzzled her cheek.

"I'm married. I had no right."

Matthew pulled back and stared at her for a long moment before he found the power to breathe again.

"Jesus Christ!" he choked out as the unsuspected fact

nearly staggered him and caused the words to stick like molasses in his throat, while an anger he had never known before spread a burning rage throughout his body. He wanted to smash his fist into something. How the hell could she be married? What kind of a man allowed his wife to tear across the countryside, unescorted, dressed like a boy, and riding her horse astride? Definitely not a husband who knew how to kiss, he reasoned, for he could not believe her innocent longing for his fiery kisses an act.

The hunger in her body had never been appeased. He was certain of that. She would not have responded so violently had she been satisfied.

Good God, what kind of a man takes a woman such as this to wife and then keeps his distance? Was he made of steel, never to touch her, never hold her in his arms, never bring her to the heights of ecstasy that he knew existed? Matthew knew that if she were his wife she'd have trouble getting herself out of bed. Her husband must be only half a man not to keep her there.

Suddenly his eyes widened with dawning knowledge. It was possible . . . more than possible. He was only a few miles from the Darrah farm. His voice, like his body, was stiff with dread when he finally found the strength to ask, "Would you be the wife of Caleb Darrah?"

Maggie's brandy-gold eyes misted with unshed tears of remorse, and her face grew as red as fire as she nodded miserably.

"Sweet Jesus," Matthew groaned as the truth hit home. She was the wife of a cripple, and he was about to take away her home. Did she know? Did that bastard of a husband tell her he had lost their farm? What in God's name had he gotten himself into?

He had been under orders to find a suitable piece of land along the Post Road between Sag Harbor and New York and to build an inn on it. It was a stroke of pure luck that he had walked into Peggy's and found a game of chance in progress.

Damn it, if he hadn't won the farm that night, someone else would have. And he was going to build that inn right on the land he had won, and damn the consequences. Why the hell should he be feeling this guilt? What was it to him anyway?

His dark eyes moved hungrily over the beautiful woman standing before him. She was tall for a woman. In her boots, her head came almost to his chin. She was easily the most beautiful creature he'd ever seen. If he lived to be a hundred he'd never forget how she looked with her thick mahogany hair falling past her naked shoulders. God, she could make a man forget his mission—and above all he must remember. *Stop! Stop thinking of her. You have a job to do. It would only bring suspicion down on you if you were to hand her lands back and build elsewhere.* Nay, no matter how badly he might feel, he would do as he must.

"My apologies, madam. I fear my behavior was most remiss."

"For God's sake, do not apologize," she groaned painfully. Her humiliation was almost more than she could stand, yet she forced herself to go on. "It only makes it all so much more horrid."

"As you wish," he returned with a quick nod of his head. He gathered the reins of her horse in his hand and offered them to her.

Without another word, Maggie grabbed at the leather and swung herself into the saddle with one fluid motion.

"Till we meet again," Matthew stated with an almost formal nod of his head.

"Sir," she responded from atop her horse in a voice that did little to disguise her need to be gone from his company. "In truth, I pray never to see the day."

She was gone with a touch of her heels to her horse's sides, leaving Matthew amid a shower of flying grass and stinging pebbles, alone with the haunting memory of a morning he'd not soon forget.

His dark gaze followed her slim figure as she bent low over the racing animal's back. A taunting smile curved his lips, for he knew his words had been more than an idle comment. His whispered words were a pledge of things to come. "You may, of course, pray all you wish, madam, but I doubt it will suffice in this case."

═══ *Two* ═══

Maggie never noticed the indignant squawks of scurrying chickens as she leaned forward and whispered the familiar words into Red's ear, words urging him to jump the split-rail fence that separated her farm from Old Man Johnson's land. Suddenly, and with little apparent thought to her safety, she dismounted in a cloud of swirling dust and prancing hooves just as she reached the huge barn doors.

Her lips were pulled back in what looked to be a permanent grimace of disgust. Her mind refused to stop its continuous accusations for her part in that morning's fiasco. What in the world had come over her? From the moment she had learned of the loss of her family's farm, her actions had been nothing less than deranged. Added to the dismal future that faced her, she knew she would forever remember this day with staggering shame.

Perhaps she had gone insane, at least momentarily. She had heard of such things happening. Of course, she reasoned, that was it. It was the shock of losing her home that had driven her into the arms of a stranger, nothing more. But then the picture of a big, dark man leaning over her, his expression stern yet filled with concern before softening to undisguised yearning, came to fill her mind and dared her to deny the truth.

For an instant Maggie allowed the sweet memories to

invade her being. Her chest swelled, filled with a throbbing ache, a longing she had only just come to know, and she realized it was not insanity but lust, pure and simple, that had driven her to commit such unspeakable transgressions. No, she corrected, not simple, this emotion. Not when it could fill her with terror, the force of which drove all other thoughts from her mind. Not when she knew she had not a chance of winning against such temptation. Not when it dared her to gamble with the keeping of her soul.

From the corner of her eye Maggie saw Elijah come running. His usually stooped form was straight, his slow, measured movements suddenly as quick and as agile as those of a man twenty years his junior. "Good God almighty!" the black man cried, his tone a mixture of relief and anger. "I swears you is aimin' to break that scrawny neck of yours."

Maggie grinned at her stableman. Elijah and his wife, Hannah, had been with her family since before she was born. Maggie had long ago forgotten the fact that they were her slaves. In truth, she had grown up with their son, James, and felt as close to him as she would to any brother. Together they worked hand in hand, seeing to the running of the farm. And she was proud of the fact that James knew as much as she about the planting and harvesting of a wheat crop.

Despite the turmoil of her mind, Maggie couldn't suppress the burst of laughter that erupted. "Why, you evil old scoundrel. Scrawny neck indeed! That's a fine way for you to be talking to the lady of the house."

"Lady?" Elijah taunted. "Nope, all I seen is some skinny ragamuffin swaggerin' around this here yard makin' out like sometin' she's not, dressed in her man's cut-down breeches. No lady I knowed would be found dressed like dat."

"Elijah, for God's sake!" Maggie snapped as she slammed the reins into the old man's gnarled hands. "I know well enough your opinion of my dress." She turned from him then, intent on ignoring any further jibes, but just before she stalked toward the house, she stopped, unable to resist a final word. From over her shoulder, she continued with no little sarcasm, "When I no longer find the need to ride my fields, I will dress in the petticoats and lace of which you are so fond. If that doesn't suit you, 'tis a shame indeed."

Maggie suppressed a smile as her six-year-old bundle of pure energy slammed the kitchen door against the wall and dashed out of the house, straight into his mother's arms. "Joseph," she admonished gently, "have I not told you again and again about the abuse you lend to that door? Where are you going that you must hurry so?"

"Aunt Matilda wants me to fetch a pail of boysenberries." In his excitement, he nearly jumped free of her hold. "We have a guest, and she wants to make a pie for dessert."

"Have we?" Maggie asked absentmindedly. Just what she needed. No doubt, another dragoon of soldiers was at this moment making themselves at home in her keeping room. If they kept this up, she'd soon have nothing left for her family.

A wry grin touched her soft lips as she remembered the farm no longer belonged to her. It mattered not who came uninvited to sup. Let the new owner worry about it.

"Our guest will be staying for supper then?" Maggie asked, never for a moment expecting to hear the deep, horrifyingly familiar voice that sounded directly above her.

"If you've no objection."

Maggie closed her eyes, wishing away what she knew to be true. It's not him! The fates could not be this cruel. Denying his presence to the end, she forced her eyes to take in the brown boots planted wide apart before her. Slowly, her gaze lifted and, despite her reluctance, ran with no little appreciation up the long length of muscular thigh.

Maggie blushed as she realized her gaze had lingered. Cursed wretch, she groaned in silent fury, what was the matter with her that the cut of a man's pants should set her chest aflutter? *For God's sake, Maggie,* she returned as she sought a silent excuse, *'tis embarrassment you feel, nothing more. Why, the man dresses as close to indecent as you've ever seen.*

Maggie struggled against the wide range of emotions that assailed her senses. Her intent was to face this brute down if it took every ounce of her strength.

Maggie almost gasped aloud as she realized who the man was. He was the one who was about to take away all she held dear, beyond her family. Maggie suddenly knew he was the scoundrel in question. Why else was he there? And what was she doing about it besides mooning over the cut of his pants? Good Lord, where had her common sense run off to?

She'd beat this flimflam man at his own game. He'd not steal her life's work, making her simply walk away, while he never gave another thought to his disgraceful actions. If this beggarly bastard had a glimmer of conscience, she'd soon see to its pricking. With luck, she'd see to that and more. In truth, had she her way, she'd see him swing on the end of a rope.

Maggie dreaded the need to show him an amicable face and forced a smile to her stiff lips as she rose and extended her hand in cool welcome.

Matthew bit back a sharp curse as his hand reached out and closed over hers. The contact of flesh brought a sudden and overwhelming urge to pull her into his arms. For an instant this morning's events flashed through his mind, and Matthew realized with dread that he had yet to know suffering in its fullest form.

His head nodded toward the boy as he spoke to his mother. "Joseph was just about to show me the best place to find berries." And then, for the benefit of any who might overhear, he added, as though they had just met, "Matthew Forrest at your service, ma'am."

"A pleasure, I'm sure," Maggie finally managed over the strangling sensation that suddenly gripped her throat. With a will of iron, she wrenched her gaze from his and kept it on his collar, lest she forget where she stood and do something insane like lean against his warm body. Forcing aside these errant thoughts, Maggie's mind raced ahead to her appointment that afternoon with Samuel Landsing, her old friend and solicitor. When at last she found the strength to pull her hand from the warm comfort of his, she wasn't surprised to find her voice trembly and soft. In truth, she had wondered at her ability to speak at all. "You will excuse me, won't you? I've just remembered an important errand."

"Certainly," Matthew acknowledged, with an expression that came very close to smug.

Joseph flittered excitedly at her side. He grabbed at her hand as he jumped up and down. "Come with us, Mama, please?" he begged.

"Not this time, darling. Mama has business to take care of."

"Oh, you always have something to do." He began to whine.

"Joseph," Matthew interrupted, "mind your manners. Your mother said she's busy. Perhaps she'll join us another time."

"Yes, sir," Joseph returned a bit sourly. Maggie realized for the first time how much she was spoiling her son.

Maggie smiled at the boy and then flushed a deep red as she lifted her gaze to the man before her and watched him mouth the word "Coward."

"Are you sure there is nothing I can do?"

"Maggie, Mr. Forrest is completely within his rights. He has done nothing but win a hand at cards. The man cannot be held at fault if your husband was so foolish as to wager your home. What would you have me do?"

"Caleb said the man cheated."

Samuel Landsing's lips tightened as he watched with helpless frustration the beautiful lady sitting across his desk. He and Maggie had known each other all their lives. They had played together as children, held hands and kissed, each for the first time, as young adults. When her parents had died, it was him and his family she had turned to for comfort and help. There was a time when he had believed they would be spending the rest of their lives together, but that was not to be. While he was away at school a man had come looking for work, and Maggie had fallen under his considerable charm. Within but a few weeks she was Mrs. Caleb Darrah, and Samuel could only curse his stupidity for leaving a ripe young beauty without the protection of his name. He should have insisted on a wedding before he left. No matter that they were both young; they would have managed somehow.

Samuel almost groaned aloud. *Damn it, Landsing, are you going to allow this to haunt you for the rest of your life? Christ, it's been years, and still she has the power to drive you mad with wanting her. Are you never to forget and get on with your life? There are others who could make you happy. You need but to stop this self-pity and useless longing and look around you.*

Samuel leaned toward Maggie, his light blue gaze tender, his sympathy apparent. "Maggie, I've played games of chance with Caleb on more than one occasion. Believe me, one does not need to cheat to win against him. The man is a fool."

Maggie sighed, knowing Samuel spoke the truth. Her husband had no head for gambling. And worst of all, he knew not when to stop.

Caleb lied to her more often than not of late. Maggie knew this as fact. Why then did she so eagerly believe he had spoken the truth this time? *Because you wanted to hate Mr. Forrest,* she answered with complete honesty. *Like a coward, you wanted to believe the worst of him, so you might explain away your wicked impulses whenever he is near you. God in heaven, what else but hate will keep you out of his arms?*

"Have you given any thought to what you will do now?"

Samuel felt his heart wrench at Maggie's brave smile. "Samuel, I've thought of little else, and yet I see no answers. I have nothing left and less hope of finding a solution."

"You will not starve, Maggie, nor will any of your family, as long as I live."

Maggie's smile was radiant, her eyes filled with tears of gratitude. "Samuel, I know not what I would do without you. You have always been there for me. I consider myself blessed with you as my friend. I only wish . . ."

Samuel came to his feet and without thought found himself lifting her to stand before him. His arms closed gently around her slender form, his hand pressing her face to the hollow of his shoulder as her tears broke in a torrent of sorrow.

"I know, darling," he dared to whisper above her sobs. "I've wished for much the same these many years past. Come away with me, Maggie. I will take care of you, honor you, cherish you. I swear, as long as I live you will never again have cause to cry."

Maggie was not altogether ignorant of Samuel's feelings toward her. He had been her first love, after all, and she suspected from his tender looks that some degree of emotion remained. Still, his words caused her more than a little surprise.

"Samuel, you cannot be serious! What of your reputation, your work?"

"They mean nothing without you."

"You cannot mean this. 'Tis pity you feel, nothing more."

Samuel smiled as his arms tightened their hold. "Do you believe me so sterling in character as to offer away my life's work to any and all in distress? Nay, my love. I've not been ignorant of the misery you so valiantly try to hide. Think on it, Maggie. I'd not bring pressure to bear, but imagine, if you will, a time when you will never again feel sadness, when every day will bring a smile to your lovely mouth."

Samuel lowered his head then and brushed his lips across

Maggie's trembling mouth. A low, anguished moan sounded deep in his throat as he licked her salty tears into his mouth.

Maggie felt herself soften within his warm embrace, her soul filled with contentment. He was right, she'd always be happy with him, but she knew it was not to be. A wave of sadness filled her being; she felt she was giving him up for the second time. He released her then and sat himself on the edge of his desk, watching as she began to pull on her gloves. "I have yet another proposition for you. I need someone to keep my files in order, to pen letters and see to countless odd errands. Do you know of someone you might recommend?" He grinned. "The wages would not be great, but I could supply lodgings."

Maggie grinned, knowing full well the man's motives. "Samuel, do you consider me such a simpleton not to know the workings of your mind? You will not manufacture work for me. I shall find my own way."

"I speak the truth, Maggie. I do need help."

"And you would supply lodgings no matter who was working for you?"

"Nay, on that point you are correct, but I'd offer that to any of my friends."

Maggie shook her head. "I thank you, Samuel, for your generous offer, but I am not qualified to work in your office, and you know it."

"Nonsense, Maggie. You know your letters and have a graceful hand. What more could I want? The possibility of seeing your lovely face every day is but an added bonus."

Maggie smiled, not certain that accepting his offer would be the wisest of moves. "Let me think on it, Samuel. Now I must return home. I have much to do."

Samuel nodded as he walked her toward his door. "Do not forget. I am here if you need me," he said as he helped her into the carriage seat.

"I'll not forget, Samuel. Thank you." A moment later the

reins were snapped above the horses' backs, and the small carriage was speeding down the dirt road toward the Darrah farm.

Maggie listened to the excitement below as she dressed for the evening meal. It was obvious that the house welcomed the presence of this man. Were he a visitor, as all below believed, Maggie too would have felt a lightening in her heart at his company. In truth, any visitor would have been most welcome, for her family seldom entertained. The atmosphere in the house was not conducive to light conversations and afternoon teas.

Maggie shook her head sadly as she gazed at her reflection in Aunt Matilda's mirror. It was in the past and best not endlessly dwelt upon. In truth, Mr. Forrest was not a visitor but the rightful and legal owner of this land, come to lay his claim, and Maggie had no doubt that by the evening's end all would know of his intentions to see them banished from the farm.

Maggie adjusted the dark pink ribbons that were threaded through her gown's neckline and smoothed the gentle folds of heavy green silk that fell from her slim hips to the floor. Her dark red hair was caught up and held on top of her head with ivory combs. A tiny dab of precious vanilla between her breasts and at her wrists, and she was ready to face whatever she must.

She was straightening the linen napkins at each place setting when the back door opened and Matthew stepped into the kitchen. Maggie struggled against the need to lift her gaze to him, but it was beyond her power to ignore his presence.

She felt her insides grow warm as his dark gaze ran appreciatively over her best dress. He too was dressed in his Sunday finest. His hair was damp from the quick bath he had taken in the river, and Maggie felt the most insane need to move toward him and . . . and what?

Maggie shook herself free of the thought. It mattered not that this man outshone any other of her acquaintance. What was it to her if that magnificent body was lean and muscular? It was no concern of hers, to be sure.

Matthew's dark eyes twinkled with humor as if he were able to read her thoughts. Maggie forced aside her sudden embarrassment, unwilling to reveal his effect on her.

"Good evening, sir," Maggie remarked. She sighed with relief at the steadiness of her voice. A smile touched her lips as she watched Joseph, who had been waiting most impatiently for Matthew's arrival, jump into the man's arms.

"Mistress." Matthew nodded toward the lady of the house, his warm gaze lingering on her even as he managed to catch the youngster who leaped toward him.

"I wanted to come for you, but Mama said to leave you in peace. I thought you might have forgotten."

"To eat?" Matthew grinned as he swung the boy into the air and laughed at his childish shrieks. "Not likely. No one gets to be my size by forgetting to eat." Matthew addressed Maggie over Joseph's head. "'Tis no bother if the lad comes to visit. I promise you, I prefer it to being alone."

"The way you've taken to the boy, Mr. Forrest, one would think you had plenty of practice with children," Aunt Matilda remarked, to Maggie's silent groan of horror. "Would you be a father yourself?"

Matthew noticed the darkening flush of Maggie's cheeks and smiled as he addressed her aunt. "Nay. As yet, I've not been so fortunate." And with a devilish grin and a lifting of a black brow, he continued, "'Tis best, they tell me, to find a wife before one embarks upon that role in life."

"Indeed," Aunt Matilda returned with a girlish giggle as a soft blush added luster to her skin and a twinkle of excitement to her eyes. "The notion makes uncommonly good sense."

Good God! Maggie almost gasped aloud. Her gray-haired aunt was actually flirting with this man. A total stranger! How could she? Why, she hadn't even laid eyes on him until this afternoon, and here she was simpering and cooing as if they had long been friends.

Maggie, Maggie, she sighed in abject misery as her mind filled with disgust at her evil thoughts. *Indeed, you are a sorry excuse for a niece. Must you see wickedness in everything? Simply because you were so inclined upon this very morn, do you truly believe your aunt to be contemplating any of your sinful tendencies? In truth, you are sadly lacking in many of the fine attributes of your aunt and would benefit greatly should you follow her lovely Christian example and simply make the man feel welcome.*

Maggie's thoughts were interrupted by Hannah's loud announcement, "That's enough of dis chitchat business. You folks be sittin' yourselves down. I'm puttin' the food out *now.*"

Maggie laughed at the bossy black woman and allowed Joseph to seat her after he had observed Matthew and copied the attention given to Aunt Matilda. "You will have to forgive us, Mr. Forrest," she offered as explanation. "We are an unconventional household by some standards. Hannah has been with our family since before I was born, and there is little hope that I, or anyone else for that matter, can force her to remember her place or keep a civil tongue in her head at this late date."

All present but for Joseph kept a tight rein on the laughter that threatened to erupt when a loud snort sounded from the woman as she splashed a ladle of hot stew onto Matthew's plate.

"Worry about it no more, mistress," Matthew managed, instantly in control of his merriment upon meeting Hannah's fiery black gaze. With absolute certainty, Matthew knew the next ladle of food would somehow find its way onto his lap if he didn't squash his tendency toward laughter. "In these troublesome times I find it refreshing indeed to hear any speak their mind, no matter the subject," he continued, and almost sighed with relief as the Cook grunted her approval and moved on to the next to be served.

The whole table breathed an audible sigh of relief as they recognized Hannah's acceptance of Matthew Forrest.

"I take it you are not happy with the present situation in these colonies, Mr. Forrest?" Aunt Matilda asked.

"Aunt Matilda," Maggie offered gently, "perhaps Mr. Forrest would rather not tell us his particular beliefs."

"Nonsense," the elderly lady returned. "This is not a hotbed of spies, after all. Mr. Forrest will be perfectly safe if he should tell us to which side he professes loyalty. As long as his side and ours are the same, of course."

"Of course," Maggie laughed and turned to face the man who sat opposite herself. "I hope my aunt's comments have not given you cause to find offense."

"You need not worry, mistress." Matthew grinned across the table at Maggie's beautiful smile. "I do not offend quite so easily, and in any case, if I were to mention my beliefs and they be for the wrong side, I am sure Mrs. Brandon would soon persuade me to see the error of my ways."

"You speak well, sir," Aunt Matilda commented, "but as yet have told us nothing. Could it be you hold some public office?"

"Aunt Matilda!" Maggie gasped. "I believe you go too far."

"Nay," Matthew laughed. "She speaks the truth. I've had a bit of practice speaking while saying nothing and will, I believe, grow more proficient in the art, at least until these cursed English see fit to leave our shores."

Aunt Matilda's soft laugh held a touch of relief. Still, she managed to shoot Maggie a smug "I told you so" look before she turned back to their guest with a conspiratorial nod. "Indeed, the English occupation has not lent an air of freedom to these parts. I fear we've yet to see the worst of it. One can only hope to see the last of them soon."

"To say the very least, madam."

"Might you be staying on in these parts, Mr. Forrest?"

Maggie gave a soft moan at her aunt's question. Was she the only one who knew the man now owned her farm?

Hadn't he told everyone the moment he arrived? A glimmer of hope was born. Could she have been mistaken? Was this only a passing stranger and not the new owner of her home? It was not unusual for a traveler to be taken in and treated as a guest. Indeed, they had done so innumerable times.

Maggie's newfound hope was instantly dashed as she watched Matthew nervously clear his throat and reach a finger to loosen his suddenly tight cravat. It was apparent he was not at ease with what he was about to say, when Caleb's voice sounded with evil mirth from the keeping-room doorway.

"Haven't you told them yet? Why the wait, Forrest?"

All heads turned at the sound of Caleb's voice. They watched as his obviously inebriated friend Jack staggered under Caleb's weight as he brought him further into the room.

Simultaneously, Maggie and Matthew jumped to their feet as Jack swerved dangerously close to the fire. "Not to fear," Caleb chuckled at the worried frowns on everyone's face as Jack dumped him unceremoniously into the chair at the head of the table. The chair wobbled sickeningly and threatened to overturn until Caleb caught the table with his hands. "We've been through this often enough, Jack and me."

Jack muttered an unintelligible goodbye to the silent assembly and stumbled out in much the same manner as he had come in.

"My, my, is this not a cozy setting? Why, at first sight one would surely believe this to be a loving family." And then he continued with a sneer, as his hate-filled glance fell on Maggie, "Mama, Papa, and baby."

"I'm not a baby, Father."

"Shut up, you whining brat," Caleb snapped at the child. "You're any goddamned thing I tell you."

Maggie's cheeks burned with mortification as she came to her feet and took Caleb's plate, filling it with the heavy rich stew Hannah had left warming over the fire. But, as she made to leave his side, Caleb's arm shot out and clutched her tiny waist, dragging her back. "How do you like my wife, Forrest? Is she not a beauty?"

"Indeed, sir," Matthew returned as he glanced at Maggie's tortured expression. "You have much to be thankful for."

Caleb's answering laughter was a horror to Maggie's ears as he jeered, "Oh, indeed I do."

Maggie couldn't lift her gaze from the floor as she prayed to God that Caleb would fall into an instant drunken sleep.

"What would you imagine her worth?"

"Sir?" Matthew asked, positive he could not have heard correctly.

"Well"—Caleb leered at his wife—"if I were to wager her in a game of chance, what amount do you suppose might be put up against her? What, in fact, would you offer for her?"

It sickened Matthew to think that this lovely lady was the brunt of her husband's contempt. With great effort, Matthew finally managed to say calmly, "I'm afraid, sir, I do not see the humor in your question."

"Indeed, Forrest, I meant not to be clever. I was serious in my offer."

"If that be the case, Mr. Darrah, I feel nothing but pity for you."

"How dare you!" Caleb choked, his lips thinning into a vicious snarl.

"I dare all I please, Mr. Darrah," Matthew countered, no longer bothering to contain his anger. "This is my home."

Maggie heard Aunt Matilda's gasp of surprise.

"You are sitting at my table and you have insulted my guests. Should you ever again come to my table, do so without ale to bolster your courage and with proper respect to the ladies present. When you insult my guests, you insult me. And I do not take insults lightly. Have I made myself clear?"

At first there was no answer forthcoming. Caleb sat in stony silence, his fingers tightening on Maggie's soft flesh, while she stared in amazement as the two men fought a silent battle of wills. No one had ever before dared to raise his voice to Caleb or question aloud the righteousness of his actions. Suddenly the dishes jumped with the force of Matthew's fist as it made contact with the table, and Caleb released Maggie with a force that nearly sent her flying into the wall. "Have I made myself clear?" Matthew repeated.

"You have," Caleb returned sullenly. His gaze moved to Maggie as she regained her composure and seated herself once again. His eyes narrowed with the promise of retaliation for this degradation, for he had no doubt that she was entirely to blame.

For a long moment the only sound in the room above the crackle of the fire was Joseph's soft whimpering.

Finding a need to break the ominous silence and to take the attention from himself, Caleb snapped, "Woman, take your son from my sight. My head aches, and I've no need to hear his caterwauling."

Maggie jumped to do his bidding, anything to be gone from there and not be witness to the pity in Matthew Forrest's dark eyes.

"And tell that good-for-nothing Elijah to bring his arse in here. I want to go to bed." And then, nodding toward Matthew, Caleb asked in a voice dripping with sarcasm, "I trust that meets with your approval?"

"It does, Mr. Darrah," Matthew stated flatly.

Three

MATTHEW BREATHED A LONG, weary sigh as he leaned against the rough wood of the barn. The warm night air carried his pipe smoke into a blue cloud of smoke that momentarily swirled above his head, only to vanish on the soft spring breeze, gone forever in the silvery, silent night.

His gaze wandered over the still fields beyond the house, and a feeling of dread filled his heart. He had to speak with Maggie, and he had no doubt that she would refuse his proposition.

Matthew was tired, and his leg ached abominably. A fall from a horse as a child had left him with a noticeable limp whenever he pushed himself too hard. And the long ride from Washington's headquarters the night before had done little to soothe the throbbing muscles.

But the discomfort in his leg was minor compared to the torment that wracked his head. For the first time he wished like hell to get out of this assignment. How long was he supposed to watch Caleb's abuse and do nothing to jeopardize the plan? God damn it! What could he do? Orders were orders, and he had no choice but to obey and bear the torture along with her, for already he felt something he had no business feeling, something that went beyond the simple need of a man for a woman.

Matthew cursed the mockery of the gods for their timing.

How they must be laughing. For a score and thirteen years he had kept himself free of personal entanglements, interested in only the most frivolous of encounters. Indeed, it had been easy enough to take what was so generously offered without a flicker of conscience, never fearing or understanding the hold some men professed their women had over them. But no longer could he deny the emotion, and, damn it, it was just his luck to find a woman so agreeable to the eye, so luscious to the touch, so delectable to the taste, and so irrevocably married.

Jesus, he'd never be able to carry on his assignment if he kept up this train of thought. He'd have to make a determined effort to keep her from his mind, lest the cause suffer. And he had no doubt about which was more important.

From the moment he had realized her identity there had been no question about his taking the farm. Even before he had met the beautiful owner, he had wondered about putting an entire family out on the street.

Actually, he needed no more than an acre or two that fronted the Post Road for an inn. He couldn't have planned it better had he offered for the land. Halfway between Sag Harbor, New York's largest and busiest seaport, and New York City, it was a perfect place for stagecoaches to stop for travelers to stretch their legs and cleanse their throats of dust. And while the horses were being fed and watered, who's to say that the travelers might not take part in little friendly discussions? Indeed, this location would do most satisfactorily for keeping a close eye on all who entered the country. Plus, and most importantly, it would enable him to hear any piece of information that might prove vital to Washington's final victory. And he did not doubt that they would succeed in the end. No people who desired victory so desperately could lose.

Matthew was just about to knock the tobacco from his pipe and return to his room at the back of the barn when, from the corner of his eye, he saw the white material of a nightdress flutter in the soft breeze. The night was clear, and the moon gave all he needed in the way of light. Matthew's heart began to pound; a vein throbbed in his throat, nearly choking him. It was as though all his good intentions had never been thought. His legs moved without his knowledge, and he found himself standing unnoticed within the shadow of the house. He watched her as she moved along the wooden porch and then rested her head against one of the posts that supported the overhanging roof.

Maggie gazed out over the short distance that separated the house from the barn and wished herself a thousand miles away. A soft smile touched her lips. Who said wishes didn't come true? By this time tomorrow, she and her family would be gone, perhaps not thousands of miles away, but far enough never again to see the pity in his eyes. There wasn't much Maggie could not bear. Life had handed her many tribulations, which she had faced bravely, but the emotion in his dark eyes made her want to run and hide.

By all rights he should be sleeping in the master's bed-chamber, yet he had said nothing when Caleb had taken it. What kind of a man was this? He owned this land and all it contained, and yet he did not insist on claiming his rights.

Maggie's thoughts returned to her immediate problem. Tomorrow they would pack their few meager belongings and be gone.

Her soft, sorrow-filled sigh touched his heart, and he longed to hold her and ease her pain. With a will of iron he fought back the emotion, and without thought he broke the night's silence by asking, "Why do you not leave him?"

The low, unexpected voice nearly caused Maggie to shriek as she whirled around to face the sound.

"Do not be afraid," Matthew said quickly as he moved from the shadows into the silvery moonlight. "It is I."

"Oh God." Maggie sighed with relief as her hand came to rest on her fluttering heart, but her fear soon changed to annoyance as she continued, "Do you know the fright you caused me? What are you doing prowling around at this hour?"

Matthew chuckled at her anger. "I might ask the same of you. 'Tis apparent, I think, that neither of us could sleep."

Maggie clutched her shawl closer as if to protect herself from his view. "I simply stepped out for a breath of air. I shall sleep now."

Matthew knew he was flirting with fire. A moment such as this might prove to be dangerous, but he found himself helpless to stop asking, "Will you stay a moment?"

Maggie's body gave a shudder at the mere thought of spending a stolen moment alone with this man. It would be so easy to lose herself in his arms, to forget the fear of approaching hardships, to lean into his strength and gain comfort from his slightest touch. But to what avail? Maggie forced aside the weakness that made her yearn for a repeat of that morning's tenderness. She shook her head as she replied, "Nay, I think not. The night is damp, and I fear a chill."

Matthew smiled at the obvious lie, for the night was almost oppressively warm and dry. "I've a need to speak with you, Mistress Darrah, if you would be so kind."

"'Tis unnecessary for you to bother yourself, Mr. Forrest. My husband has informed me of his actions." She shrugged a slender shoulder and waved a delicate hand in a helpless gesture. "I am aware that the farm's ownership has changed hands. Let me assure you we will be gone upon the morn."

"Nay, you need not."

"Indeed, sir, I fear we must."

"Mistress, I have no need for this land. 'Twould be put to waste if you left."

"I know not your meaning, sir. Are you offering to forgo your winnings?"

"In a manner of speaking."

"Pardon me?"

Matthew sighed. "If the truth be told, I was in the market for an acre along the Post Road when I happened upon the game of chance that made me the new owner of your farm. What if I return all but what I need?"

"Nay, I . . . I could not take it. 'Tis yours."

"To do with as I wish?"

"Indeed."

"Then I wish to give it to you."

Maggie's heart leaped with excitement and threatened to burst within her breast. Was it true? Would she and her family be allowed to stay? She'd never be able to thank him. Suddenly she understood the magnitude of his offering. No, she could not accept such a gift. This was too valuable and something that could not be tossed about so casually. Maggie's head tilted slightly, her eyes narrowing with sudden apprehension. "And what might you request as payment?"

Matthew grinned at her suspicions. "And if I said you?"

"'Tis as I thought," Maggie snapped as she turned toward the door, only to be stopped by Matthew's firm hand on her arm.

Matthew laughed softly as he turned her back to face him. "Rest easy, mistress. I spoke in jest. I did not mean it was you I wanted."

"Did you not?" she responded angrily, trying to ignore the thumping of her heart and his proximity. What in the world was the matter with her that she should react so violently to this man's touch?

"Nay. Still, it matters little if I say not the words. I'll not deny what we feel for each other." And at her obvious stiffening and the stubborn lifting of a defiant jaw, he asked, "Do you dare deny it?"

"Till my dying day," Maggie vowed, and she instantly cursed the trembling of her voice that exposed her lie.

Matthew's tender smile did not put her fears to rest. The knowledge shone clearly in his eyes, and they both knew, no matter her words, the truth of the matter. Still, he was gentlemanly enough not to press the point, for now. "Perhaps you will deny it, but that does not make it less so. I'll not deny my desire for you, but I will not ask you for the payment of which you hint. If I take you, it will be because you give yourself to me of your own will, not because of a debt owed."

Maggie gasped. "Sir, you forget yourself. I am a married woman."

Matthew's hands gripped her shoulders and lifted her face to within inches of his mouth. His lips twisted with disgust as he gave her a slight shake. "Aye, on this night I've witnessed the workings of your marriage. How else do I dare to speak to you thus?"

Maggie couldn't bear the pity she saw in his warm eyes. Unconsciously, a denial rumbled from within her throat. "You've no right, regardless."

"Perhaps," he conceded as he lowered her to stand before him again. "But it is beyond my power to watch you so abused."

"Please," she begged softly, no longer able to meet his gaze. "You mustn't say these things."

With a great deal of effort, Matthew managed to force aside the need to pull her closer, to comfort her. His eyes closed for a long moment.

Maggie knew he was on the brink of giving in to his sinful impulse, but she had her own war to wage. A voice in the far recesses of her mind suddenly taunted her to lean toward him, to dare him to try to win his battle against temptation.

Finally Matthew found the needed strength. He shook his head as if to clear away the desperate longing that had possessed him since the first moment he had seen her. He dropped his arms to his sides. This lady could not be taken lightly. The time might come, he thought to himself, but not tonight. Tonight he had to persuade her to remain, just to talk to him so that he could help her.

"Back to the point at hand, I think. Since we both know of your husband's tendencies toward the gaming tables, I will give you back your land but hold it in my name in trust for Joseph. I do this because it pleases me and for no other reason, no matter your beliefs."

Maggie shook her head. "Nay, I shall not take it. Land is too valuable to be simply given away."

Matthew gave a low chuckle that nearly caused Maggie to groan at the sudden pain that filled her chest. "Pay me for it, then, if you dare."

Maggie tried to ignore the teasing laughter in his voice and the delightful way his lip twitched as he fought to control his humor. She had to swallow and clear her throat twice before the huskiness would disappear. "I will visit the bank tomorrow."

"Nay, 'tis not necessary. You may pay me what you wish, when you wish."

"I will pay you as I would a bank, or I will not stay."

"As you wish, mistress."

With the matter settled between them, they were both momentarily at a loss for words. Maggie looked at the man who stood so dangerously near, and her voice shook as she spoke. "I think I shall go in now."

He said nothing, but his dark, burning gaze never left her as she reentered the house.

═══ *Four* ═══

MAGGIE SAT ON THE barn floor, laughing at the rapturous expression on her son's face as he cuddled a furry kitten. The mother cat eyed her unwanted company with suspicion as Joseph reached for yet another kitten.

"I wish they could stay this small."

Maggie smiled as she reached a hand into the box to pet the newborn creatures. "Sometimes I wish the same of you, Joseph. You grow closer to manhood daily, and I would halt the progress had I the power." As she watched her son, her eyes beamed with love. He was six this year and soon would be attending morning classes. How had he grown so quickly? Had it truly been six years since she had first held him in her arms? And how was she to bear his growing, knowing that adulthood would bring their separation?

Maybe she would not feel this tightening of her chest if she had another to love. If she had another child, or a man. Maggie abruptly pulled her thoughts from that dangerous notion. To love again would only bring heartache. Hadn't she already experienced love only to see it turn to hate? Indeed, she faced the truth of those words daily.

"Why do you wish me to remain a child?" Joseph asked, his blue eyes round with curiosity.

Maggie felt her heart tug at his sweet innocence. A gentle smile touched her lips at the simple question. "You're a child for such a short time, darling. I'd wish more time to love you before you grow away."

Joseph dropped the kittens back in their box and reached slender arms around her neck, the hard pressure of his small body almost tumbling the two of them to the dirt floor. "I won't leave you, Mama," he swore solemnly. "I'll always be here."

Maggie kissed his blond head and disengaged his arms from her neck. "Have you seen Mr. Forrest today? I've a need to speak with him."

At that moment Matthew walked into the room. "If Hannah sees you sitting on the floor dirtying your clothes, I can promise dire consequences."

Maggie smiled as she came to her feet, dusting at the dirt that clung to her clothes. "One hopes she will not see me."

Matthew grinned as he watched her slap at her backside. "Do you need any help?"

"Nay, I can manage," she returned, knowing, without looking up, that he was grinning.

"Mama, can I play down by the creek today? Can I, can I? Elijah promised to take me if you say yes."

"Joseph, Elijah has work to do. You must not nag him into doing your bidding."

"Why don't I take the lad? I've little enough to do until my supplies arrive."

"That would be very nice, I'm sure, Mr. Forrest, but we would not wish to impose."

Matthew shrugged. "'Twould be no imposition. Especially if you were to join us."

Despite the warmth of the day, a slight shiver ran through Maggie's body as she imagined an afternoon spent at his side watching her son frolic in the water, or better yet joining him in the cool creek.

Maggie's cheeks flushed at her improper thoughts. She raised her eyes to his and recognized the dark fire in his gaze. For a wild moment she almost agreed. But she knew she could not join them. "I'm afraid that is not possible."

"No?" he asked as he leaned nonchalantly against one of the barn's beams. A smile teased one corner of his mouth. His arms were folded across his chest, and his eyes feasted on the beauty before him.

"I've work to do," she answered determinedly.

"Work that could not be delayed?" He grinned as his glance took in her nervously fidgeting fingers.

"I'm afraid not."

Unbelievably, Joseph took just that moment to pipe in, "Mama wants you, Mr. Forrest."

And Maggie turned beet red at Matthew's low, suggestive laughter. "Does she indeed?" he asked, his gaze never leaving her face.

Again Matthew laughed as Joseph asked in all innocence, "What's the matter, Mama? Your face is red."

"Is it?" Maggie asked. She pressed her hands to her cheeks as if they could fight down a burning heat that threatened to turn her to ashes. "Perhaps the heat . . ."

"Joseph, wait for me outside," Matthew interrupted. "I'll be with you directly, and we'll go down to the creek."

A shriek of happiness was heard as Joseph ran from the barn, only to stand at its opening, jumping impatiently up and down and enveloping himself in clouds of dust.

"If you cater to his whims, the boy will never leave your side."

"Do you realize how lovely you are?"

"I wanted to talk to you." Maggie stood within a shaft of light from one of the barn's high windows.

"When the sun shines on your hair, it turns the color to flame."

"I was just informed that my house will be needed to headquarter the militia."

"It takes an effort not to touch you when I look at you."

Maggie closed her eyes and stifled the warm feelings inside her. She could not allow this man to so control her emotions, her mind. "Please," she choked out, "might we speak of one subject at a time?"

"I thought I was." He grinned.

Maggie shook her head, helpless but to allow a small smile to touch her lips. "I grow to fear you may never speak of anything else."

"Nothing else intrigues me by half."

"Mr. Forrest, please." She laughed softly.

"Ah, I was coming to believe the lady had forgotten how to smile."

"In times such as these, it is often hard to remember."

Matthew nodded his agreement. "What did you wish to tell me?"

"I'm afraid I will be forced to take away your room. The militia are commandeering my home, and my husband must have a bed."

"And what of yourself?"

"Nay, I don't sleep . . ." Maggie bit back the rest of her thoughtless admission.

Matthew's spirits lifted. His eyes shone with satisfaction. "'Tis as I thought. You do not sleep with him."

Maggie had no way of knowing that Matthew had already guessed as much the morning before. Flustered that this man, this stranger, should know her deepest, most personal secrets, she moved away from him and looked at her feet.

"Nay, mistress, you need not suffer so. Above all else, I could not hope for more, and I'd not banter such knowledge about."

Maggie ignored his words. She couldn't allow herself to think of their intended meaning. She could never allow it. "Mr. Forrest, I must ask you to give up your room. I'm afraid I shall need it immediately."

"And where will you sleep? Certainly not in the house."

"Nay. The loft will be comfortable enough."

"And myself?"

"Indeed, Mr. Forrest, that depends on you, does it not?"

Matthew grinned. "Does it?"

Confused, Maggie blinked. "Do you believe I should find you a bed?"

"You need not if you share your own," Matthew replied as he eyed her with wicked humor.

Maggie laughed. "Oh, I see now your meaning. I'm afraid you are doomed to disappointment, Mr. Forrest, for Joseph shares my bed."

"And you would not contemplate changing your current arrangements?" Matthew grinned.

Maggie's laughter echoed sweetly throughout the barn. "I think not."

"'Tis a pity, mistress, but I think not a condition to last overlong."

"Mr. Forrest," Joseph's impatient voice called out, ending their teasing conversation.

Maggie watched with a light heart as her son and the intriguing stranger walked side by side toward the wooded section of her land. She wished it were possible to have joined them, but she had already spent too much time thinking of the man, and spending the afternoon in his company was out of the question.

Maggie jumped and spun around as Elijah's voice spoke out of the silent barn. "Why didn' you go wit dem? I can see you wanted to."

Maggie gasped for air, her heart pounding a little faster. "What is it with the men on this farm? Can not one of you warn of your approach?" she asked. "One of these times my heart is going to give out."

"Your heart is just fine. Why didn' you go?"

"Why don't you mind your own business, old man?"

"There ain' notin' you got to do that cain't wait."

"Elijah, I'm warning you. I grow weary of your constant interference."

"Little miss," Elijah returned, using her childhood name, his black face twisting into a scowl of disgust, "you is without the comfort of a man for dis last six years. You think I don' know you sleep on the floor in the kitchen every night?"

Maggie's mouth hung open with shock. Was nothing private? Did the whole town know her business? "Are you telling me I should seek comfort elsewhere? With a perfect stranger?"

"How'd you know he's perfect 'less you give him a try?"

"Oh God!" Maggie cried in frustration. "I cannot believe I'm hearing this. Do you want me to go against a lifetime of moral beliefs for a moment of physical satisfaction?"

Elijah shook his head. "I'm tellin' you you is going to shrivel up and die like a old flower if'n you don' do sometin'. God ain't no fool. He knows every last one of us needs lovin', and you ain't no exception. Do you think he would condemn you for taking comfort from another of his children?"

"Elijah, stop it this minute!"

"You're afraid we'll think you ain't perfect. Is dat it?"

"Elijah, please," Maggie managed in a strangled voice before her strength seemed to vanish and, to her mortification, her face suddenly crumbled and tears ran freely down her face.

"Dere, little miss," Elijah soothed as he took her in his huge arms and pressed her face into the warmth of his thick shoulder. "I knowed you suffer sometin' fierce. You jus forget what I said. Dis old man, he don't know enough when to shut his fool mouth."

Maggie blew a damp mahogany tendril from her forehead with a short puff of breath and sighed as she surveyed the results of an afternoon spent in backbreaking work.

"It's almost livable," she mused to herself, and then cursed for the hundredth time the English presence in her home. How long were she and her family to remain living under these conditions? Indefinitely, she presumed, for she had been told only to vacate the house and to do so immediately.

Maggie knew of several others who had been forced to

share their homes, but those were larger establishments with enough space should the owners wish to remain. Perhaps the militia would soon tire of their cramped quarters and find more suitable living arrangements. She could only hope.

At least the barn was fairly clean and dry. Thank the Lord, it was spring, and the horses could be settled in the corral or put to pasture with no hardship. If it had been winter, she might have been forced to abandon her home entirely, possibly till the conclusion of the hostilities.

Maggie heard the sounds of a buggy as it drove into her yard and groaned at Caleb's early return. Why did he have to pick today, of all days, to come home early? Damn! She had a half-dozen officers to contend with, and the house was in an uproar as the British soldiers moved their belongings into place. The very last thing she needed right then was her bitter and probably drunk husband underfoot.

Maggie stepped outside into the late-afternoon sun to remind Caleb about their new living quarters. A warm smile of welcome and relief lit up her face when she spied Samuel lowering himself to the ground.

"You've had a few additions since yesterday," he commented, nodding toward the house. An aide staggered under the weight of a large trunk perched precariously on his back, while a red-coated officer stood by, dusting imaginary specks of dirt from his palm with a snowy white handkerchief.

Maggie grinned at the scene. "One cannot help but wonder how this lion has managed to subdue whole continents. Surely the idea of breaking a nail must have put them off, don't you think?"

"Maggie," Samuel returned, his voice telling of both his wish to laugh and the danger of speaking thus, "have a care. 'Tis best, I think, to keep your opinions to yourself. These are not the times to speak out, lest your whole family suffer."

"Aye, Samuel." She grinned. "You are right, as always. Come inside. I have something to tell you."

"What is this?" Samuel asked as he took in a freshly scrubbed table and benches that stood a few feet from the door. The floor had been covered with fresh hay, and the few chairs and small tables scattered about lent the barn an almost homey quality. "Has Forrest put you in the barn?"

"Nay, Samuel," Maggie laughed softly. "In truth, Mr. Forrest has been most generous in allowing the return of our farm. I was ordered out of the house by the redcoats."

"What is this you say? Forrest has returned your property? Just like that?" Samuel asked, amazed.

"Well, not exactly."

"I thought as much. What does he ask for payment?" he asked snidely, his jealousy apparent.

"Samuel, please," she countered. "You're not being fair."

"Am I not? Are you telling me he offered to return your land and asked nothing of you? Indeed, 'tis hard to believe."

"If you would allow me a moment to explain, we shall soon be done with this nonsense."

"Explain."

"Mr. Forrest has asked us to stay on. He is not a farmer and has no need of this property except for a parcel of land that borders the Post Road. He has intentions of building an inn, and he asked no more than an acre or two for that purpose."

"He asked?"

"Aye."

"And he requires no payment? He is offering you a gift?"

Maggie was clearly annoyed at the tone of his voice, and she snapped, "Samuel, I believe you have been a solicitor for far too long. Your mind sees only the criminal element."

Samuel had the grace to blush at her sharp rebuke. In truth, he had no right to cross-examine. Instead of unwarranted anger, he should be feeling happy for her. But he couldn't forget the fact that, had the man not been so generous, she would now be needing his help. Perhaps by now she would be setting up her things in his home.

Jesus, was he to be thwarted at every turn? Would he never have her for his own? He had had the opportunity to keep her near, but instead this *savior* had to come, destroying his hopes.

Maggie felt contrite at Samuel's hurt expression. He was, after all, her friend. She need not be so sharp with him simply because he worried about her welfare.

Her voice softened to a gentle murmur as she continued, "We've worked out the means for payment. 'Tis not a gift, but a business arrangement."

Samuel nodded dejectedly. His arms ached to reach out and hold her again. It had been so long. Yesterday, thanks to Caleb's gambling, he had thought she would eventually be his. She had let him hold her, kiss her, and he knew she did not feel disgust at his touch.

Why had this goddamned man interfered? Of course, he reasoned, Forrest, in his sly way, was planning on having her. He knew it more certainly than he knew his own name. It did not occur to Samuel that his own motives were equally base.

Suddenly Samuel reached out and pulled her into his embrace. "Maggie," he sighed, "I had hoped you would come to me. I waited all day."

Maggie leaned her head against his chest and momentarily allowed the comfort of his embrace to ease away her weariness. "I know, Samuel, and I would have come to let you know the change in plans had not the militia caused some delay."

From the doorway Matthew couldn't hear the softly spoken words, but he could not mistake what his eyes saw. Unaccountably his heart filled with anger, and he longed to smash his fist into the face of the man who dared to hold the beautiful woman he already considered his own.

It took a moment to clear away the red mist, but when he

spoke his voice was cold with suppressed icy rage. "Excuse me, I did not mean to interrupt."

Maggie jumped at the sound of Matthew's voice, feeling very much like a child caught in an evil act.

"Could you tell me where my things were put?" Matthew asked, while glaring at an obviously annoyed Samuel.

"Hannah moved them to the last stall in the back, Mr. Forrest," Maggie returned, her voice trembling with nerves as she watched the two men exchange looks of pure hate.

Maggie, hoping to soothe whatever was troubling them, quickly performed the introductions. Introductions, however, did little to ease the tension.

A few moments later Samuel left, claiming he had an appointment, while Matthew stormed through the barn mumbling curses.

Before he entered the stall, he kicked the door and, upon leaving, with a fresh shirt flung over his arm, he kicked it again.

"Is something amiss?" Maggie asked as she watched Matthew's anger-darkened face, unable to understand his reaction.

"Why?" he asked as he came to stand before her.

"Why?" she echoed. "I can see you are upset. What has happened?"

"You should take care, mistress, to embrace your lovers only when and where there is no chance of being caught," he returned viciously.

Maggie ignored the reference to their first meeting, angry that he should so dare to presume. "Mr. Landsing is not my lover, Mr. Forrest, he is my friend," she stated nastily.

"Is he now? Are you as generous with your favors to all your friends?"

Maggie bit her lip, trying not to overreact, and answered with a strained calmness. "Mr. Forrest, Samuel and I grew up together. I've known him since I was a child."

"Does that make it all right?"

"Does it make what all right?"

"Kissing him, damn it! Or do you make it a habit of kissing all your friends?"

"I was not kissing him."

"Weren't you?"

"I said I was not. And since when do I owe you an explanation?"

"Fine," Matthew grunted, his anger growing in strength the longer he was in her company. "You owe me not a thing, except maybe to treat me as well as you would your friend."

Matthew suddenly shoved her against the wall with a force that stung. Before she realized what he was about, he pressed his hips into hers. "Why, you . . ." Maggie's attempted slap was stopped in midair by a quick block of his arm. Instantly he had her hands pinned behind her as he pulled her up firmly against his obviously growing passion.

His voice was a low, menacing growl as he pulled her hair back so her face tilted up. "If I were you, I'd not try that again. I don't appreciate being slapped."

Maggie felt a moment's fear but refused to give the emotion full rein. He would rot in hell before he'd see her cower. "And *I* don't appreciate being spoken to in this manner."

"Perhaps you'd rather I do this than speak," he returned as he lowered his head and suddenly took possession of her soft mouth in a kiss that held no trace of the tenderness she had experienced the day before.

Maggie tried to twist her head, to free herself of the contact of his mouth, but the movement only caused his arms to tighten until the breath was nearly squeezed out of her. Maggie's heart thudded with dread. What had she done? How could she ever have allowed him to touch her? Who was he, after all? What was he going to do to her?

But a moment later Maggie's fearful thoughts evaporated into nothingness as the pressure of his mouth began to gentle, and a suffocating heat rose to engulf her within its flame. Maggie's heart still pounded, but no longer in fear. Now she fought against the raging desire he so easily brought to the surface. She wanted him despite his rough treatment, despite all he had said and implied. She wanted him despite the anger he inspired. Perhaps because of her anger she only wanted him more.

Matthew felt her body soften. A groan came from deep within his throat as he felt her rub her hips against his. His tongue sought out the sweetness of her mouth and found no obstacle to his rediscovery. Kissing a woman had never felt this right before. It had never been so sweet.

Matthew released her hands so that he could hold her hips still. If she kept moving against him, he'd explode. But, when he had released her hands, Maggie proceeded to let him know just how hungry she was to touch him, and Matthew couldn't prevent the hard shudder that suddenly wracked his body.

Their mouths twisted, each hungrily taking what the other offered. Both felt the aching splendor of passion denied. They moved on instinct, wild for the taste and feel of each other.

Matthew was the first to come to his senses. God, he had to stop, and it had to be now, lest he lose all control and take her here in the open where any and all could come upon them.

Matthew tore his mouth from hers and looked into her passion-filled eyes a long moment before finding the strength to mock, "So it seems I too am a friend." An instant later he flung her away and walked outside.

Matthew knew his temper was out of control. He also knew that he wasn't being fair, but at the moment he couldn't think rationally. He had wanted to hurt her, simply for being so beautiful that others wanted her. He knew the embrace he had witnessed was not as harmless as she seemed to believe.

Matthew gave off a steady round of vile curses, for it was Landsing he wanted to hurt but Maggie who suffered. Sweet Jesus, he never knew he had such jealousy within him, and the knowledge left him less than happy.

══ *Five* ══

ABIGAIL WARREN'S FEET ACHED as she walked briskly along the Post Road toward her home. The sun was nearly set, and the idea of being on the road at night made her uneasy. It was known that the soldiers who patrolled the area would not resist the temptation to ravish a young girl if they had the chance.

Her stomach growled as she hurried along, hoping she'd be in time for the evening meal. She couldn't be certain that her mother had kept something aside for her. If her father or brothers saw it, they'd more than likely finish it off without thinking of her empty stomach.

Abby fingered the few coins in her skirt pocket with a satisfied smile. She'd be able to buy Lizzy shoes for Sunday with the added coin Mrs. Hale had insisted she take, and her father and brothers would be none the wiser till the deed was done.

It was a disgrace, she mused, the way the menfolk of her family took to the taste of ale. Instead of seeing to the care of their women, they spent their days at the Fox and Hound Inn some ten miles south of their home, cajoling and wrangling and sometimes cheating a fellow patron so their afternoon might be spent within the numbing comfort of drink.

Abby sighed with disgust. Her father and brothers would

never reform, regardless of their constant promises, and she must accept the fact that as long as she lived at home they would forever take her last coin.

Abby smiled as the beauty of the setting sun reminded her of the vivid bolt of cloth Mrs. Hale had shown her, cloth that would remain intact and in the closet until this wretched war was at an end. For, Mrs. Hale declared, no true patriot would spend time working on such frivolity when there were bandages to roll and shirts to make for our fighting men.

The fashion book that had accompanied the fabric was also pushed to the back of the closet. It was filled with pictures of pretty ladies in beautiful clothes, and Abby could have cried with the longing that filled her heart when she looked at its pages.

Mrs. Hale couldn't help but notice the look on the young girl's face and had promised that on the day the war ended she would begin to make Abby the most beautiful dress she had ever seen. They would copy one of the patterns from the book.

Remembering Mrs. Hale's promise, Abby suddenly stopped her hurried pace and spun around. She was almost beside herself with the sheer joy of someday owning something so lovely. She had seen ladies in beautiful dresses now and then, but they were the women who lived at Peggy's rooming house, and everyone knew what they were. Still, she had noticed the way the men in her village looked at them, her brothers in particular. Perhaps the women were not so wrong in their chosen way of life, after all. It did allow them a luxury she knew she'd never have. Their white skin was unmarred from daily chores. Their backs didn't ache from overwork, nor did their feet burn from miles of walking to their places of employment.

Last week Peggy herself had noticed Abby when they were both visiting the Hewlett farm for supplies. After some moments of conversation that was uncomfortable on Abby's side, the two women had struck up a friendship of sorts, and Peggy had mentioned her need for a laundress. It seemed the last one had run off with Peggy's coachman.

Since that chance meeting, Abby hadn't been able to shake her mind from the idea of working at the bawdy house. She wouldn't have to do anything she didn't already do, she reasoned. It wouldn't be up to her to entertain the men. Still, Peggy had hinted that if Abby had the inclination, the possibility of more substantial wages existed.

What would it be like to be with a man, Abby wondered? Would it be horrible? Would he make those awful animal sounds she sometimes heard coming from her parents' bed? Would she be able to keep her mind on the monetary rewards and not show her revulsion? For that matter, would she feel revulsion? What would her mother think? What would her father do if he found out? Probably nothing more than to visit occasionally to ask for a handout, Abby mused with a cynical twist of her lip.

At the sound of an approaching carriage, Abby turned and moved a bit off the dirt road. It was getting darker by the minute; if she didn't step up her pace, it would be pitch black before she got home.

Abby watched as the buggy swerved toward her, and she smiled and waved as she recognized the driver.

He was pulling the horse to a stop. Abby couldn't believe her luck. He was going to talk to her, and her heart pounded with excitement. Perhaps she would tell him about the dress.

Abby did not realize how pretty she looked as the last rays of the setting sun cast a warm pink glow over her. The light emphasized the snowy whiteness of her mobcap, bedecked with dark blue ribbons that exactly matched her eyes, while tendrils of golden curls had fallen free to frame her pretty round face.

Abby's smile turned her face from pretty to radiant as the man nodded gallantly and said, "Evening, Mistress Warren. Could I tempt you with an offer of a ride home?"

Abby laughed aloud at the formality with which he

addressed her. No one had ever treated her like a lady before, and she fairly beamed as she gave a short curtsy and replied, "Indeed, sir, you may."

The carriage moved along at a brisk pace, and Abby soon forgot her aching feet as she and the man at her side passed the time of day.

"Would you mind terribly if I made a quick stop before bringing you home? I promised the widow O'Shea that I would check on her house while she's gone to Pennsylvania."

Abby thought that an odd request. Why would the widow ask him to keep an eye on her property? He didn't live nearby. Still, it was none of her concern, and another moment or so spent in this man's company could only bring her more delight.

"You need not rush on my account." Abby smiled prettily, while enjoying immensely the simple privilege of being with him. "I rarely have the chance to ride in a carriage."

The carriage turned off the dirt road onto an overgrown, narrow path.

"This is not the way," Abby remarked as she noticed the error in direction. "The widow lives further on down the road."

"Aye," he agreed easily. "This is but a shorter route to her place."

Abby nodded, a slight smile tugging at the corner of her lips, for she knew there was no way they could get to the widow's house by this road. He was taking her to a place that provided more privacy. Perhaps he wanted a kiss. Well, she would see about that, she thought primly. She wasn't the kind who gave freely of her favors. If he wanted to kiss her, he'd have to make a few promises first.

The night was perfect for romance, and Abby's heart skipped with delight. Who would have thought this man would be interested in her? He was so much older, so much more sophisticated. She hoped he didn't think her a child.

Surely he did not, she reasoned, for he would not be there with her if that were so. He would not have pulled off the road but would have taken her directly home.

Once they were a hundred yards or so from the road, he pulled the carriage to a halt on a grassy knoll.

"I'm afraid I've made a wrong turn. I'll have us out of here in a minute. Don't be frightened."

"Oh, I'm not," Abby said, her voice trembling slightly with excitement. "I could never be afraid with you at my side."

His eyes glittered in the shadows. Thick overhanging branches blotted out the last of the day's light. "Would you like to watch the moon rise?"

Abby's smile was all he needed for an answer.

They sat in silence. Sweetly scented clover covered the ground, giving off a delicious fragrance that promised a delightful summer. He put his arm around her shoulders, to ward off a chill, he explained, and Abby sighed with contentment, easily convincing herself that not another two on the planet could feel this exquisitely close bond of companionship.

After a few minutes his hand tipped her head to rest upon his shoulder, and they both sighed as he pulled her soft, small body more firmly against him.

Abby had never been kissed before, and although the gentle touch of his mouth to her forehead was as far from passion-filled as one could get, Abby, in her innocence, instantly imagined herself in the throes of a great, all-consuming love.

"Oh darling," she murmured into the warmth of his neck as her young body trembled with anticipation of a first love.

A low growling sound came from deep within his throat as he spread his fingers into the luxuriously thick blond curls that cascaded down her back when her mobcap was flung aside.

Abby smiled, proud that her hair should bring him such

delight. She lay back against the strong arm that encircled her and watched as his dark face came ever closer to her own. He was going to kiss her! Her first real kiss, and she couldn't wait! Abby's lips parted slightly in anticipation, and a soft moaning sound came from her throat as his mouth covered hers.

Abby was caught up in a young girl's dream of romance. Never before had a man treated her so tenderly, touched her so gently, or whispered such loving words, and she had no doubt that before the night's end he would beg for her hand.

"I've wanted to do this for so long," he murmured against her throat as he pushed aside the fichu she had neatly tucked inside her neckline.

"Have you?" she breathed softly, her mind in a fog of delight, her heart nearly bursting with happiness. Abby, in her innocence, would have been shocked to know his true thoughts. For his words meant nothing more to him than a means to vanquish his raging lust. And her shock would have turned to horror had she known that it mattered not at all whom he slaked it upon.

An instant later his fingers were reaching for the soft flesh of her breasts, uncaring that the tenderness he had been so careful to exhibit before had vanished.

Abby tried in vain to push his hand away. "'Tis not proper," she whispered sweetly, fully expecting a sincere apology. But when her softly spoken words were ignored, Abby felt the first stirrings of anxiety.

A moment later her body stiffened as a chilling fear overrode the sweet sensations she had previously known. Uncaring of the pain he inflicted, he brutally squeezed her breast and bit the tender flesh of her lip till her soft protests grew into screams of terror.

"No!" she cried as she squirmed to free herself. Her heart pounded with dread that she should find herself alone with a man who didn't hesitate to show his cruelty.

"Bitch!" came the thickly garbled reply as his lips left

hers and his hand closed over her mouth, cutting off all sounds of protest. "You're just like *her.*" He sneered. "I should have waited for Peggy. She knows how to treat a man."

"Please," Abby begged frantically, but the word went unheeded as his fingers tore at her clothes until they hung in tattered shreds from her shoulders.

In a panic now, Abby bit his hand, and for her efforts she felt the back of the other come crashing into her face. Again he hit her, this time with his fist, not concerned that the force of the attack nearly rendered her senseless. A front tooth broke, its jagged edge dug into her lip, but she hadn't the time to feel the pain it would cause before her lip split from yet another blow.

He couldn't stop. Somehow, every time his fists struck her, he grew harder and his need to possess her grew more urgent.

Some part of Abby's mind wondered dully that she was still alive. But she never managed to finish the thought as another blow slammed into her face and cracked her jaw.

The next ruthless punch caused something to snap in her neck, and she found herself gagging on her own blood as it gushed into her mouth. But his hand covered her mouth again, and she could do naught but swallow the warm, obnoxiously sweet fluid. Her stomach threatened to rebel, but Abby soon forgot its uneasy condition when a horrible pain ripped into her breast.

She moaned in helpless horror, her voice thick with shock and pain, as she realized he was biting her. With relief, Abby gratefully welcomed the blackness of unconsciousness and never knew his teeth were sinking deep enough into her flesh to cause blood to run in tiny rivulets across her chest.

A moment later his eyes lifted with a maniacal gleam. He smiled as he watched her face, so pretty and sweet in sleep. But she shouldn't be sleeping, he reasoned. Nay, she should be enjoying this as much as he.

"Abby," he commanded, "'tis not the time for a nap."

Stupid bitch, he groaned to himself in annoyance. *What the hell kind of a woman falls asleep in the midst of such love making? This will revive her soon enough.* He grinned as he swung her limp, nearly naked body onto his lap. It took but a moment to release the throbbing heat from between his legs and ram his body into hers.

A low groan escaped his throat at the pleasure. She was so tight, so goddamned tight, he could hardly bear it.

Abby's nearly unconscious body stiffened as fiery agony suffused her being. She had never known such horror. She wanted to scream, but the sound was no more than a soft cry as it passed between her swollen lips. She lapsed into blessed nothingness.

"God, this is good," he grunted unevenly as he pumped his body with ever-increasing speed. It was happening too fast. He wasn't going to be able to hold back. It wasn't going to be good for her, but he couldn't stop.

A low groan rumbled deep within his chest. It was coming. It was ecstasy. He'd never known such pleasure. His body jerked convulsively, and a choked cry broke the quiet of the night as he held her in a bone-crushing embrace.

Abby lay limply in his arms. Her head rested against his shoulder. Her body gave a last violent shudder before collapsing completely.

It took a long moment before his breathing returned to normal. With a tender smile, he held her close against him. "'Twas good, Abby," he sighed as he snuggled his face into her neck. "Was it not?" He chuckled softly. "Fall not back to sleep, Abby, love. The hour grows late, and your mother will begin to worry."

But when no answer was forthcoming, he gave her a gentle shake. "Abby?"

Still nothing.

He pushed her from him so he might look into her face and gasped with shock at the sight that greeted him. My

God, had he done this? Had he so violently bruised her face
and ripped her clothes? It couldn't be! He had to get her
some help, but from where?

His heart pounded in his chest as he fought against panic.
Nothing but disaster would be accomplished if he didn't
think clearly. What was he to do? He couldn't take her home
like this. He couldn't calmly deposit her on her doorway
and depart, leaving her bloodied and almost naked. No one
could know what he'd done. Could he talk to her? Could he
convince her to keep her mouth shut?

Impossible. He couldn't take the chance. He had much to
lose if all were found out.

He didn't want to do it, but what choice did he have? He
had to protect himself.

With slow determination, he ran his hands to her neck
and closed them around her slender throat. Slowly, he
began to squeeze. He held her like that for a long time until
he realized she was not breathing. She had never fought
him. She had already been dead.

With a small shove, her body toppled to the ground,
bruised and beaten. He hastily dumped the bits and pieces
of her clothing he found around him.

He suddenly realized that his cheek smarted. The bitch
must have scratched him! How had he not felt her doing it?
A vicious curse broke the silence of the night when he
realized that his coat and shirt were damp with her blood.
God damn it! Even in the moonlight, his trousers showed
the telltale stains. How was he going to get into the house
without being seen? He had to burn those clothes. He felt
panic grip his chest and close over his throat with icy
tentacles until he could barely breathe. *Wait, damn it, think!
Think!* his mind screamed.

Finally, a slow smile lifted the corners of his mouth. Of
course. He grinned. There was always Peggy. Peggy would
help without asking questions.

He gave the buggy a final check, lest he overlook some

damning piece of evidence. Then he grabbed up the reins and swung the buggy around.

His gaze lingered for just a moment on the half-naked form sprawled across a carpet of clover. He shook his head with regret. An instant later he shrugged his shoulders and left.

═══ Six ═══

M AGGIE HEAVED THE LAST of her belongings from her shoulder to the floor of the loft. After she finished arranging Caleb's impromptu room, Hannah would have to see to making the linens into sleeping pallets. Maggie did not have the time. Even now Aunt Matilda was beside herself trying to complete the preparations for the evening meal.

It was amazing how those cursed British could come into her home and take over, regardless of the inconvenience they caused. What did they care, after all? They were not forced to endure the scent of animals while they ate and slept.

It was beyond her understanding how those prettily dressed peacocks and their simpering lackeys could have beaten Long Island's rugged forces. Maggie knew the sheer size of the English army had brought about the only outcome possible. Still, the knowledge did not sit well, for she knew any colonist could take on a Britisher and beat him soundly. Maggie smiled as her imagination allowed a lone man to stand before the whole of the British army and beat them one by one.

Maggie grinned at the ridiculous thought, but her smile did not fade as she thought again of the final outcome of the hostilities. New York might now be firmly in the hands of its occupiers, but in the end the patriots would win, of that she had no doubt. And, until that time, she could do naught but obey whoever might be currently in charge.

Maggie shook her head, forcing aside her dangerous thoughts. If she were smart, she would not let the occupying force know of her resentment. It was well within their power to treat her and her family in a most hostile fashion.

Maggie knew she was not alone in her distress. Since the battle of Long Island, the English had swarmed over her small village, strutting in their finery, taking what they would, and punishing those who objected.

Others had had their homes commandeered, and Maggie knew better than to speak out against her own unjust treatment. She would not put her family in danger, no matter what was asked of her. Even if it meant moving their sleeping quarters to the barn.

Weary from a day spent toiling for the strutting, powdered fools, she slowly descended the ladder from the loft. Her back ached, and Maggie knew it would be hours yet before she could retire.

The sound of a buggy careening into the yard instantly freed her thoughts from the chores that awaited. Maggie stopped midway between the house and the barn, a worried frown marring her beautiful face. Her first thought was of Joseph and his safety. A quick look around relieved her, for the boy was nowhere in sight. But Maggie had no further time for thought. She watched, horrified, as the horse and buggy dashed madly toward her.

Clearly, the animal was out of control, for it ran as if crazed. Its eyes bulged with fright, its coat was slick with sweat, and foam dribbled from its mouth as its sides heaved in a struggle for breath. Maggie then realized with a shock that the horse was being savagely lashed with a buggy whip.

Her gaze moved past the wild-eyed animal to the driver. Caleb's maniacally gleaming eyes could be seen even from that distance. That the man was mad was obvious. Maggie found herself frozen in place. She could not breathe. She could not think. And, worst of all, she could not move.

A scream lodged silently in her throat, and Maggie felt the world tip crazily as she stared helplessly into the eyes of certain death. In her frozen horror, she could do no more than pray for a speedy end.

As the horse sped closer, unseen hands flung her with dizzying force into the unyielding wall of the barn.

Maggie cried out as her shoulder slammed against the inflexible wood. For a long moment she lay inert against the firm body that held her pinned to the wall. She was somehow, miraculously, still alive! Next to her ear, a breathless voice asked, "Are you all right?"

Maggie gasped as she realized that an English officer was holding her almost tenderly against him. An Englisher! Good God, he had saved her life! Until now she had believed them to be naught but vile creatures, capable only of leaving horror and death in their wake.

His frown of worry smoothed, and his mouth curved into a charming smile as his blue gaze took in the pretty woman he held so closely in his arms. "For a minute I thought we were both done for."

Maggie's mouth opened with wordless horror. The realization of what had happened suddenly crashed upon her. Her own husband had tried to kill her! And she had been so dumbfounded that she could do no more than stare. She had never even moved.

Maggie started to shake. The enormity of what had just happened left her suddenly feeling helpless, and tears of despair ran down her cheeks. Her body was shaking. She couldn't hold on. She was losing control and started sliding from the man's arms. His frown appeared again, and a low curse sounded somewhere near her ear. Just as his face went strangely out of focus, a drifting sensation left her peacefully calm.

The next thing Maggie knew, she was sitting on the first

step of her porch with her head between her legs, while a heavy weight pressed firmly against her back and soothing words were whispered from somewhere above. She must have made a sound, for the officer released his hold and allowed her to lift her head. She was dizzy and weak and didn't refuse the flask that was brought to her lips. Maggie gasped and choked as the burning liquid filled her mouth and seeped down her throat, leaving fire everywhere it touched.

She was still sputtering and gasping for air when Matthew turned the corner of the barn to find her almost nestled in the arms of an English soldier.

Jesus Christ! He choked, his body filled with sudden rage. Was the woman never without the comfort of a man's arms?

Matthew's face was dark with fury. He hated to expose his annoyance at her behavior, but he couldn't resist the almost casual taunt as he moved closer. "Yet another friend?" Before Maggie could respond, he continued, "I hate to interrupt, but that husband of yours is riding like a wild man through your precious fields. If you listen, you can hear him laughing from here."

Maggie lifted her head and faced her tormentor with a threatening scowl. For the moment, she couldn't have cared less if Caleb ruined her whole crop. After so narrowly escaping death, she did not have to take anything from this beast. No matter what he was doing for her and her family, she didn't have to listen to his abusively snide comments. But the sudden ear-splitting screams of an injured horse stopped any words that might have come.

Matthew emitted a stream of curses as he turned on his heel and dashed toward the sounds of agony with the young officer following close behind. By the time Maggie had gained control of her wobbly legs, the two running men were hundreds of yards away.

She came upon the buggy in a distant field, lying ominously on its side, but she could find no sign of the horse. None, that is, until she moved closer . . .

By this time, Maggie's skirt was in ruins. Soaked with foam and sweat, caked with newly plowed soil, she cradled the horse's head in her lap. Her soothing words of comfort and calm stroking hands belied her grim expression as she looked across the animal's prone body into Matthew's dark, angry eyes.

The horse jerked with pain as Matthew ran his hand down its foreleg. His low, barely heard curse sounded as the horse screamed. The disgusted shake of his head left Maggie with little doubt about the animal's fate.

Matthew lifted her away from the animal when he returned with his gun. An instant later, the horse suffered no more.

Maggie turned away, wanting to be alone, when her husband's drunken whine stopped her in her tracks.

"Are you going to leave me here?"

"I'll send Elijah back for you," Maggie managed brokenly. She knew he was gloating over the loss of the animal, even though he lay helpless in the mud.

Matthew turned his pent-up anger on the drunken fool at his feet. He wanted to smash his fists into the ugly face, but he remarked coldly, "You, sir, owe me a horse. I care not how you manage to repay me, but I expect it to be done within the week." And before he took his leave, he finished with, "You will not again take an animal from this farm. If you've a need to go about, have your friend Jack take you."

Maggie listened to Aunt Matilda's gentle snores as she lay cuddled next to Joseph in the dark. It had been hours since the last candle had been extinguished, and still sleep would not come. She was going to be exhausted during the long day that stretched ahead, but no matter how she shifted she could find no comfortable position and therefore no sleep.

You lie, Maggie, she berated silently. *You know the cause of your sleepless night is right now in the last stall below.* She sighed as she disengaged Joseph's thin arm from about her neck, knowing it useless to lie abed any longer. It would be light in a few hours. She might as well get dressed. Hannah would, no doubt, be in the kitchen, already preparing the morning meal. With the soldiers to feed, Maggie knew Hannah would welcome her help.

Maggie had reached the last step of the ladder when her skirt tangled around her foot. She gave a soft gasp, knowing she was about to fall, when arms as hard as steel pulled her against a warm body.

Maggie almost screamed. Her heart pounded with terror until his harshly spoken words sounded above her ear. "I've a need to talk to you, mistress." And when Maggie struggled to free herself of his hold, he continued, "Right now!"

Matthew dragged a very unwilling Maggie from the barn. For a moment she thought of screaming, but that would bring her family and the soldiers upon them, and she had no wish to be found in the dark with this man.

"Let me go," she grunted as she fought against his superior strength.

Matthew ignored her words and struggles until he got her some yards from the barn. There, beneath the darker shade of an old oak, he turned her to face him and shook her till her teeth rattled.

"You barbarian!" she gasped as she tried to work herself free.

"You fool!" he grunted as he shook her again.

"Take your hands off me!" she insisted.

Matthew pulled her close against him. "Why didn't you tell me?"

"Why don't you stop sneaking up on me?"

"He tried to kill you today. If I'd known, I'd have . . ."

"I promise you my heart can only take so much."

"Why didn't you move?"

"God, it pounds still."

"Do you want to die?"

"What?" Maggie asked, since these were the first words that penetrated her fear and anger.

"Damn it, haven't you listened to a word I've said?"

"Have you?" she countered.

Matthew grinned, and although Maggie could not see his smile, she could tell by the way his body suddenly relaxed that his anger had passed.

"It appears we are destined forever to carry on two simultaneous conversations."

"That's because you are a thickheaded bull," Maggie snapped as she finally found herself released.

Matthew chuckled softly. "You've found me out, mistress. I had hoped to gain your trust and more before you knew the truth of it."

Maggie ignored the meaning behind "and more" as she brushed off the sleeve of her shirt just as if her eyes could see through the pitch blackness that surrounded them. At his lengthening silence, she finally prompted, "Well, you were anxious enough to bring me here. What did you want to talk about?"

"Are you going to report his actions to the constable?"

"And if I do?"

"I understand that according to law you cannot testify against him, but Bretton certainly can. The man was eyewitness to the incident."

"Mister Forrest, what Colonel Bretton saw was a man deep in his cups. No court in the world would hold him liable for a near accident. And no one, not even you, can say it was anything more."

"And what say you?" His deep voice came out of the darkness, and Maggie was grateful he could not see her as she lowered her head and refused to answer.

"I asked you a question."

Still nothing.

"Maggie," he growled, his tone a clear warning. "You will answer me."

"For God's sake!" she finally returned, knowing the fruitlessness of her silence. The man was not going to allow her a minute's peace until she answered. But she couldn't admit, even to him, the horror of the truth. "What does it matter? 'Tis finished, done. I'll not speak of it again." She turned to leave him, but Matthew sensed her movement and reached out to pull her toward him.

"Maggie, Maggie," he breathed into her hair as he held her within the warmth of his arms. "How can you stay with him? How much more are you to suffer at his hands?"

"He is my husband," she spoke softly into the warmth of his chest, while his tenderness caused her eyes to mist inexplicably. "Shall I throw him, a cripple, into the street and take up with you?"

"'Tis a thought." He grinned. At her obvious stiffening, he soothed, "Fear not, Maggie, my love, I tease, no more."

"You are a wretched beast," she groaned into his shirt, unconsciously pressing her face closer to his warmth as she breathed the scent of his skin deep into her lungs.

"Aye," he agreed easily as his arm pulled her closer.

"A bully."

"Aye," he grinned as his hand slid down the length of her back and cupped her hips, bringing them hard against his.

Maggie gasped as she felt his desire. "And a man of one thought."

"Aye," he breathed as his lips came to brush against the silkiness of her cheek, her jaw, her neck.

"I should go," she breathed shakily. "Hannah will be needing help in the kitchen."

"Aye," he groaned, his voice growing deeper, huskier, pulling her closer to a fire that threatened to burn out of control.

"Can you say naught else but aye?" Maggie sighed, barely able to think past the knowledge of his mouth as chills ran over her shoulder and down her spine, and his mouth moved over her cheek ever closer to her own.

"Are you ready to hear the things I want to say?" he asked, his mouth hovering an inch from hers.

"Nay," she groaned just as his mouth covered hers at last.

Maggie gasped with the shock of the heat that suddenly filled her being. In an instant all thoughts of decorum had fled, gone as though they had never existed. She was wild for his touch, an eager participant in this mind-boggling need.

Maggie felt as though she had been starved and was at last allowed to feast. She answered his kisses with her own. She needed this man. She needed his touch to soothe away the horror of the day. She needed his softly spoken words to erase the lingering pain.

Her mind was lost to reality, her body pulsed, filled with sensation. She knew not how the buttons of his shirt had come undone but groaned with pleasure as the parted fabric allowed her fingers the luxury of moving over the firm flesh of his chest. Her mouth tore free of his and moved to follow the warm caresses of her hands.

Matthew gasped as her lips left a trail of fire searing his exposed flesh. He knew beyond a doubt that this woman had ruined him for all others. She was driving him wild. He couldn't let her go on, but he couldn't find the strength to stop her.

"Maggie, Maggie, my love," he groaned as he lifted her head so his mouth might once more taste her sweetness. He coaxed her lips to part as his tongue eagerly sought hers.

A sentry making his hourly rounds heard the softly spoken murmurs as he neared the huge oak. The young soldier's heart pounded with terror as he imagined a platoon of cutthroat rebels lying in wait, ready to pounce on him.

Quickly he flattened his body to the opposite side of the tree. His heart pounded in his ears as he breathlessly listened for further evidence of foul play. A moment later a small smile creased the thin line of his lips as he realized he was interrupting something quite different from what he first supposed.

He sighed in silent relief, but he still hated this duty. Why was he unlucky enough to pull the last watch? And what the hell was he doing in this country in the first place? Anyone with half a brain could see these people wanted nothing more than to live in peace.

It was so dark, the soldier thought to himself. Without his lantern, he wouldn't be able to see his hand before his face. His mouth split into a grin, for he knew the two behind him would not be happy to find their privacy interrupted.

The sentry pushed himself from the tree and silently moved in a large arc to the opposite side of the tree. He had to clear his throat three times before the dazed couple finally broke apart with a guilty start. The sentry recognized the man as the new owner of the farm, but the man's body protected the lady in question from the sentry's view, even though the soldier raised his lantern for a better look. For a moment he thought he might have seen red hair. Was it the cripple's wife? God, if it were, he'd give much to trade places. It had been a long time since he'd seen such a beauty. Even the painted ladies in New York could not compare. Another grin threatened but was held in check when the young man caught the fierce look of her protector. The sentry shrugged, knowing better than to voice his thoughts. It was no concern of his who the man dallied with.

"You ought not to be wandering about on a night so dark," he remarked, hoping his voice held the right amount of authority. "There are some more prone to shoot first and apologize later for their mistake."

At Matthew's silent nod, the sentry shrugged his shoulders and moved on. It was not his problem if another of a more jittery nature should come upon them. He had warned them, and beyond ordering them back to bed he could do nothing more.

Maggie's low moan caused Matthew to turn to her once more. Gently he pulled her into his arms and soothed her as he breathed in the clean scent of her hair. "You've naught to fear. He did not see you."

But Maggie's suffering was not caused by fear of discovery. She was mortified that she should have been so wantonly aggressive, that her sinful tendencies grew in strength at every encounter. Being caught only brought home the error of her ways.

Maggie knew these stolen moments could not continue lest disaster follow.

"Matthew, we must talk," she finally managed as she forced aside her embarrassment.

"Aye," he agreed, pulling her closer.

"This cannot happen again."

"Aye."

"Will you promise?"

"I will promise only to wait until you are ready."

"But I will never be ready," she cried as she raised her face, trying to see him in the darkness. "Would you want me so desperately after I broke my vows?"

"Maggie," he breathed shakily. "Can you not understand? I want you. It matters not what you do. I will always want you."

"Nay," she groaned miserably, moving out of his arms. And just before she left his side to walk into the house, she repeated, with a shake of her head, "Nay."

Matthew lounged against the tree and watched her silhouette, formed by the light from the kitchen window, move away from him. Absentmindedly, he reached into his shirt pocket for a cheroot and grinned as he found the tattered remains of a would-be smoke.

The lady might deny her desire, but he knew it was only a matter of time before she would come to him.

═══ *Seven* ═══

Maggie wiped her red hands on her wilted, rumpled apron and blew away a stray curl that had fallen from her mobcap. She walked out of the kitchen, smiling, to greet her longtime friend, who was eyeing the huge pot of boiling water with a wicked gleam. "I knew if I waited long enough, I'd find out you preferred the more feminine arts to riding a horse."

Maggie's grin turned into a low laugh as she wielded the heavy laundry stick and pulled a pair of pants from the pot. "Sally, we've been friends for a score of years and more. Have you ever known me to forgo this most pleasant of pastimes?"

Sally, skirts flying, jumped from her carriage and laughed at her friend's sarcastic comment. The teasing twinkle in her eye belied the solemnity of her tone. "Indeed, the sight of you makes one hunger for home and hearth and, of course, her own pot of laundry."

The two women laughed at this outrageous statement as they joined forces, quickly emptied the pot of its few remaining articles, and finished the chore by dumping the water over the small fire.

A red-coated soldier stepped out of the house and leaned lazily against one of the porch beams.

74

"You too?" Sally asked as her gaze caught the movement from the corner of her eye.

Maggie nodded.

"No wonder you're not riding your fields. When?"

Maggie gave a sigh. "Yesterday."

"But . . ."

"I know. My home is not large enough to supply quarters to more than one of King George's elite, never mind six and their aides. Behold"—she gave a wry grin as she waved her arm toward the barn—"my new place of residence."

Sally followed her friend inside the barn and listened to Maggie point out the many fine points of her new living arrangement. "You cannot fault it for airiness, although the air is sometimes more pungent than one would prefer. The roof does not leak. The doors close securely. It needs little in the way of cleaning." Maggie shrugged. "No floors to scrub, and, thankfully, the windows are too high to worry over." She shrugged again and lowered her voice appreciatively. "With the Lord's help, my visitors will take their leave before the onset of winter, and we'll not freeze to death."

"Word has it Colonel Thompson is building a fort in Huntington. In a few weeks time we could all lose the pleasure of our guests' company."

Maggie nodded. "Aye, the rumors abound. One can only pray they hold some truth."

"'Tis true enough. Steven's business often takes him through the area. He tells me the people suffer greatly." Sally shrugged as if her comments were of no importance, but Maggie knew the depth of her friend's feelings. Sally continued, "It seems our *friends* have not the respect for the dead that we would have wished. The fort is being built upon the town's graveyard, while the parsonage was dismantled and the wood used for stables."

Maggie sighed with disgust. "All in all, I've no cause to complain. In truth, this is but an inconvenience compared to most."

"Aye," Sally agreed as her eyes misted. She herself had suffered greatly during the hostilities. She wondered if she'd ever forget the horror of finding her father's body along the roadside last December. Those in Sally Townsend's family were educated, well-to-do merchants, distinguished leaders in their tiny community. It was no surprise to her to find her brother and father actively, although secretly, supporting the rebel cause. And after her father's murder, she herself had continued his work.

Sally smiled and sat at a rough wooden table, watching Maggie retrieve a simmering pot from the tiny potbelly stove. "Domesticity suits you, I think. It's been some time since I've seen you attired thus and a mobcap to boot! Will wonders never cease?" she teased.

Maggie grinned as she poured the piping-hot brew into cups and sat across from her friend. "I'd not give these English something to gape at. No doubt they'd find my usual garb a bit disconcerting."

"To say the least," Sally teased. "How goes it since their arrival?"

Maggie sighed. "Hannah and Aunt Matilda have had their work load multiplied by twelve. You'd not believe the amount of bread alone that must be baked. In only one day our monthly rations have been sadly depleted, and I will not touch our hidden supplies." Maggie tipped her head toward the house. "If they expect to eat, they'd better see to other means of filling their bellies."

Sally smiled. "I take it James is working the fields."

"Aye," Maggie sighed. "Luckily, most of the planting is done. He and the two we've hired for the season are finishing the west field. All should be done by the end of the week."

Sally nodded and took a sip of her coffee. "Ugh!" she gasped and shivered at the bitter concoction. "I wonder when I will ever acquire a taste for this brew. I'd almost prefer a cup of hot water to this vile potion. At least I could then imagine myself drinking weak tea."

"Indeed, I've often had cause to witness your imagination." Maggie's brandy eyes glittered with amusement. "I can attest to its greatness."

Sally grinned at her friend's comment, but an instant later all joking ended as she lowered her voice to a mere whisper. "Do you think I could inconvenience you by borrowing your trousers just for tonight?"

Maggie knew Sally was deeply involved in the rebel cause, more so than most. Still, she had never hinted at just what it was that she did. Obviously, Sally would not ask her if it were not important.

"Your brother is out of town, I take it," Maggie commented, knowing Sally would not have come there were that not the case.

"Aye, and I've a special need to meet someone on this night. Someone who has something I hold very near and dear to my heart." She grinned devilishly.

"What time?"

Sally whispered, "Twelve. Meet me near the stream where we swam as children. All should be abed long before then."

After her friend's departure, Maggie sat thinking for a long time. For months the English had occupied the Townsend home. Of course, Sally's house was very large, and because of the Townsends' standing in the community, the family was not asked to leave but simply to use one side of the house while the officers used the other. However, it was inconceivable to Maggie that the English thought the Townsend sisters to be so inconsequential. The soldiers spoke freely around them and never worried that important information might be passed along to rebel forces. In the meantime, the women were expected to see to the officers' needs and wait upon them as if they were servants.

Maggie grinned as excitement caused her heart suddenly to pound. She wondered what Sally had in store for the charming gentlemen tonight and could hardly wait to find out.

* * *

Caleb was bored and miserable. All day long he had been stuck in his hole of a room with nothing to do but stare at four bare walls. His face was swollen and stung from the injuries he had received when the buggy overturned. He needed a drink. Where the hell was Jack? Didn't the stupid bastard realize he should have been there hours ago? He'd never felt more a cripple.

Now that Forrest had forbidden him the use of a buggy, he had nothing to do but wait for his friend. This morning he had ordered Elijah to carry him to the buggy, but the sneaking servant had only muttered, "Sorry, sir, but the master, he says no one can take his buggy or horse without askin'."

That was a shock. What with the state he was in yesterday, he remembered Forrest growling out something, but for the life of him he hadn't known what. Now that he remembered, he dared not simply override Forrest's orders. Not that he could in any case, not with that worthless Elijah always watching.

Jesus, he had to get out of there! He'd go crazy if he stayed even one more minute.

Suddenly a black face peeped around the corner. "Miz Maggie says it's time to eat."

"Well, what the hell are you waiting for? Get me up."

Caleb muttered all the way to the table until his eyes met the murderous black gaze of the farm's new owner. Knowing better than to push his luck, lest he find himself with nowhere to sleep that night, he wisely quieted. Still, the anger and bitterness he felt toward Matthew quietly grew.

The conversation around the table was pleasant, if a bit stilted, as Caleb sat moodily picking at his food. Everyone seemed to be on edge over the events of the day before.

Caleb admitted to himself that he had been deep in his cups but not so deep that he hadn't known he had nearly killed that bitch of a wife of his. If it hadn't been for the interference of that goddamned Britisher, today he would have been the happiest of widowers.

"Have you too had an accident, Mr. Forrest?" Aunt Matilda inquired gently as she noticed the angry red scratch along his cheek.

Matthew nodded somewhat sheepishly. "Aye." Keeping his gaze on his plate, he continued, "It appears at the time my mind was on other matters, and I didn't notice a branch that blocked my path." Matthew grinned as he lifted his gaze to the gray-haired lady. "Once my supplies arrive, I'll not have the time for idle strolls in the woods."

"When do you expect them?" Aunt Matilda asked.

"Before the end of the week, I'm told."

"One wonders," Caleb began with an air of total innocence as he played listlessly with his food, "how, during times such as these, one can manage supplies for an inn."

Matthew shot Caleb a look of pure hate. "I imagine one does," he returned.

"We are under such constraints here. How will you manage, Mr. Forrest?" Aunt Matilda asked. Every face, including Hannah's, turned toward him, waiting for an explanation.

Caleb almost shouted with glee. So their charming host was not exactly what he professed himself to be. His lips curved into an evil grin, and he fought a losing battle to keep his merriment at bay. It was obvious from the growing silence that suddenly filled the barn that everyone present had just become suspicious of Matthew.

Matthew almost groaned aloud. By the looks they were giving him, he hadn't a doubt they thought him a Tory, for no one but those loyal to the crown could possibly embark on such an expensive undertaking. And it was impossible for him to tell them the truth. To do that would clearly jeopardize the whole operation.

Why hadn't anyone thought of this problem before? Of course, the town folk would question the means of his acquisitions! How could they not, when they were reduced to the barest existence, and he appeared beyond all monetary worries?

His compatriots had been wise enough to foresee problems with the English, and he had purposely made British friends in places of authority in order to overcome any problems that might occur, but no one had thought of the townfolk and their opinion.

After a long moment of total silence, Matthew knew the matter would not be laid to rest with a simple shrug of his shoulder. He had to come up with some sort of a story. With a silent prayer that those present would believe his tale, he began, "My family owns some acreage east of here. Most of the supplies will come from there." He allowed a conspiratorial grin as he leaned back in his chair and continued with a nonchalant shrug, "The rest will be cajoled out of the trusting souls who have so graciously established themselves as our guardians."

Matthew breathed a long, silent sigh of relief as, one by one, every frozen face relaxed, and sheepish grins began to soften what had been only seconds before tight masks of mistrust.

Matthew had to force himself not to grin in triumph as he shot Caleb a look and saw the naked hatred in the man's eyes. He believed this man was a threat to his cause. He hated family and country alike and would not hesitate to see either destroyed if it suited his whims.

Caleb's nasty voice once again broke into the family's mealtime chatter. "I believe I've never seen you looking more lovely, my dear." Everyone at the table held their breath waiting for the final cutting word. They were not to be disappointed.

Caleb's evil grin belied the sweet tone of his words and delight that crossed his face as he watched his wife's eyes close in torment. "One wonders why, after years of trying to act the part of a man you should so suddenly acquire a taste for feminine trappings." He laughed as he watched her cheeks darken with color. "With the exception of Sundays, of course, I had my doubts I'd recognize you in skirts."

He grinned as he leaned forward. "Would you care to let us all in on the secret?"

"Caleb," Maggie hissed between clenched teeth as she strove to control the rage he could so easily bring to surface, "'tis no secret, in fact. Since the arrival of our English friends, Aunt Matilda and Hannah are in need of my help. 'Tis easy enough to ensure our gentlemen guests do not overstep the bounds of propriety, by changing my usual manner of dress."

Caleb made an ungracious sound, his expression clearly one of disbelief. "Oh come now, since when have you cared for propriety? You, a lady of such free spirit? You ride a horse astride, do you not? You swagger about your fields caring not what others think upon seeing your womanly form, do you not? You rule this house as if you were the man, deferring to no one—especially not to me, do you not? What care you about propriety?"

Maggie shot her husband a pleading glance. "Caleb, need we air our differences before others?"

Caleb shrugged, "I harbor no secrets, my dear. Can you say the same? Could it be the real reason you've taken to skirts, of late, is the fact that they are so much easier to lift when the need arises, particularly when certain innkeepers are about."

Aunt Matilda's gasp, Hannah's choke of rage and Maggie's soft groan of horror were all lost in the sudden clatter of dishes and savage roar that filled the barn to the point of shaking the high windows as Matthew jumped from his seat. His chair was sent flying behind him as he lunged across the table, his hands clutching at Caleb's collar as he dragged the man over the spilled tankards of apple juice and half eaten plates of food.

Matthew gave him a vicious shake. His face, dark with fury, was only inches from Caleb's suddenly terrified expression as he spat out, "If you ever again dare to insult this lady in my presence, I will kill you."

He shook him again. Caleb was hanging limp and helpless from his neck, his arms relieving only a portion of the choking sensation Matthew was inflicting as he desperately clung to the raging man's thick shoulders. Caleb's skin was turning sickly blue from lack of air, but Matthew was oblivious to the man's suffering as he waited for an answer. "Do you hear?"

Maggie ran around the table, trying to pull Caleb free of Matthew's hold. Joseph began to cry in fear, and Aunt Matilda quickly spirited the boy away from the table and out of the barn.

It took a long moment before Maggie realized her efforts to bring about Caleb's release were futile. In truth, she only managed to increase his suffering as she tugged at his body. It was obvious from the glassy look in Matthew's eyes that her cries of protest were having no effect on his murderous rage. For an instant she wondered if anything short of a blow to his head with a cast-iron pot would break his hold. Knowing the fruitlessness of her efforts to help Caleb, she gave up her tugging and turned instead to Matthew. Beating at his arms with all her strength, she finally got him to notice what he was about.

"Matthew, please, stop!" And then, noting the bluish color of her husband's face, she continued, with no little horror, "He cannot answer you if you will not allow him to breathe."

By this time, James and Elijah had run into the barn, and Maggie was shoved roughly aside as the two men saw to the lengthening of Caleb's life rather than his neck.

A short while later, Matthew was standing outside beneath the same tree where Maggie and he had shared a tender moment the night before. Even though the night was warm, a shiver of revulsion ran up his spine. God, he had almost lost all control. What was the point in pretending? He *had* lost control and had come closer than he cared to admit to killing a fellow human being—although in his opinion, calling Caleb Darrah a human being was taking great liberties with the word.

He sighed silently. Caleb could tempt a saint to murder. How the hell was he to sit at the same table and listen to the man's evil comments night after night and not finish the job he had started?

Another thought crossed his mind. If Caleb were dead, Maggie would be free to come to him. If he were dead, if he were dead . . .

God damn it, stop! he berated himself with a vicious curse. *He's alive, and wishing otherwise is a waste of time. If you want her so badly, persuade her to overcome her moral objections on the matter. Convince her that being with you would be worth her loss of self-respect.*

He groaned aloud with total disgust. How could he do that to a woman he loved? Matthew's whole body stiffened with the truth of the sudden thought. He loved her. Damn, how had he allowed it to happen? It could only complicate everything. He didn't need this.

What the hell are you going to do about it, Forrest? a voice in his head queried. *Not a goddamned thing,* another barely heard voice answered in the back of his mind. He loved her, but he could not, would not, drag her away from here. He couldn't even think of starting a new life somewhere else— not until he was finished with this mission, and that could take years.

There's nothing for you to do, Forrest, but bear the pain of it.

"Nothing," he whispered aloud.

"Are you all right?" came a softly spoken question in the dark night. Matthew watched her shadowy form move toward him.

"Hadn't you better ask that of your husband, madam?" Matthew snapped, fighting the instant flood of longing that filled his being.

Maggie was shocked into silence by his vicious tone. Her head snapped up. Her eyes glittered dangerously. "Mr. Forrest, I've another who is proficient in the art of nastiness. I need not stand here and listen to your insults." Maggie suddenly spun on her heels, more than anxious to depart his company.

"Wait," he hissed, his arm moving against his will. What the hell was he doing pulling her back? Why didn't he just let her go?

The sudden impotent wanting that filled him seemed only to fuel his anger. He lifted her by her shoulders, his fingers digging cruelly into her soft flesh as he brought her close to his snarling face. "Come to bring a measure of comfort to the less fortunate, mistress?"

Maggie gasped with shock at the biting words. Her first impulse was to slap his face, but her position restricted all movement. "Mr. Forrest, you are, without a doubt, the most obnoxious beast it's been my misfortune to encounter."

"Perhaps," he conceded, "but, more importantly, are you really the sweet abused wife who tears at everyone's heartstrings? Are you deserving of the pity bestowed?"

"Spare me your pity, Mr. Forrest. I want nothing from you."

"Do you not? I grow to believe your husband has ample cause to accuse you."

"I care not what you believe." She sneered as she eyed him coldly. "You are a rutting rogue, ready at a moment's notice to fall upon any female, the willingness of the lady of no consequence."

"Aye," he returned, his sarcasm unmistakable, "I've had to fight to the death to get you in my arms."

Maggie was beside herself with rage. It took every ounce of her control not to scream out the curses that threatened. She fought a desperate battle for calm and was finally able to look into his eyes with a deadly chill that would freeze any heart. Her icy stare might have worked had there been enough light beneath the overhanging branches. She felt the need to curse at him after all. "You beast, you bloody, rutting beast!"

Matthew only laughed. "Is that the best you can do? Am I not deserving of more passion than that?"

"Let me go!" she warned between clenched teeth as she struggled to free herself.

"And if I do not?" he dared to ask.

"Mr. Forrest, I know not the reasonings of your anger and less so your need to make me the brunt of it. If you do not release me this instant, I shall scream until all in the house come running."

"Will you?" he laughed without a shred of humor. "And how, may I ask, will you accomplish that feat when your mouth is otherwise occupied?"

He took her mouth then, without further warning. He kissed her with all his pent-up, misdirected rage that longed to find its release in pure violence. He felt a small measure of guilt at her soft groan of pain when he ground his mouth almost viciously into hers. But his guilt was instantly overshadowed by the deliciousness of holding her close against him.

His anger was now forgotten, replaced by a desire that threatened his sanity, if not his very life, and he knew then that he'd have this woman, no matter what it took to get her . . .

Maggie cried out against the sudden desire that raged throughout her body the moment his mouth touched hers, while a tiny part of her mind marveled at how easily he managed to overcome her anger. It wasn't pain that caused her to groan, but a savage need that would surely condemn her to hell. Still, no matter the consequences of allowing this emotion full rein, she found herself answering his devastating kisses with an urgency that left neither in doubt about her desires.

Matthew lifted her hips against his and moved her against him. He groaned as he felt her instant response. He was losing control.

Suddenly he shoved her from him and watched as she struggled to regain her composure, with her back against the tree, her chest heaving with emotion. He had to clench his hands together lest he reach for her again.

Matthew's voice was unsteady as he said brusquely, "If you still feel the need to scream, mistress, feel free." And he turned and walked away.

=== Eight ===

Maggie stood hidden within the dark curtain of an overhanging weeping willow, listening with growing fright to the eerie sounds of the night. Why had she never before noticed that these sonorous night tunes were so ominous? At the simple croaking of a frog, gooseflesh formed along her arms, and a shiver of fear ran down her spine. Her heart thudded with something close to terror at the distant hoot of a watchful owl. A gentle rustle of underbrush brought to mind grotesque images of dastardly demons rather than the small animal who was, no doubt, searching out the darkness for safety. Maggie shivered with apprehension. She wished Sally would hurry.

Had she in her anxiousness misjudged the time? Was she early? She groaned in silent frustration as she cursed Caleb's thievery. Sometime back he had taken her timepiece, probably in order to settle a gambling debt, she mused with disgust. Without it she could only guess at the hour and pray she had not too much longer to wait.

Maggie breathed a long sigh of relief when she heard the softly muffled sounds of a horse's hooves prancing at the water's edge. "At last," she laughed aloud, finding it impossible to keep the relief she felt from her voice. "I thought you'd never come," she continued as she moved from her protective covering. "I must have been waiting for . . . oh my God!" she gasped, her hand reaching for her throat as she realized it was not Sally but an English officer who sat upon a suddenly jittery horse. And if he was a bit unsteady in his seat, neither seemed to take notice, for the surprise both felt left little else to reckon with.

If Maggie felt unnerved at the unexpected arrival of this stranger, the young man was totally confused. He blinked stupidly toward the sound of her voice.

Deep in his cups, he had ambled toward the river, intent on answering nature's call. But the sound of a female voice instantly made him forget his heretofore pressing need.

He stumbled from the saddle and staggered toward the alluring female sound.

More than a little confused, he thought himself back at the bawdy house. He must have taken a wrong turn, he mused, and shrugged off his apparent mistake. No matter, he reasoned, surely a final toss wouldn't take that much time or effort. There was no telling when he'd make his way back there again, and he'd be a fool to pass up this opportunity.

Maggie was frozen in place as she watched the officer make his way toward her. Good God, what was she to do? What kind of excuse could she give to be dressed as she was and about at this hour?

"Darling," a low voice sounded close to her ear. Maggie turned in alarm, her scream of shock registered as no more than a muffled cry against a warm mouth as the huge dark shape held her securely in his arms.

"What the bloody hell?" The soldier stared stupidly. He stopped in his tracks and watched the lovers embrace. In his drunken state, it had not occurred to him that the lady was dressed in a most unseemly manner. His mind had centered only on the sound of her voice, while his eyes registered little.

Maggie's heart pounded with terror that turned instantly to rage as she struggled to push herself free of this unwanted shelter of safety. Within the time it took to take a breath, she knew that no one but Matthew would dare to take such liberties. And when, a moment later, his tongue forced her lips to part with a definite lack of tenderness, she had no doubt of his fury.

Maggie did not cower in fear but found herself matching him in anger. Still, her struggles, meager at best against his strength, proved to be of no consequence as he merely tightened his hold. She couldn't breathe and wondered if her ribs might crack within his so-called embrace.

Locking his wobbly knees, the soldier stiffened his back and held to the lapels of his red coat, trying to portray the epitome of an English gentleman and officer. He did not know that the propriety for which he strove was lost because he swayed like a reed in the wind. "Now see here," he admonished in what he presumed to be a steady and authoritative tone. "You two know better than to disregard the hour of curfew. What is the meaning of this?"

Matthew whispered threateningly against her lips, "If you've a need to live through this night, say not a word."

Maggie was amazed at his acting ability. He turned from her as if surprised at the officer's sudden presence. "Oh, it's beggin' your pardon I am, sir."

Despite her anger, Maggie suddenly wanted to burst out laughing as Matthew answered with a meekness that would have put those on the stage to shame.

His grip suddenly tightened on her arm, and all thoughts of the ridiculous fled. He continued, "The missus and me meant no harm. What with the passel of younguns at home and all, we've nary a moment to enjoy the more pleasurable sides of marriage."

Maggie gasped in outrage that he should take it upon himself to spout such utter nonsense. How dare he? she ranted in silent fury. But the angry words that threatened to explode were suddenly stilled and forgotten as Matthew's arm tightened on hers yet again.

Matthew waited, every nerve alert, for the officer's next move.

The young officer, now feeling very much in control, muttered an order to see to their getting home at once.

The moment the officer managed once again to gain his seat, Matthew dragged Maggie some yards away and shoved her beneath a tree. His tone conveyed, in no uncertain terms, his barely controlled rage as his hands held her to the trunk. "What the hell are you doing here?"

"What business is that of yours?"

"Damn you, woman, you chance much by furthering my anger. I said, what are you doing here?"

Maggie felt a chill of fear race up her spine at his threatening growl, but she forced the cowardly emotion aside. If the English did not cause her heart to cower in fear, she'd be damned if she would allow this man the satisfaction. "Mr. Forrest, 'tis apparent you have taken it upon yourself to be my watchdog. Still, I believe I owe you no explanation. Leave me be."

Matthew lunged for her. Amazingly, even though their bodies were but a foot apart, his hands never contacted with their intended destination, which seemed to be somewhere in the vicinity of her throat. Instead, his low growl of rage died suddenly in his throat as a puzzled look replaced the fury in his eyes. He took one wobbly step forward, and Maggie jumped away just before he fell flat on his face.

Maggie stifled the urge to scream by holding her hand over her mouth. Her whole body stiffened in shock as a young boy was suddenly visible in the dark. Maggie watched in terror as the boy slipped a pistol into the waistband of his trousers.

"Who is he?" a low whisper sounded.

Maggie almost cried out her relief as she recognized Sally, who was dressed, much like herself, in boy's clothing. "Good God, you gave me the most awful fright!"

"Keep your voice to a whisper. We chance much should another come upon us." Again she asked as she lowered her gaze to the huge man on the ground, "Who is he?"

"Matthew Forrest. He's the one I told you about this morning."

Sally grinned. "It appears our Mr. Forrest is somewhat protective of the lady of the house."

Maggie, seeking to deny any involvement with the man, shook her head. "I've no idea why . . ."

Sally interrupted her with a shake of her head. "It matters not. We've a chore to see about. Let's go."

Sally turned from her and moved toward the dense foliage which hid her horse from view. "Wait," Maggie called softly. "What about him?" she asked, nodding toward Matthew.

"What about him?" Sally inquired.

"Are we just going to leave him there?"

"Shall we wait for him to awaken?"

Maggie shook away the cold dread that filled her, knowing the fury she would face when he regained consciousness. "How can you be sure he's all right?"

"Maggie," Sally said with an impatient sigh, "even now the man begins to moan. If we should wait for his recovery, I will only be forced to inflict yet another blow, for he seemed reluctant to see you about your business on this night, and I cannot do this chore alone."

Maggie nodded and, following Sally's lead, mounted her own horse.

Matthew moaned again as consciousness came slowly to his befuddled mind. Was it his imagination, or had he heard the sound of horses galloping away? Where the hell was he, and why in God's name did his head feel like it had been caught beneath a horse's hoof?

Someone had dealt him a mighty blow. He had not heard a sound but suddenly found his world swallowed in darkness. His head pounded with a dull ache, and touching behind his ear brought a groan to his lips. Suddenly alert, he remembered what he had been about before the blow fell. Maggie! Where the hell was she? Sweet Jesus, had the same man who had laid him low taken her? Or had she run for safety? He groaned as a sudden pain ripped into his chest. He couldn't bear the thought that she might come to harm.

Matthew cursed as he felt himself stagger, his legs as weak as a babe's. His mind might be alert, but no matter how fiercely he willed it, his body rebelled against movement. He cursed again, forcing himself to hold on to a tree for support as the blackness threatened to overtake him once more. He had to find her! And, regardless of his present condition, he had to be quick about it.

Maggie lay uncomfortably on her stomach along the shoulder of the dirt road, thankful for the shelter of the overhanging foliage which counteracted the brightness of the clear moonlit night.

With her position and very possibly her life precarious at best, she nevertheless found herself fighting off the sudden need for sleep. Desperately, she tried to keep alert, but the constant sound of chirping crickets had a mesmerizing effect on her.

She turned to her back, trying to clear her mind, breathing deeply and stretching. No good, this only brought her more comfort, while the spicy scent of pine needles and the warmth of the summer night left her drowsy. She moved further into the underbrush and sat upright, ignoring the temptation to lean on a scub oak. Better, she mused as she bit down hard on her lip, hoping the pain would help thwart any remaining desire for sleep.

Maggie looked around. The spot Sally had chosen for their ambush was perfect in its desolation. They were miles from town and even farther from the nearest farm.

Sally was stretched out on the opposite side of the road. Between them, on the dirt, lay a heavy rope that would, when strung tightly from tree to tree, see to the immediate dismounting of their patiently awaited adversaries.

Maggie breathed a sigh of relief. Even though she knew Sally's exact position, she could not see her colleague in the foliage. It was imperative to their plan that surprise be on their side. With it, their sex and stature made little difference against the superior odds they were bound to face.

Sally had related the facts as known. A squad of men would be traveling this road sometime after midnight, heading for the governor's mansion in New York. One of the men was carrying some papers which could considerably shorten the hostilities.

What could they possibly contain? Maggie mused as she moved aside an annoying leaf that was tickling the side of her face. The sudden sound of a lone rider tore her mind from the imagined contents of the papers. Her heart thudded with fear, apprehension, and, to her surprise, a certain amount of excitement.

Maggie's job was simple. She was to follow Sally's lead. Breathlessly she waited. Nothing happened. Sally was going to let the rider pass unassaulted. Maggie gasped as she recognized Matthew speeding by. *Go home, damn it,* she wanted to cry. *You're about to ruin everything with your infernal meddling.*

Soon after Matthew's appearance came the sound of many horses approaching. Maggie saw the rope begin to rise from the dirt road. Instantly, she was on her feet. A moment later the rope was strung across the road and fastened between the two trees. Silently the women waited.

Maggie had never realized how easy it was to unseat a rider. She watched in amazement as three were instantly lifted from their saddles as if an invisible hand had simply reached down and plucked them free. The next three tried, to no avail, to avoid what had befallen their comrades. They too ended up sprawled upon the road.

The last two brought Maggie a moment of dread. Having had more time, they managed to pull back. Although their horses inflicted more injury on the downed men, they ignored the clear moans of pain and called out orders for an immediate search of the area.

The explosion of Sally's gun split the silent night, causing three of the unmanned horses to lunge wildly down the road, while one soldier slumped forward and cried out in pain as he clutched at his shoulder. To Maggie's amazement, Sally's efforts had the desired effect. The remaining soldier lifted his hands in instant and wordless surrender.

"Throw down your weapons," ordered the low voice from within the protection of the underbrush. "Be quick about it," Sally warned when his hesitation proved obvious. "I've not the patience to play with fools tonight."

The man did as he was told, as did his wounded companion, although for the injured man the effort was a good deal greater. Maggie could see the man suffered as he continued to hold his shoulder, but she kept her gaze, as ordered, on the others, who were more capable at the moment of giving resistance.

Maggie's eyes widened with surprise as she watched one of the downed men slyly remove his pistol from its holster. She aimed and fired. Her shot went wide, as she had intended, for she had no urge to kill any of these men, be they friend or foe. Still, the shot managed to swirl the dust at his side and persuaded him to throw the gun aside with a muttered oath.

"Now, if you would be so kind, help your men to their feet."

With many curses and groans, the men finally managed to form a haphazard line across the road.

"All of you, take off your clothes."

Maggie gasped when she heard Sally's menacing whisper. What was she about? Why was it important for these men to be unclothed?

More grumbling curses filled the silent night as, one by one, they stripped down to their drawers.

"Everything," the husky whisper sounded when it became apparent that the men were not about to continue unless further coaxing was provided.

Reluctantly, they did as they were ordered, but not before

vile curses were rained down on their unseen assailant's heads.

Maggie choked back a giggle as Sally commanded the men to walk back in the direction from which they had come. The sight of eight stumbling, cursing men, barefoot and every bit as naked as the moment they were born, was sure to start more than one tongue wagging. And Maggie gave silent thanks it wouldn't be she who first tested their good humor.

Maggie and Sally watched until the men were a respectable distance away before they dared to scramble into the road and pick up the discarded clothing and weapons.

A quick search of pockets proved futile. Annoyed, Sally kicked a boot and then laughed when she saw a packet of papers fall free.

Maggie couldn't hide her respect for her friend as Sally safely deposited the packet in her own boot and began to fling the clothing and guns around. "Should they be brave enough to return, I'd not make it easy for them to follow us." With those last words, Sally mounted her own animal and slapped the backs of the soldiers' remaining horses, scattering them into the night.

═══ Nine ═══

Maggie lay wide awake as the soft sounds of the night gave way to morning. Amazingly enough, earlier she had been hard pressed to keep her eyes open. And now, while lying comfortably on a bed of straw, sleep proved to be elusive.

A twinge of guilt caused her to stir restlessly. She knew she should be up and about. Aunt Matilda had risen at least an hour before to start the fires for the day. Already the mouth-watering scent of warm bread and fresh coffee filtered from the open kitchen windows to tease her senses.

Maggie groaned. She didn't bother to deny that Matthew had caused yet another sleepless night. She had heard him come in almost immediately after she had settled herself beside Joseph. Her heartbeat had accelerated alarmingly. Would he insist on a confrontation?

She could hear him walking about below and wondered at her sanity as she was tempted to join him. What could she have been thinking? The little she knew about the man left her with no doubt about his anger. She owed him no explanation or apology, she reasoned. If his head throbbed, it was of his own doing.

What gave him the right to follow her, to interfere in her business? Three days ago she hadn't even known of his existence. Now he presumed her answerable to him. Well, he presumed too much.

Maggie groaned and turned to her side as she remembered the night's ending. She had felt great trepidation before he had come to her to check on her safety. He shouldn't have taken it upon himself to do such a thing. But he had.

Maggie had heard him making his way to the loft and had closed her eyes, feigning sleep. She smiled at Fluffy's low, menacing growl and then frowned as her protector apparently recognized the visitor and simply lowered his head to the floor once again.

Matthew had moved silently to her side. For a long moment he had simply knelt there watching her. Maggie could hear him breathing, and her skin tingled, knowing he was close enough for her to reach out and touch. She dared not open her eyes. She had to make him believe she slept, for she knew there would be a tremendous argument—or worse—should he learn the truth.

Maggie had almost jumped when his fingers gently brushed aside the heavy lock of hair that hid half her face from his view.

She had heard his long sigh and refused to wonder at its cause. She didn't want to know his thoughts, his feelings. She wanted only for him to be gone.

Maggie had fought a valiant battle as she felt his fingers against her skin. *Please God,* she had given a silent prayer, *now that his curiosity has been sated, let him leave.* But he hadn't left.

She had been amazed that he couldn't hear the thundering of her heart, for it grew in volume and strength with each lingering touch. And by the time his lone finger had touched the rapidly pounding pulse at her throat, she could deny her needs no longer.

She had heard his sharp intake of breath. Regardless of her act, he knew she was awake, and, worst of all, he knew his nearness did not leave her unaffected.

His warm mouth had covered hers, and Maggie had given up any pretense of sleep. With a soft cry, her lips had opened beneath his, and her arms had reached out hungrily to pull him to her.

Gently he had lifted her to kneel before him and gathered her into the haven of his arms as his lips covered her face with short, desperate kisses.

Surely she had lost her mind. This couldn't be happening to her. Why in only three days had she abandoned her moral upbringing and a lifetime of good behavior? Where had Maggie Darrah gone? She tried to think, yet all thoughts had fled as she lost herself in the magic of his touch.

"Maggie," he had murmured against the warmth of her neck. "Oh God, Maggie."

His body had trembled against her own, and his arms had tightened to almost a strangling hold. Maggie realized that he had been worried for her safety.

How had they become so close in such a short span of time? Maggie had no answers. All she knew was that she wanted this man, wanted him above all else and with every fiber of her being.

Her breathing was ragged and gasping as he had slowly lowered the straps of her chemise, letting the material fall to her knees. She hadn't even thought to stop him as, bathed in silvery moonlight, she watched his eyes darken with the fires of passion and burn against the smooth golden flesh he had bared.

The rough texture of his palm against her softness had sent her mind whirling. She couldn't bear this pleasure. Her head fell back, her long hair brushing deliciously against her naked hips, as Matthew's hands slid gently from her legs to her rounded hips and small waist.

Maggie had almost cried out as he cupped the softness of her breasts and brought his mouth to linger and taste until she thought she would die from wanting. She did not have the strength to stop him. If he had wished, he could have taken her then, beside her sleeping family, and Maggie knew she would not have objected.

With a shuddering sigh, it was Matthew who had finally pulled away. From the blazing desire in his eyes, Maggie knew it had cost him a great effort. Weak and trembling, she had silently watched him leave her side.

Maggie knew that she'd find untold ecstasy should she succumb to his tempting charm. But she also knew that a moment or two of gratification would not be enough. No, she wanted all this man could give. She wanted it forever, and it could never be.

Maggie laughed at Joseph and Fluffy's playful antics. She leaned against the thick trunk of a huge oak, her legs stretched out comfortably before her. It had been a good idea to spend the warm afternoon with her son. It had been too long since she had allowed herself this innocent pleasure. Running her farm, she rarely found the time to do the things she enjoyed most.

Joseph was getting so big, and she had missed so much. Next year he would already be starting his lessons. Her chest swelled with pride as she watched his tall, slender body weave through the high grass, and she prayed that with God's help he'd not become like his father.

A sudden hunger overtook her. How she longed for another baby. A look of pure disgust crossed her brow. *You fool yourself, even in your most private reflections, Maggie, for 'tis not a babe you long to possess, but the man who could give you one.*

There was truth in the thought, she mused. Had she someone to love, she would not feel this constant emptiness or the need to fill it with babies.

For God's sake, stop it! she berated herself. *It does not help your peace of mind to long for what can never be. Accept the truth, Maggie. Accept the role you have in life. And if it is not the most favorable one, think then of others who have nothing, and count your blessings.*

She shook off her melancholy notions determinedly and came to her feet, eager not to let another enjoyable moment pass her by.

Maggie scrambled through the tall grass, arms outstretched, chasing Fluffy in circles. Joseph's squeal of laughter rang out over the treetops as he watched his mother lunge for the dog and end up rolling toward the shorter grass that bordered the creek.

Maggie laughed at her son's enjoyment and came to a stop. Standing again, her hands placed firmly on her hips, she gave Joseph a look of warning, but the laughter in her voice belied any attempt at anger. "'Twould benefit us both were you to help rather than laugh, Master Darrah. For I see no chance of playing this game lest we retrieve the ball."

Joseph joined his mother in what proved to be a quarter of an hour of nothing but laughter in their quest to corner the frisky animal.

At long last, Maggie, breathless from exertion, felt the end in sight. Fluffy was as winded as she. It wouldn't be long now, she reasoned, trying to follow the dog's sharp turns of evasion. She quickened her pace and gave a final lunge, only to find herself precariously off balance.

Maggie stifled a helpless scream. She was rapidly sliding in the mud toward the water's edge.

An explosion of glistening droplets bathed her face and arms. She desperately tried to halt her slide, but she could not.

She felt the creek's pebbly bottom beneath her boots as she tumbled deeper into the water. Suddenly she found herself face down, staring, with no little surprise and quite stupidly, she thought, at a few terrified fish that were anxiously trying to avoid this invasion of their home.

Maggie pushed her heavy wet hair from her face and laughed as she tried to stand in the water. Her son doubled over in fits of merriment on the shore. "One can only hope all will find an equal measure of enjoyment in my mishap," Maggie chided him.

"In truth, mistress, I, for one, can attest to it," came a deep male voice filled with laughter.

Maggie grinned, knowing full well who was the owner of the voice before lifting her gaze to Matthew's smile. "Indeed, sir, I can see as much."

"Might you be in need of some assistance?" he asked as he ambled slowly toward the water's edge.

"I might," she chuckled and raised her hand.

"Do you think we should help her, Joseph?" Matthew asked conspiratorially while resting his hand on the boy's slender shoulder.

Joseph, who quickly understood the teasing mood between these two adults, only shrugged, his enjoyment apparent.

"If we do not," Matthew warned, "I'd venture dire consequences await us."

Joseph nodded yet gave no opinion, save a giggle.

"Joseph!" Maggie laughed. "I'd not dally overlong if I were you."

Matthew reached a strong hand toward the bedraggled lady and pulled her free of the water.

"Traitor," she mumbled as she moved past her laughing child.

Maggie couldn't remember when she had last seen Joseph laugh so wholeheartedly. She could see he was weak from giggling. Still, he sat on Matthew's bared chest and pinned the man's muscular arms over his head. "Yield," Joseph ordered.

"I yield, I yield," Matthew allowed, and then, just as Joseph sent his mother a triumphant look, Matthew laughed and the boy squealed as he was easily rolled over and pinned beneath Matthew's body.

"Help! Mama, help me," Joseph screeched with gasping breaths from Matthew's tickling.

Maggie grinned and came to her feet. Her struggles to dislodge her son proved useless as she tugged on Matthew's shoulders.

Suddenly Matthew grunted, and before Maggie realized his intent, she was flung to her back. She blinked with surprise as she realized she and her son had exchanged places.

Joseph offered happily, "Her knees are ticklish."

"Are they?" Matthew asked while grinning down at her laughing face. And then, for her ears alone, he murmured, "I'll have to see about that at a later date."

"Joseph," Maggie chuckled, "'twould no doubt further your cause to help me rather than give advice to this villain."

Suddenly Joseph lunged and landed his body with full force on Matthew's shoulders. With much grunting and groaning, he managed to pull Matthew off his mother but not before Matthew's tongue erotically licked Maggie's soft, smiling lips.

Unable to stop the soft gasp that lodged in her throat, Maggie was still for a long moment, watching with sudden, aching desire as his mouth hovered only inches from her own. For one wild moment, she almost forgot Joseph was there. And when Matthew finally gave in to Joseph's shoving and rolled away, Maggie cursed the emptiness he had left behind.

It wasn't until sometime later, when all three were comfortably sitting around after finishing a huge picnic luncheon that Hannah had packed, when Joseph asked, "Why did you lick my mother's lips, Mr. Forrest?"

Maggie turned every shade of red. She had no idea that Joseph had seen him. Damn the man. Couldn't he hold his passions to more private moments?

The laughter in Matthew's eyes did little in the way of

relieving her annoyance. He merely shrugged aside her anger, knowing embarrassment to be the cause. "There was a smudge of dirt," he lied easily.

Joseph nodded his satisfaction at what he perceived to be a proper and reasonable answer, since Hannah had often licked at her finger before rubbing dirt off him. A few moments later he stretched out lazily in the warm afternoon sun and, using his mother's still damp lap for a pillow, was soon fast asleep.

After leaving the water, Maggie had accepted Matthew's offer of his shirt. In the privacy of the bushes, she had discarded her blouse and underthings, leaving them to dry over a tree branch. She was comfortable enough, and her skirt was rapidly drying.

Matthew reclined near her feet with his head resting on his hand. He watched as Maggie idly fingered the laces of his shirt. It gave him an odd sense of comfort to see her wearing his clothes. She was not a tiny woman, but she appeared small and even more delicate when covered by a shirt so large. And Matthew had to look away, for the ache to surround her, like his shirt, was almost more than he could bear.

Maggie brushed a lock of golden hair from Joseph's forehead. Her eyes never left her son's flushed face as she spoke. "'Tis apparent Joseph lacks male companionship. You must forgive him if he was a bit unwilling to see the wrestling come to an end. I believe he has not wrestled before, for I cannot imagine Elijah sprawled on the ground with Joseph astride his chest." She laughed softly at the odd picture her words brought to mind. She lifted her gaze to Matthew's as she added, "My son has come to hold you in the highest regard, Mr. Forrest. For that I am thankful."

"And what of his mother, mistress? How does she perceive me?"

Maggie laughed. "I'd warrant any opinion of hers would

be a bit premature since their acquaintance has been so short."

"I know her to be quick of mind. Surely she is of some opinion?"

"Perhaps." Maggie grinned.

"But she is not of a mind to let me know of it."

"Apparently not."

"It matters not." He shrugged with a wicked grin. "There are times when actions tell more than words."

Maggie couldn't resist a grin. "I should wring your neck for the last of your actions. How could you be so bold while Joseph was so close at hand?"

Matthew's dark gaze met hers, and Maggie couldn't hide the sudden longing that filled her at his words. "When you are in my arms, I forget others exist."

Maggie licked at her suddenly parched lips as her heart thudded uncomfortably in her chest. "Don't," she whispered weakly.

"You ask for the near impossible when you look at me thus. You too forgot he was there, didn't you?"

"Nay," she answered breathlessly.

He simply nodded at her answer, for neither believed the lie. With an effort, he pulled his gaze from hers and nonchalantly brushed a bit of dust from his pant leg. "Speaking of neck wringing, 'tis possible I know of one who is in dire need."

Maggie lifted her gaze as he moved to sit at her side. Her eyes were clearly suspicious.

"One hears tell of unusual goings-on last night."

"Indeed?"

"Aye, 'twas reported that a dozen or so bloodthirsty rogues attacked a squadron of our favorite king's soldiers. By their own words, they were fortunate to escape with their lives."

Maggie grinned.

"In truth, it was most opportune that the attack was

conducted under the cover of darkness, since these poor souls were forced to walk to the nearest dwelling in their altogether."

Maggie gasped. "You mean they were naked?"

"Aye." He nodded, his dark eyes searching her face with obvious suspicion. "One wonders why these soldiers would be invited to disrobe."

"Perhaps someone intended to search their clothing," Maggie offered as a reasonable excuse, "and realized the prudence of doing so without the interference of the clothing's occupants."

"Perhaps." He shrugged. His eyes narrowed dangerously as he continued, "It couldn't be that a certain lady of my acquaintance was involved in the escapade, could it?"

Maggie grinned, her eyes rounding with professed innocence. "I fear I have little knowledge of the ladies of your acquaintance. How would you expect me to know such a thing?"

"Maggie," he warned, his low voice carrying a definite threat.

"Are you suggesting myself as the culprit?" Maggie asked, her supposed surprise a worthy act indeed.

"Should I not?"

Maggie gave a soft laugh, " 'Tis pure folly to put the blame at my feet, Mr. Forrest. You said yourself their assailants numbered a dozen or so."

"I said 'twas reported as such." Gently he touched the tender spot behind his ear. "My head, even yet, holds proof enough that you were not alone. There was at least one other."

"Do you believe two capable of outmanning a squadron of soldiers?"

"If the two were cunning in their tendencies."

"Indeed, sir, I wish I could settle your mind."

Matthew sighed as he lifted his arm and circled her shoulders, bringing her weight to rest on him. "I confess to wishing much the same, mistress." A long moment of silence passed between them before he continued, "It would make me sleep easier if I had no cause to fear a repeat of a night such as this one past."

Maggie looked up into his grim expression. A soft light of warmth shone in the depths of her brandy eyes as a smile curved her lips, and she whispered, "I'd not worry of it overmuch, for I doubt such a happening."

Ten

Maggie did not realize how her brandy eyes softened, turning to shimmering gold, as she looked at Matthew. He was busy checking the wheel of the buggy, oblivious to her gaze. Apparently, the officers and their staff were about their business of war on this fine Sunday morning. Except for the two of them, the yard stood empty.

Maggie allowed herself to savor the delicious sight of him squatting before the buggy wheel. His thick, muscular thighs bulged almost indecently against the beige material of his tight trousers. Her heart quickened as she watched his tan arms, sinewy and corded with muscles, reach beneath the buggy. She knew that since Caleb's destructive ride the vehicle had been completely overhauled, but for some reason one wheel refused to stop squeeking.

Maggie desperately tried to calm her racing pulse as she noticed the muscles beneath his shirt flex and strain when he reached for something.

Matthew, sensing her presence, raised his eyes and watched with obvious admiration as the lady of the house walked toward him. "Good morning, mistress."

"Good morning," she returned, unable to stop the smile that was nearly always in evidence when she was in his company. Maggie's eyes widened with appreciation of the quality and fit of his Sunday suit as he stood before her, rolling down his shirt sleeves and sliding his arms into his coat. If she thought the cut of his trousers a bit bold for church, she said nothing. Still, she couldn't prevent the flicker of disturbance that clouded her eyes.

"Is something amiss?" Matthew asked, noticing the slight frown that marred her features.

"Nay," she returned, a bit too brightly. "All is well."

"I know you better than that, mistress. I can see something troubles you."

Maggie's cheeks flamed with mortification. She turned quickly away, suddenly finding great interest in the fields beyond her house. Never, never could she be so bold as to tell this man that the tight fit of his trousers caused an unexplained trembling in her knees and a certain testiness in her temper. An uncomfortable flutter, not unlike jealousy, settled in the pit of her stomach, and Maggie cursed the errant emotion, for she had no right to suffer this possessive sensation.

She did not doubt that at first sight the Johnson twins would be all over him, their eyes raking his manly form. And although they posed no threat to her—for Maggie would deny to the death that she cared who might feast their eyes on him—she couldn't prevent the uneasy sensation in her stomach. Maggie forced a shrug of nonchalance. If the man wished to flaunt his obvious masculinity, so be it. Who was she to say nay? It was no concern of hers, after all.

Matthew grinned, knowing that whatever her problem was, he'd find out soon enough. "Are they ready?" he asked with a nod toward the barn.

"Aye. Aunt Matilda is searching her chest for a hatpin, and Joseph is finishing the last of his breakfast. They'll not keep us waiting long."

"That's too bad," he remarked, coming to stand at her side.

"Is it?" Maggie grinned, looking up and reading the

merriment in his eyes. She knew she shouldn't, but she was unable to resist his teasing. "Why?"

"I've a mind to wish you a proper good morning. And for what I'm thinking, privacy would be most appropriate."

Maggie shook her head, unable to stop the devilish gleam of answering laughter in her eyes. "No doubt, sir, for what you are thinking, the rack would be most appropriate."

Matthew agreed with a laugh. "Perhaps." His dark gaze caressed her face with a dark, hungry look, and he continued, "Indeed, 'tis fortunate for me they have done away with that particular brand of torture. Still, I'd venture to say, even with the rack as a deterrent, it would not lessen my desire to discover the ticklishness of your knees."

Maggie giggled like a young girl, feeling suddenly very pleased to be alive. Her soft laughter turned into a low chuckle as she watched Matthew give a mock villainous leer. "You need not take such a heavy chore upon yourself, for I am perfectly willing to admit they are very ticklish indeed."

"Mistress," Matthew said, grinning, "'tis not that I doubt your word, but over the years I've come to believe that to experience some things firsthand is to know the truth of the matter."

Maggie laughed. "Mr. Forrest, you are a scoundrel of the first order." And then, hearing her aunt and her son coming up behind her, she continued, "Please help me into this buggy." And as she watched his smile widen, she warned, "And take that nasty grin from your face."

Today, for the first time since her father's death, she and her family were going to church with a man. Caleb had never accompanied her. Even when he was well, he had found no need to give a few moments to God each week.

Maggie forced aside the condemnation that so easily came to mind. She was being unfair. She knew many good, decent people who shared her husband's lack of beliefs. In truth, it did not matter how one sought to honor their maker, and she had no right to judge. Still, she often wondered if Caleb might find some peace of mind if he allowed God to bear some of his life's burden.

Maggie shrugged aside her thoughts. It was too beautiful a day to explore the dark depths of her husband's miseries. The sun was shining, the sky was clear, the company promised to be excellent, and she was determined to enjoy it.

In church, Maggie felt like a hypocrite indeed as she fought against the desire to lean toward the man who sat far too close to her. She tried to concentrate instead on the minister's words. The usual discomfort of the hard benches and stifling thick air went unnoticed as she strove to hear the sermon. But she did not hear a word as she stared straight ahead, fighting the desire to look to her side.

Apparently, Matthew was also having trouble concentrating on the minister's words, for he seemed unable to sit still. From the corner of her eye Maggie could see his easy grin as he brushed his thigh against hers with supposed innocence. And later his fingers lingered to caress the inside of her wrist as he handed her the prayer book and passed the offering tray.

Maggie breathed a sigh of relief when the last words of the hymn were sung and the parishioners began to file out of the pews. She was unable to resist a quick jab in his ribs as payment for his teasing.

"Oh, I beg your pardon," Maggie responded to his look of suspicion with wide-eyed innocence. "I seem to have lost my footing for a moment."

"Perhaps you need a helping hand," Matthew offered cheerfully. He slid his arm around her and, regardless of some of the congregation's raised eyebrows, pulled her close to his side.

"Release me this minute!" Maggie said between clenched teeth, her eyes spitting fire yet her voice so low even Aunt Matilda, who followed close behind, had not a notion of her scandalized tone.

"Are you sure?" Matthew grinned, leaning low, his words whispered somewhere in the vicinity of her jaw and neck. And as Maggie's answering glare promised murder, Matthew continued with barely suppressed laughter, "I'd not see you fall."

"Mr. Forrest," Maggie warned, her tone low and menacing, while flashing him her sweetest smile, lest any onlookers see the degree of her anger, "if you do not take your hands from me immediately, I will not hesitate to use violence."

Maggie's eyes gleamed with devilry as a plan of retaliation came to mind. She never thought she had it in her to be so heartless, but if anyone deserved his just reward it was the man at her side. It only took a moment for her to spot the Johnson twins. Watching them with their heads close together, whispering and giggling charmingly, Maggie had to admit that they were a lovely sight indeed decked out in their Sunday finery. But prettiness was not enough in their case; they were incorrigible chatterboxes. Added to this fact was the alarming sound of their laughter. Maggie had known them all their lives, and even she almost jumped when she heard them laugh. Charity forbade her to compare the sound to a horse's whinny, yet she could think of nothing else in the way of description.

Maggie almost felt sorry for him as she purposely led an unsuspecting Matthew toward the two overeager women and made the introductions—almost, but not quite.

After a long, hard week of endless chores, the ladies of the town were loath to rush home after Sunday services. Having little time to chat with friends and acquaintances, they used what was left of the long morning to socialize. So nearly an hour went by before Maggie had a free moment to see to the results of her efforts.

Maggie's wide grin bespoke her triumph. Matthew was trapped between the twins' fancy bonnets. His glare of promised retribution only caused her to laugh aloud and receive odd glances from her neighbors.

It was only the obvious glazing of his eyes that finally caused Maggie to take pity and come to his side. "Mr. Forrest, I'm sorry to have to interrupt, but I'm afraid we must go. Aunt Matilda has been cooking a roast, and if we aren't soon on our way it will be rendered useless for dinner."

With barely another word spoken, Matthew almost dragged Maggie from the two twittering females, anxious to escape their company. And when Maggie looked up into his thundering expression and inquired sweetly, "Did you have a pleasant chat?" his eyes narrowed and his lips tightened further still.

"Do not dare say another word, for I believe the sound of one more female voice will be the end of me."

"I'm afraid I have news that will not cheer you overmuch."

"Being?"

"Aunt Matilda has invited Samuel to Sunday dinner."

Matthew groaned sarcastically, "Wonderful." And at her obviously happy smile, he continued, "Will you not feel just a bit uncomfortable? Your husband, your friend, and myself all at the same table?"

"I see no reason for discomfort." Maggie returned in self-defense. "You are the new owner of my farm. I can hardly ask you to dine elsewhere."

"Hardly," Matthew agreed.

"Aunt Matilda has invited a longtime friend, and I can hardly rescind the invitation."

"Hardly," Matthew repeated.

"What would you have me do?"

Matthew raised one black brow and grinned.

Maggie quickly cut off his response. "You need not answer. I know well enough your train of thought, and you may keep your unsuitable suggestions to yourself."

Maggie thought the meal would never end. The thick slices of tender roast beef and potatoes oozing with freshly

112

churned butter stuck like straw in her nerve-tightened throat, and she found herself reaching time and again for the tankard of ale to dislodge it. Caleb, although perfectly sober, was in one of his most obnoxious moods, and no one could ignore his presence.

Matthew and Samuel, while not exactly at each other's throats, were barely civil to each other as they vied for her attention.

Maggie silently wished for the meal to be done. How had she gotten herself into so uncomfortable a position? She breathed a sigh of relief as the sound of a carriage outside the barn brought Matthew from the table. Joseph, bubbling with excitement, followed close at his heels.

A few moments later Joseph came running back, shouting, "It came! Mr. Forrest's supplies are here. Mama, come see."

"Don't worry about it, dear. Take your time and finish your meal. I'll see to everything." Aunt Matilda smiled with relief, happy to find an excuse to be gone from the suffocating atmosphere.

Making one final attempt to include Caleb in conversation, Samuel asked, "Have you heard the fort is finished? No doubt we will soon have our homes to ourselves."

Caleb muttered a sullen "Aye." And then, to Maggie's mortification, he continued, "I'll be glad to see them go. The bed in back"—he nodded over his shoulder—"is too narrow, and my wife is forced to sleep in the loft." Caleb's eyes shone with glittering hatred as he watched his wife's face darken with telltale guilt. "There's no tellin' what kind of riffraff wanders about at night. Even if I heard someone sneaking up to the loft, what could I, a cripple, do about it?

"'Tis not right that a man and his dear wife should be forced to separate. Do you not agree, Landsing?"

Samuel muttered something unintelligible.

It didn't seem possible, but Samuel's face grew deeper in color than Maggie's. If Caleb didn't know better, he'd think the bitch was servicing this bastard along with Forrest.

Caleb couldn't imagine what the two saw in her, but it was obvious they both fancied themselves in love. He gave a mental shrug. She was a comely wench, but as cold as a frigid winter night. He preferred a warm woman in his bed, and to date none could compare with Peggy.

Still, it couldn't hurt to see what all the fuss was about. Caleb gave a low, evil chuckle. He hadn't touched the bitch in years. Maybe it was past time to claim his husbandly rights.

"Well, I thank you for a delicious meal, Maggie, and for your hospitality, Caleb," Samuel said as he came to his feet. "I'm afraid I've work to do, and I'd best be going before the hour grows any later."

Maggie left Caleb to finish his meal alone while she walked Samuel to his buggy. "I'm sorry your visit proved to be so awkward. Caleb is most often in these moods and treats all horridly." Maggie gasped and bit her lip, astonished that she should show such blatant disloyalty. "Pardon me, I did not mean . . ."

"Do not worry, Maggie, I understand." His arm linked with hers as they walked. "We've been friends for as long as I can remember. It does not sit well with me knowing you are at his mercy." Samuel nodded toward the barn. "I'd not take it kindly if some harm should befall you."

Maggie gave a weak smile and patted his arm as he released her. "Fear not, Samuel, I am in no danger."

Samuel nodded again and glanced up at the dark, menacing clouds that drifted overhead. "I'd best hurry before the storm comes. Remember, my offer stands. My home is open to you."

Maggie reached up and kissed his cheek. "Thank you, Samuel. I'll not forget."

Maggie listened for a long moment before she gave up any hope that Elijah would see to Caleb's care. It had taken her a few moments to distinguish between his moans and the raging wind outside the barn's thin walls. She didn't want to go to him, but it would be unfair to awaken Elijah at this time of night. Perhaps Caleb was merely in the throes of a nightmare and a gentle nudging or a glass of water would suffice.

"Go back to sleep, Joseph," she whispered gently as she heard the boy mutter in his sleep. She left his side and crept carefully down the ladder steps to the darkened barn below.

She had waited too long for Caleb to grow quiet and knew she'd have to hurry to him before Aunt Matilda and Matthew awakened.

Maggie struck a flint and lit the lantern. She hurried toward the tackle room and opened the door. Caleb lay tangled in his sheets. His naked chest heaved as if he had done some great physical labor. From the doorway he looked flushed and feverish.

Maggie moved closer. She put the lantern on the bedside stand and reached out a hand to his forehead. Suddenly her wrist was caught in a viselike grip, and Caleb's eyes filled with evil mirth.

"It took you long enough," he muttered as he pulled her closer.

"Release my hand," Maggie ordered stiffly.

"Oh, come now. Is that any way for a wife to speak to her beloved husband?"

"Caleb," Maggie threatened, "let me go. I warn you."

"Do you?" he chuckled. "What will you do if I refuse?"

"I will scream."

Caleb laughed again. "Maggie, even your lover would not dare to interfere between man and wife."

"Caleb," she said, trying to control the tremor in her voice, "Samuel is not my lover."

Caleb smiled. "Aye, but he has intentions of taking up where Forrest leaves off, has he not?" He caught her free hand when she tried to pry his fingers from her wrist. "I've been wondering of late, what is it about you that so appeals to them? What is it they see in you?" He gave a hard tug and laughed when she fell helplessly across him. "Then suddenly I remembered how remiss I've been in my husbandly duties. I think 'tis past time for me to see to that oversight. Do you not agree?"

Maggie took a deep breath. Nothing would be gained should she panic. Caleb was right. No one would intercede, and, worst of all, all would know of her shame if she cried out.

"Caleb, stop it this instant," she demanded as he chuckled evilly. "You will not have an easy time of it," she grunted as she fought to free herself.

"I care not if it will make you suffer."

Maggie knew he spoke the truth. She should calmly submit, but her body shivered with disgust and recoiled at his touch. It was as if a total stranger were handling her, and she knew she could not allow it. The panic she had tried to forestall suddenly came to life. She'd die before she'd let this animal take her.

Caleb, fooled into relaxing his hold by her calm demeanor, cursed as she pulled her hand free and left a long bloody welt down the side of his face.

"Son of a bitch!" he growled as his fist hit her. "You can whore for them, why not for me?"

Maggie didn't recognize the low groan that escaped her throat as his fist connected with the side of her jaw. The whole world suddenly went hazy, and she thought she might black out from the force of the blow. But Maggie fought desperately to keep her wits about her. She couldn't allow herself to pass out. If she succumbed to unconsciousness, Caleb would then have his way.

At least he'll not bring you further harm, a soft voice offered from the far recesses of her mind. *Aye, but in any case, you'll know what he's done,* she returned, *and as long as you breathe, you'll not make it easy for this monster.*

Maggie heard the sound of material ripping and realized he had torn her gown open to her waist. Her two hands were pinned above her head in his one as he reached cruel fingers of his other hand to her breast, squeezing until she moaned in pain.

She twisted and struggled, her legs kicking out uselessly as he laughed. "I'll . . . kill . . . you," she threatened.

Caleb laughed again, rolled over, and pinned her firmly beneath him. Maybe this wouldn't be so bad at that, he reasoned with some surprise. The bitch had some spirit after all. Maybe that was what her lovers found so stimulating, for it was doing fine things to the piece between his legs. Jesus, he was growing as hard as a rock. He couldn't remember when he'd been so damned excited. He'd forgotten how soft her skin was. He was ready to come, and he hadn't even gotten her gown off.

An instant later her nightdress was torn to its hem, but Caleb had yet another problem. The sheet was still between them. He tried to lift himself and pull it free, but her constant struggling was driving him to the brink of ecstasy. His mind clouded with desire. He couldn't stop it. Jesus, the bitch was making him come before he could get near her.

He was desperate to enter her before it was too late, but his legs were tangled in the sheet, and it wouldn't move no matter how desperate his wrenching.

"You bitch," he cried out as his body suddenly shuddered and jerked and spilled his seed upon the sheet and her one bare leg. "You goddamn whorin' bitch," he groaned as he desperately continued to seek entry.

Maggie didn't hesitate. The moment she felt him in the throes of climax, she shoved him aside and scrambled to the door as fast as her shaking legs could carry her. Caleb gave a frustrated groan, and the curses came like his seed, helplessly vented upon his sheet. He never realized she was gone till the last shudder shook his body.

Matthew paced the barn floor, knowing full well what was happening inside the small room but helpless to do more than curse the bastard. He had no doubt that Caleb was forcing himself on Maggie, but he could not interfere between husband and wife. And, no matter how desperately he wished otherwise, she was another's wife.

Scream, Maggie, scream! he raged in silent agony. *Give me a reason to interfere.*

Matthew punched the table when he heard Maggie's soft moan, welcoming the pain as his knuckles split, for it momentarily took his mind from beyond the closed door. Helplessly he ran his fingers through his hair for the hundredth time. There was nothing he could do to help her, nothing he could do to relieve his own torment. He was going to go insane if he had to keep hearing the sounds from that room. And yet he couldn't bring himself to leave.

The wind continued to howl, wailing like a banshee gone wild. It dared the barn to withstand its powers, while crashes of thunder echoed through the night, almost rocking the building from its very foundation. But Matthew heard nothing but the muffled sounds from the tackle room.

A low stream of vile curses filled the air inside the barn just as Maggie finally stumbled from the room.

Matthew held his breath. His heart thumped wildly in his chest. He said nothing as he watched her for a long, silent moment. Her eyes shone vacant and huge in her white face. Her split lip was dripping blood, and a bruise was beginning to discolor her jaw. Her hair was wild about her shoulders and face, and her gown gaped open, leaving her exposed to his searching gaze. *I'll kill him,* he vowed silently as he spied the red bruises from his fingers and the teeth marks on her breasts.

Helplessly he watched her lean against the closed door and give a violent shudder.

Maggie stared blankly ahead, not seeing Matthew come toward her. Suddenly and with a choking cry, she was on her knees, her back heaving as she vomited on the barn floor.

Neither noticed the little boy silently crying at the bottom of the ladder, nor did they see him as he ran out into the wild night, terrified at the sight of his injured mother.

"Jesus Christ! I'll kill him!" Matthew groaned as he gathered Maggie into his arms and held her hair from her face.

"Go away," she begged between wrenching heaves.

"Hush, Maggie, 'tis over," he soothed, taking a clean handkerchief from his pocket and wiping her face. "He'll never touch you again."

Matthew held her close within the circle of his arms, crooning soft words long after her tears dried.

"I love you, Maggie," he breathed into her hair. "Do you know that?"

Maggie nodded, but instead of his words creating a soothing balm for her soul, her tears started afresh.

"Does knowing I love you hurt so very much?"

"Oh, Matthew, do not," she cried into his chest, her words muffled against his warm skin. "There can never be a life for us."

"There can, Maggie." He smiled as he ran his hands over her hair. "I'll find a way. I swear before God, I'll find a way."

═══ *Eleven* ═══

Matthew wondered at the emotion that gripped his chest and caused his throat to constrict. Is this what it was to love? To feel another's pain? To suffer as though the other were but an extension of one's self?

Matthew wasn't pleased at the thought that this emotion should bind him to a woman already spoken for, but it was far too late to change that. He'd loved her almost from first sight.

Gently he gathered her into his arms and brought her to the stall he used for sleeping. He knelt beside her as he laid her upon his blanket and covered her with an extra quilt. He was hesitant to leave her even for a moment, for she trembled as if palsied, but the woman needed care more than pity.

"I'm going to get you another nightdress. Where do you keep them?"

Maggie tried to lie very still while he was gone. It was almost as if she were afraid to move, afraid to feel, afraid to think, or she'd lose what little control she had gained and begin to scream. And she knew that if she started, she'd not be able to stop.

Her body ached. Even beneath the quilt she couldn't get warm and couldn't seem to stop shaking. She longed to slip into unconsciousness, to forget even for a short time the trauma this night had brought, but despite her wants her mind was alert. Again and again, she reminded herself that Caleb had not completed the act, but there was no relief in the knowledge.

In Matthew's absence, Maggie had heard Caleb call out. Perhaps resisting the temptation to exact revenge, Matthew had wakened Elijah and ordered the man to see to Caleb's wants.

A few moments later Maggie heard Caleb outside. He was cursing at the laziness of the black man as Elijah prepared the buggy. Soon after, a whip cracked, and the buggy sped off into the dark night.

It seemed forever before Matthew returned to her side. "You heard?" he asked softly, noticing she was wide awake.

Maggie nodded. "You let him take the buggy. Why?"

Matthew breathed a long sigh as he deposited a basin of water, clean nightclothes, and another blanket near her. "Let's just say I want to see him gone from my sight."

From the corner of the stall, Matthew retrieved a bottle of rum. "Drink this," he ordered, giving her a half-filled cup and lifting her to a sitting position.

Maggie gasped and choked as a mouthful of the fiery liquid burned a path down her throat. Tears came to her eyes as she struggled for breath. "Why, in God's name, does anyone drink this brew?"

Matthew grinned but insisted, "All of it," when she tried to hand it back to him.

"Please, it's awful."

"Drink it, Maggie. It will warm you and ease the trembling."

Maggie saw the determination in his eyes. It was easier to do as he asked, for she seemed to have lost the will to fight. With a shrug, she lifted the cup to her lips. Slowly this time, she sipped at the rum. Amazingly, it had lost its power to burn. Perhaps her throat was numb from the first swallow, she reasoned. She took another sip and felt the warmth spread inside her. By the time she finished, it had done a remarkable job toward relieving her trembling.

"Good girl," Matthew remarked as he took the cup and pressed her back to the blanket.

"No arguments now, Maggie," Matthew continued. "I'm going to see to your comfort."

"Nay," she returned. "I need but a moment's rest and I will be myself again."

"I said no arguments."

Maggie gave a long, weary sigh of acquiescence and allowed his ministrations. She had no strength to protest, in any case. Right now she did not care what he might do; she wanted only to sleep.

Maggie felt oddly lethargic and a bit dizzy. A soft giggle suddenly escaped her throat as Matthew dipped a small cloth in the basin and ran the cool soapy fluid over her face and neck. "The Johnson twins would be green with envy if they saw me now," she giggled.

Matthew smiled, knowing full well that the rum was having its desired effect, for her words were just slightly slurred. "Would they?" He grinned. "Why do you suppose?"

"They'd wish themselves in my place, of course."

"Do you think so?" he asked while a smile played around the corners of his mouth.

"Play not the innocent with me, Mr. Forrest. I saw their hungry looks. No doubt, given the chance, they'd eat you up."

"In truth?" Matthew laughed and gazed down at her annoyed expression. "Would that bring you some distress?"

"Just keep away from them," she ordered bossily.

"Indeed, mistress, I have every intention of doing just that."

"Good," she grunted, never noticing that he had lowered

the blanket and was pulling her arms free of her torn nightdress.

A long moment of silence followed as Matthew sucked in his breath, forcing his hands to administer to her needs rather than give in to the desire she inspired.

"Oh, that feels good," she almost purred as he washed her shoulders and lowered the cloth to soothe away the injury to her breasts.

"Does it?" Matthew managed, although his voice sounded strangely strangled.

"I'm sure you should not be doing this," she murmured, slipping closer to the edge of sleep.

"Do you believe if something feels good it must be wrong?"

Maggie giggled again, her voice coming thicker and still more slurred. "I'll not answer that, for I know the dev. . . dev . . . deviousness"—she stumbled over the word —"of your mind. Why is it I cannot see you clearly?" she asked, her mind a bit confused, for even though the lantern was left on the table, its light should be reaching them.

Matthew smiled. " 'Tis the rum."

"Oh, now I understand why people drink it. It leaves you feeling good, does it not?"

"Sometimes. If you drink enough."

"Well," she breathed tiredly, "I think . . ." She began slowly, "I think . . ." She tried again, only to end with a gentle sigh and a soft snore.

Matthew cuddled her softly pliant body close against him. They were lying on their sides, facing each other. Her head rested on his arm, and her warm breath caressed his chest. He had been lying like this for hours. His arm was stiff, but he was reluctant to release her. The luxury of holding her close more than compensated for the discomfort.

The fires of hell could not have compared to the suffering

that had suffused his body as he cleansed away the last of
Caleb's abuse. He was almost positive the bastard had not
raped her, although by the evidence left on her leg, he had
come dangerously close. The tension in his body had
relaxed some when he finally pulled the nightdress over
her head and covered her, only to grow again with each
passing moment as he held her close in a comforting embrace.

Matthew had to choke back the groan that threatened as
she snuggled closer. Her gown had risen up to her hips, and
her naked leg was flung sleepily over his.

Beads of sweat formed over his brow and lip, and his
body stiffened as he realized he needed only to shift his
position an inch or two to enter her, for their bodies were
unmistakably naked and pressed tightly together.

Her low, sleepy moan of pleasure and the almost imper-
ceptible lifting of her hips as she moved against him was
nearly his undoing. He bit down hard on his lip, his hands
clenched into tight fists, as the desire to press her to her back
upon the blanket threatened to overcome all reason. He
wanted her more than he'd ever wanted any woman, but he
would not take this sweet, sleepy offering. He wanted her
fully awake and conscious of her own desires.

Matthew groaned as his hand came unthinkingly to the
roundness of her hip and slid beneath her gown. He pressed
her still closer to him, and his mind reeled at the sensation
of naked flesh against naked flesh. God, he'd have to move,
or at the very least lower her gown, for he'd not be able to
control himself much longer.

Maggie stirred sleepily and rubbed her face against his
chest. Her arm slid over his shoulder and settled around his
neck.

Matthew trembled. God, if he were upon the rack, he'd
not feel suffering such as this, and still he could not find it
within him to move.

Maggie slowly opened her eyes to a wall of dark, furry
chest. She smiled as her fingers brushed idly through his

long black hair. She had wanted to do this for so long. She knew it would feel like this—crisp, clean, and so very Matthew.

His chest was so near, and he smelled so delicious. She wanted only to rest her mouth against him for a moment . . . just for a moment.

Suddenly Maggie jerked away. Her eyes opened wide. Her shock and confusion were apparent. "Oh dear," she exclaimed. "Oh my." She felt herself pressed up against his maleness.

Matthew feigned sleep. It was easier, he reasoned, than to explain their current position. He allowed Maggie to squirm loose from his hold. Once she had adjusted her nightdress, he deemed it safe to awaken.

Maggie lay startlingly wide awake. Her cheeks flamed as she remembered her close contact with this man. And her delight in it. Her body was shaking, and she knew it was not from shock but from a feeling of aching loss.

She had purposely blocked out the knowledge of how dangerously close she had come to indiscretion. She longed to flee, yet she ached to return to her previous position. God, had she ever known such torture?

How could it be wrong to love this man? He was so good, so kind, so decent. Did God truly demand that she stay with a husband who hated her? Would He not understand if she gave in to this temptation?

You fool yourself, Maggie, she berated herself silently. *If you break your marriage vows, you do so of your own free will. Do not hide behind your merciful God.*

Matthew sighed sleepily and stirred. A moment later he opened his eyes and grinned to find her some inches away, feigning sleep herself.

Slowly, and with some exaggerated groaning, he left the makeshift bed and slid into his pants. Kneeling again at her side, he touched her shoulder and almost laughed at her startled jump, which she turned brilliantly into a sleepy movement.

"Maggie," he whispered as he rocked her gently. "'Tis nearly dawn. You'd best not stay longer. Aunt Matilda will soon awaken and find you gone."

Maggie groaned and opened her eyes. She gave a silent nod and came to her knees, careful to keep the hem of her gown at her feet.

As Matthew helped her to stand, Maggie bit at her lip with indecision. She couldn't just walk away, not after the tender care he had given her, not without a word of appreciation. And yet her feelings ran so deep, she knew not how to phrase her words.

"Matthew," she began softly when he abruptly took her into his arms.

His voice was low and filled with pain as he whispered into her hair, "Do not thank me. Berate me instead for allowing it in the first place."

"You know you could have done nothing. He is my husband and has every right."

"I'll kill him if he touches you again," he growled, his arms tightening. "I care not who he is."

Maggie pulled away slightly and looked up to see the pain that filled his eyes. Hesitantly her hands came to frame his face, and her warm, comforting fingers soothed away the hard lines of his frown. Her smile was gentle, her words low and filled with hopeless tears. "I will thank you in any case."

"Kiss me instead, Maggie," he begged, his whole body throbbing with the pain of wanting her in his arms. His eyes filled with a yearning that pleaded for her not to deny him.

Maggie had no conscious thought of moving toward him. But with a soft cry she was in his arms, her mouth seeking the pleasure of his lips as her arms clung to his neck.

Matthew did not realize that the touch of her mouth had the power to shake him to the core. He had made a mistake in asking for her kiss, for he knew it wouldn't be enough.

"Maggie," he groaned desperately into her mouth, his lips never parting from hers. His arms tightened with bruising strength, crushing her to him, and Maggie found herself welcoming the roughness of his caress, yearning for more.

She wanted to melt into him, to become part of him, and the kiss only served to deepen her need.

His hands were all over her as his tongue probed her mouth.

She moved against him and heard his gasp of pleasure as he pulled her more firmly to him. He was holding her in place, his hips and tongue imitating the act of love they both longed for.

Their mouths broke apart to gasp for air and then immediately rejoined.

Her mind was lost in a fog of desire, more powerful and dizzying than the pint of rum. She loved this man and had no strength to pull away.

His hands were beneath her gown, running freely over her smooth flesh, exploring the softness of her breasts, and Maggie thought she'd die from the sheer ecstasy of it. She had never known a man's touch could overwhelm her senses.

Whimpering sounds escaped her throat as his hand moved from her breast along the smoothness of her belly to finally brush against her aching need.

She was warm and moist, and his body screamed to take her now, but he had other plans for their first time. It wouldn't be quick, and it wouldn't be now.

He felt her legs buckle as he thrust his fingers into the heat of her and almost smiled with satisfaction at her soft moan. His arm came around her waist and held her against him.

Maggie breathed a quick, sharp gasp at his sudden entry and groaned as his scent and taste flooded her senses. Her knees gave way, and had she been free she would have fallen. She was nearly incoherent as his fingers moved, causing her pleasure beyond belief.

It was like nothing she had ever experienced. And the wildness of her response caused her a moment of panic. She was about to lose control, and she was afraid. She tried to hold back, to break away, for the aching in her grew to agony, building toward a higher yet more terrifying pitch, and she wondered if she'd survive.

But Matthew felt her fear and increased his pace, his movement wiping the last thoughts from her mind.

Her body tightened around his fingers, and Matthew groaned, imagining himself inside her. She felt so lusciously sweet.

Maggie gasped for air, but he refused to release her mouth and, like a man dying of thirst, drank in all he could taste.

She was being absorbed into him, losing herself, no longer Maggie but an extension of his mouth and hands. Her scream was lost in his growl, and pleasure crashed down upon her. She thought she would surely die as his fingers continued to move and her body tightened and pulsed around him. And as the waves of pleasure began to roll over her, consuming her mind and spirit, she knew no greater love could exist than what she felt for this man.

Matthew released her mouth and breathed ragged, gasping breaths into her neck. Maggie cried softly into the warmth of his chest. His arms held her gently against him as he smoothed her long hair back from her damp face.

"I didn't know," she murmured, still lost in the moment just past. Unknowingly, she increased his agony as she brushed her cheek against his and ran her hands over his bare chest. "I never knew."

Maggie felt his nod.

"Go, Maggie," he choked out brokenly as he put her away from him. "Go now before I cannot stop."

Maggie's legs trembled, and for a second she thought she

would fall. Her chest heaved from the emotion that had rocked her senses, and tears ran freely down her cheeks. She stumbled to the door of the stall and stopped. Not daring to face him, she stared straight ahead and whispered, "I love you, Matthew."

Matthew felt his heart twist at her softly spoken words. His body tensed, and he helplessly watched the door swing back into place, leaving him more alone than ever.

Twelve

HE COULDN'T STAND MUCH more of this. She was tearing him apart. Lately she was in his thoughts every waking minute of every day, and he had yet to find release. Tonight he wouldn't chance a repeat of the last disastrous episode. He'd have to be careful. He'd have to hold on to his control.

If only he didn't want her so damn much. His heart thudded against his chest as he thought of her long red hair and creamy skin. He didn't doubt that he'd have her, but a man shouldn't be forced to wait for his woman. He had waited long enough, longer than any man should have to.

A soft chuckle escaped him as he looked down and saw the results of his thoughts. The sheet was pitched high above his hips, leaving little doubt about his present needs.

No doubt the whore he awaited would believe him hot for her. He gave a careless shrug as he stretched out comfortably on the feather mattress. It mattered not what she thought. It mattered only that he find release before another uncontrollable urge overwhelmed him.

They had found Abby's body three days ago, and the whole town was abuzz with speculation. It was clear most thought a drunken soldier to be the culprit, and he was pleased to let the blame fall where it may.

He leaned back and watched as the whore entered the room. A smile of anticipation hovered around his handsome mouth. She was perfect. He could feel himself growing even harder at the mere sight of her. It didn't matter that this night would cost him a tidy sum. Her long red hair might have come from a bottle, but the thought bothered him not. She had skin much like the one whose place she took; and if he imagined hard enough he had no doubt it would be as soft. And if her eyes were not brandy-gold, he'd lower the lamp so as not to notice.

Flo walked toward the bed. Her diaphanous robe parted as she moved, leaving nothing to the imagination, while her hungry eyes took in his obvious condition. She leaned her shoulder against the post at the bottom of the bed, her hand slid into the opening of her robe, and she fondled her lush breast absentmindedly as she asked, "Would you care for a brandy? Peggy stocks an excellent vintage."

His eyes were drawn to her nipple, and he nodded as he watched her roll the tip between two fingers until it was hard.

Flo grinned as she watched his eyes darken with lust. She walked toward a table that held a decanter and two glasses. Oblivious of her near naked state, she moved to his side and smiled as she darted her tongue into the glass. "I've been waiting a long time for you to ask for me. I was beginning to give up hope."

He shrugged. "Peggy's been seeing to my needs. If I'd known . . ." He left the sentence unfinished.

"After tonight, you'll have no further need of her," she promised as she dropped the robe to the floor and lay down at his side. "After tonight it's going to be you and me."

He leaned against the headboard of the bed and sipped at the brandy as he watched her. Flo positioned herself at his side, but when he made no immediate move toward her, she merely shrugged and began to run her hands over her breasts.

He grinned as he looked up to the mirror overhead and watched her slip her fingers between her legs. It was getting harder to pretend to be enjoying the brandy as she spread

131

her flesh and played with the hard nub of her passion with such obvious enjoyment.

Flo looked at the man at her side. "You want to do this for me?" she asked, her breathing growing choppy and labored.

He shrugged and smiled down at her. "You seem to be doing just fine." Idly he reached over and fondled a swaying breast as her fingers moved with ever-increasing speed.

Suddenly he poured the remaining brandy over her breasts and, removing her hand, between her legs.

He gave a soft laugh as her look of surprise turned to one of sudden intense interest. "Have I wasted a perfectly good glass of brandy?"

"I don't think so," she smiled in return, stretching languidly and arching her back toward him. "Brandy, like a woman, should be warmed and savored slowly to appreciate its full value."

"Do you imagine it to be warm enough?"

Flo laughed. "Were I to venture a guess, I'd say it's near ready to burst into flame."

"Well, we wouldn't want that, would we? 'Tis best, I think, if I remove it before some damage occurs." He grinned as he leaned over her, more than eager to combine the tastes of brandy and heated flesh.

This was a nightmare! She couldn't know, she couldn't! It would be the end of everything if this got out! In an instant his satiated body tensed as he carefully kept his face blank while listening to her ramblings. Perhaps she was guessing. It would be wise to let her go on, he reasoned. He couldn't make a decision about what to do until he knew all in her surprisingly devious little mind.

"I've been wanting to leave Peggy for some time now," Flo remarked casually. "With a little backing I thought I could set up a house in New York," she went on, oblivious to the rage that filled the man at her side. "Of course, my backer, besides sharing the profits down the middle, would have the sole rights to my company."

Bitch! Did she think her particular piece of ass so good he'd blindly fall into her trap? Granted, she was good in bed, but so were a dozen others. She had to be out of her mind if she thought he'd ever trust her. A whore! Jesus, he'd have to be stark raving mad before he'd allow her such control of his life.

His voice was steady and smooth when he finally calmed down enough to answer her. "Judging by my current circumstances, it might take me some time before I could lay my hands on the kind of money you're talking about."

Flo shrugged as she turned toward him and gave him her most seductive smile. "In the meantime you'll have to find a goodly sum to get Sampson out of town. You know how the man babbles on when deep in his cups." Her finger trailed down the length of his chest and stomach, not stopping until she cupped his spent manhood in the palm of her hand. "We wouldn't want him telling anyone else."

"How is it he was supposed to have seen me?" he asked as he allowed her to bring the object of her pleasure back to its former rigidity.

Flo shrugged. "It seems he was sleeping along the side of the road when you pulled your buggy into the dirt path and woke him up. He was too scared to say anything. You know, him being the town drunk and all, who'd believe him?"

"You seemed to have little trouble."

"Oh, sweetie, I never said I believed his story. I only told you what he told me."

"So now you're servicing town drunks?"

Flo giggled. "Are you jealous? Truth is, I felt sorry for the old man. He's always hanging around, hoping to make a few pence doing odd jobs for Peggy. I've seen his pants bulge often enough and thought he'd appreciate a little treat."

"Did you do this for him?" he asked as her tongue caressed his swollen manhood.

Flo laughed happily, her eyes shining with pleasure. "You are jealous. Rest easy, darlin', I only do this to my special friends."

"Of which I'm one?"

"Honey, you're going to be just about as special as one can get."

He couldn't prevent his low groan as she took him deep into her mouth. For just an instant he was almost sorry for what he was about to do. There were few others who knew what a man liked best. But the thought died a quick death when he recalled the danger she posed. He had little choice in the matter. He had to survive, and he'd do whatever was needed to ensure it.

It was dark. He could barely see his hand before his face as the wind and rain slashed at his form, nearly knocking him from the crate he sat on. Luckily, although the storm was fierce, it was nearly as warm as a bath, or he'd never have been able to wait this long. It had been hours, but he knew, regardless of the wild elements of the night, she'd have to make use of the outhouse sooner or later.

The problem of Sampson had earlier been taken care of. Once he was finished with her, he could rest easy.

Christ, she must be working her ass off tonight. He suppressed a threatening chuckle as he imagined the literal truth of his thoughts.

It was nearly dawn, and most of the whores had already seen to their nightly call of nature. Unseen, he had watched them pass by. Hidden as he was by the shrubbery and the storm, he had gone unnoticed.

Inside the house, Flo remained on the bed and smiled as the last of her customers prepared to leave. The man grinned as he watched her hands run seductively over her breasts and slip between her legs. "You be wantin' more, honey?" he asked.

"You be willin' to give it?" she teased, spreading her bent knees to give him a clear view of what she was doing.

Her customer laughed. "Sorry, not tonight. As it is, there's going to be hell to pay if Molly's waitin' up for me. I'd best be headin' home."

Flo nodded and watched him slide his arms into his heavy coat. "See you next week?"

"Sure as hell will, darlin'," he promised as he bent to kiss her goodnight.

After he left, Flo sighed with contentment and allowed her mind to rehash the night's events. A sly smile curved her usually pouting lips. She hadn't realized how easy it would be. She had been a bit nervous telling him Sampson's tale but had covered her apprehension with sultry promises. And it had worked! She had her backer. She was leaving the country bumpkins and going where there was big money.

A warm feeling washed over her when she remembered his touch. Damn, but he was good in bed. She wet her lips with her tongue and imagined him at her side again. The idea of working her own house lifted her spirits, leaving her with an almost permanent grin. This was the financial security she had always longed for, and she would have a handsome man as her lover.

She smiled, knowing she'd have no more sweating farmers asking for things their wives refused to give. What stupid women they were. Didn't they realize that to deny their men only sent them to another's arms? Didn't they care?

Flo shrugged. Her man would never have need of another. She'd make sure of that. There was nothing he could ask of her that she wouldn't do.

Just the thought of him was bringing her to a climax. Her fingers worked furiously over the sensitive flesh between her legs. Flo's body stiffened as her release grew closer.

She wished he had stayed the night. A low moan escaped her throat as she shuddered and came, lifting her hips, imagining his final thrust.

Flo breathed a long, satisfied sigh, stretched out, and watched her hands move over her naked body. No one could make it as good as she, not even him. She chuckled as she got to her feet. But he certainly came in a close second.

Flo gave a weary sigh. She had to use the privy. Her lips tightened with annoyance. If she worked one of the fancy houses in New York, she'd have a maid to empty her commode, and she wouldn't have to brave a storm just to answer nature's call. Judging from the sounds of the storm pounding against her windows, when she got back she'd be cold and wet and definitely in the mood to snuggle up against a warm body. She groaned, wishing she had talked him into staying. She wrapped her naked body in a cloak and left the room.

Flo couldn't be sure, what with the howling wind and all, but she stopped and listened. Sure enough, she heard it again. Someone was calling her name. A slow grin curved her mouth, and she imagined a man so desperate that he'd brave the storm for her.

"Where're you at, honey?" she asked as she peered into the darkness.

"Here," came a low voice, almost lost in the rush of wind.

Flo moved toward the sound, never even noticing or caring that her cloak blew open as she eagerly searched the blackness for her admirer. Suddenly a flash of lightning split the dark night, and Flo saw him sitting behind a bush. "Why you waitin' out here, sweetie?" she asked as she moved to stand before him. "If you be needin' some more of what I can give, why didn't you come into the house? I got plenty left." She grinned as she held open her cloak and began to move her hands over her warm, wet body. But the action was wasted, for the darkness of the night prevented him from seeing her.

Suddenly she was pulled onto his wet lap. "You really are anxious, aren't you?" she giggled, raising her face for a kiss. But her bubbling laughter caught in her throat as she realized he was menacingly silent. Before she could say a word or raise her hands to protect herself, he slid his fingers around her neck and squeezed.

Flo had already passed into the next world by the time he heard the faint sounds of her bones crushing. With a sigh of disgust, he shoved her away from him. Satisfied, he looked at her crumpled form lying amid the puddles and mud and smiled. He couldn't have chosen a better place for the slut to die.

He breathed a long sigh of relief, happy to put this night behind him.

═══ Thirteen ═══

Maggie flung herself into Matthew's arms, heedless of Aunt Matilda's surprised gasp and Hannah's knowing gaze. "He's gone! Oh God, he's terrified of storms, and he's out there somewhere!"

Matthew's whole body stiffened with dread. He knew before he asked, for only one person could bring her to this hysteria. "Who's gone, Maggie?"

"Joseph," Maggie sobbed as the tears she had fought for hours came suddenly to surface at his compassionate gaze. She pressed her face into the wall of his warm, wet chest. Her mind was oblivious to his saturated clothes, registering only the thickness of his soothing arms as they came around her and the warmth of his hands as they moved familiarly over her back.

"How long has he been gone?" Matthew's deep voice rumbled in his chest and brought a measure of comfort to her ears.

"I don't know," she whispered brokenly. "When I returned to the loft he was gone. I thought he might have gone to the outhouse, but he wasn't there. He wasn't anywhere. We've been searching for hours. Where were you?" she demanded, not thinking the question unseemly.

"Walking."

"Did you not see him?" Maggie knew her question was

futile. If Matthew had seen her son, Joseph would now be at her side.

Matthew simply shook his head. "Did you search the house and barn?"

"Aye," she cried, "again and again. The vegetable cellar, the smokehouse, the linter, everything." With pleading eyes, she looked up to the strength shown so clearly in his face. "Matthew, please," she whispered. "He's just a child. He'll be so afraid. Find him for me."

He nodded. "Stay here. I'll bring him to you."

Maggie nodded and did not object when, before two pairs of inquisitive eyes, his mouth swooped down to capture hers in a short, hard kiss of promise. Their eyes held for a long moment after he released her mouth, and Maggie knew deep in her heart that she'd never again feel this connection to another human being.

He didn't bother to change, for the viciousness of the pelting rain would only resoak his clothes in a matter of seconds.

Matthew lunged out into the wild night, as terror for the child's welfare tore at his heart. He prayed Joseph was hiding in a safe place.

Rain slashed across his face, all but blinding him as he moved between the trees, toward the river. To conserve his energy, he didn't bother to call out, knowing his voice would be lost on the wind. Joseph would likely be found closer to the creek than the house. Determinedly, he bent his large frame into each endless gust, praying he'd not be too late.

Matthew groaned as a jagged streak of lightning lit up the sky, allowing him to see what was once a gently flowing creek. To his horror he found its banks had overflowed by at least ten feet, and yesterday's lazy trickle was now a wild roar of white, rushing death.

Curses flowed as freely as the raging water, while he struggled against the raging winds. His feet slid in the mud as he moved closer and closer to the wild waters. Still, he refused to give up. His eyes squinted against the wind and flying debris; his voice was raw as he now called fruitlessly into the pelting rains.

Although the heaviness of the clouds prevented a true dawn, it was beginning to grow lighter. And the murky light at last enabled Matthew to walk around the trees rather than into them.

Almost blinded by wind and rain, gasping for breath, he leaned for a moment against a thick, swaying pine to recoup his energy. He turned his face away from the worst of the storm and helplessly cursed his weakness against nature's force. His legs felt as if he had walked for miles rather than the few hundred yards that separated the barn from the creek. And his arms throbbed and shook with exhaustion as though he had cut a cord of wood. He could only thank God that the rain and wind were warm, or Joseph would be in even greater danger.

As it was, if he did not find the lad and find him soon, the chances of his being alive were slim indeed. Whatever had possessed the boy to run out into a storm? Had he seen Maggie and himself together? No, he would not have run on that account. For there had been no real intimacy between them until he had brought her to the stall.

No doubt the storm had awakened him and he had seen the damage done at Caleb's hand. God damn her husband, he raged in silent fury. How he wished him out of their lives.

With his back to the tree and partially sheltered from the wind, Matthew was able to see a bit more clearly. He jumped as a tree snapped in half and crashed to the ground. The sound was not unlike the crack of a rifle shot. Forcing away his growing panic, he took a careful look around. Slowly his eyes searched out the surrounding shrubbery and tall, swaying grass, sometimes completely flattened in the wind. His brain did not register the sight of a tiny blur of white. Again he looked, slower this time. It took a long moment before he realized that what his eyes had passed over was some sort of material and not part of the natural surroundings.

Matthew lunged forward and reached out for the cloth, only to find it a much larger piece than he first thought. He tried to lift it but found it attached to a heavy object. He bent, pushed aside the wide evergreen, and laughed when he saw Joseph curled into a tight ball.

Quickly he gathered the sleeping boy into his arms. Joseph stirred as Matthew pressed him close to his warmth.

"Cold," came a sleepy murmur.

"I know, boy," Matthew soothed as he held him closer still. "I'll have you warm and dry in a minute."

Matthew burst into the barn amid cries of thanksgiving when the women spied Joseph. In an instant the boy was stripped of his soaking nightdress and cuddled in a thick quilt before the glowing potbelly.

Joseph choked as Aunt Matilda insisted he take a spoonful of sherry followed by a steaming cup of hot broth.

"Where is she?" Matthew asked as he pulled his shirt from his pants and began to undo its buttons.

"She left," Aunt Matilda answered. "I begged her to wait, but she said she had waited long enough." The women looked into Matthew's angry face, his eyes dark with fury. "We couldn't stop her," she continued weakly.

A string of curses filled the barn. "Did she say where she was going?" he asked as he ran to the back of the barn and disappeared into the stall he used as a bedroom. The door had barely closed behind him when he burst out again, clutching a bottle of rum and his oilskin.

"Try down by the creek," Aunt Matilda called over the roaring sound of wind. "She knows Joseph loves it there."

Again he cursed as he realized the storm had caused him to miss her. Why hadn't she waited? If anything happened to her . . . He left the thought unfinished.

The storm was growing in intensity. Matthew watched in amazement as a huge oak, topheavy from accumulated water, was ripped from the ground, its thick roots grotesquely snarled.

His heart hammered with fear. He had to find her. "Jesus, please," he begged aloud as he bent his body into another angry blast of raging wind.

He didn't even want to think of how Maggie was faring. If a man his size had no more strength than a babe against this force, what might it do to a woman so delicate and slender?

The mud sucked at his boots, making every step an effort of will.

He had been searching for an hour when he found her crumpled at the base of a tree. In all likelihood, he would have missed her had he not ducked a flying branch. Her cloak was blowing wildly about her, while her muddied, soaked nightdress clung to every curve of her body.

Until that moment, Matthew had never realized what it was to know true relief. Had the rain not already trailed water down his face, traces of dampness would surely have been detected in the vicinity of his eyes.

Summoning the strength to move forward, he knelt, reached his arms around her, and lifted her so he might see her face. Matthew sucked in his breath when he saw blood. It was everywhere, covering her face and caking with mud in her hair. The panic that gripped him caused his mind to suddenly go blank, and he simply stared as if befuddled.

It took him a long moment, but with sheer force of will he managed to push aside his terror. With a pounding heart, he searched out her injury. She had a good-sized lump on the side of her head and a small cut inside her hairline.

He breathed a sigh of relief. Something had hit her and knocked her senseless, but he doubted that she was seriously hurt.

"Maggie, can you hear me?" he asked, bending over her. She did not respond, except for the slight fluttering of her eyelids.

His chest tightened with apprehension as terror squeezed

his throat. Could he have been mistaken? Was she seriously hurt? "Maggie!" he shouted. He gave her limp form a violent shake.

Suddenly she seemed to realize he was there and opened her eyes. "I cannot find him," she sobbed in torment as Matthew pulled her close with a silent prayer of thanks. "I cannot," she muttered brokenly, the sound muffled against his chest.

"I found him, Maggie," he soothed as he wiped the blood from her face with his fingers. He bent his head and spoke into her ear. "He is safe. At this moment Hannah is forcing hot broth down his throat and cuddling him near a blazing fire. No doubt he is already complaining of the confinement."

Maggie looked at him for a long moment before his words seemed to sink in. A slow smile began at her lips, transforming her fearful expression to one of contentment. Her laughter was lost in the wind. She reached for him and hugged him close.

"I'll never be able to thank you," she whispered in his ear.

Matthew smiled down into her golden eyes, bright with tears. "We'll think of something," he teased, his heart suddenly light at her joy.

Maggie giggled at the look of smoldering promise in his dark eyes. "'Tis best, I think, if we find shelter before you put your thoughts into action."

"We'd best hurry, love, for the danger grows with each moment."

Matthew lifted her to her feet and held her protectively close to his side as they left the shelter of the tree and moved out into the wind.

Rain slashed with near explosive force, rocking the wobbly couple, while the wind tore viciously at their hair and clothes, daring them to ignore nature's awesome power gone berserk.

Matthew breathed a premature sigh of relief as he spied

the dark forms of rain-drenched buildings ahead. They were only a hundred yards or so from shelter. He and Maggie would soon be safe, warm, and dry. "Thank God," he breathed aloud, then fell suddenly to his knees. The last thing Matthew remembered was the softness of the black, sucking mud as it cushioned his face.

Maggie had lain upon the soft, wet earth some moments before she realized Matthew had fallen and taken her down with him. The weight of his body pinned her beneath him, and she found herself using the last of her strength to simply turn on her side.

Blinded by the torrential rain, Maggie found no evidence that he had been hit. Although he was surely exhausted, it was inconceivable that Matthew had simply fallen asleep, and yet she could see no injury. How had he gotten hurt?

Maggie groaned as she struggled to free herself. Why did the man have to be so big and so heavy? If she didn't hurry and roll him to his back, he would surely suffocate in the oozing mud.

Desperately, she pushed with the last of her strength and slid out from beneath him.

Maggie lay gasping, half on top of him, as she sought to regain her strength with a minute's rest. "Oh no," she groaned when she spied the blood running from the side of his head. What in God's name had hit him? And then she groaned again when she noticed a branch as thick as a man's arm lying close by.

"Matthew," she said as she shook his unconscious form. "Matthew, can you hear me? You've got to get up!"

Nothing.

Maggie sighed. There was no hope for it. She had no strength to move him. She'd have to leave him and go for help.

Inside the barn, Hannah and Matilda's ears were alert for any unusual sound, and Maggie's soft knocking and low groans of effort did not go unheard.

Before she allowed the threatening blackness to enclose her in its blissful comfort, she managed with the last of her strength, "He's out there. Please help . . ."

Maggie knelt by Matthew's side and moved the soapy cloth over the stubble on his cheeks and neck. After three nights his fever had finally broken, and Maggie had at last trusted Aunt Matilda to sit with him for the rest of the night, while she enjoyed her first peaceful sleep since the storm.

The sun was now shining, and the heavy air of summer held a clean, cool scent. Maggie hummed a happy tune as she continued about her task. Her humming faltered only when she had completed washing his arms and chest and debated the wisdom of lowering his sheet and continuing on.

"You need not hesitate on my account, mistress," came a deep voice.

Maggie didn't miss the slight movement of the sheet below his waist, and with cheeks beautifully pinkened with embarrassment she turned to face him. "It appears you are more healthy than one would think, Mr. Forrest."

Matthew chuckled, knowing the reason for her red cheeks but unable to quell the reaction of his body to her gentle touch. "I'd have to be dead, mistress, before I could withstand your tender ministrations and show no response. Were you to continue, I'd voice no objection."

"No doubt," she grinned, finding herself hard put to resist laughing at the daring twinkle in his dark eyes, "but I think you are now well enough to see to your own toilet."

When she made a move to come to her feet, Matthew's hand reached out and stayed her. "Nay, do not leave."

"You have been very ill, Mr. Forrest. You need to rest."

"I'd never ask to be well if I could always awaken thus."

Maggie grew flustered. "Are you hungry?"

"Do you realize how beautiful you are?"

145

Maggie smiled. "You'd do well, sir, to think of food. There is less danger in filling your stomach."

"Aye, but more pleasure in filling yours."

"Matthew!" Maggie gasped.

Matthew chuckled at her expression. "Do my words shock you?"

"You've no right to speak to me thus."

Matthew smiled as his hand slowly began to draw her to him. "Why did you stay at my side while I slept?"

"You were hurt. Someone had to see to your care."

"Why you?" he breathed as he drew her closer.

"Because I . . . because . . . I don't know. I cannot think when you pull me so close."

Matthew laughed. "One wonders why. Could it be the two questions have but one answer?"

"I know not what you mean."

"Do you not? Couldn't it be because you love me?"

"Nay," she breathed as her lips brushed against his. "Matthew, you must not listen to the ravings of a woman so distraught. 'Tis most unfortunate, for I spoke without thought."

"Will you tell me now you did not mean it?"

"Nay." She smiled as she brushed his hair back from his forehead. "But I will tell you this, your breakfast will be cold if you do not allow me to get it."

Laughter sparkled in his eyes. "I believe you to be quite heartless and cruel. Here I lie upon my sickbed"—he looked around and amended—"sick floor, and you can offer me not a word of kindness."

"I thought I heard you talkin'," Hannah's voice boomed from the doorway to the stall. "Seems to me this lady's worries were for nothin'. I told her so, but would she listen?"

Maggie, red-faced at almost being caught in Matthew's arms, jerked away at the sound of Hannah's voice and almost jumped to her feet. Her mumbled "I'll get your

146

breakfast now" brought a knowing smile to Hannah's broad face. Had Maggie seen the conspiratorial wink that passed between the two the moment her back was turned, she would have understood why Hannah nearly wrestled her to the ground to get the man his breakfast herself.

═══ *Fourteen* ═══

Maggie put the heavy bucket on the ground and wiped the perspiration from her forehead with the hem of her dress. If she had realized the bucket was so heavy, she would have called Elijah for help. But Aunt Matilda had been so insistent that the men have something cool to drink while working in the broiling sun that Maggie hadn't felt its weight until she was almost halfway to her destination.

She smiled as she heard Matthew teasing Elijah and James. Maggie grinned at the sound of male laughter, and a lightness filled her soul. She had not felt so complete in a long time. In fact, she barely remembered when happiness had been so tangible in her home.

Only Caleb remained unaffected. Maggie shivered as she remembered their last encounter. Thank God there had been whole weeks recently when she barely saw him. Often as not, he stayed in town, sometimes for days at a time. When he did return, he did so in the small hours of the morning, only to leave again while Maggie was about her chores.

The sound of hammering, sawing and good-natured laughter filled the silence of the small wooded area that separated Maggie's farm from the inn.

The inn itself was complete. Today the men worked on

the outbuildings and put the finishing touches to the barn, while Matthew anxiously awaited the arrival of the supplies that would enable him to open for business.

Maggie felt her face grow even warmer when she spied Matthew lifting a heavy length of planking. He was naked to the waist, and the muscles of his back and arms bulged under tan skin. Holding the plank high, he took a nail from between his lips and secured the wood to the side of the small building.

Maggie couldn't move. She had never but once seen him without a shirt, and the sight brought on a powerful ache of longing.

Elijah, noticing her, spoke a word to him, and Matthew turned to find her watching. A wide grin lit his handsome face as he reached for his shirt, slipping it over his shoulders and moving toward her.

Maggie watched the slow, easy movement of his hips. His sweat-dampened trousers clung to every delicious muscle and corded tendon in his powerful thighs. Her heart thumped with instant desire as his sex showed blatantly, almost taunting her to reach out and touch him.

She groaned softly. She had thought it safe to meet him here. Surrounded by three hired hands and two of her own men, she never imagined her reaction could be so overwhelming.

With an effort, she tore her eyes from his body and met the laughter in his eyes.

"Is there something you're in need of, mistress?" he asked, his words innocent enough, his look lecherous.

Maggie had to clear her throat twice before the words would come. "Aunt Matilda thought you might enjoy a moment's respite. She sent along a bucket of cool lemonade."

"Looks appealing indeed," he remarked. A slow smile teased his mouth, and his tongue moved enticingly over his parted lips. Maggie had no doubt that the man knew his effect on her.

Desperately she searched for something to say that would lighten the tension between them. "Are you thirsty?"

"Aye," he nodded, his eyes never leaving her face, "but more than thirsty. I hunger. If we were alone, I'd show you just how much I hunger."

Maggie felt her knees weaken, and she swayed. Matthew reached out a steadying hand, but Maggie dared not let him touch her. Quickly gaining control over her turbulent emotions, she moved out of his reach.

"Where is Joseph?" she asked, her voice amazingly steady.

Matthew grinned as he grabbed the pail and followed her. He knew his effect on her. Damn her stubbornness in denying it. Did she really believe all was finished between them, simply because she thought it improper? It had been weeks since he had touched her. Weeks since she had allowed them to be alone together.

An almost evil grin touched his mouth. Enough! he thought. This torture was about to end. It was obvious she'd not come to him of her own free will; therefore, he'd simply have to show her the folly of her ways . . .

"Where is Joseph?" she repeated, interrupting his reverie.

"Beyond the smokehouse," he responded. "The lad practices the use of a hammer."

Maggie grinned down at her son. "Aye, Joseph, you did a good job of it indeed."

Joseph skipped along beside his mother as she returned to the farm. Again he held up to his mother's admiring gaze the small piece of lumber and the more than two dozen nails that had been driven into it.

"And I didn't hit my thumb, not even once. Mr. Forrest showed me how. He can do anything."

Maggie murmured an unintelligible reply. *Indeed he can,* she mused silently, *especially . . . Stop it, Maggie!* she commanded severely. *You will not think on it.*

150

"Hurry along, Joseph," she urged as she quickened her step. "Hannah has a cough again, and I promised Aunt Matilda I would go to the apothecary. If you like, you can accompany me, and if you're very good, perhaps Mr. Goodwin will find you a licorice stick."

Maggie pulled hard on the reins, and the gentle horse came to a stop before the general store. A moment later she and her son were inside Mr. McMahan's establishment. After handing her list to Mrs. McMahan, Maggie made her way to the small building across the rutted dirt street.

"Good day to you, Mr. Goodwin," Maggie remarked as the door chime announced her entrance.

"Mistress Darrah." Mr. Goodwin smiled as he looked up from the bowl in which he mixed his medicines. "How do you fare on this morn?"

"I am well, Mr. Goodwin. But Hannah has once again come down with that nagging cough."

The chemist nodded and walked toward the back of the store. "I mixed a new potion just this morning." From the back room he called out, "Would you be wanting the Squire's Elixir for your aunt?"

"Aye, Mr. Goodwin, 'twould save me a trip if you include it."

Joseph looked longingly at the selection of sweets, trying to decide between licorice sticks and cinnamon drops, while Maggie waited for Mr. Goodwin's return. She was always mesmerized by Mr. Goodwin's collection of shelf after shelf of delightfully colored ceramic bowls and glass jars filled with exotic ingredients. And, of course, the sweetly scented sugars, cinnamon, cloves, and nutmeg added a special aroma to the apothecary.

A short time later, with her son in tow munching on a rum and butter candy stick, Maggie returned to the general store to await her small order of supplies. As she idly browsed among the shelves of foodstuffs, her eyes came to rest on a jar of tea. Since the English occupation of her town, it was once again possible to buy the substance, but like most of her fellow compatriots Maggie would not. Still she couldn't help but gaze longingly at the container of black shredded leaves, and her mouth watered as she imagined a deliciously steaming dark cup of the brew.

"I'd tell no one if you bought an ounce," came a familiar voice from behind her.

Maggie smiled as she turned to face Matthew's teasing smile. "Aye, but I would know, and that would be enough."

"Do you never sway from your beliefs?" he asked, his gaze warm and admiring.

"Indeed, Mr. Forrest. I claim no qualities of sainthood. All I can do is try."

"So there's hope," he murmured, not quite beneath his breath.

Maggie tried to laugh away his words, for it was obvious he spoke not of tea. But the laughter died in her throat. How could she brush aside as nothing the pain she saw in his eyes? A pain that so closely mirrored her own? Her mouth opened twice to speak, but no sound came forth. She knew she was behaving scandalously, but she couldn't pull her gaze from his. If she didn't soon regain control, Mrs. McMahan would notice her staring at this most handsome man, and the whole town would be gossiping about them. Trying to relieve the tension, she finally managed, "What brings you here today?"

Matthew shrugged and fought against the urge to reach out and touch her. He had watched her head the wagon toward town, and like a magnet to steel he had followed. "I'm in need of tobacco."

"Ah, 'tis fortunate indeed you came." She smiled. "I nearly forgot I was to get Hannah a sack."

A good sign, he mused silently as he smiled into brandy-gold eyes. *At least I can make her forget something.*

* * *

Maggie held the rifle to her shoulder, her eyes glowing yellow with rage as she aimed it at the uniformed soldier. "If you value your life, you will release her and put the vegetables back where you found them."

The young soldier's eyes widened with surprise. At a nod from his superior officer, he shoved a sobbing Aunt Matilda away.

"'Tis a serious offense, this hoarding," the officer remarked authoritatively. "No doubt my commanding officer will not take kindly to the notion."

"I care not what your superiors think. My family needs this food. Without it we shall surely starve."

"Do you mean to kill all of us? How else do you propose to keep us quiet?"

Obviously Maggie hadn't thought that far ahead. "Damnation," she groaned in disgust. What on earth was she expected to do? The idea of killing them was ludicrous, and yet if she did not they would take all the food she had till harvest.

"A suggestion, sir, if you've a mind," Matthew remarked as he silently moved from behind Maggie and gently but most determinedly relieved her of the gun.

Maggie spun around and gasped with surprise. How did the man always manage to sneak up on her like that?

"If you don't mind . . ."

"But I do," he interrupted, glaring at her stubborn expression. "Now step behind me and hold your tongue, or you will feel the palm of my hand where all children need it most."

"How dare you!"

"Maggie," he warned, his voice as hard as granite, his eyes promising dire consequences should she disobey. "Shut up and do it."

Maggie reluctantly did as she was told. From the clear threat in his eyes, there was no telling what the beast might do if she refused. Still, her body was stiff with indignation and barely contained rage.

Maggie fumed. This was more than she could take. What gave him the right to speak to her thus? Ignoring his direct order, she glanced around and found to her utter mortification that all the men were smiling. Her hands clenched into fists, and Maggie couldn't remember a time when she was so near violence. Several deep breaths later she managed to gain some control. Smarting with pride and barely controlled tears, she vowed, *At the first opportunity, I'll put the beast forever in his place.*

Matthew emptied the gun and handed it to Aunt Matilda. "Would you see to this, madam?" he asked gently.

Aunt Matilda breathed a sigh of relief, nodded, and disappeared into the barn, more than a little thankful for Mr. Forrest's rescue.

"Gentlemen," he began, "'tis obvious, I fear, the lady did not think before she acted. A common occurrence among her sex, I'm told." He shrugged. "We all know of their general lack of intelligence. Indeed, most often we could accomplish more when speaking to a child."

Matthew almost smiled at the distinct sounds of gnashing teeth he heard behind him. Silently he prayed that her control would last till he got her away from these men. He continued, "Surely 'tis possible to forgive her this one indiscretion?"

After a long moment of silence, the officer replied, "I'd take the gun."

"The gun belongs to me," Matthew returned. "In the future I shall make sure it is kept safe from her reach."

The officer nodded. "We will take the vegetables."

"Nay," Maggie blurted out, unable to stop herself. She lunged toward the men in a wild but hopeless effort to stop them. "You cannot!"

In the next second Maggie could only gape in silent surprise as her world suddenly turned upside down. It took her a full minute to realize that Matthew had grabbed her waist and flung her over his shoulder. But when, to every man's utter delight, he landed a powerful blow to the softest

154

part of her anatomy, Maggie answered their roar of laughter with an angry curse on all things male.

Knowing he needed to get her as far away from the soldiers as possible before her temper completely erupted, Matthew nearly ran toward the inn, with Maggie bouncing on his shoulder.

"Release me this instant, do you hear me?" she shouted. When he chose to ignore her order, she punched his back with all her strength. "You bloody beast, I said release me!"

For her efforts Maggie only received yet another smack on her bottom.

"Ow!" she yelled. "Damn you, Matthew, put me down!"

Matthew never hesitated until the door of the deserted inn slammed behind them. Suddenly she was flung from his shoulder to stand dizzily before him.

Maggie groaned as the room swayed about her, and she clung to his arms for support.

"You little fool!" he ranted and shook her until her teeth rattled and her neck threatened to snap. "What did you hope to gain by that nonsense?"

"S-s-stop it!" she finally managed to stutter, gasping for air as her stomach lurched.

"My God," he groaned, pulling her tightly against him, his heart thudding with a terror he only now allowed himself to acknowledge. "Do you realize what they could have done to you?"

"You monster!" she raged as the dizziness finally abated. She swung a weak-fisted punch at his chest as tears of despair filled her eyes. "We will starve, thanks to you."

"Nay, Maggie," he soothed as he slipped her mobcap from her head and caressed the long, flowing mahogany curls. "Don't worry. I shall see to it."

Maggie sniffed and dried her eyes with the back of her hand as she moved away from him. "I'll not take another farthing," she insisted proudly. "'Tis enough we owe."

"You owe me nothing, damn it!" he growled and pulled her to him again.

In truth, Maggie knew she had no choice in the matter. What he gave, he gave freely. Recognizing this should have pleased her, and perhaps it did. Still, oddly enough, instead of happiness she wanted to cry, and her emotions left her more than a little confused. Her eyes filled with mist. Suddenly she was sobbing into his chest.

Matthew sighed as he gently soothed her. "Maggie, love, do not cry. All is not lost."

"But it is." And she cried all the more at his tender ministrations. "I've worked so hard," she sobbed. "I try . . . I try."

Matthew gave a sad smile as he realized the toll it had taken for this slender woman to have borne alone the weight of her family's responsibilities.

"You need not fear, my love. I'm here. I'll always be here."

Fifteen

Maggie sighed as she sipped the frosty lemonade. Imagine ice taken in huge chunks from the Hudson in the dead of winter to be used for cooling drinks on a warm summer day. What utter luxury!

Maggie listened to Sally's chatter and leaned back on the thick cushions of her friend's porch swing. "Why, I wouldn't be surprised if you could move back into your house within the next day or so. 'Twill be a relief, I imagine, to sleep without the scent of animals."

Maggie shrugged, her family's sleeping arrangements of little consequence at the moment. "I've lived so long in it, I doubt if I'll notice the difference."

"Like the fort, I hear the inn is also ready for use."

"It is."

"So Mr. Forrest is gone then?"

"Well, actually, he waits for the last of his supplies. He'll move his things in then, I imagine."

Sally laughed and shot her friend a knowing look.

Maggie lifted a thin brow and glared back. "Is that laugh supposed to have some meaning?"

Sally shrugged. "I'd think you'd be sorry to see him go. I know half the women in this town nearly swoon if he simply wishes them good day."

"Sally." Maggie tried to admonish her friend, although

her voice was softer than usual. "Shame on you. I am a married woman."

"Does marriage mean you've become suddenly blind?"

Maggie laughed. "Do not think you can induce me into admitting such nonsense with no more than ice in my lemonade."

"Tell me, then, what *would* it take?"

"Sally." Maggie laughed again. "Truly, you are terrible. Does Mr. Williams know what a minx you are? One can only feel sorry for the gentleman, knowing the disturbance you are sure to cause once he marries you."

"Nonsense." Sally smiled as she gave Maggie a look of feminine confidence. "He shall love every minute. Indeed, I shall see to it."

Maggie shook her head and laughed again. How lucky she was to have this woman for a friend. No matter what the problem was, Sally could find something to laugh at.

"Now tell me, why have you come if not to talk about your delicious Mr. Forrest?"

Maggie didn't bother to correct her this time. "Yesterday the English found our secret vegetable cellar. They took everything. I don't know what I will do if I can't get some supplies. The crop won't be ready to harvest for months yet, and I dare not slaughter any of the animals we've hidden away. They are sure to notice the scent and the smoke once we cure the meat."

"And there are just so many rabbits one can eat, correct?"

"Aye."

Sally smiled. "I see no problem. We have stored enough away for years. Have Elijah dig another cellar, this time deep in the woods. When he is finished, send him over, and one of our men will help him move in a new supply."

"Sally, I don't know how to . . ." Maggie began, with tears of gratitude blurring her vision.

"Please," Sally groaned, "do not thank me. If you do I shall be greatly insulted. I expect you would do at least as much if I were in need."

Maggie nodded her head.

"Well then, keep your thanks for strangers. We've been friends since childhood, have we not?"

"Aye," Maggie agreed.

"Then why won't you tell me about Mr. Forrest?"

At first Maggie stared with surprise at the abrupt change of topic, but then, noticing the twitching of Sally's lips, she laughed and shook her head in dismay.

"Very well," Sally returned easily. "I can see you are harboring some deep dark secret, and although it will probably kill me, I'll not nag you into telling me." Suddenly she gave Maggie her most charming smile and continued silkily, "At least not so you'll notice."

Caleb groaned as the blinding pain penetrated his skull and lingered with burning needles behind his eyes. Jesus, at this rate he would soon find himself sleeping for good, planted in a pine box.

A smile softened his usual sulky features and creased his unshaven cheeks. For a moment he almost appeared handsome. Regardless of the pain, he had to admit last night had been one of his best.

"I can see by that grin you are awake," Peggy remarked as she pushed a brush through her long fire-red hair.

Caleb fought against a wave of dizziness as he opened his eyes to bright sunlight. Jesus, he was still drunk. Drunk and hung over at the same time. Even for him, this was a first.

His blue gaze moved toward the sound, and he watched Peggy brush her hair until she was satisfied that the long silken tresses glowed. "So, you've decided to join us again, have you?" she asked, her soft Irish accent a balm to his throbbing head.

Caleb could feel himself growing hard at the sight of her sitting across the small room, naked but for a tightly secured corset and black silk stockings. The corset left her bottom bare and caused her huge, soft breasts to lift enticingly toward the mirror she faced.

"Come back to bed," he growled as he fought back the pain in his head and gut. "I'm not finished with you yet."

Peggy laughed softly. "So you'd be wantin' more, would you?" She turned in her seat and faced him, her eyes shining with delight that she could so easily bring this man under her spell. "Is it these you be wantin'?" she asked with supposed wide-eyed innocence as she cupped her breasts in her hands and began to roll the nipples into hard buds. "Or this?" she asked, parting her legs and moving her hands between them, splaying the soft flesh for his view.

Peggy leaned back against the small dressing table and smiled as she opened her legs farther. Slowly she dipped her fingers deep inside for moisture and began to massage her most sensitive area. "Mmm," she sighed, thoroughly enjoying herself as she watched his eyes move hungrily over her.

Just knowing what Caleb could do to her made her blood pound in her ears. Even without legs, he was the best damned lay she had ever known.

"Come over here, and I'll finish that for you," he promised, his voice husky with lust, his ailments miraculously vanished. He pushed aside the sheet and ran his hands over his enormous sex.

Peggy smiled and moved toward him, her eyes on his throbbing manhood, eager to feel his pulsating thickness fill her. In her mind, this was the true mark of a man, no matter the condition of his legs.

With his massive arms, he lifted her above him and held her as if she were weightless, and his mouth continued the work her fingers had started. When he heard her cry out and felt her body shudder, he suddenly impaled her on his aching rod. Peggy gasped her pleasure as he entered her with one sharp thrust, filling her until her ache became a torment she had only known with him.

For a long time she lay gasping atop his body. Their skin was damp, their breathing still harsh and unsteady, as she felt her throbbing ease and then cease. He was the only man she knew who could make her go wild like that. If it was up to her, she'd never even look at another. When was he going to realize they were good together? Good enough for him to forget his wife and stay?

Caleb sighed tiredly. "I'll have to use your buggy again, darlin'," he said as the bitterness that was never far from his mind flooded his being. *Damn that bastard Forrest to hell!* he raged in silent frustration. *Who does he think he is to keep me from using my own carriage? Damn him to hell for taking everything!*

"Why do you have to leave? Why can't you stay here?" she asked, her mouth pouting beautifully.

"Peggy, you know I can't," he countered easily. "I've a wife at home."

"You told me yourself she's whorin' for Forrest. If that's the case, she won't be missin' her husband."

Caleb laughed. "No doubt you are right, my dear, but I'd not miss a chance to add my delightful company and wit to their table. I've been gone too much of late. I want to know what's been going on."

Peggy shrugged, rose from the bed, and slid her arms into a diaphanous dressing gown. "I've been thinking about moving to New York. A friend of mine tells me there's big money to be made there."

Caleb's eyes narrowed at her words. This wouldn't do at all. He'd never be able to get out of that godforsaken house if he didn't have her and the use of her buggy. Jack, constantly drunk, couldn't be depended on. Christ, he'd rot in his bed if he had to wait for that one to come and get him. And if he did, what then? This town had little enough in the way of entertainment. She couldn't leave him there.

"When were you thinking of going?" he asked with a deliberate show of calmness, as if his very life and sanity didn't depend on her staying.

"You could always come with me." She shrugged, not at all fooled by his show of nonchalance.

A plan began to form in the far recesses of his mind. He'd have to think on this. Maybe he could go with her. After all, why should he have to stay with a bitch of a wife who didn't even realize what kind of a man he was? But to go as he was, penniless, with no more than the clothes on his back, and a cripple to boot, would be unbearable.

He might not be the proudest of men, but even he had his limits. What he needed was money, and he knew where to get it. Somehow he'd find out where she stashed it. More than likely they had a tidy sum left from the sale of last year's crop, for the tightfisted bitch guarded every cent.

He gave a low laugh as he imagined the look on her face when she found it gone. Would she run with teary eyes to Forrest? Of course she would. Let the bastard take care of her. He'd had more than enough of them all.

═══ *Sixteen* ═══

"JESUS CHRIST!" CALEB SWORE in a loud whisper. "If you keep banging into everything, you'll have that old hag awake and there'll be hell to pay."

Caleb had waited patiently for Joseph and Aunt Matilda to retire for the night. Only moments before, he had watched his wife leave the house and head toward the creek with a towel and a bar of soap, but there was no telling how long she might be gone. For all he knew, she could walk in at any minute.

Jack mumbled a drunken "Sorry" as he reached out to still a tottering dish, sending yet another cup flying from the mantel to smash on the hearth as he continued his search. "What is it we're looking for?"

Caleb groaned at the sudden noise and the man's stupidity. Thank God his son slept like the dead. "Money, damn it! I've told you again and again, I need to find out where she hides it."

Caleb grumbled with disgust as he watched his drinking partner stagger and fall against the fireplace. Banging his head on the thick wooden mantel, Jack slipped to the floor and lay dangerously close to the fire in a drunken stupor.

Jesus, Caleb ranted in silent frustration, couldn't he have stayed sober for one night? It was hard to believe, but he was even more useless than Elijah.

163

Thank God he was getting the hell out of there. He'd go crazy if he had to spend one more day with those idiots.

"Jack, Jack, you stupid fool, wake up!" Caleb whispered from a chair across the room. The urgency in his voice was unmistakable. He had to get out of there before that bitch Maggie returned to find them with their hands in the till, so to speak. "For Christ's sake, wake up!"

Jack muttered drunkenly, unaware of both the danger of being caught and his proximity to the fire.

Even though it was the middle of summer, no one ever extinguished the cooking fire, since it took so long to start another. So the kitchen was oppressively hot. Sweat slid uncomfortably down his back as Caleb struggled to rise from his chair. His arms bulged at the effort it took to move his useless legs. Trying to hold to the wall proved to be wasted effort. His legs crumbled beneath him and sent him sprawling on the floor. Caleb cursed as he crawled slowly across the floor, his upper body dragging the rest of him toward his happily sleeping cohort.

Caleb was drenched with sweat by the time he reached the fireplace. He shoved Jack and received a drunken mumble for his efforts. Cursing the uselessness of the man, he continued the search himself.

One of the bricks had to be loose. He had seen Maggie enter the kitchen more than once when in need of cash. He doubted she was foolish enough to use one of the many jars that lined the shelf over the dry sink. She'd be too fearful of losing her money to leave it where anyone could get their hands on it. But no matter how he twisted and pulled, no bricks seemed loose. Where the hell did she keep it?

It would be just his luck that she had hid it high and out of his reach. He grunted in determination. A pair of useless legs were not going to stop him. He was going to get that money if it killed him!

Caleb groaned and pulled himself up, his hands bleeding as they sought to hold on to the rough bricks. With superhuman effort, he managed to cling to the fireplace, holding himself erect with one hand as he began a careful search with the other.

Suddenly his body began to slip. Desperately, he tried to stop his fall. His hand reached out and grasped the mantel, only to wrench it from its wooden braces. Helplessly, he watched as it and all its contents smashed to the floor.

Disaster might have been averted that night if the lantern perched on the mantel's edge had not been lit. Or perhaps if Aunt Matilda had not assuaged her cold symptoms with a generous dose of sherry. Or if Maggie had returned the basket of rags to a place of safekeeping.

As it was, the lamp fell directly into the rag basket, and Caleb watched with dumbfounded fascination as the flaming whale oil seeped like hungry fingers of death over the fabric and onto the wooden floor.

The room filled with acrid, violently bitter smoke almost before Caleb could blink an eye. The fire spread like gushing water, greedily absorbing the wooden beams that lined the walls and ceiling.

But Caleb had no thought for the horror of what he had caused as his gaze fell on the handful of gold coins that had tumbled from the ceramic jar, now smashed at his side. Greedily he scooped them into his pocket and began to crawl from the burning building. Suddenly he remembered the sleeping people within. The old hag who slept above the kitchen was no concern of his, and that stupid Jack deserved what he got, but Joseph . . . A twinge settled in the pit of his stomach. Joseph, no matter how annoying he could sometimes be, was still his son.

"Joseph!" he called, watching the flames run up the frilly curtains and crack the thin glass of the window. "Joseph!" he screamed again as the boy began to stir. "Get up," he ordered. "Get out of here!"

Used to being yelled at by his father, Joseph took no particular notice of Caleb's panic-stricken voice and moved sleepily to his feet. But it was already too late; black, choking smoke engulfed him. With his first gasp of surprise, smoke filled his lungs, burning a painful path of fire within his chest and leaving him strangely dizzy. He couldn't stop coughing, and with every gasping breath he took more smoke entered his lungs. He tried to run, but for some reason his legs weren't working like they should. He tried to see, but his eyes filled with tears as he strained against the wispy black clouds. He felt a moment of fear and fell weakly to his knees, but he quickly pushed the thought away. It was only a dream, after all, he reasoned, and hadn't his mama always told him he shouldn't be afraid of dreams?

Joseph crumbled to the floor and snuggled close to the warm body at his side. A slight smile touched his childish lips, and he sighed peacefully. Soon he would awake cozy and safe in her arms, and she would make it all right.

Maggie smiled as she slid under the black water to rinse the lather from her hair. Although she originally had been annoyed with Caleb—his presence in the house had forced her to bathe at the creek rather than in her kitchen—she was now quite happy. Indeed, he had done her a favor. In all the years she had lived on this farm, she had never once bathed naked outdoors, and the feeling was blissful.

The cool water ran over her naked body, and Maggie luxuriated in its sensual touch, wondering why it had taken so long for her to find this pleasure.

She was clean now, but the water felt so good that she was loath to return to the house. She would stay on a few moments. Just the thought of the breathless heat coupled with the uncivil company that would greet her upon her return grated sharply on her nerves, and she knew she would have a time of it simply controlling her tongue.

Maggie sighed, leaned back, and allowed the water to gently lift her to its surface. The moonless night caused the stars to twinkle in a brighter pattern than usual across the velvety black sky. All was peaceful and silent, except for the occasional hoot of an owl and the constant chirping of crickets. Fluffy gave a low growl at a passing squirrel, and Maggie felt happy just being alive.

As was prone to happen when she had a moment to herself, Maggie's thoughts soon turned to the man who still occupied the tack room of her barn. Although his belongings were few and it would have been no great effort to move, he had not yet done so. She was happy just knowing he was close by.

Maggie knew now that no matter the distance between them, she would always feel near to him. She imagined his touch, the exquisite taste of his mouth, the scent of his skin. She loved him as she would never love another. In her ignorance of this new emotion, Maggie had once harbored the notion that after a time her needs would abate. But to her surprise they had grown tenfold.

Her eyes glowed luminously in the black night, reflecting the shimmer of the sky. Maggie smiled at the tall, shadowy form suddenly standing at her side. Indeed, her imagination was quick to conjure him up from the depths of her mind. For conjure him up she must surely have done, since his presence caused not a ripple to disturb the glassy sheen of black water. Suddenly he was there where moments before he was not. Her heart thudded violently in her chest as she stood to face him. Afraid to blink lest the movement cause the vision to vanish before her eyes, she raised her hand as if to touch him but pulled back at the last moment. Her words sounded whispery soft and distant as she sighed, "God, how I wish you were real."

A deep, warm chuckle came to caress her ears. "Am I not?"

"Nay." She smiled, knowing, of course, at the sound of his voice that this man was no figment of her imagination. She faced him unashamedly naked, reveling in the hunger that shone in his eyes. Water swirled deliciously about her hips, and if she but closed her eyes she could imagine it to be his touch. "I have called you from my mind."

"Am I so often in your thoughts that you perceive me where I'm not?" He grinned, his eyes glowing with pure manly confidence.

"Aye." She smiled again, and an evil glimmer came to her eyes. "You come particularly to mind when I assist Elijah in cleaning the horse droppings from the stalls." She laughed at his astonished expression and splashed a handful of water in his direction as she suddenly turned and raced toward the shore.

Maggie had moved only three steps, the weight of the water hampering her movements, when she screamed as his powerful arm snaked around her slim waist and hoisted her up in the air, only to release her to fall with a giant splash at his feet. "You little wretch." He grinned as he pulled her free of the water and into the heat of his arms. "And here I thought you to be speaking from your heart."

Maggie sputtered and gasped at the sudden dowsing, but at the look in his dark eyes she giggled. "Was I not?"

Matthew groaned. "I fear you were."

Maggie laughed. "Is your confidence so fragile, your manly ego so unsure, that you must hear the truth of it?"

"Aye," Matthew groaned when he felt her wet, slippery hips brush against his own as she tried to lean away from his embrace.

Maggie didn't miss the evidence of his growing desire as he lowered one arm and pressed her firm hips more tightly to him. A soft moaning sound came suddenly to her throat, a sound that dared her to deny her hunger to be in his arms. "What would you have me say?" she asked, her voice suddenly low and thick with yearning, her eyes half closed with the ecstasy she felt.

Matthew shrugged. "The truth will suffice," he said as he lowered his mouth to hers.

"Matthew, we shouldn't do this," she whispered against his lips once her mouth was free to speak again. Her arms clung to his neck as dizziness assaulted her senses.

"Tell me to stop, Maggie," he groaned, raising her body

so his mouth might linger at her breast. "Tell me, and I swear I'll try," he choked out as his lips and tongue moved to caress her sensitive flesh with pure liquid fire.

"I cannot," she gasped, lowering her face to his hair and breathing in his special scent. "Oh God, I swore I'd never let this happen, but I cannot." *Just this once, please, God. If I'm doomed to remain forever in this sham of a marriage, let me have this one moment.*

═══ *Seventeen* ═══

THEY WERE, FOR A time, lost in that beautiful moment of eager anticipation, a delicious prelude all lovers savor, for its passing would move them to a different type of union. So it was some moments before either heard the screams.

Fluffy was suddenly on his feet, barking as if crazed, jumping and howling, trying to get the couple's attention.

Matthew released her so suddenly that Maggie almost fell. A moment later he was out of the water, forcing his wet legs into his pants and running toward the incessant screaming.

Maggie felt the terror squeeze her throat. *Smoke! Oh God, please, not smoke!*

Matthew lunged forward, heedless of the branches that slapped against him as he instantly realized what might await them.

Even through the dense foliage, Matthew could see the glow that lit up the black sky and silently prayed it was the barn that burned. His breath was labored and harsh as he hurried forward, while a fearful ache started at the pit of his stomach as the sounds of Hannah's screams filled the night.

He could see her form outlined against the burning house as he broke through the last of the woodland, and his heart sank with dread. He knew without asking that the boy

170

remained inside; if not, Hannah would have him clutched close to her side.

The house was aflame, its glow surely visible for miles. Matthew never hesitated as he rushed past Hannah, who was clutching hysterically at Elijah. With one last gasping breath, he lunged into the inferno. He could see nothing. In a second his eyes were tearing from the dense smoke, and he fell to his knees, hoping to avoid the worst of it. Blindly his hands explored the wooden flooring, searching for Joseph.

His lungs ached, and his mind screamed out for air, but he dared not breathe, lest he fall forward and never get up again. His hand touched something soft, and he instantly realized Caleb was before him. If Caleb was here, perhaps the boy . . . He never finished the thought as his searching hands found Joseph nestled close to his father's side.

Instantly Matthew had the boy in his arms. Blinded by smoke, he had to stop a moment and think before he could retrace his steps to the door. Matthew turned and left the unconscious man to his destiny. He could not manage both, and he knew the fire would prevent his return.

Meanwhile, Maggie had been right behind Matthew as he rushed through the woods. In the distance she could hear Hannah's screams, but she refused to allow the horror to invade her mind.

Maggie's footsteps faltered when her gaze took in the blazing building. She had never seen or heard such a roaring blaze before. She had no time to think. All she knew was that she had to get to Joseph and she had to do it now.

Heedless of her own safety, she ran toward the flaming house. But strong arms held her firm, dragging her back before she could go inside. "No!" she screamed as she clawed at James and tried to break free of his hold.

"Mr. Forrest is already inside. You would only get in his way," came the voice of her longtime friend.

"Joseph!" she bellowed, kicking and clawing the man who was trying to save her from certain death.

Suddenly Matthew burst out of the flaming doorway. Maggie cried out with relief when she realized he held her son in his arms. Matthew would long remember her smile, for he, like the others, knew she had no reason to smile.

"Joseph," she crooned softly as Matthew placed the boy in her open arms. "Oh, Joseph," she murmured gently, tenderly brushing his singed hair from his face. "I'm so sorry I left you, darling. I'll never leave you again."

Maggie's stomach lurched at the smell of burnt flesh, but she pushed the queasiness aside. He needed care. She would soon make him well. For just a second Maggie wondered at the stillness of his form. But this too she reasoned away. The boy was injured. It was a blessing that he could sleep.

Hannah's low sobs increased in strength as Matthew's sorrow-filled eyes met hers.

Silently, except for the sound of Hannah's soft weeping, they stood around her. Their hearts wrenched in pity as she cooed lovingly to her son, softly spoken words Joseph would never hear.

"Hannah, would you get me a wet cloth and some salve for his burns?"

"Hurry along and do as she asks," Matthew said to Hannah's confusion.

Hannah returned moments later from her small house with a pan of water and rags to wash away the black soot. "Gently now, Hannah," Maggie warned. "I'd not see him suffer."

"Child . . ." Hannah sobbed as she handed the soapy cloth to her mistress.

"There now, sweetheart. Is that not better?" she asked as she cleansed his burned cheeks. "I love you, Joseph. You know I'll not let any harm befall you. Rest now," she soothed and nuzzled her face into his lifeless neck. "Mama's here."

It was daylight, and Maggie's arms and legs were numb, but she never thought of releasing the boy. She smiled as she watched Fluffy move into a more comfortable position. The dog had whined through most of the night. Now he slept with his head on Joseph's leg.

Matthew, his burns bandaged, knelt before her, trying to gather the courage to tell her the truth. "Maggie," he began gently, his hands cupping her face, forcing her gaze from the boy to him. "Maggie, can you hear me?"

Maggie lifted her slightly vacant innocent eyes from Joseph's peaceful face to the warm, loving gaze of the man before her and smiled gently. "Of course I can hear you, Matthew."

"Maggie." He breathed deeply, steeling himself for what lay ahead. "The boy died last night."

Maggie's expression grew confused. "What boy, Matthew?"

"Joseph, darling. Joseph is dead. You must let us take him from you."

Instantly her gentle expression turned to disbelief and then to rage. "Matthew!" she snapped viciously. "That is a horrible thing to say!"

"Maggie," he sighed, "can you not see? He does not breathe."

"But he does! I can feel it!"

Matthew pressed his hand to the lifeless chest and slowly shook his head. "He does not."

"It is horrible of you to say such things," Maggie said as she steadfastly denied his words. "I'll not listen." Maggie turned to her son again. "Joseph," she asked softly, "would you like something to drink, dear?" When no answer came, she simply smiled and whispered, "He's sleeping."

Matthew sighed and rose to his feet while Maggie began the same lullaby she had sung throughout the night. He turned and watched her rock the lifeless form in her arms. His heart wrenched with pain, knowing she was unable to face this horror.

The sun was high, but no one even thought of food, while Maggie still rocked Joseph. Matthew downed a tankard of apple cider as he spoke to Elijah and James. "There is no

173

hope for it. Maggie cannot admit to the boy's death." He looked toward the blazing sun and remarked, "Before too many more hours, his death will become apparent, even to her."

The two men sighed and gave a solemn nod.

"We've no choice. We'll have to take the boy."

Matthew approached Maggie again. "May I hold him for a time? Your arms must ache, and I'm sure you thirst," he coaxed her gently as he knelt before her.

"You will be careful?" she asked.

"I will," he promised. He took the boy and walked toward Hannah and Elijah's house.

Maggie was in a daze. She did not know why all these people kept coming toward her to whisper low words of comfort. What had happened? Why was everyone there? Was there a party? If so, why did everyone seem so sad?

Gently she disengaged herself from the small group of women in the house and searched for Matthew. He could explain the situation to her.

She found him a few moments later, standing beneath a thick oak near the barn and talking with two men. "Matthew," she ventured softly, "might I have a moment of your time?"

Matthew nodded and joined her as she walked toward the fields. "Something most peculiar has happened."

"What is it, sweetheart?" he asked, taking her hand in his.

"Samuel has asked me to marry him."

"And your answer?"

"I've not answered him, Matthew," she stated softly as she gazed up into his dark eyes. "How can I agree to marry anyone? I'm already married."

"Maggie," he sighed, "do you know why everyone is here today?"

"Nay, I hoped you could tell me."

"Caleb died in the fire last night. Do you not remember?"

"Of course." She breathed a long sigh of relief. Then, for

some reason, a breathless terror had clutched at her heart, and she thought he was going to say something else. Maggie shrugged aside the fear and smiled. Suddenly her eyes clouded with shame, and her cheeks turned scarlet. "What must you think of me smiling at such a time? 'Tis just that I feel this great relief. I know not why."

"He was not the best of men, to be sure, Maggie. You need not feel guilt that there is no remorse in his passing."

"Nay, that is not the case. Indeed, I do feel remorse, but more than that I feel sorrow for what could have been. We were so happy at the beginning. He changed so after the accident. Perhaps if I had been more understanding . . ."

"I'll not let you take the blame, Maggie," Matthew insisted, looking deeply into her eyes. "Remember, I was witness to his treatment of you."

Maggie lowered her eyes again and silently nodded. Her voice was barely audible as she hesitantly asked, "There's more, isn't there? So many would not have come for Caleb."

Matthew could not bear to tell her about her son. Suddenly he realized she would remember when she could stand the pain. For now, as long as she did not mention it, neither would he.

"They came for Aunt Matilda," he finally managed.

"No! Oh God!" Maggie groaned and slumped against him.

Her voice was muffled with pain when the sobbing finally eased. "How could I have been so lacking in feeling not even to have missed her?" She dried her eyes with his handkerchief.

"'Twas shock, Maggie," he soothed as he took the handkerchief back and wiped at the tears she had missed. "Do not berate yourself overmuch. Each of us handles the loss of those we love differently."

Maggie smiled as she patted Fluffy's head. Her brow creased as she tried to understand his actions. It had been three weeks since Aunt Matilda and Caleb had died, and he still acted so strangely. He had followed her to the creek today and sat at her side as she leaned her back against a sturdy oak. But he was not his usual frisky self. He seemed sad, if that was an emotion possible for a dog. She had heard of dogs pining for their masters, but surely Fluffy did not miss Caleb. The man had hated all animals. And Aunt Matilda, although she was a kind and sweet lady, was never Fluffy's playmate. That was Joseph.

Maggie's heart suddenly twisted with terrifying pain as images of Joseph playing with his dog flashed in her mind. Where in God's name had Joseph gone? She hadn't seen him in ages.

The ache in her chest grew, but Maggie denied its existence. Why was she feeling this panic? Surely nothing had happened. He must be away. Perhaps he was visiting someone. God in heaven, why couldn't she remember?

"I thought I might find you here," came a familiar voice from behind her.

Maggie breathed a sigh of pleasure, happy to relinquish her terrifying thoughts. "Did Hannah send you looking for me?" At his nod, she continued, "I grow to believe the woman thinks me dim-witted, for she rarely lets me out of her sight."

"She tells me you ate no morning meal again and, it is now long past noon."

Maggie laughed. "Were Hannah to have her way, I'd be bigger than she. I eat, believe me."

"But not enough. You have lost weight, Maggie. I do not want to see you ill."

Maggie smiled. "Come sit beside me, Matthew. Your presence is needed more than food."

Matthew settled himself comfortably at her side and closed her within the warmth of his arms. "A bag of bones," he teased as he rubbed his face against her hair.

Maggie chuckled and then sighed peacefully. "Is it not beautiful here?"

"Aye," Matthew murmured, "almost as beautiful as you. When are you going to come and live with me at the inn?"

"Matthew," she sighed, "we've been over this before. I cannot. What would the townfolk say? Why, they would snub me at every turn."

"No one need know. Who would dare ask about our sleeping arrangements? You will simply be in my employ."

"Nay, Matthew, 'tis unseemly."

"Then marry me, damn it!"

Maggie laughed. "When has a lady ever received such a romantic proposal?"

"Maggie, 'tis not the first time I've asked. I want you for my wife. I'll not wait a year."

"But you must, darling. Imagine the scandal should I marry sooner."

Matthew spit out a round of frustrated curses. "Why the hell must you care about talk? Can you never do something simply because you want to and let the gossipers be damned?"

"Matthew, I've not just myself to think of."

"Who else matters?"

"What about Joseph?" she asked. "Would you have others shun him because of his mother's loose ways?"

"Maggie," Matthew replied, his voice low, his eyes dark with pain, "think of what you're saying."

Maggie studied his face for a long moment, her heart suddenly thudding with fear as a rush of pain gripped her insides. Panic was clear in her golden eyes when she finally whispered a soft plea, "No, Matthew, do not make me . . ."

"What were you thinking of before I came?" he wisely interrupted.

Maggie sighed and leaned against him again, relieved that the terror had passed. "I was remembering how Joseph and Fluffy played in the tall grass. How Joseph would laugh when the dog found out his hiding place. The more he laughed, the more Fluffy would lick him." Suddenly her voice broke, but she instantly gained control. Pictures of him ran through her mind—running, swimming, riding a horse, licking his fingers after a honey treat, laughing with the sun shining on his beautiful blond head—intermingled with those of a limp, fire-blackened form being rocked in her arms . . . She had to press her hand to her chest, for the pain threatened to take her breath away.

Her voice trembled as she continued, "Sometimes we would play ball and Fluffy would steal it and run away. It often took us some time to find it again." She wiped her tearing eyes with the backs of her hands. "Do you remember the time we were wrestling here and you licked my lips? Joseph thought they were dirty." She laughed at the memory. Suddenly her face grew somber, and great tears rolled silently from her eyes. "He's dead, you know."

"I know, my love."

"He was such a good boy, and I loved him so much."

"I know you did, darling."

The tears came then in huge, wracking sobs. "The pain tears at my heart, Matthew. It grows stronger with every passing moment," she gasped. "I fear I'll not live through this."

"You will, Maggie," he declared. He tightened his hold on her, his dark eyes fierce with determination. "I do not know the pain of losing a child, but I love you, and you will live through this. You'll do it for me."

"For a long time he was all I had." She struggled to talk through her tears. "We were a team, he and I. He'd be sorry to see his kittens grown. He wanted them to stay small, but nothing stays the same, does it?"

"Only the love we feel for each other, sweetheart," Matthew said as he pulled her onto his lap. "Nothing can ever change that, no matter what might come."

"Do you think he knows I love him?"

"Oh, darling, he knows, be sure of it."

══ *Eighteen* ══

IN THE BACK ROOM of an ale house, four men wallowed in their woes over frothy tankards. They had signed loyalty oaths to the British, but they were still not trusted. So many colonists had signed out of pure self-preservation. And because of that fact, these men were treated as any other colonists, suspiciously.

Richard Marshall, the richest of the four, was the most bitter. He brought his tankard to his lips after wiping away the foam with the sleeve of his coat. "Something must be done, lads. Before long I'll be left with nothing. There must be a way to prove my loyalty and get these bastards off my back."

"Aye," three others commented in unison.

"There's been nothing but trouble ever since these rebel fools started," one of them grumbled.

"Good God almighty," Marshall continued, "whatever possessed them to think they could fight against the power of the crown and win? Sweet Jesus, they'll be lucky to get out of this without getting their necks stretched."

Samuel Landsing listened from a nearby table, and a speculative gleam grew to life in his blue eyes. From the deep recesses of his mind an idea came forth. Could it be that he might rid himself of that son of a bitch Forrest and gain the trust of the English with one simple cunning act?

Since the start of this conflict, his clients had been nearly nonexistent. Unlucky enough to be born a colonist, he was treated as one by his English cousins despite his loyalty. The British had added nary a penny to his coffers. He might as well have joined Washington's starving forces.

And Maggie. Samuel breathed with a long, weary sigh. Christ, but his guts turned every time he had the slightest contact with her. If he didn't win her soon, there was no telling what might happen. If he could only get her alone for a moment—but no, Forrest was forever there, hovering about, never giving them a moment's privacy. Jesus, what did the bastard think he was going to do?

A humorless smile touched his lips. He knew something was going on between those two. Did they believe him dim-witted? God damn it! He had to do something, and he had to do it now, before Forrest took her to bed.

It was bad enough knowing Caleb had had her, but Forrest! Good God, he couldn't bear the thought.

An evil grin curved his hard lips into a grotesque smile as he approached the disgruntled group. It didn't matter if he had not a shred of evidence. The English would be sure to listen in any case. If nothing else, it would get Maggie out from Forrest's protection, for a time . . .

"Gentlemen, mayhap I have an answer to your worries," Samuel said, as four pairs of eyes settled on him. "If we were to capture a rebel spy, would not our government then know us to be loyal and treat us accordingly?"

"I've no doubt, sir," Marshall returned. "Might you be in possession of such information?"

Samuel shrugged. "It appears I might," he remarked, anxious now to take his leave. He needed to settle his thoughts so his plan might be put into effect. "I shall look further into the matter and let you know."

Matthew paced the floor of his room, and for the hundredth time he pushed his fingers through his thick black hair. *Had I known what torture this love would bring, I'd have run at the sight of her,* he groaned inwardly. *Jesus, when will I be able to claim her as mine? How much longer is this to go on?*

Maggie had agreed to come work for him, at least for the time being. But what good did the move bring? For weeks now she had worked at his side, and her close proximity kept him in a constant state of pain. He longed to touch her sweet lips with his, to hold her in his arms, to love her, but had anything but suffering come to pass? No! Fate had thrown one obstacle after another in his path. Was this love doomed from the start?

Damn you, Maggie, for your stubbornness, he ranted in silent frustration as he punched at his thigh. *I'll not let you win. I know you love me. 'Tis naught but your sorrow that keeps us apart. And it will no longer suffice. If you must know this guilt, from this moment on, you will know it in my arms.*

Matthew slammed the door to his room and dashed up the few steps to where Maggie slept. Quietly he opened her door and entered. His breath caught in his throat at the lovely sight that greeted him. The bed was bathed in a shaft of silvery moonlight. Maggie slept, her mouth slightly parted, her thick lashes forming half moons on her high cheekbones, her heavy dark curls fanned the pillow about her head. Matthew knew he had never seen a sight half so lovely.

Silently he discarded his shirt and pants and slid in beside her. His body trembled with longing as he reached for her and brought her into his arms. It had been months since he had touched her, and he had to steel himself against the urge to take her in quick selfish relief.

Maggie murmured and sighed as she cuddled herself closer to him. In her sleep her hand slid to the evidence of his passion and cupped him.

His body jerked at the contact. This was torture. He almost groaned aloud. He couldn't think, not while she touched him thus, and unless she moved away he'd take her regardless of his resolve to talk things out first. Gently he brought her hand to rest against his chest and allowed a sigh of relief.

"Maggie," he murmured as his lips caressed her cheek. "Wake up and talk to me, love. There are things that need to be said."

"Matthew," she sighed as she snuggled closer. Suddenly her body stiffened, and she jerked herself into a sitting position. "What are you doing in my bed?"

Matthew gave a low laugh, happy to have finally gotten her attention. He placed his hands beneath his head and grinned as he stretched out comfortably. "'Tis past the time for us to talk."

Maggie leaped from the bed, her whole body shaking just at the thought of him lying at her side and, by the looks of it, wearing not a stitch. "Matthew, I want you to get out of here. We can talk on the morn."

"We will talk now," he said, slowly shaking his head. "Get back into this bed."

"Nay," she insisted, "I will not."

Matthew cursed as he watched her ignore his order and sit in a chair near the window. For a long time there was total silence in the room as each struggled for the words to set things right.

Maggie was the first to speak. "It is over between us, Matthew," she said on a long, weary breath. "What we both once longed for can never be, not after all that has happened. Had I not been with you . . ." She left the sentence unsaid, her pain unbearable at the thought. After a deep, steadying breath, she finally continued, her voice dull, "Joseph's death was my fault."

"Why in God's name must you take the blame?" he snapped as he came from the bed.

"If I hadn't left the house. If I hadn't dallied at the creek. If . . ."

"*If* Caleb wasn't at home," he interrupted, "you'd never have left to bathe. *If* Aunt Matilda wasn't sick, she wouldn't have taken the sherry and would have awakened in time. *If, if, if.* Can you not see it was an accident and no one was at fault?"

A gentle smile curved Maggie's lips, but what struck Matthew's heart with terror was not her next words but the calmness of her voice when she said them. "You may rave all you wish, Matthew. You will not sway my thoughts. 'Tis finished."

"Maggie, please, do not do this to us. I love you. Do not throw away what we have."

"We sinned, Matthew, and God punished me. Can you not understand?"

Matthew stood and scooped Maggie into his arms. He sat in her chair and settled her on his lap. "Maggie, my love," he soothed as he brushed her hair from her face, "the God I worship would not have been so cruel. 'Tis your own misplaced guilt, not God who punishes."

She said nothing, but stared silently out the window.

Matthew sighed. "He is your heavenly Father, is He not?"

"Aye," she nodded.

"Would a loving Father so abuse His darling child?"

He waited a long moment, and when no answer was forthcoming he asked, "Would you?"

She turned to face him. Tears glistened in her eyes. "Matthew, you know I would not."

"Do you not believe He loves us more than we can imagine?" he asked as he tenderly caressed her cheek. "Surely a being with such love cannot bring harm to another. I doubt He has the capabilities. Nay, only we humans can harm each other."

"Then why, Matthew?" she asked so pitifully that he thought his heart would surely break. "Why did he die?"

"Oh, Maggie," he sighed and pulled her head down to rest against his chest. "I do not have all the answers. I know only this. Our God is a God of free will. He puts us here to do what we will. What we make of our lives is up to us."

Maggie cried with her face pressed to his chest. "I want to believe you, Matthew, truly I do," she whispered brokenly.

"You can believe me, love. I swear you can."

Moments later, while still holding her in the warmth of his arms, he settled her on the bed. "I will stay with you, Maggie. I need to hold you." And when she gazed questioningly into his loving expression, he continued, "You need not fear, love. I only wish to bring you and myself a measure of comfort."

Maggie voiced no objection to sharing her bed but sighed and cuddled closer to his warmth, her sorrow forgotten till the morn.

Matthew fought to contain the laughter that threatened as Maggie dumped a full tankard of ale on the lap of an overly ardent admirer. Matthew's eyes had narrowed dangerously when he saw the patron reach out and casually caress her rump as she leaned over the table. But before he had a chance to do more than frown, the man was on his feet, brushing at his suddenly soaked trousers.

"Oh, I am sorry, sir," Maggie offered as she watched the man's surprised expression turn to anger. "I fear I'm overly clumsy today."

"Nay, mistress," he said, thinking better of the curses he longed to bestow upon this stupid ingrate as Matthew moved protectively to her side. "Worry of it not. Perhaps you were startled."

"Perhaps," she agreed, with only the slightest of smiles belying her apology.

"Mayhap you'd fair better at another inn, sir," Matthew said as Maggie began to clean the ale sodden chair and floor. "Shall we say one where the ladies are less comely and the service less damp?"

Later that same night, Maggie was in the back room gathering the soiled clothes for the next day's laundry, when thick brown arms encircled her waist from behind and pulled her close to a warm, hard form.

Maggie glanced up from her chore and remarked with a decidedly evil laugh, "Oh, it's you."

"Wretch." Matthew groaned with delight as the pain of holding her close threatened to wreak havoc with his control. "Have the wandering fingers of some now become such a habit that you can only mutter, 'Oh, it's you,' when in my arms?"

Matthew's breath teased the side of her neck as he lowered his head and went on. "In the last week alone, I've asked three never to return. Should this keep up, I'll soon be forced to close my doors for lack of customers."

Maggie giggled as he nuzzled her neck, asking, "Have you a solution to my dilemma?"

"Are you accusing me, sir, of being the cause of your present difficulties?"

"Indeed I am, mistress."

"Shall I then take to wearing a pillow sheet over my head?"

Matthew's voice was heavily laced with humor when he returned, "The idea is certainly deserving of some consideration."

Maggie tipped her head and shot him a look of wry disbelief, while her elbow found his chest to be a perfect target.

Matthew gave a low laugh, ignoring the blow. He appeared to think on the matter. "Still, with a cloth over your head, you might spill more than you serve or, worse yet, walk right into their greedy arms. For, like myself, not one among the horny assemblage can keep his eyes off you, while a few even have the audacity to touch."

"Like this?" she asked, pointing to his hand, which was now cupping her breast.

"I'll kill the first one who tries," he replied.

Maggie smiled as he turned her to face him. "Mayhap Hannah and myself should trade places. I've no objection to working in the kitchen, and I doubt your customers would dare to fondle that lady."

Matthew laughed. "Indeed, I feel a pang of sympathy for any who might try. But I'm afraid that arrangement will not suffice, for although you excel in many qualities, I've tasted of your cooking efforts."

"You beast!" Maggie laughed as she punched his shoulder. "So I fare well enough in some rooms but not the kitchen?"

"Mistress, I've not tested you in all rooms to swear to the fact, but I believe you'd fare best in the bedroom."

Maggie laughed again. "'Tis lucky for you, sir, I do not offend easily, for your words are most insulting."

Matthew felt his heart swell with love at the sound of her laughter. Although they had shared the same bed for almost a week, they had not yet made love. Each night they lay in each other's arms, sometimes talking well into the early hours of dawn before they fell asleep, while Matthew wisely waited for her sorrow to ease. Each day a smile seemed to come more easily to her eyes, and he knew he'd not have much longer to wait.

"Am I insulting?" Matthew grinned as he removed the mobcap from her mahogany hair, spreading his fingers through the heavy mass of curls that fell down her back. "I think not, for a man can only consider himself most fortunate if his woman excels in their bedroom."

Maggie poked his chest with her finger and warned, "If you keep up this conversation, you may never find out."

Maggie stirred sleepily in the dull light of early morning as a crash of thunder seemed to rock the room. Rain beat a monotonous, soothing tempo against her window, tempting her to return to the deliciously warm comfort of sleep.

She tried to move her leg and found it pinned in place by a heavy weight. Something was tickling her nose. Slowly, not wanting to disturb her position, she opened her eyes to a wall of thick, dark fur and a deeply tanned chest.

A soft smile curved her lips as memory returned, and she sighed, languishing in the pleasure of being held in his arms. Although Matthew had no qualms about stripping naked before her and did not seem to notice her startled gaze the first few times he slid into her bed, he did not turn to her with passion ablaze in his eyes. He was most patient and apparently content to wait for her to make the first move. Perhaps it was his patience, above all else, that caused him to rise higher in her regard. Whatever the reason, she knew she could not love him more.

She did want this man, of that she had no doubt. But could she turn to him? Was he right? Was she suffering only from her own guilt? Could it be God had not punished her?

Joseph is gone, Maggie, a soft voice sounded from the far recesses of her mind. Her eyes misted with sorrow as she allowed a new thought: *Children are merely on loan to us. Not ours to keep. Be thankful you had him, at least for a time. Will you live out your life in limbo, never to know this man's love, because of your guilt? Will that bring Joseph back? He is a man, Maggie, a man who loves you. How much longer will you force him to wait?*

Maggie couldn't deny the love she felt for him. She knew it showed in her eyes. He had said God could only do good. Perhaps this love she felt was a special gift. If so, would she not be a fool to chance its loss? She'd not throw away this chance at happiness. She'd take it as she was meant to and give thanks every day for the rest of her life.

Maggie hungrily took in his sleeping features. His gentle snore comforted her as his warm breath brushed against her cheek. The heavy weight of his arms held her securely. She now knew the time for sorrow and guilt was past. It was time to live again.

With no further thought, she allowed her lips to touch his heated flesh. Slowly her mouth and tongue tasted, greedily absorbing the scent and texture of his skin until she was overcome with a burning need to know more of him. Hungry now, she shifted, lowering her mouth to his stomach, and gave a soft sigh. This was ecstasy. How long had she wanted to touch him, to kiss him? She couldn't remember a time when she had not wanted it, and she reveled in the pleasure. God, how she needed this man. She needed his strength, his tenderness, his teasing laughter. She needed all he could offer.

Her mouth lowered farther still, her lips grazing the warmth of his flesh, teasing as they brushed over his desire, feeling his muscles tighten and strain at the effort to remain still.

A choking moan lodged in his throat, the sound causing Maggie to pull slightly away as she realized at last what she was about. On her knees, she silently looked up to eyes gone black as pitch. Maggie felt her cheeks heat with the boldness of her actions, for there was no way of disguising the fact that she was making love to him, nor the fact that she found great satisfaction in doing so.

All embarrassment fled as his next words brought a smile to her lips. "I was afraid to move lest I awaken from this beautiful dream."

He smiled and reached for the hem of her gown, bringing it slowly up and over her head. His hands lingered at her shoulders, while his eyes, ablaze with yearning, moved slowly over her nakedness.

Gently he eased her forward, so sensuously that Maggie couldn't prevent the low moan that escaped her throat. She was lying half over him, her breasts brushing his chest. His huge hands cupped the sides of her face, holding back the heavy mass of tangled curls. "It was a dream, was it not?"

Maggie lowered her gaze and smiled, amazed at her boldness. "I've heard tell certain men prefer their ladies to excel in the bedroom rather than the kitchen. I was simply seeing to that task."

"In that case, mistress, you may proceed," he returned, easily joining her in her lighthearted mood.

"May I?" She grinned.

"Oh, indeed, you may."

A cloud of doubt passed over her bright eyes. "One wonders if this particular woman might be found lacking in this room too."

"Mistress," Matthew said, "you may relieve your mind of that worry."

"Indeed? But how can you know?"

"I know that I love you, and anything we might do together will be all I could have imagined." He rolled her to her back and positioned himself above her.

"Will you love me, Matthew?" she asked, her voice soft and pleading. "I've waited so long."

"Oh, Maggie," he sighed as her arms encircled his neck, gently tugging until he lowered his mouth to her offered lips. Matthew groaned at the giving he felt in her. He gladly surrendered to the desire that pounded like a drum in his brain. "'Tis not in me to deny you anything. And most especially this."

At the touch of her lips, his mind flamed with need. God, how long he had wanted this woman. The contact of female curves against male hardness caused a simultaneous groan the moment he pulled her against him. Bodies clung and breaths mingled, with an intensity that defied anything on earth to separate them.

Her mouth sought out the taste of his and dared him to control the need he had for so long held at bay. This woman was his for the taking, and he didn't care what had prompted her to initiate this act. He could no longer find the strength to question or resist her offer.

"I love you, Matthew," she whispered. "Please, I've waited so long."

Matthew groaned as her words penetrated the fog of desire that had claimed his mind. He pulled her tighter against him, drinking in the sweetness of her mouth.

Rain slashed at the window, growing to near explosive force, daring the thin glass to withstand its mighty power. But the ferocity of the sudden summer storm was lost on the lovers. Neither noticed the driving torrent, so inflamed were their senses, so frenzied their need for each other.

This time there'd be no teasing of the senses, no tempered

control, no hesitation. The moment had come for their final commitment.

"I've wanted you forever," he gasped as he tore his mouth from hers, his breath heavy and labored against her neck.

"I know." She smiled, delighted at his low growl as she ran her nails over his back. "I too have wanted."

"I imagined our first time to be slow, Maggie," he whispered as his lips and teeth teased her neck. "I wanted to kiss you and touch you everywhere until my hands and mouth memorized all of you . . . But I've waited too long . . . too long."

Maggie's back arched, and she gave him easy access to the secrets of her body. Her heart sang with joy, knowing his need was as great as hers.

"Later," she gasped breathlessly as his fingers ran the length of her, only to retrace their path and linger at the junction of her legs. "Oh God, Matthew," she moaned as if in pain, her hips lifting despite her words, as his fingers sought to enter her. "I'm done with waiting. Torture me no more."

Maggie's pleading was all it took to release the savagery he held just barely under control. And, although some segment of his mind warned caution, he was beyond the point of rational thought. His body ached with a longing he had never known, a longing he was powerless to deny.

A hiss of indrawn breath sounded sharply above the crazed storm as he entered her at last. She was so tight, so tight! Could such ecstasy truly exist? For a moment he doubted his sanity. But the sounds of pleasure from the woman beneath him instantly convinced him he was not alone in this delectable sensation. He watched as her golden eyes opened in wonder.

"I love you," she moaned almost drunkenly as he began to move within her.

"Maggie, oh God," he rasped between short, labored breaths as she answered his movement with her own. His eyes closed, unable to bear the beauty of the moment, as sensation, so wondrous it almost brought pain, suffused his body until he thought he must surely die of it.

Sweat glistened on his skin as his straining muscles desperately fought to prolong these last moments, lest he leave her wanting.

He drove harder and deeper, squeezing his eyes closed as he forced his body past the point of pain to wait until she was ready. And it wasn't until he heard her cry out and felt the aching tight throb of her moistness engulf and draw him closer to agonized paradise that he gave up his fight and took her with almost brutal strength.

They gasped for breath, their eyes wide with wonder, unable to believe the magic that had passed between them. The sky was suddenly cleared of all clouds, and for a moment the early dawn held a silence so intense it seemed almost an eerie.

Maggie's golden eyes opened wide with astonishment as she listened for the crash of nonexistent rain and wind. "Do you suppose we did that?" She grinned.

Matthew's dark eyes sparkled with pleasure as he rolled to his back and pulled her close to his side. "Considering our passion, I'd not disallow the notion."

Maggie raised herself to her elbow and looked down at his satisfied expression. A wicked gleam danced in her catlike eyes as she idly traced her finger through the heavy mat of dark hair on his chest. "Imagine what we could do with this newfound means of harnessing nature. Why, if word got out, we might be called on to stop monsoons or prevent volcanos from erupting."

"Would you have all know of the power we have amassed?" he asked, a smile teasing the corners of his mouth, his finger tracing lazy circles around the tip of a tempting breast.

"Matthew," she sighed softly, her tone much like that of an adult intent on having a child see reason, "if it should serve such exalted purposes, I see no choice."

Matthew laughed at the seriousness of her tone and tried to ignore her sultry teasing as her fingers moved down his chest, intent on following the ever-thinning line of black hair to more interesting pastures.

Matthew groaned as his body responded to the movement of her hand. "Do you think it prudent to test this newfound power yet again?"

"Aye." She grinned. "'Tis important, do you not agree? After all, there may be a storm in Europe that needs our attention."

═══ *Nineteen* ═══

MAGGIE SIGHED WITH PLEASURE as she slid beneath the cool water. Before too many more days, the crisp air of autumn would show itself, and she would be forced to cart water to her room to bathe. A laborious job to be sure, especially when one must climb two flights of stairs.

She was clean now, but Maggie was reluctant to leave the delight of the water. There was no need for her to hurry. Matthew had gone to New York the day before to see about supplies for the inn, and he wasn't due to return until late that night.

With expert ease, she moved through the water, hardly making a ripple as she swam from shore to shore. The chirping crickets and the soothing feel of the water lulled her into an almost dozing state as she turned on her back and allowed the water to lift her to its surface.

Maggie gazed up at the heavens and smiled. The moon shone brightly in a cloudless sky, causing the stars to appear as pinpoints of light against black velvet.

Maggie sighed, almost annoyed that she should feel this intense sense of loss. He'd been gone only one day, but the few hours had seemed endless. Maggie sighed yet again, willing him to hurry back.

Matthew pulled his horse to a stop near the front of the

barn. Anxious to see Maggie, he let Elijah tend to the animal.

After a quick look around the inn, he knew where she could be discovered.

Matthew grinned as he moved silently from the edge of the creek and slid beneath its surface. The water was pitch black, but, like a homing pigeon, he had no trouble finding her.

Maggie gave a short scream as a long, thick arm encircled her waist and pulled her under. She struggled against the heavy weight of the water and tried to escape her attacker, but his mouth suddenly fastened itself to her own.

Maggie instantly recognized who held her, but the knowledge did little to relieve the thunderous beating of her heart.

A moment later he stood and brought her above the water's surface. The second he released her mouth, she gasped, "You beast!" and smacked his shoulder. "You frightened me half to death. My heart is pounding!"

"Can I feel it?" He grinned.

"Is this what I have to look forward to?"

"I think it would be wise if you refrained from bathing here, at least unescorted."

"Will you forever sneak up on me?"

"Anyone might happen by."

"God, I've not long to live if this keeps up."

"And you're too sweet a morsel to resist."

Maggie giggled. "You're doing it again."

"Indeed," he agreed as he lowered his hands and cupped her smoothly rounded hips. Gently he pulled her within contact of his rising passion. He lowered his mouth to her ear and breathed seductively, "And since I've every intention of doing it again, and quite possibly still again, I suggest we begin this arduous task."

Maggie smiled and shivered as his warm breath teased the damp flesh of her neck. She couldn't control her tremble of hungry anticipation. Her voice was soft, her words suddenly thick, as she said, "You are incorrigible. What am I going to do with you?"

"Hopefully much the same as I'm doing to you," he returned as his mouth slid with aching slow torture across her cheek.

"Matthew," she groaned. A surge of desire raced through her body. Her arms clung to his neck, and she pressed herself closer to his warmth. Her lips parted as she hungrily accepted the thrust of his tongue. It was never enough—no matter how many times they came together, she wanted more.

"I've waited all day for this," she groaned as he tore his mouth from hers.

"Maggie, my love," he murmured and brought her body higher so that his mouth might again sample her sweet delights, his heart nearly bursting with joy as she easily admitted her need for him. His mouth moved to her shoulder, across her chest to the throbbing, aching flesh that longed for the heat of his mouth.

Maggie arched her back and gave a low sob as he suckled and bit down on her, only to run his tongue over the supposed injury. The beauty of his lovemaking caused her belly to tighten with a longing that would find no release but in his total possession.

Her movements were anxious, almost desperate, her need apparent as she sought a release of this aching torment.

But Matthew did not have a quick taking in mind. On his long journey to the city, his mind had refused to relinquish the thought of having her at his leisure. All day he had envisioned the touch and feel of her against him, and now that he finally held her in his arms, he'd savor this delight.

Slowly he eased her silky, warm body down his, standing her before him again as his mouth ravenously explored the sweet depth of hers. His hand slid unerringly between her legs, and Maggie moaned as his fingers splayed her warm flesh. Gently he massaged the tiny, stiff proof of her passion, and Maggie felt a wave of delight so intense that she couldn't prevent the soft cry that escaped her lips.

"Matthew," she moaned. She knew nothing but the wonder of his touch. Desperately she clung to his neck, for all strength had left her body.

The dull ache grew. She knew nothing but the need for him to continue. She'd die if he stopped now, and when he lifted her up against him and whispered, "Put your legs around me, Maggie," she could only murmur brokenly, "I cannot. Oh, please God, I cannot!"

She was farther along than he had imagined, and Matthew knew that if he didn't hurry she'd lose the pleasure he had in store. With one hand he slid her legs around his waist, never ceasing in his erotic massage, desperate to join with her before it was too late.

"Oh God," Maggie cried as he drove into her body. A long hissing sound escaped her throat as she felt his heat, and the dual pleasure of his constantly moving fingers and the thickness of his passion left her mindless and gasping.

"Now, now," she urged as an ache not unlike a heavy cramp began to tighten her lower body, and she knew if relief wasn't far off she would surely die of this pleasure. "Matthew, please," she sobbed, rocking wildly against him, her passion so intense, her pleasure so great, she wondered if she could stand much more.

Maggie was lost to all reason but to press closer, to take him deeper, to give even more and thereby gain it all. The pressure was building, building, and she feverishly fought him for more, sucking his tongue deep into her mouth, scratching at his neck and shoulders, clutching at his hips with her legs, searching for a release of this tormenting anguish—until she suddenly stiffened and cried in ecstasy.

But his mouth was there to absorb her cries, and Matthew growled out his pleasure as he felt her shudder against him, her body greedily sucking his seed deep inside.

She was gasping for air as she buried her face into the warmth of his neck and savored the delicious echoing throbbings that continued on. Too weak to release him, she cuddled softly against his strength and wiped at her suddenly misty eyes.

"What's this? Tears?" Matthew asked as he heard her sniff. "Did I hurt you, love?" he asked. He slid her body down until she stood leaning against him and lifted her face for his view.

"Aye." She grinned. "You gave me the most delicious hurting I could imagine. What is this magic you do?" she whispered, her mouth and tongue tasting the tangy salty flavor of his chest.

Matthew smiled and nuzzled his face into her hair, breathing deeply of its sweet, fresh scent. "'Tis not mine alone, Maggie, but between us, and it will only grow more powerful each time we come together."

Maggie grinned. "I'll not guarantee my survival should it grow in strength."

"Aye, Maggie, you will survive. We will live a long, happy life. I long to grow old with you."

Suddenly she smacked his shoulder and tried to glare at him. "Not if you keep sneaking up on me. One of these times my heart is sure to give out." Maggie gave a soft laugh. "I'm beginning to think you have Indian blood. How else can you explain the silence in your step?"

Matthew grinned. "My parents hail from Ireland, and as far as I know no Indians lurk in the background. Then again"—he shrugged—"since I was not present at the time, I'd not swear on it."

Maggie shook her head, one brow arched with reproach. "One wonders what your mother would say at such defamation of character."

"When you meet my mother, you'll realize she'd more than likely laugh."

"How did you know to find me here?"

"Mistress, do you think I had nothing else in mind but to search you out the moment I returned?"

"Did you not?"

"My, my, what arrogance. Actually, I was taking a walk." His eyes filled with devilry. He continued on with a deliciously evil leer, "You see, sometimes the exercise relieves the stiffening of certain parts of my body."

Maggie laughed. "And to what parts might you be referring?"

"I'll show you in a minute."

"Not now?" she asked, her eyes wide with supposed innocence as her hand began to move over his chest. "Then let me guess," she murmured as her fingers slid past his waist to linger at his reviving passion. She felt him grow larger in her hand. "I begin to see your meaning. Does the stiffness bring a degree of discomfort?"

Suddenly he captured her hand in his and brought it to rest against his chest as he chastised her. "I've something to tell you, mistress. If you're not going to be serious, I doubt if I can continue."

"Please, do proceed. I shall behave."

"Well, here I was, taking my nightly stroll, when lo and behold, what should appear?"

When it seemed he would not continue, Maggie asked, "Shall I guess?"

"No! Ask me what," he prompted.

Maggie giggled. "What?"

"You'll not believe this, but I found a mermaid in your creek."

"A mermaid! In my creek?" Her voice echoed his apparent amazement.

"Aye." He grinned. "But if you feel some degree of surprise, imagine my astonishment. Why, I was hard put"—his voice lowered as he emphasized his words with a slight movement of his hips—"and I do mean *hard* put, to take my eyes off her."

Maggie smiled and answered his movement with her own. "And what did you think of this mermaid?"

Matthew gave a long sigh, his eyes half closed in remembrance. "Mistress, I doubt my ability to relate her perfection."

Maggie knew she was comely but doubted anyone could be as beautiful as he professed her to be.

"Oh sir, please do try," she purred ever so sweetly.

Matthew smiled, his voice lowering with tender emotion as his finger traced an imaginary line from beneath her ear, down her neck and shoulder, to her naked breast. "I thought her the loveliest sight I've ever seen. Her body glistened white amid the dark swirling water, and I found it an effort just to breathe while watching her red hair . . ."

"Mermaids don't have red hair," Maggie interrupted.

"Mistress, is this my story?"

Maggie laughed. "Indeed it is, sir. Pray tell, what happened next?" Then she gasped as his finger and thumb caught the dark tip of her breast and teased it into a hard nub.

"Well, you can imagine my trepidation at disturbing this elusive creature. Why, I hear tell not one has ever been captured. And I did so fear frightening her away."

"So what did you do?" she asked a bit breathlessly as she moved her hips against his.

"Silently, I eased myself into the water, after I took off my clothes, of course."

"Of course," Maggie agreed as she ran the palms of her hands across his damp chest, threading her fingers through the mat of thick, dark hair. "It would not do to get them wet."

"Indeed not," Matthew acknowledged so primly that Maggie burst out laughing.

"And then?" she prompted.

"And then, upon touching her, I realized she was not a mermaid after all."

"How disappointing for you," Maggie commiserated in a strangled voice, her eyes half closed, her body tensing as his hand traveled down her side to the firm flesh of her hip and leg, only to retrace its movements and linger at the junction of her thighs.

"Nay, for I much prefer legs to a scaly tail. And the scent of a woman to a fish."

"Any woman?"

A tender smile touched the corners of his mouth as he reached down and took her up in his arms. "Do I look the kind of man to have no preference of taste? Only one woman will suffice, thank you."

"Indeed, sir? And who might that be?"

Matthew smiled, his face very close to hers, his eyes clearly speaking of his love. "There is only one woman whose scent mingles so lusciously with soft vanilla. Only one whose hair is so thick and lustrous it seems to have a life of its own. Only one whose skin is so clear and soft my fingers constantly ache to touch her." And as his lips lowered to hers, he whispered, "There is only one who can set a fever in my soul."

Maggie smiled and caressed the hollows of his cheeks with her fingers as he moved to the shore and laid her on his shirt. "I fear we suffer much the same ailment."

"Aye," Matthew murmured as his lips brushed against her mouth. "I suspect this is an illness that will linger on for some time."

Son of a bitch! Samuel smashed at the foliage that blocked his path, imagining that each blow was hitting Maggie's lying face. He had seen Maggie walk in that direction more than once and imagined her to be bathing. Today, with Forrest's protective presence finally gone from the inn, there had been no one to stop him. Patiently, he had waited for her to leave the inn and had followed some distance behind. The lust she inspired was almost too much to bear as he watched her disrobe and step into the water.

Samuel had had no notion of joining her. He was content to wait for her to finish. A smile of anticipation had curved his handsome mouth, and he knew he would have her that night. After all this time, he would finally have her.

So single-minded had he been that he never noticed another's presence. It wasn't until Maggie was drawn under that he had realized he was not alone with her. About to dash to her assistance, Samuel had found himself standing knee deep in the gently moving water, his mouth opened wide with astonishment as Maggie surfaced again, now in Forrest's arms. Had she put up some sort of struggle, Samuel would have instantly been at her side, but she offered none. She had laughed instead. Samuel had watched in amazement as she allowed the bastard to kiss and fondle her. It was then he had realized what a fool he had been.

A white-hot flame of pure rage suffused his being with such sickening pain that he almost doubled over. Jesus, had he been armed he would have gladly killed them both. A moment passed, and reason took control again. Silently he retraced his steps, his eyes never leaving the entwined couple. He had something better in store for them, something better than a quick death.

She was whoring for the bastard and probably had been all along. God damn it! How could he have been such a fool to believe her pure and, but for Caleb, untouched?

His body shuddered. God, how he had suffered while controlling the urge to take her. The rage came again as he remembered the times he had taken others, others he had pretended were Maggie.

He cursed as he remembered the danger, the needless deaths. If he had known, if he had only known.

═══ *Twenty* ═══

Samuel casually jumped from his buggy and tied the reins to the post outside the large inn. He behaved as if his whole life did not hinge on the next few moments. He smiled and tipped his hat to a small group of travelers exiting the inn. Mentally, he patted himself on the back for his playacting. God, he was getting good at disguising his true feelings. Not even the skeptical Forrest would suspect his motives or doubt the fabricated story he was about to relate.

He almost laughed out loud with excitement and had to hold his hands firmly to his sides, lest his anxiety show. He took a deep, calming breath and made his way up the three concrete-slab steps to the inn's entrance. If he was going to talk Maggie into going with him, he had to act naturally. It wouldn't do to arouse any suspicions, not now.

He grinned. Later it wouldn't matter. After his plan was set in motion, the couple's communal bliss would be ended. Within hours, Forrest would be resting, he hoped not too comfortably, in prison, and Maggie would be Samuel's whore for as long as her appeal held.

He probably should have waited until the British came for Forrest. Maggie would have been ripe for any comfort he could give by then. But his need was so torturous after

202

watching them together the night before that he knew he
had to have her now. He'd not wait any longer.

He shrugged. It mattered not. In a few hours' time,
Forrest would be gone forever from their lives. Samuel
grinned and wondered how many times he could have her
before word filtered back of Forrest's capture.

"Good afternoon, Samuel." Maggie greeted him with a
smile as she walked toward the table at which he had
positioned himself. "You've come just in time," she remarked. "Hannah has made the most delicious roast."

Samuel's mouth opened in silent amazement. Good God,
the woman grew more beautiful as each day passed. He had
never seen her so lovely. Idly he wondered if a good stiff
cock was the reason for the bloom in her cheeks. If so, she
was sure to grow even lovelier once he got her alone, for he
intended to ride the bitch until his ever-present need was
vanquished.

"I've not come to eat, Maggie, but to tell you some
important news."

Maggie leaned slightly forward, giving him her full attention.

Her cheeks were flushed from the heat of the day, and
tendrils of mahogany hair had escaped her mobcap. Samuel
had to hold his hands forcibly to the table, lest he reach out
for her and ruin his careful plans.

Samuel prayed that his voice sounded calm and his words
believable as he started. "I've received papers from your
husband's family solicitors. It seems you are the sole
beneficiary to a tidy sum of money. The papers have to be
signed and sent back right away, before another comes to
claim what is rightfully yours."

Maggie gasped with surprise. "But how?" she asked, the
shock making her voice a mere whisper. "He was not well
off. Nay, he depended on me for everything."

Samuel easily developed the lie. "An uncle has died.
Caleb was named his heir." Expanding further yet, he

continued, "There are other cousins, but they were not in the uncle's favor."

Maggie shook her head. "Nay, Samuel, let the cousins share it. I want nothing to remind me."

Samuel leaned back in his chair, his mouth open in astonishment. *Jesus Christ! She's refusing the money.* Rage suddenly filled his being. How could anyone be that stupid?

"Maggie, you cannot be serious!" Samuel gasped as he strove to contain his anger. "You'd not give it all away."

Maggie gave a weak imitation of a smile as she shook her head. "Samuel, I have no claim. 'Tis not truly mine to keep."

"You are Caleb's widow. It is yours."

Maggie's voice softened as she tried to make her friend understand. "Samuel, that part of my life is over. I want nothing to remind me of the years I've suffered or the horrible ending to it all."

Samuel thought quickly. It would not do to press his case. Perhaps it would have been wiser to wait for the British to come, after all. Suddenly a new idea formed, and he continued, "Very well, if you are adamant about refusing the inheritance, you'll have to sign papers to that effect."

Maggie nodded her agreement.

"If you've nothing to keep you here, perhaps you might accompany me back to my office. I'd like to post the documents as soon as possible."

"Aye, this is a slow time of the day," Maggie acknowledged as she came to her feet. "They can manage without me for a spell."

Samuel waited at the door while Maggie spoke a few quick words to Forrest. It was obvious from the look that spread over Forrest's face that he did not like the idea of Maggie accompanying the lawyer. Samuel's heart almost fell to his stomach as he watched Forrest untie his apron. Good God, he was going with them! Why hadn't he thought of the possibility? Now what was he supposed to do? *Oh*

Jesus, he groaned inwardly as beads of sweat broke out along his upper lip.

But Maggie, conscious of the animosity between the two men, insisted, "Nay, Matthew. You need not join me. I shall be back momentarily."

"I don't trust him, Maggie," Matthew remarked, ignoring her words. "I'm going with you."

"Matthew!" Maggie whispered forcefully as she moved to block his path, her hand pressed lightly to his chest. "Samuel has been my friend since I was a child. I trust him implicitly."

"I've seen the way the man looks at you. He looks ready to eat you up."

Maggie smiled. "Matthew, can you say his looks differ greatly from yours?"

"Exactly my point!"

Maggie laughed. "Do you trust me so little?"

Matthew's hand reached out to caress her soft cheek. "Maggie, I'd trust you with my life."

Maggie nodded and smiled. "Then you know you have nothing to worry about."

Matthew nodded. "Very well, but if you're not back within the half-hour, I'm coming for you."

Samuel breathed a sigh of relief as he watched Maggie's solitary figure move toward him. Forrest was staying behind. *Thank God,* he muttered to himself.

As Samuel's buggy moved slowly down the dirt road, Maggie's brow creased with thought. "'Tis odd, is it not, that Caleb had an uncle of means? I wonder why he never mentioned the fact?"

Samuel shrugged and looked straight ahead. "The man was in truth his father's uncle. Mayhap he had no knowledge of any wealth."

"No doubt." Maggie smiled in agreement. "Else he would surely have made regular visits."

"I've been meaning to speak with you for a long time,

Maggie," Samuel remarked as he changed the subject. "But I've not had a chance to approach you in private."

Maggie smiled, knowing Matthew rarely allowed them a moment alone. "Samuel, you've been my friend since I can remember. You need only have asked."

"And you would have told the bastard to leave us in peace?"

"Samuel!" Maggie gasped with surprise, for he had never before used profanity in her presence.

"Did my harsh words offend your ladylike senses?" he asked, his voice heavy with sarcasm. "If so, I shall apologize." He laughed then, his mouth curving into a grimace that Maggie would later remember as a sneer.

Maggie felt a chill of bewildering fear race down her back. What in the world had come over him? He was acting so strangely. "Samuel," she ventured at last, "is something amiss?"

Samuel gave a hearty laugh at her question. "You might say that . . . 'Is something amiss?'" he repeated quite nastily as if he was enjoying some private joke.

Maggie felt a stirring of annoyance. "Rather than mimic my words, you'd better tell me the problem."

"Problem? Have I a problem?" He laughed horribly. "What makes you think I've a problem?"

Suddenly Maggie was downright horrified at his strange behavior.

"Samuel, I think it best if you take me back to the inn. We can continue this business when you are more yourself."

Samuel laughed and placed his hand on her knee. "Maggie, I've never been more myself." He shot her an evil leer as he squeezed her leg painfully. "What I want is for you to act more yourself. Like you do with Forrest, perhaps?" And then, giving her an all too knowing look, he finished with, "Mayhap I should head the buggy toward the creek."

He knew! Oh God, had he watched them make love?

Maggie shivered with revulsion. Gaining some control over the desire to strike his leering face, she finally managed, "Samuel, turn this buggy around!" and then gave a silent curse as she realized just how clearly her panic showed in her rising tone.

Samuel grinned as he pulled the buggy to a stop before his house. "All in good time, my dear. We have some unfinished business to catch up on, do you not agree?"

"Samuel, I'll not accompany you inside. Not in your present mood."

"Oh, but you will, darling," he insisted. He grabbed her and dragged her protesting body inside.

Maggie's heart was pounding furiously.

"There we are," he said horribly, sending gooseflesh up her arms as he settled her on her feet. "Just like newlyweds," he added.

"Samuel, what has come over you? I've never known you to act so odd."

"I fear you've never known me at all, my love." And then he chuckled almost conspiratorially. "But you shall. I'd venture to say from this day on you will know me better than anyone on this earth." Before she had a chance to move away, he closed her in his arms, and, almost crooning, he rocked her stiff form against him. "You will be my whore, darling. And we shall both love every minute of it."

"Samuel, this is madness," she grunted, her arms caught between their bodies. She fought to free herself from his embrace.

"Nay, Maggie, I quite agree. I have been at fault in the past, but no more. I'll not let you slip through my fingers yet again. I realize I've been remiss. I did not make a move and allowed that bastard Caleb to take you from me, but that is over. It matters not that you've whored for Forrest, my dear. I have not remained virginal while waiting for you. I used many as substitutes . . .

"But there'll be no more substitutes, Maggie," he promised with terrifying finality. "Now that I've got the real thing, there'll be no need. Ironic, isn't it?" His eyes glittered horribly, and his mouth formed a grotesque grin. "I could have had *you* all along, just like Forrest. There was no need to indulge in whores and that mess with Abby." He gave an elaborate shrug. "Well, I confess to being a bit rough. But the bitch tried to fight me at the last minute." His eyes softened as he caressed her back. "I'd never do that with you."

He laughed suddenly. "Too bad I didn't believe your husband's accusations of infidelity. It would have saved me so much pain and suffering." His voice lowered measurably with yearning. "So much suffering."

Maggie's mind spun in confusion. Samuel was ranting. His low voice droned on and on, most of his words making little sense. What in God's name did he mean about Abby? Had he been the one who raped her? Her heart was pounding furiously, almost strangling her with its intensity as she allowed the thought, *Had he murdered her?*

"Samuel, please," Maggie whispered, her voice breaking as she tried to force some distance between their bodies with her arms. But her efforts were wasted as he easily held her in his unwanted embrace. "You must listen to me."

"Nay, darling," he responded as his fingers moved to cup a heavy breast, his eyes closing with delight. "The time for talking is past. I will have you now."

Maggie's body stiffened. "Samuel, stop it this instant," she snapped, panic overwhelming her.

Samuel only laughed, ignoring her protests as his mouth closed over hers. He knew what she really wanted. He knew, no matter their denials, what they all wanted. A good stiff cock was the answer. As his tongue forced her lips apart, he mused, *They might profess their dislike of the act, but in the end you can't tell a lady from a whore.*

Maggie fought down nausea as his tongue moved deep into her mouth, almost gagging her. Her first instinct was to bite, but she instantly thought better of the idea when the mere grazing of her teeth against his flesh made his hand tighten ominously on her breast.

She had to talk to him. Dear God, she had to make him see reason. But from somewhere deep inside, Maggie knew there was no hope. This man, her longtime friend, was surely mad. And in his madness he would use her body as he pleased.

Maggie twisted her head, trying to free her mouth. But his hand yanked hard on her hair, stilling all further movement.

He was ravaging her mouth, the harsh thrusts of his tongue causing her shivers of revulsion, as he greedily sucked at the moisture he found within.

Maggie gasped for breath. Her knees weakened with shock, and Samuel followed her sagging body to the floor.

In his sickness, he thought her weakness a sign of submission. He did not notice that her moans were of horror, not desire. He almost laughed as he easily disposed of the buttons of her bodice and dipped his hungry mouth to suck on her quaking flesh. His heart soared with delight. He knew he could convince her. He had had no trouble getting others to bed. Indeed, once there he often had a time getting them to leave, for the size of his member was a true delight to all who had come before her. All she had ever needed was a moment alone, a moment spent in his arms, to realize his true worth.

Maggie suddenly stilled. Gasping for breath and trembling from exertion, she realized she could not hope to win out over his superior strength. It was obvious that he was going to rape her.

Amazingly, Maggie's mind grew suddenly clear, her fears receding as a daring plan took hold. Her only chance was to escape. And to do that she had to keep her senses about her and convince him of her acquiescence.

"Samuel," she managed, and if her voice trembled with fear, she prayed he would imagine its source to be desire.

"Aye, darling, aye," he returned, more than anxious to comply to the urging he thought he heard in her voice. He cursed as he struggled to undo the buttons of his trousers. His swollen passion pressed tightly against the material.

"Would we not be more comfortable on a bed?" she asked, her heart thudding as she awaited his answer.

Samuel raised his somewhat bewildered eyes to hers and stared for a long moment before he realized they were lying on the floor. Suddenly a beautiful smile lit up his face, and Maggie almost groaned with relief as the old Samuel seemed to return.

"Indeed we would," he agreed. He rose to his feet and brought her to stand before him. "You must forgive me, darling," he whispered against her neck as he lowered her torn dress to her waist and gently caressed her naked breasts. "My only excuse is that I've so long endured this need to hold you . . . to touch you."

Maggie now realized that Samuel had not gained control of himself; he was merely convinced by her act. Silently she prayed that her shiver of disgust would be mistaken for desire as she turned her face from his mouth. Oh God, how was she to stand it?

His fingers were sliding to her waist, and his mouth moved over her shoulder. A moment later the tie to her petticoat was released. With a slight movement, both dress and undergarments fell to the floor. An instant later she was relieved of her torn chemise and drawers.

Maggie shivered with shame as his hands moved over her. She had never exposed her body to any man but Matthew. Even Caleb had taken her half dressed in the shadows of the night. Stiffly, she stood naked in his arms, but for her stockings and shoes. She willed herself to relax, and her gaze sought out the cloak that hung on a peg by the door.

If she could get him to disrobe and somehow move out of his arms, there was a chance she could grab the cloak and make her escape. Samuel would have no choice but to dress again in order to follow her, and she would be long gone by then.

Maggie gave a silent prayer as she moved her hands from his shoulders to the buttons of his shirt. "Take it off," she whispered, never lifting her gaze from his chest, lest he read the disgust she knew showed in her eyes.

Samuel quickly complied, his eyes never leaving her lush, naked body. A few moments later they stood facing each other, their hearts beating furiously, each for a different cause.

"Touch me," he whispered as he moved his hips within easy reach of her hands.

Maggie steeled herself against the desire to rush past him and grab for the cloak. Her body trembled as she watched his eyes move over her, and by sheer force of will she managed to push aside the revulsion that assailed her senses.

Maggie's eyes widened with shock as she allowed her gaze to move down his body and rest upon his swollen manhood. Never in her entire life had she imagined anything that huge. Good God, if her plan failed he would rip her apart.

A soft chuckle escaped his throat as he watched her expression. "Do you like it?" he asked confidently, his feet spread, his hips angled slightly forward, as he reached for her hand and guided it toward him.

Maggie shuddered as he moved her hand on his engorged member, but she forced her lips into a semblance of a smile. "'Tis huge." If she didn't faint with disgust from this, she surely could stand anything.

Samuel laughed at the amazement he chose to read in her expression. "Imagine how good it will feel inside you," he urged as he dipped his fingers between her legs. "Right here," he whispered near her ear as he wiggled his fingers back and forth.

"Samuel," she groaned, disgusted by his probing fingers. "Samuel, might we share a glass of brandy before we retire to the bedroom?"

Samuel laughed so softly and so menacingly that gooseflesh formed over her entire body. "Maggie, you need not invent means to prolong this. Indeed, it has been prolonged all too long."

"Aye, 'tis true," Maggie returned as he closed her in his arms and moved his nakedness against hers. "But it's been so long since I've been with a man, a real man"—she corrected herself as she felt him start—"that I long to savor every moment."

A flicker of doubt touched his eyes, and Maggie felt her heartbeat accelerate. She had to make him believe she wanted this. Her very life might well depend on it. After his confessed murder of Abby, she had little doubt of her fate should he suspect her real motives.

Gently her fingers moved to his face and began to caress the stiff muscles of his cheeks. "I want you, Samuel," she murmured as her lips brushed lightly as feathers against his mouth. "I want you so much." She leaned back, her hips sitting on the edge of his desk, her arms supporting her weight as she leaned back, and hoped her smile was filled with sexual promise. "Get us a drink."

Samuel watched her for a long, breathless, heart-stopping moment before he smiled and nodded. It wasn't until he had moved to the other side of the desk that she realized she had held her breath as she awaited his response.

Behind the desk stood a table that held various bottles. Maggie waited for Samuel's gaze to leave hers and turn to one of the bottles of brandy before she made her move. In the blink of an eye, she was across the room. Her one hand was on the coveted cloak, the other on the door handle, when she heard his roar of fury.

Maggie pulled on the handle and blinked in amazement as it remained closed. She had no time for further thought as his hands gripped her shoulders and flung her across the room. Maggie fell heavily against the desk, a small moan escaping her lips as the side of her head hit a sharp edge of the sturdy oak. Dazed, she watched as papers, pen, inkwell, and lamp went flying, not realizing that the warm stickiness running over her face and neck was blood.

Before she could lift a hand to ward him off, he was on her.

"Bitch!" he snarled as he forced her legs apart and buried his body deep inside hers. "I'm going to kill you, just like the others. Only I'm going to take particular pleasure in watching you die."

Samuel almost reeled with joy as the ecstasy took hold, his anger forgotten as the blinding beauty of the moment suffused his body. God, how long he had wanted her, needed her, longed to find himself deep inside her smooth body. Surely there was no pleasure to compare.

A tortured scream tore itself from her throat and ended in a guttural moan, not unlike that of a wounded animal. Her body was unprepared for him, and her pain was unlike any she could have imagined. Samuel quickly reached for her mouth, lest any passerby hear her anguished cries.

Samuel's hand over her mouth impeded her breathing. A blackness began to form around the edges of her consciousness and promised momentary release from horror. For a moment she welcomed the deliverance it offered, but suddenly she knew she could not afford the luxury. If she fainted, he would surely kill her when he had finished his dastardly deed. If she were to have a chance of survival, she must remain conscious.

Maggie was desperate to free herself. Her fingers tried to pry his hand from her mouth; when that failed, her nails raked a bloody welt down the side of his face.

Samuel cursed and with his free hand dealt her a stunning blow. Maggie relaxed for a moment, and Samuel believed her incapable of further resistance. He underestimated her pain and determination.

It wasn't little Abby or lazy Flo he fought this time.

Maggie was a woman used to physical labor. Her muscles were strong with constant use, her legs powerful from daily rides. When she struck his jaw with her fist, Samuel knew he had been hit.

Her blow was surprising and disconcerting in its strength. He hesitated for just a moment, and Maggie leaped on the opportunity. Instantly she brought her leg to his chest and shoved with all her strength. She watched with amazement as he toppled from the desk to the table, dragging the liquor bottle with him as he crashed heavily to the floor.

Maggie expected him to recover quickly. Now she was in for it. She had no doubt he would beat her senseless once he stood up. She waited a long moment.

She looked over the edge of the desk. He was struggling to come to his feet. Her heart pounded with terror as she watched his stiff progress. But a moment later he groaned and crumbled back onto the floor. He rolled to his back, and Maggie gasped as she saw a jagged broken bottle protruding grotesquely from the middle of his chest. He gave a last moan, and suddenly all was quiet.

There was an eerie stillness within the tiny office. Maggie could hear her own labored breathing and nothing else. He was dead. Maggie stared dully at the man she had once thought of marrying, the man who had been her longtime friend and confidant. He was dead. Tears of remorse and pity filled her eyes.

Slowly, she came to her feet. Her knees buckled, and she clung to the desk for support. Her eyes wildly searched out the cloak, and she breathed a sigh of relief when she found it crumpled near the door.

Maggie had barely settled the woolen cape over her trembling shoulders when she heard the sound of a horse thundering across Samuel's open yard. Within seconds someone was pounding on the door.

"Open this door, Landsing," Matthew bellowed as he

tried the handle and found it locked. Instantly he was alternately pounding and shoving his shoulder against the door.

Maggie felt her tears of sorrow grow into huge sobs of relief. With a cry of joy, she unlatched the lock. Naked and bloody, she fell into Matthew's astonished arms.

═══ Twenty-One ═══

He's DEAD," MAGGIE MOANED as she pressed her face to the
neckline of Matthew's open shirt.

Kneeling at her side, Matthew moved the soapy cloth
over Maggie's bruised body. His mouth twisted into a
grimace as his eyes took in the many marks that now
marred her skin.

A fresh wave of rage filled his being when his hand
lingered momentarily between her legs and he heard her soft
cry of pain. Matthew's hands trembled with emotion, and
he knew a biting sense of failure. He had not been able to
protect his love from suffering at the hands of another. For
the hundredth time in as many minutes, he wished Landsing were alive so he might have the pleasure of killing him.

He retained a measure of control but still was unable to
conceal the suffering in his husky voice. "Are you feeling
better, darling?" he asked as he helped her stand, wrapping
her in a soft towel.

"He's dead, Matthew, and I killed him."

"Maggie, love, he died at his own hand."

"Nay, I pushed him, and he fell into the bottles."

"Perhaps, but what alternative had you? He was trying to
force himself on you, was he not?"

"Aye," she mumbled, averting her eyes, lest he read a
truth she could not hide.

"He only tried, Maggie? He did not succeed?" His heart suddenly pounded with dread as he awaited her response. And when there was none, his imagination began a scenario of exacting detail. Grizzly pictures of monstrous depravity danced wildly through his mind. Momentarily lost in his own helpless agony, he buried his face in her damp hair.

"Would it matter very much if he had?" Her eyes filled with fresh tears as she raised her gaze to his. "I did not look for his attentions, Matthew," she whispered softly.

Matthew's heart twisted with pain, knowing he had not been there when he was most needed. While cursing himself for forcing her to recount her noncompliance, he groaned, "Maggie, sweetheart," and pulled her more tightly into his arms. "It matters to me for your sake. I ask only so I'll know to what extent you suffered."

"He did not finish the act," she answered wearily, her voice dull.

But he started it, Matthew continued silently. His arms tightened around her again, and his heart cried out in sympathy for her suffering. He felt as if he himself had received a mighty blow to his stomach. And he longed to join her in the release of helpless tears.

Why had he let her go? Damn his stupidity! He should have been there. He should have taken better care of her. It was his fault, all his fault. How was he ever going to make it up to her?

"I'm so sorry, sweetheart. I'm so very sorry."

Again he brought her into his arms and sat on the bed, cradling her as she allowed her tears to wash away the last of her hurt. She was deep in the comforting, forgetful warmth of sleep before Matthew dared to leave her side.

With no little amount of dread, he headed his horse toward the constable's farm. In the past, there had been little cause for Stirling to abandon his daily chores and take on the duties of a constable full-time. Barring an occasional argument over property boundaries or a lost animal, there was no need—at least not before the British had taken up residence.

In the last few months there had been two murders, and the gentle townfolk had assumed a drunken British soldier was the culprit. Now Matthew wondered if their assumption had not been a bit hasty. If Landsing had been crazed enough to force himself on Maggie, could he not also have been responsible for the killings?

Matthew's heart twisted again with pity as the picture of Maggie came to mind. When he found her at Landsing's, her face had been covered with blood, her eyes wild with fright. If he lived to be a hundred, he'd never forget the sight of her.

A quick examination of Landsing's body had confirmed his death. Maggie professed to have killed him, and, though she might have been the one to coax him toward that path, he had to make her realize her actions were self-defense before he'd allow the constable to question her.

Filled with pain and remorse, there was no telling what she might admit to. The constable would not question her, not just yet.

Hannah had given Maggie a light sleeping draft. Matthew breathed a sigh of relief, knowing it would be hours before Maggie awakened.

But Matthew had underestimated the depth of Maggie's torment and the weakness of the laudanum dosage.

Maggie stirred as the last effects of the sleeping potion left her system. A moment later she was fully awake.

Her mind was clear, all too clear. The picture of Samuel lying dead amid the broken bottles came back with terrifying clarity.

Maggie sat up straight in bed, her body suddenly covered with a fine film of sweat as she relived every moment of the fateful day. Again the horror came to assault her senses. She could not stay in bed. Each moment she remained inactive left her mind more vulnerable to the memories.

Quickly she scrambled into her underthings and shoes. She pulled a simple linen dress over her head. After buttoning the bodice, she ran a brush through her thick hair, tying it into a knot at the top of her head and covering it with her mobcap.

She felt no lasting ill effects from the day's happenings, except for a few bruises and a general trembling that would soon disappear once she got to work. Luckily the cut on her head was high enough to be covered by the cap.

For a moment Maggie remembered Hannah's hysterics as Matthew had carried her in the back door of the inn.

Maggie mentally prepared herself for Hannah's tongue-lashing, but she knew Hannah would be needing her help. Regardless of her competence, the woman could not both cook and serve, and Matthew was as clumsy as a bear with a tray of hot food in his hands. She could not imagine a man less able to cope with the domesticity demanded of an innkeeper, for it was obvious he lacked the simplest of skills.

Maggie, seeing his ineptitude, had often suspected the truth: he was a spy. His frequent disappearances while she was sleeping did not go undetected. He was often gone for hours without explanation. And he was always alert to the drunken ravings of a British soldier or a whispered conference between patrons. It was obvious he was working with Washington's forces and using the inn as a cover for his activities.

"What are you doin' up?" Hannah exclaimed, as Maggie walked into the room. Hannah's impatience was obvious.

"Hannah, I cannot lie about while there is so much to be done." A quick look around confirmed her suspicions that the woman worked alone. "Where is Mr. Forrest?"

"He went to talk to the constable. Now get back to bed!"

"Hannah," Maggie sighed, "I've no time to argue with you. You need my help, and I cannot bear the thought of lying down. It does naught but cause me to remember."

Maggie shrugged her shoulders. "In any case, Mr. Stirling is sure to want to talk to me, and I'd best make myself available."

"God almighty, you is the most stubborn girl! I'm goin' to get my James. Then we'll see," she warned as she stalked out of the inn's back door.

Maggie sighed. There was no way anyone was going to get her back to that bed. She couldn't stand another minute lying there alone with her thoughts.

Maggie was busy wiping up a table, readying it for its next patron, when a small contingent of British soldiers stormed inside. Their spurs scraped the floor, and their swords clanged into the chairs and tables as they elbowed each other for ample room.

The man in front, obviously in charge, came toward Maggie. Her eyes grew wild with sudden fear as they darted from one red-coated uniform to the next.

They had come for her! Good God, she hadn't imagined the British would involve themselves in this, but of course they would. The constable had no real authority. They lived under military law, and everything came under British jurisdiction.

Maggie was desperate to escape. They'd never listen to her. She had no proof of what had happened, nothing but her word, and she knew how much the British trusted a colonist's word.

She started to run. In a flash, she was out the door, running through the lean-to, her skirt catching on one of the tubs stored there. She ripped it free and was suddenly outside. Fluffy was barking at her heels. He thought she was playing. He followed her as she made for the woods, but the jangle of spurs and the curses of the men followed close behind. Her skirts were hiked up to her knees, and she ran with no clear destination in mind. She knew only that she had to get away.

"Stop her!" came a shout from behind. Maggie's heart

pounded. She dared not look back. Even a moment's hesitation could prove disastrous.

Maggie was quick, and she imagined the soldiers' speed impeded by the heaviness of their equipment. She was wrong.

The woods were just ahead. A few more feet, and she could lose herself in them. She would be safe.

A heavy hand touched her shoulder. Its weight pulled her back, preventing her from going on. She struggled to break free. She had to get away. She had to!

But the squad of British soldiers surrounded her, allowing no hope of escape. She considered begging but knew the futility of the notion. These men had been sent to perform a duty, and no amount of feminine beguiling would suffice.

Gaining some control, she stared straight into the stern face of one of her captors. The officer's gray eyes clearly showed his distaste for the assignment imposed on him. If Maggie had not been so riddled with guilt, she would have read sympathy and admiration in their smoky depths.

"Why did you run?" he asked. "Were you trying to warn him?" And then he cursed to himself as he realized the woman might have led them to the suspect had they not stopped her. Damn it, he had not thought of that. "Are you his accomplice?"

Maggie stared at the man questioning her. Unable to comprehend his words, she asked, "What?"

"Why were you running? Where were you going?"

Maggie smiled slightly at the ridiculous question. "What does it matter?" she asked, her voice dull with resignation.

Major Harry Harding was enraged that this woman could have fooled them so easily. In all likelihood Forrest had been in the inn and by now was safely in hiding thanks to her ruse. Jesus, he was going to catch it for this.

Major Harding caught his lip between his teeth as his quick mind desperately sought a face-saving solution. Suddenly a smile curved his lips. If he returned to New York with Forrest's accomplice, who would find fault? Surely the woman had given herself away by running. He had no doubt of her guilt. Let his commanding officer get the truth out of her. His job had been to get Forrest, and, failing that, he had managed the next best thing.

Now believing himself victorious, Major Harding ordered his men to bind the prisoner and bring her along.

═══ *Twenty-Two* ═══

Maggie GROANED AS SHE was shoved into the damp, unyielding stone wall. Desperately, her hands clung to the stones, her knees locking with determination and pride. From the force of the shove, it was obvious they had wanted her to fall, but she would not. She'd not give those beasts cause to laugh at her expense.

The door to the dank cell slammed behind her, leaving her alone in the stench-filled darkness. Maggie stood absolutely still and listened to the chilling sounds of scurrying feet and occasional squeaks. Her heart pounded so hard it seemed to drown out the sounds, and sweat broke out across her upper lip and forehead. She now knew that she was not alone, and the knowledge brought shiver after shiver to her spine.

She couldn't imagine a greater horror. If one of these rodents touched her, she knew she'd go stark raving mad. How could they have shoved her into this hole? Regardless of her crime, she deserved to be treated as a human being. It took some time before she realized the charges against her were not of murder. She was accused of being a traitor to the crown in rebellion. It was apparent from her interrogation that they thought Matthew a spy and Maggie his accomplice. Since the English did not admit that the hostilities with the colonies amounted to a war, she was not considered a prisoner but a traitor; therefore, in their estimation, she did not deserve fair treatment.

Maggie wondered if all soldiers were as heartless as these brutes, or if the English had simply mastered the art of barbarism. She breathed a long sigh and admitted that she might be hasty in condemning all the British soldiers. Captain Steele, one of the officers who had questioned her, had been decent enough. Perhaps men were men, after all. It mattered little if they were dressed in fiery red or the tattered rags worn by the rebels; some were kind, others were not. She'd heard stories of horror from both sides, and now she believed them all.

Maggie's stomach growled, and she gave a small wry smile. Apparently the body did not care about the mind's suffering and fears, for despite her present circumstances and the obnoxious stench she was forced to endure, she was undeniably hungry. She had not eaten since early that morning, if, in fact, it was still the day she had been taken prisoner.

What more could happen? Maggie trembled, wondering what her fate might be. The horror she had known with Samuel dimmed into nothingness compared with these new circumstances. Good God, was it only today she had suffered at his hands?

Maggie listened long and hard. The sounds were gone. Had her unwanted visitors found more accommodating dwellings? She hoped so. With a long, weary sigh, Maggie slid down the wall and sat. The floor was wet, much wetter than the walls. Already she could feel the dampness seeping through her skirt and petticoat, but she was too tired to care. The cell was totally black. She could not see her hand held before her eyes. The fleeting glance she had taken of her surroundings when she arrived had revealed that not a stick of furniture or bedding was available for her comfort.

Maggie shivered from the cold. It was August, and she was freezing. Idly she wondered just how far below ground she was. Coming to her feet, she examined the cell with her hands. Four stone walls and, of course, a door, but no windows. She was in the dungeon. She wondered if it was still night. She had no idea how long the exhausting, endless questioning had lasted.

Maggie considered the time of day to be the least important of her problems. She shivered again and sat huddled against the wall, her knees bent, her arms holding her legs tightly to her chest.

So this is the notorious Sugar House, Maggie mused as she closed her eyes and rested her head on her knees. She'd have much to tell her grandchildren when she got out of there. That is, if she did get out and lived long enough to have grandchildren.

Maggie opened her eyes to total blackness. She had no idea how long she had slept. Was it morning? She groaned as her stiff arms released her equally stiff legs and stretched them out before her. Was there any place she did not ache?

Maggie shuddered as she remembered the cause of her many pains. On the long trip to New York, she had been treated roughly. They had forced her to walk for countless miles. When at last her legs had crumpled beneath her from exhaustion, she was dragged some distance before the man holding the other end of the line noticed she had fallen.

While the soldiers made camp for supper, they treated her like an animal, prodding her with gun butts, pinching her, and knocking her down. Occasionally some of them fondled her simply to watch her shudder with disgust.

They had had much enjoyment at her suffering, but now Maggie would gladly have returned to their company if she were allowed a drink of water and a biscuit or two.

She had to relieve herself. Although she knew no facilities existed, she nevertheless searched the tiny cell for a convenience. There was none.

Finding the door, she banged hard and long before a gruff voice grumbled sleepily, "What the hell do you want?"

"Please," Maggie returned, her desperation causing her voice to become shrill, "a bucket, if you will?"

"If I will," he returned, his voice dripping with hatred and anger at being so rudely awakened. *"If* I will, it won't be till the morning. Now shut up!"

There was no way she could wait until morning. She couldn't wait another five minutes. "Wait! Don't leave!" she called from her cell as she began to pound again. "A bucket, please!"

There was the sound of a key in the door. Maggie felt a rush of relief. An instant later the door swung open forcefully on squeaking hinges, moving so hard and fast it almost knocked her to the floor. Maggie quickly backed up. She tripped on the hanging hem of her gown and stumbled against the wall. Her heart was hammering in her chest. The guard was coming toward her, and, from the glitter in his dark eyes, she had no doubt of the menace he had in mind.

Still, Maggie did not foresee his next move and was caught off guard when his fist swung out from the surrounding blackness. Suddenly a crushing blow contacted with her jaw. The last things she remembered were the beautiful bright lights that danced and flickered behind her lids and his satisfied grunt, "I said shut up."

Maggie was neither concerned nor conscious of her needs, as her body did quite naturally what it had threatened.

Maggie had no notion of how long she had lain there. Her first thought upon awakening was of the painful ache in the side of her face and the back of her head. In addition to the guard's savage punch, she had probably banged her head when she fell.

As Maggie came slowly to her senses, she realized she no longer needed the bucket. Her face suffused with color, and for the first time she was glad to be alone in the dark. She was mortified. How could she have allowed that to happen? Maggie gave a soft moan and rose to her feet. She clung to the wall for support until the dizziness passed. The material of her skirt stuck damply to her legs. With a disgusted groan, she tried to shake the fabric away, but it continued to cling every time she moved.

Maggie hid her face in her hands and at last gave in to the crushing despair she had fought so hard to keep at bay. She cried harsh, wracking sobs that themselves brought further aching, until she was gasping for breath. Then, no longer having the strength to stand, she sank onto the cold slime that covered the floor.

Maggie gave the guards no further trouble. When she next felt the need to relieve herself, she did so in the corner of the cell rather than chance further abuse.

After the sixth time she had awakened and fallen asleep again, she stopped counting. Time stretched on endlessly. She had no idea how long it had been since she was brought to this hole. More than a week, she reasoned. Had they forgotten her? Would they never bring her food and water?

Maggie had never known such discomfort. Her tongue was swelling from lack of water, making it difficult to breathe. She was so hungry, her stomach rumbled almost constantly now. She daydreamed about catching one of the rats that often sought out her company. Perhaps its blood would ease her thirst, for she thirsted most of all. God, she had never imagined such thirst.

She was filthy and smelled as putrid as the cell. But she no longer cared. After a time, she realized with some dismay, her disgust for the place was diminishing. She now eagerly licked the walls, seeking moisture from any means.

As the days wore on, she began to hallucinate, but the knowledge that her dreams were not real did little to stop the eerie happenings. Quite suddenly she would burst into tears, believing herself a child. Her raspy voice came from parched lips as she begged her father to forgo a childhood punishment. In her ravings Maggie would often see her mother and longed for the comfort she knew she would find in her arms. But when she reached out, the elusive figure would disappear like mist on a summer morning.

And then she was laughing, feeling the fresh spring air rush through her long hair as she pushed Red to his limit, her heart swelling with joy as she felt the horse beneath her and the freedom of the ride.

A soft, teasing grin shaped her lips, her eyes sparkled with devilry. She was in the apothecary shop, reading a sign hung near the door:

> How merrily we live that Doctors be,
> We humbug the public and pocket the fee.

A moment later she was remembering that disgracefully forward but delicious Mr. Forrest, and she asked the empty cell, "I wonder whatever became of him?"

Maggie was sick, terribly sick. She burned with fever and shivered with cold. She was dying. She knew it but could not find the will to care. It was justice, after all, she reasoned when her thoughts would now and then become more rational. She had killed a man and deserved no less.

Someone was lifting her. Maggie snuggled into strong arms, aching for the warmth they hinted at. Someone was talking to her. Was she no longer alone? Had they remembered her at last?

"Just a sick little girl," came a deep voice from far away.

Something hard was pressed to her mouth. Maggie groaned as cool water trickled between her cracked and bleeding lips, bathing a throat that felt as if it were filled with a thousand fragments of glass. Desperately she sought out more, for she never thought to be free of her thirst. "More," she croaked weakly.

"Nay, you'll sicken further," came a warning voice. "I'll soon give you more."

When Maggie awoke, she saw with no little surprise that she was lying in a large dirty room, beside a grizzly gray-bearded man, while men and women dressed in every manner of rags wandered about. The man's heavy arm was thrown protectively over her waist, as he snored loudly near her ear.

Maggie had no idea where she was. How long had she been sick? How had she gotten there? Had the man tended to her while she was ill? Was it his voice she had heard?

Maggie moaned, all her effort focused on moving out from beneath the weight of his arm, but it was impossible. She was so weak. She was so thirsty.

"Well, I see you've finally come around, little girl," the man said. His face was so close she could see the pores of his skin and the wrinkles around his cheery blue eyes. His voice seemed pleasant, and he smiled reassuringly.

"Do you have some water?" she asked as she ran her tongue over her dry lips.

The man smiled. "Aye, a bit."

Maggie choked as she greedily swallowed the fluid, and he pulled the chipped cup away. "Just a little at first, girl. Lest it come right back up."

"Have I been ill?" Maggie asked, exhausted by the simple act of drinking.

"Aye, that you were, and for a mighty long time."

"How long?"

The man shrugged. "A week or more."

"And you've been taking care of me?" Maggie asked hesitantly, her face coloring as she imagined the intimacies involved in caring for someone so ill.

"You need not worry on that account," the man responded gruffly, reading her embarrassment correctly. "I've doctored my lovely Lisbeth and our three girls more times than I could count." He shrugged again as if it were of no importance. "I did what I must."

"Is Lisbeth your wife?"

A beautiful smile lit up his eyes. "That she is, girl."

It was growing dark. Maggie could see others preparing to bed down on the floor of the huge room. Each one held close a filthy rag of a blanket.

"Where are we?"

"In Sugar House," the man whispered. "They brought you up from below some days ago." A gentle smile curved his thin lips. "These cursed English offer most comfortable accommodations, don't you agree?"

Maggie smiled at his wry sense of humor. "I want to thank you, Mr. . . ."

"Ames, little girl, John Ames. But there's no need for that. My Lisbeth would skin me alive if I left you to die. 'Twas no bother to share this ragged blanket and give you a drink now and then." He gave a low, conspiratorial laugh, his eyes aglow with devilry, as he continued, "Besides, I've a need to let that nagging wife of mine know I've been sleeping with another."

Maggie chuckled. "Then I thank your Lisbeth too, sir. Indeed, she is a lucky woman to claim you for her husband."

"'Tis as I have thought all along," he agreed, his lips twitching with humor. "My problem is getting *her* to admit it."

Sally handed the letter to Matthew only moments after his arrival at the deserted cabin. She sat by the cold fireplace and waited for him to read it through.

My Dearest Sally,

I've permission to write you at last, but just this once. Mr. Corbet has been so kind as to assure me the immediate and correct dispensation of this letter. Forgive my presumption, but I promised him your payment upon receipt.

My dearest friend, I hold no hope. I pray only that a quick death will release me from my torment. In Sugar House, everything is much worse than I ever could have imagined.

Smallpox is rampant, and had I not had a mild case as a child, I would have long left this earth for my final reward. A pity. As it is, the air is pregnant with fever, including my own, and dysentery has left me terribly weak.

Sally, I would not ask this of you had I another, but you are my last and only hope, lest I die the horrible death of the starving. The water is foul and is suspected of being the guard's castoff. There is no eatable food unless it is bought. Unfortunately, I was taken without a coin in my possession. Yesterday, I watched a man eat his shoe. Only a month ago, I would have laughed at the mere notion, but I salivated instead. Fresh meat is one shilling per pound, milk fifteen coppers per quart, turnips a shilling a half a peck. Anything you could spare would be greatly appreciated.

There is no glass in the windows, and the dampness on even these warm nights leaves me hoping for a reoccurrence of the fever. This time I pray I'll not be able to fight it off. Only then will this suffering end.

Sally, I implore you to let no one know of my dire straits. I'd not risk another's life to save what is left of mine. Should he find out my whereabouts, I fear greatly for his safety, for I know not what he might do.

I thank you in advance, for I doubt we will meet again in this life. May God have mercy on all our souls.

I remain your most affectionate friend,
Maggie

"Jesus Christ! What have they done to her?" Matthew raged as his hand swung out and hit the wall. "She sounds more dead than alive."

Since the night of Maggie's arrest, Matthew had been in touch with every contact he knew, and he had found no one who could offer a clue to Maggie's whereabouts. It was as if she had simply vanished from the face of the earth.

He knew she was being held in one of New York's prisons, but where? He had made endless inquiries, but the fools who kept the records had apparently forgotten to add her name to the list of poor souls held at Sugar House.

He had gone almost mad with worry in the month she had been missing. In that time he had died a thousand deaths imagining the horrors she would be made to endure. At least he could be thankful they had not sent her to the *Jersey,* for escape from that hellish prison ship was impossible and death inevitable.

Matthew was a sad caricature of the man he had been but a month ago. His cheeks were sunken, his skin a sickly gray, his eyes wild with fright and rimmed with black circles from endless sleepless nights.

"If she dies, I'll kill every last one of them."

"She'll not die, Matthew," Sally countered. She came to her feet and faced him. "We could not act until we knew where she was being held. Now we will simply get her out."

"Indeed?" Matthew asked, his thick brow raised in disbelief, obviously doubting her confidence. "And how might we accomplish this task, with the whole of New York occupied by that cowardly lot?" His lips twisted into a humorless grin. "Shall we walk right in and take her out?"

Sally smiled. "As a matter of fact, we shall."

═══ Twenty-Three ═══

M AGGIE'S SMILE WAS RADIANT and her eyes glowed with joy
as she carefully rewrapped the loaf of bread and tucked it
beside the bag of potatoes. It was a sad state of affairs when
a week's supply of food could bring her to near euphoria.
But as of this moment she couldn't imagine anything better,
except perhaps freedom.

Thank God for Sally, she mused as her fingers lovingly
caressed a thick blanket. Maggie marveled as she realized
her mental health had returned almost to normal. She
hadn't known the depths to which she had sunk. Each day
had nibbled at her spirits until she was devoid of emotion.
She hadn't cared then whether she lived or died. Actually,
she had, for a time, preferred death over the effort it took to
remain alive.

It was amazing that in only two days her whole outlook
had changed. Now she could think only of the happiness a
sack of potatoes brought. Apparently all it took was a full
stomach, and John at her side, and she could once more face
all that life handed her.

They rarely bothered to question her now. Perhaps they
finally believed she held no useful information. Her murmured nays, as they asked the same questions again and
again, were annoying to both parties involved. Maggie

could only hope they would soon give up and allow her some peace.

"So, little girl," John Ames remarked as he sat himself comfortably at her side, his back leaning heavily against the wall, "is that a smile I see?" He grinned as he eyed the many packages spread out around her. "Now, I wonder what could have happened to bring about such happiness?"

"Oh, John," Maggie exclaimed, her excitement equaling that of any child on Christmas morning. "Look at what I've got for us."

"For us?" he asked, his amazement obvious.

"Of course, for us," she chided gently. "Do you believe me such a glutton that I would buy all this for myself alone?"

He smiled, his eyes warm with undisguised love, his warning but a gentle censure. "Little girl, you'll have nothing but empty sacks if you continue on this way. I saw you give Mistress Blake enough produce to last a week or more. What will you do when all is gone?"

"John," Maggie returned with a determined shake of her head, "Mistress Blake was in dire need. She has no one to come to her aid." She gave a careless shrug of her slender shoulders. "I did no more than anyone else would have done." A soft smile touched her lips as she faced him. "Mayhap the others will also share when they receive an answer to their letters."

John Ames smiled at the young woman's innocence. He himself knew human nature a good deal better than she. Of course, it was possible for some to share, but most here knew the fear of hunger, and he doubted one among this ragged group capable of the charitable act. His keen blue eyes moved skeptically over the other occupants of Sugar House and noted, with no satisfaction, the mistrust and downright belligerence with which most guarded their meager possessions. Once Maggie's supplies were gone, she'd see little kindness from her fellow man.

John sighed with sorrow, for he couldn't find it in his

heart to condemn those poor souls. It was the need for survival that drove all to act in an inhuman fashion. And if their actions disgusted him, at least he could understand their motives.

"I'll not fault your charity, little girl," John returned, lifting her stubborn chin with his finger, "for you are the best of the lot."

"Nay, John," Maggie countered, her brandy eyes responding warmly to his obvious affection. "'Tis merely your example I follow. For weeks you've shared everything with me—even the warmth of your blanket." Maggie gave him a stern look. "I'll not hear another word on the subject."

But Maggie was soon to regret that she had not heeded her friend's advice.

Maggie cuddled closer to John's body as the first rays of the sun shone shyly through the glassless window. But no matter how she snuggled within the confines of the two blankets, she could not find her usual warmth and comfort.

A louse was making itself at home in her hair, and Maggie sighed with annoyance as she sleepily reached up to scratch. She wondered idly if she'd ever again be clean and free of vermin. She had always been so fastidious about her person. Never in her life had she been bothered by lice, although she knew many who had. She almost smiled at the amazing change in her. Now, picking at the ugly, tiny creatures and crushing them between her nails did not even make her shudder.

Maggie pushed her rump closer to the curve of John's body, only slightly puzzled that she received no answering pressure. A gentle smile curved her lips, and she wondered how many other men would treat her so gently. It was obvious John loved her, and yet he had never taken advantage of her sleepy form.

In her heart Maggie knew she'd not refuse his advances. They had no one now, no one but each other. Maggie knew of the burly seaman's love for his Lisbeth, but it mattered not. She too had once loved. But as each day passed it grew increasingly clear that they would never see their loved ones again. In truth, they were as dead to them as if their souls had already left their bodies.

On more than one occasion, Maggie had felt John's obvious arousal, an arousal that slowly began to taunt her own body's needs, yet he had only rolled away—saying nothing, doing nothing, waiting for her to make the first move.

Maggie's heart filled with emotion, for she knew no other to compare with this man's gentleness. Always protective, he would hide her from curious eyes, standing before her and spreading his coat, when she needed to use the corner pail. Twice he had warned Jacob Darning away when the man's manner proved to be most offensive, his intentions obviously the most basic. And when her monthly flow had come upon her, filling her with dismay, for she had not a scrap of cloth to absorb it, he had seen her discomfort and suggested that she apply strips torn from her petticoat and do so beneath the protective cover of his blanket.

Vaguely she wondered what she would do next month, since the fabric could not be saved and cleaned, water being too valuable to waste on washing.

Maggie sighed. She loved him, it was true. How could anyone not? But the love she felt was different from any she had previously known. It soothed and comforted her, wrapping her in its warm protection. John's gentle compassion drew them closer than she'd ever felt to another human being. And if it did not drive her wild with uncontrolled passion, it brought the only pleasure she was likely to know for the rest of her days.

Maggie felt a twinge of guilt as Matthew's laughing dark eyes came suddenly to mind. *No,* she almost moaned aloud as the vision grew clearer. *Do not let him into your thoughts. To do so only brings more suffering. Be thankful he got away. Pray for his safety, but forget what you once had together. There is no hope.*

Again she moved in John's arms. Around her she heard others beginning to stir. God, but it was cold this morning. There was a dampness surrounding her that left her feeling more than just uncomfortable. She was truly wet.

Maggie glanced up at the high ceiling. Had it rained during the night? Did the roof leak? She groaned in disgust.

"John," she murmured gently as she reached her hand behind her to give his hip a shake. Her brow furrowed with puzzlement. She had never known him to sleep so heavily. "John, wake up. We are lying in a puddle of water."

And when she still received no reply, Maggie quickly looked to his face.

The scream started as a low, anguished moan. It spewed forth in ungodly torment, intensifying with each passing second, until the wailing sound brought pity to the hardest heart. The agony of what she saw twisted her chest and clutched at her bowels until she was one writhing pain.

She never knew that the demented sounds she heard were her own. In a blur of tears, she could see a red-coated arm as a firm hand continuously struck her face. There was blood everywhere. It had puddled her bedding and covered her bodice and neck. It had hardened her already filthy hair into stiff strands and stuck disgustingly between her fingers.

Maggie couldn't take her eyes off the man at her side. His throat had been cut. She had never imagined skin to be so thick, nor a gaping wound so bloody and grotesque.

His lifeless blue eyes stared almost accusingly, and Maggie shuddered with guilt, instantly knowing the reason for his death. Their supply of food was gone. She did not need to look to verify the fact. John had forfeited his life because of her stupidity.

Maggie was sobbing with the last of her energy. A guard was lifting her to her feet. She did not notice or hear the knife as it tumbled from her lap, clattering noisily to the floor. Her eyes made contact with Jacob Darning's gloating smile, and Maggie knew who the murderer was. Her heart sank with despair: to accuse him would have afforded her no good. She had only her word and, much to her horror and distress, had long ago discovered the guards took no notice of anything she might say. At any rate, Jacob Darning's punishment would not have brought John back.

The guard grunted with disgust when he picked up the knife. He gave a humorless smile and a short nod of his head as if solving a mystery. The bitch had sliced the poor bastard's throat while he slept. Jesus, what kind of animals were these rebels? It was enough to give a man the chills knowing he endangered his very life by bedding one of these whores.

Two guards half dragged a subdued Maggie from the room. A few moments later she was thrown once again into the dungeon. But Maggie, so thoroughly immersed in sorrow, voiced no objections. She never realized what was happening but almost immediately fell into a dreamless sleep.

Maggie awoke to total silence. Her face felt swollen and sore. It took only a few moments before she realized why. She remembered the screaming now and the excellent work of the guard who had tried to quiet her. He must have worn a heavy ring, for the bruises were accompanied by deep cuts. Her eye was swollen shut, and one of her front teeth felt chipped. Maggie knew the injury to her tooth was slight, but nevertheless it ached every time she allowed the cold air of the cell to hit it.

Oh God, she moaned in silent horror. *I can't go through this again. I don't want to live if I have to do it here.*

She wouldn't try to stay alive this time. She'd not lick at the moisture the wall afforded. She'd die of thirst in three or four days. So be it.

Matthew gave a low round of vile curses as he helped the tiny lady at his side down the dark steps to the bowels of the prison. The air was stagnant and foul with the overpowering scent of human feces. Matthew's chest twisted with helpless rage, a rage that had not lessened since Maggie's capture nearly two months ago.

His heart thudded with anxiety. Nothing must go wrong. He had to get her out.

The guard stopped before a thick door and slipped his key into the lock. A moment later Matthew and Sally were standing inside. His stomach lurched as he fought against the suffocating stench, while his eyes took in the pitiful sunken woman huddled in a corner of the cell.

Maggie blinked at the sudden harsh light of the lantern. Why had they come to bother her? Couldn't they just let her die in peace? But no, it was not her lot in life to know a peaceful death. No doubt they had divined a means to prolong her torture. But she'd not allow that. If they brought her water again, she'd not drink it. Like before, she'd dump it onto the floor, lest she be tempted.

The door clanged shut, and Maggie sighed with relief. At least they had left her alone. Her brow furrowed. They had not taken the light. Why?

Someone was holding her, lifting her into strong arms, murmuring low, soothing words near her ear. Maggie looked up into Matthew's worried face, but she knew it to be a hallucination. She closed her eyes and commanded herself to sleep again. Still, the feeling that others were present would not abate. Again she forced her eyes open, only to find her imagination once more playing tricks. Maggie almost smiled at the sight of a beautifully dressed young lady. Was she an angel? Surely she was beautiful enough. Was it her time at last? Was God calling her home?

"Have you come for me?" she asked weakly. "Will you take me from here?"

"Aye, Maggie," Sally's whisper echoed in the small cell. "I have come to take you home."

"I'm not sorry," Maggie mumbled as she closed her eyes again. "I've been waiting for you."

Sally smiled. "Have you? Were you so sure I'd come?"

Maggie's smile nearly brought tears to Matthew's eyes. She was so horribly thin. Her cheeks were hollow, and purple discoloration was evident around her eye and along her jaw. There was no doubt she had been beaten, and Matthew prayed that the man who had dared to touch her would someday fall into his hands.

"I knew our Father'd not forget His child."

Matthew and Sally exchanged puzzled looks. "Maggie, do you not recognize us?"

Maggie stared at her visitors. Suddenly her heart swelled with joy as her senses took in the sight of her lover and her best friend. A moment later she asked hesitantly, "You're not dead too, are you?"

Matthew found his throat closed to her pitiful question and could not bring himself to answer her, lest he burst into tears.

Sally smiled at her friend's confusion. "Nay, Maggie, we are not, and neither are you."

Sally was lifting her skirts. Maggie couldn't keep from staring. Her mouth hung open in surprise, wondering what in the world she was about. Could she be mistaken? Was there a pair of boots hanging from a rope and tied to Sally's waist? "Sally, what are you doing?"

Sally glanced up at her friend's startled expression and quickly divested herself of the unusual array of clothing hidden beneath her wide panniers. "I am getting my friend out of here, of course."

The heavy boots fell to the floor. A red coat, white blouse, belt, and trousers were held out to her.

"We must hurry," Sally urged. "We've little time."

The reality of their presence finally hit her, and Maggie gasped, horrified that Matthew was holding her. She knew she looked horrible, for her face was still stiff from the beating, and she was mortified to know that she smelled worse than she looked. She had soiled her dress and underthings a number of times, having neither the strength

240

nor the inclination to walk to the corner. Maggie's face flamed with embarrassment. "Please," she begged, "put me down."

Matthew did as she asked but hovered close by, lest she show any sign of falling.

Maggie lowered her gaze to the cell floor, her voice muffled with shame. "Matthew, I'd not have you see me thus."

He was pulling off her dress and underthings as he shook his head. "Maggie, it matters not. We must hurry." His fingers moved quickly, buttoning buttons and tying ties. A moment later he gathered her hair on top of her head and pushed a tricorn hat in place, while Sally forced Maggie's feet into high black boots.

"Guard!" Matthew called. "Guard!"

The turnkey must have been waiting directly outside the cell, for no sooner had Matthew called than the man opened the door.

Maggie's heart pounded with terror as she finally understood the plan. She was dressed as a British soldier, but the idea of her passing as such was ludicrous. It did not matter how far Matthew pushed her hat over her eyes. It could not totally hide her face. They'd never make it. Once they had walked through the lighted areas of the prison, they'd be recognized and stopped. And once caught, they would all be held in the building's hellish hole.

"I cannot," Maggie murmured as she tried to pull back. "They'll find us out, Matthew."

But Matthew's strong arm was around her waist, propelling her forward, his words soothing her fears. "Nay, my love. The guards have been paid well to look the other way. They will see to the others."

It couldn't be this easy, Maggie reasoned. Someone was sure to stop them. But, as Matthew had promised, not a man glanced their way as they moved from guard post to guard post. Filled with terror, Maggie only stared straight ahead, waiting with each drawn breath for the command to halt, but none came. Miraculously, they were outside. Tears filled her eyes as she savored the clean, fresh evening air.

The guards at the prison door gave no flicker of notice to the three, and Maggie felt her knees weaken with joy. She slumped against Matthew's side, and he half lifted her into a waiting carriage.

If any passerby noticed the peculiar sight of an officer holding his enlisted man so intimately at his side, one glance at the man's grim face would discourage any from voicing an opinion.

═══ *Twenty-Four* ═══

MATTHEW'S HANDS GENTLY SMOOTHED the ointment over the last of the rash. Maggie seemed to be healing nicely. At least her skin showed definite signs of improvement, for the inflammation grew paler as each day passed. Now, if she could manage to recover her strength as well, he would be able to breathe more easily. A curse slipped from his lips, for he realized all too clearly to what degree this woman had suffered.

Relentlessly, and despite her painful cries to cease, he had administered her care. Almost immediately upon entering the house, Maggie was stripped and made to sit in a tub of hot water. The pain of the soapy water against her raw and inflamed skin caused her to cry out, and she would surely have tried to leap free if Matthew's strong hands had not kept her in place.

Again and again, her hair had been doused with a burning, malodorous concoction, until she had begged to allow the little creatures a safe haven, for their removal was not worth the price she paid.

Sally visited often, but her visits were necessarily short. She did not want to tax Maggie's strength.

During the long weeks of Maggie's recovery, Matthew talked to her almost endlessly. The silence of the room seemed to hold demons for her, and she often cried out, even in her deepest sleep, unless she heard the soothing sound of his voice.

He talked until he was exhausted, until his voice grew raw, and he talked on every subject he could think of. He told her about his childhood, his schooling, the years spent working his family's farm, the farm itself, reminding her that one day it would be theirs. He talked of the terror he had known upon finding her gone, and, of course, he talked of his love and need for her as he silently willed her to regain her strength.

"She improves daily," Dr. Steward announced to Matthew with a gentle smile directed at his patient. He replaced her covers and patted her hand. "She'll be up and about soon. A few more days at the most, I'd wager."

Matthew beamed, and Maggie smiled at the softly spoken words of assurance.

"In truth?" With a wicked gleam in his eyes, Matthew's gaze rested lovingly on his lady. "I had hoped to keep her abed for some time to come."

"Matthew," Maggie admonished with a soft smile and a gentle pinkening of her cheeks. "What will the good doctor think?"

Matthew laughed as he watched Maggie's cheeks color beautifully. "The good doctor knows I tease, my love."

Dr. Steward chuckled, his wise old eyes not missing the look of love that passed between the two. It reminded him of what he felt for his long-dead Annie. He sighed and wished the couple more fortune.

"I'll be back in a few days, Mrs. Forrest. See to it you listen to your husband." Noticing her look of astonishment and the stubborn set of her jaw, he laughed and then added, "Just till you are well, my dear. After that, you will, in all likelihood, do as you wish."

Maggie watched Matthew reenter her room after seeing the doctor out. A decidedly sheepish grin curved his mouth when he saw her eyes narrowed with anger. Before she had a chance to speak, he forestalled her words by raising his hand. "The room thickens with indignation, Maggie. I know you need to air your vexation, but won't you grant me a moment to explain?" His grin deepened, and Maggie steeled herself against the charm of his boyish smile. "I know you felt some degree of surprise to be referred to as Mrs. Forrest. I thought it best to let Dr. Steward believe he administered to my wife, lest your reputation suffer irredeemable harm." He smiled at her look of helpless frustration. And after a moment of silence, he asked, "Would you fault me for my reasoning, love?"

Maggie shot him a sideward glance, her look telling him all. Her groan of obvious frustration brought forth a low chuckle, and she remarked, "I cannot fault you, sir, but the lie pleasures me not."

Matthew laughed. "It will be a fact before long, in any case." He shrugged a heavy shoulder. "I did no more than hurry your title along."

"You are a rogue, Mr. Forrest."

Matthew laughed. "Perhaps, but as long as I am your husband, if in name only, you will remember the good doctor's orders." And, at Maggie's look of confusion, he continued, "You must listen to me, at least until you are well."

Maggie smiled. "I warn you, sir, when I am well again . . ."

"A time I look forward to most eagerly, mistress," he interrupted. "It pleasures me not to find you weak and acquiescent. I long for the spirited lady who stole my heart."

"Is it arguments your heart desires?"

Matthew grinned, his gaze decidedly wicked as he teased, "I've no doubt that you will see to my heart's desire the moment you are able. In the meantime, 'tis time for your bath."

Maggie shook her head and sighed. "I suspect you appreciate this particular chore more than is proper."

Matthew nodded, his grin spreading almost ear to ear. "I'd not deny it, Maggie."

Matthew moved the soapy cloth over her body. His mind was tortured with a mixture of ecstasy and pain, the former outweighing the latter by immeasurable degrees. For his suffering did not matter. He'd never get enough of looking at her, of touching her.

"You are gaining weight," he announced proudly, his voice holding only a thread of the pain that wracked his body. "Your stomach is less sunken, your breasts fuller."

Trying to dispel the effects of his touch, Maggie teased, "I take it you are an authority on the female anatomy, Mr. Forrest?"

Matthew grinned at her saucy remark. "'Tis best, I think, if I ignore that question."

Maggie watched his warm gaze move over her. Her heart thundered in her chest as his fingers grazed her flesh. Her skin grew pink, her breathing shallow, as she fought to suppress the desire his touch instilled. She shuddered beneath his touch. Weak or not, ill or no, she wanted him. It had been so long since he had held her. With each day's passing she grew stronger. As her body continued to heal, so did her desire increase for this man to make her his again.

Mistaking her shivers for cold, he hurried his task. "I'll soon be done, my love. I'd not see you chilled."

Maggie's skin flushed deeper as her gaze rose boldly to meet his. Her voice was husky with desire, her eyes clouded with passion, her meaning unmistakable as she whispered, "'Tis not cold I feel when you look upon me, Matthew."

Matthew's hand froze as he grasped her meaning. He tried, he really did, but after weeks of worry, of longing, of striving to put aside his passions, his control was worn to a frazzle. He couldn't fight his need without her help. And the promise of delight he saw shining in her golden eyes was simply more than he could bear.

"Maggie," he asked, his voice thick, "I'd not bring you further harm. Are you sure?"

Maggie smiled. "Sure that I want you?" She laughed softly and raised a finger to trace the column of his dark throat, to play in the open neck of his shirt. "'Tis a fact I've long ago stopped denying." Her gaze rose to meet his. "Would you see this lady suffer still more? For I swear when you touch me 'tis worse than torture to have you stop."

Hot blood pulsed through his veins, and his heart thudded with a strength that obliterated all else. "Oh God," he groaned, his mouth lowering until only an inch separated their flesh. His warm, clean breath bathed her skin and further intoxicated her senses. Their eyes locked, each pleading for the other to yield. He murmured, "Maggie, my love, you should first be well, but as God is my witness, I've no longer the strength to wait."

Maggie gave a glad cry as Matthew's mouth closed over hers at last. Her arms came to circle his neck and drew him more tightly to her. He growled as his tongue slid deep into the dark recess of her mouth, her lips and teeth proving no barrier against his thrust. Greedily, he tasted her sweetness again.

Maggie sighed as wondrous sensations filled her to bursting, only to taunt her need for more. Her fingers undid the buttons of his shirt, and she tugged at his shoulders, aching to feel his nakedness brush against her own.

He leaned heavily against her and gathered her into his arms, but her sigh of relief at being held close at last turned quickly to a gasp of pain. The battering her body had taken had not yet healed, regardless of her assertion that all was well.

Matthew was swimming in a sea of delight, drowning in a world of beauty only she had the power to dispense. There was never a woman like this, never a time when a man could find such ecstasy closed within white silken arms, pressed against warm succulent flesh. He felt her stiffen beneath him and instinctively pulled back. His eyes were puzzled until he saw the pain she had sought to hide.

"Damn it, Maggie," he growled. "'Tis too soon. I knew it!"

"Nay, my love," she cried, seeking to keep him in her arms. "'Tis nothing."

"Do you deny that I hurt you?"

Maggie bit at her bottom lip, "I deny it," she stated evenly.

But her hesitation was enough to convince him of his suspicions.

Matthew gave a long, weary sigh and rose to his feet. He dared not remain at her side, lest he succumb again to her allure. His back was stiff as he walked to the window and looked out over the dark, busy streets of New York. His hand shook as he ran his fingers through his hair.

"We will wait, Maggie. You are not ready." Before she had a chance to voice an objection, he continued, "The matter is closed."

Maggie opened her eyes and watched the candlelight flicker in dancing patterns across the ceiling. She sighed and snuggled deeper into the soft feather mattress, nuzzling her head into the clean pillow sheet. Never again would she take the comfort of a bed for granted.

She was safe now. Matthew had assured her of the fact a dozen times since she had come there. He and Sally had brought her to a house not far from the prison. Maggie knew she would be staying there until she was well enough to travel to Mastic and Matthew's family's farm. Once there, she would have no reason to fear, for the British would not know where to search for her.

She spent most of her days up now and, if not about, at least sitting in a chair rather than lying in bed. Her body grew stronger daily, and she looked forward happily to putting the enforced seclusion behind her.

All was well but for one nagging memory. John Ames's death tormented her. She took the full weight of his death upon herself. Over and over again, she berated herself for her foolishness. Why had she gathered so many supplies? Why had she been so greedy as to buy so much at once? Had she listened to her friend, he would now be alive. Maggie knew Matthew sensed something was wrong, and she realized the time was almost at hand when she would have to tell him.

At first she was wracked with a different sort of guilt, but Maggie realized now, as she grew well again, that she had never really loved John. She knew it was natural that she should have turned to a man of his strength and gentleness, and she thanked God that she had known him.

Maggie heard the bedroom door open and smiled as Matthew entered. She watched silently as he approached the bed and placed a tray of tea and thick, hot soup on the nightstand. With a sigh, he sat at her side and gently pushed her clean hair from her face.

Marveling at the sight before him, Matthew couldn't prevent the smile that curved his lips. God, how he had suffered in fear for this woman. Every day since finding her, he thanked the almighty. Living without her was no life at all.

"I've brought your supper," he said gently.

Maggie smiled and nodded. "You need not treat me as an invalid, Matthew. I grow stronger every day. I could join you downstairs, with some small help."

"Soon, darling," he replied gently. "Humor me for a bit longer, will you? It doesn't bother me to see to your comfort for now." With a great deal of care, he raised her to a sitting position. Her back rested comfortably against the newly fluffed pillows.

After her meal, she was sipping at a steaming cup of tea. Tea was easily obtainable in the city, and Matthew insisted that she drink it, no matter her objections.

Matthew removed the cup from her hands and began, "Maggie, you are well enough now. 'Tis time for us to talk."

Maggie knew he was right, but her courage suddenly fled, and she dreaded what she must say. Silently she shook her head, refusing to meet his gaze. "I know something is wrong. I've seen it in your eyes. It does neither of us justice to deny it."

Maggie bit at her bottom lip, her heart thudding with remembered fear. "Matthew, I . . . I . . ."

Matthew stiffened, suddenly fearful that whatever was at the root of her suffering could tear them apart. His heartbeat accelerated tenfold. His palms suddenly began sweating. He didn't want to hear it, but he knew Maggie had to speak of it. If they were ever to rekindle what had once been between them, there could be nothing but truth. She had not been herself the last two weeks, and he knew the time spent in prison did not alone account for the change in her.

"You need not tell me if you were abused, Maggie. I know well enough what must have happened." He gathered her into his arms and cuddled her trembling form close against him. "Is that what has been bothering you?"

"Nay, Matthew. 'Tis not what you think." And after a long pause, she sighed and went on. "There was a man."

"Go on." He almost choked, feeling his body stiffen with dread.

Another moment of silence passed between them as Maggie sought out the words to tell him. He couldn't stop himself from asking, "Did you care for him, Maggie?"

Maggie nodded. "I did. He was everything kind and gentle in a world of horror."

"And this man, what did he feel for you?" Matthew asked, knowing the folly of the question, for he doubted a man lived who would not love her to desperation.

"He cared for me, I think, though he spoke most lovingly and often of his Lisbeth."

"And you say he treated you kindly?"

"Aye, he saved my life. I was nearly dead with fever, and he brought me back."

"And now you suffer a measure of guilt, believing you cared more than you should?"

"Nay, Matthew, 'twas true at first, but I've since grown to understand that my suffering caused me a measure of confusion." Her voice broke as she continued. "In truth, I suffer because I was responsible for his death."

Matthew forced aside his jealousy as he listened to her story. A long moment of silence followed when she finished, and Matthew sorted out what he had been told. Regardless of her confusion, he knew one thing as a fact. This woman loved him and him alone. He saw it in her every look, her gentle smile, her tender touch.

The time she had spent in prison had left her bewildered and believing for a time that consolation and friendship were love—indeed they were, to an extent. He could not deny that the idea of her seeking another for comfort caused him pain, but he understood. He rocked her in his arms as his huge hand smoothed her hair. It was only natural for two people in such circumstances to turn to each other.

He carefully thought of what he was about to say. "Maggie, you cannot hold yourself responsible for the villainous acts of others. It matters not that they hungered. You too suffered, and you did not resort to murder."

She did not respond.

"I know you feel a measure of regret, but your guilt is misplaced. You must put these feelings aside, for they bode no good. Will you promise, Maggie? Will you try?"

Matthew sighed at her silent nod, holding her closer. "I'm sorry he died, Maggie. I would thank him for his care of you, if I could."

Maggie laughed as Fluffy charged through the underbrush, intent on searching out the daring squirrel that taunted him daily. Her heart swelled with happiness and more contentment than she had dared hope for as she glanced at Red tethered close by. Matthew had seen to it that her horse and dog were waiting at his farm for her arrival. A soft light filled her eyes. His consideration never ceased to amaze her.

It had been three weeks since she had come to Mastic, and, but for an occasional nightmare, she felt more herself with each new day. Working at chores again had been a soothing balm to her injuries, both physical and mental. And, although Mary and Thomas Forrest had two slaves and three hired men to see to the running of their large farm, they made her feel at home by allowing her to take over the care of their horses. Maggie smiled as she clutched her shawl close against the chilling autumn wind. Mary and Thomas treated her as if she were already their daughter-in-law. She could never hope to know two nicer people. They had not questioned her about her past, although it was obvious she dressed in mourning. They knew she was a widow. And if it was not Caleb but her son for whom she mourned, no one was the wiser.

Maggie had at last come to terms with her son's death. She could think of him now with happy memories, the horror of his death fading with each day. She longed for the time when she and Matthew could have a child. Maggie smiled. She had come a long way toward being completely healed. Her only sorrow was the contemptible war, which all too often kept them apart.

Matthew had been away this past week again. Maggie knew he was on some assignment for Washington and prayed he was not in danger. Of late, her life had been filled with one emotional upheaval after another, and she longed only to live out the remaining years in peace with Matthew at her side.

"You seem deep in thought, mistress. Mayhap you are thinking of me?" asked a deep voice close behind her.

For once, Maggie did not jump with surprise. Somehow she had almost expected him since he often appeared suddenly when she thought of him. She did not turn to face him, but a radiant smile curved her lips, and laughter danced in her warm eyes. "Sir, do you believe I have nothing to do but think of a villainous scoundrel, who leaves me for weeks at a time to go heaven knows where, no doubt enjoying every minute we are apart?"

"It has been but one week, mistress," he returned as his arms slid familiarly around her and his face nestled in the curve of her neck. Matthew groaned as he felt his body respond to the mere touch of her. He sighed, accepting the ache, knowing it was beyond his power to deny it. "And a torturously slow one at that. Mayhap it felt longer to you?"

"Pray tell, why should it?" She sighed as she leaned into his warmth.

Matthew almost groaned aloud. God, it grew harder every day to resist her. He wanted to tumble her to the ground and take her there in the tall grass, but he would not. He had sworn he would wait until they married, and he could only pray she suffered as he did.

Maggie chuckled and turned in his arms, her eyes bright with happiness. She searched his face hungrily, reeling in the tender love she found there. "Indeed, sir, you seem to have fared exceedingly well." Her fingertip traced the firmness of his jaw. "I see no marked signs of dissipation marring your handsomeness. No sunken cheeks, no dull eyes, nothing, in fact, to prove your claim to have suffered at our parting."

Matthew grinned, his eyes aglow with delight. "So you perceive me handsome, do you?"

Maggie shrugged, a smile teasing the corners of her mouth. "Passably so."

"Only passably?"

Maggie laughed. "Are you in need of a compliment, sir?"

"It would not overinflate my ego to hear one occasionally, mistress."

Maggie smiled. "Would it not?" Her eyes danced with devilry as she continued, "Nay, I think many have told you of your handsomeness. I'd not be accused of bringing more swelling to your head."

Matthew grinned wryly. "Mistress, you may rest assured on that account."

Maggie giggled. "I love you, Matthew." Suddenly she danced out of his arms and eyed him shamelessly from his face to his toes and back again. A moment later she gave an elaborate shrug and sighed sadly, "What does it matter if you are a bit homely?"

Maggie tried to dart away but was instantly caught in his arms. With a short shriek, she found herself flung over his shoulder and the recipient of a smack to her bottom.

Maggie laughed, reached down, and pinched his backside, only to feel yet another well-placed blow. "You are a beast," she cried, desperately trying to control her laughter as she hung helplessly upside down, "to so abuse a lady!"

"And you, mistress, are a wretch." He smiled as he lowered her to stand before him again. "But I know when I've met my match," he sighed. "I yield."

Maggie smiled as she slowly raised her arms to encircle his neck, drawing his mouth closer to her lips. His eyes glowed with daring promise as she murmured, "Will you, sir? Will you, the handsomest of men, yield to this woman?"

Matthew's heart thudded painfully in his chest, and he closed his eyes, almost crying out as the agony came to wrack his body. How he managed, he never knew, but he smiled at her obvious attempted seduction. "Aye, mistress, I'll yield some five minutes after we leave the church."

Jacob Darning was coming for her. Even though she could not see his face clearly in the mist, she knew by the low sound of his evil laughter that it was he.

He was wearing a long, dark cloak again, his form blending almost invisibly with the night. But she could make him out. She knew it was he. Terror clutched at her heart. She had to get away. She had to hide, but where?

The bloodied knife came closer and closer still, until it filled her vision and she saw naught else. A hand raised the dripping weapon high above her head. He would plunge it now, deep into her heart, and yet she did no more than watch. Why couldn't she make her legs move? Why did she stand there waiting to die? . . .

He was there again, and she felt a rush of warmth and safety, knowing he would protect her. He moved between Darning and herself, but as she touched him he fell dead at her feet . . .

Sightless eyes stared at her. His throat was cut. There was blood everywhere. But it wasn't John. It was Matthew! It was his blood that covered her, his blood! . . .

"No!" she cried. "Matthew, please, no!"

"Maggie, wake up. You are dreaming. Can you hear me, darling? Wake up."

Maggie's arms were around his neck, desperately holding on, clutching his body to hers. She was sobbing into his naked chest. Her nightdress was soaked with perspiration, and the bedclothes were twisted from her terrified struggles. "Matthew." She shivered and sighed with relief as she finally realized she had been dreaming again. His arms tightened and pulled her closer. "I thought it was you. I thought he had killed you."

"Nay, my love. 'Twas only a dream," he assured her.

"When will they stop, Matthew? I grow fearful of sleep, lest another should assail me."

"In time, my love," he crooned as if to a child. "All will fade in time."

He held her for some time before her trembling ceased. Finally, she seemed to notice that he was in her room and without a stitch of clothing.

"Matthew!" she exclaimed. "You are not wearing anything."

Matthew laughed. "Maggie, my prim and proper miss. You know it is my habit to sleep thus."

"Suppose someone saw you?"

Matthew shrugged for an answer and then offered, "If it offends your sensibilities, I'll go back to my room and dress."

But Maggie had no wish to be alone. The dream was still too real in her mind, and she very desperately needed him with her. "Nay, stay with me."

Matthew nodded. "Let me see to the fire. 'Tis cold in here."

Maggie watched him squat to his haunches before the nearly extinguished flames. Completely unconscious of his nakedness, he added a log and poked at the embers, soon bringing some warmth to the room.

He was so beautiful. Maggie felt her heart sure to burst with the simple pleasure of watching him. Without thought, she left the bed.

Matthew turned at the sound of the floor creaking. "Get back into bed."

But Maggie ignored his order and moved toward him.

"Maggie," he warned as she stood silently at his side. Slowly she untied the gatherings at her neckline and allowed the nightshift to fall to the floor.

"Maggie, please." His eyes hungrily moved over her smooth skin. "I've sworn."

"Aye," she returned softly, "I know."

He had not loved her since before she was arrested. Maggie knew he was waiting for her to agree to marry him.

"Do you want me?" she asked, knowing his answer by the look in his eyes.

"You know what I want."

"Aye, you want me to marry you."

He could only nod, not having the strength to repeat the words yet again.

"When?" she asked softly.

"Tomorrow."

"What time?"

"What time?" he asked as if unable to comprehend her meaning.

Maggie sank to her knees before him. Her voice was soft and low with desire as her fingers ran a pattern in the dark fur of his chest. "I would know, Matthew, lest I be late."

═══ *Twenty-Five* ═══

M AGGIE," HE GROANED, HIS voice stiff with control, his mind dizzy with the promise of her words. "Have mercy, and increase not my burden."

"Nay, Matthew," Maggie soothed, her golden gaze warm and giving, her smile softly tender as she raised her mouth to his. "I'd see the end of this suffering. Name the day and time."

"And your mourning will cease?" he asked, not daring to believe he had finally persuaded her to ignore propriety.

"I'll not waste another moment worrying about others and their opinions. I want you, Matthew. I want you now." And when he seemed too astounded to do more than stare, Maggie giggled. "It appears we've exchanged roles, you and I. There was a time when you would have taken me, no matter the circumstances. And it was I who begged off." Her eyes glistened with laughter. "Mayhap I should follow your well-remembered example and speak not but act out my intentions."

Maggie's hands slid over his huge shoulders and clasped at the back of his neck. Gently she tugged until his mouth lowered to her anxiously waiting lips.

Matthew's heart raced wildly. He had waited so long for her to consent that he couldn't quite believe what was happening. His eyes closed, his brow furrowing as if in pain, as her mouth moved against his. It mattered not if she teased, for he could no longer resist her. Caught under her tantalizing spell, he growled out a feral sound as the heat of her tongue brought exquisite torture to fill his being.

His arms reached around her slim waist and caught her tightly against him. Almost rough in his sudden, uncontrollable need for her, his mouth drank thirstily of her essence, his hands hastily seeking to recapture every inch of her flesh.

What might have brought pain only a few short weeks ago now thrilled her to the core of her being. She needed this man, and if his long withheld passions caused his arms to hold her more tightly than usual, his hands to caress with more strength, and his mouth to almost punish as he sought to absorb her into him, all the better. Her senses flamed at his rough handling, and she knew naught but his touch, his scent, his taste.

His fingers moved under her hair and over her back, his heart swelling with delight as his hands cupped her rounded hips and lifted her body to brush against his arousal. This was no planned seduction on his part. He had not imagined he would find her ready to share his life at last. And he suddenly felt like a bumbling schoolboy unable to control his greedy need as he sought out what was freely offered, stamping every part of her as his with his touch.

Slowly they sank to the floor, too intent on their purpose to seek out the comfort of the bed, too enraptured with each other to notice the unyielding floor beneath the rag rug.

Maggie was dizzy and lost to conscious thought. Slowly, and with aching pleasure, his mouth, hot with desire, moved to the softness of a tempting breast.

Maggie's back arched, and she cried out as the blinding heat of his tongue slid over the tip of her breast and drew her deep into his burning mouth. She felt a fire deep within her abdomen and unconsciously lifted her hips, searching out the one means that would bring her release. Her fingers threaded through his thick black hair and pulled him closer, while her sweet, disjointed words of love nearly drove him mad.

His hands moved greedily over the familiar smoothness of her body. His fingers splayed the warm, moist flesh at the junction of her thighs, and his mind raged with but one need. He had to taste her. He had to know her again.

But Maggie was not of a mind for a leisurely taking. She had waited too long. Her need to be part of him once again was too great. And when she felt his mouth leave her breast to move down her belly, she understood his intent. Her fingers urged him back. "Nay, Matthew, I'd not dally overlong. My need, it grows to pain."

"As does mine," he murmured. He took her hands from his hair and held them to her sides. His black eyes mirrored the flames of the fire as he gazed down into his beloved's face. "I'd know all of you again, Maggie. I've waited too long for a quick taking. I've dreamed of this for months. Do not deny me this pleasure."

And at her silent acceptance of his need, he grinned. "Now, where was I?"

Maggie giggled at his look of feigned confusion. "I think about here," she returned as she pulled her hand free and pointed to a spot just below her breast.

Matthew shook his head. "You see what you've done, woman? You've made me lose my place. Now I've no alternative but to start again."

Maggie laughed with joy at his nonsense and gladly invited him to begin again, for her mouth knew no greater pleasure than the touch of his. But if Maggie felt some disappointment at his speedy release of her mouth to go on to other enjoyments, she gave no objection. The feeling of hot flame as his moist tongue tasted every part of her body soon left her mindless with the joy of his incredible love-making.

There wasn't a place his mouth didn't know, from the bottom of her feet, to the back of her knees, to her inner thighs, to the inside of her arms and between her long

tapered fingers. Maggie felt dazed. Never had she responded
so wildly.

And when his mouth came to nuzzle at the junction of her
thighs, Maggie caught the bottom of her lip and bit down
hard to prevent a cry of delight from escaping.

Somehow, she didn't know when, he had carried her to
the bed. Her hips were positioned at the edge of the feather
mattress, her feet on the floor, as he knelt between her open
legs.

Maggie was drowning in sensation. Words that once were
disjointed were no longer even words, but indistinct mum-
blings as she sought to ease the building torture that caught
her body in a vise of longing.

There were no secrets between them as his tongue slid
smoothly over her sweetness, investigating and relishing
every warm, moist crevice he found. His low moans of
pleasure filled her ears as his tongue delved deeply into the
sweet mysteries of her body. Maggie thought she would
surely die from this ecstasy. Her body tightened and
strained, begging for the release that was so near.

He felt her shudder and tremble beneath him. Her soft
cry was muffled as she grasped the bedclothes to her mouth.
Tense, tight, she was almost aching with the throbbings that
wracked her body for endless moments.

She eased back at last, taking huge gasps of air to soothe
her starved lungs, but Matthew knew, even as he felt her
pull away, that it wasn't enough. He wasn't satisfied to see
this end. He wanted more.

"Enough, enough," Maggie cried, too weak with the
aftershocks to do more than plead, but his mouth couldn't
stop. He needed to bring her again to ecstasy, to witness her
delight, for each time he mastered her body and held her
helplessly yearning in his hands, he became more enslaved.
Her taste and touch were a drug, an opiate he couldn't
resist, and he found himself a willing addict in this act of
love.

She didn't think she could bear it. She was so sensitive

that she cried out at each movement of his mouth and felt her body jerk and instinctively pull back. But the delicious ache between her legs was soon forgotten as a greater need came to take her in its hold. A tension was building again across her abdomen, tighter this time, stronger than anything she had ever known.

It was carrying her to the edge of madness, and she cared not, for if this was insanity, then she wanted never to be sane again. Her soft cries and gasps, her low moans and broken words drove Matthew on with a pride of fierce possession. He felt her harden and soften and harden again. Her body tensed, readying itself for the shock of blinding white-hot ecstasy that was at hand, and he could do naught but growl as he lifted her hips, pressing his mouth tighter and feeling the frenzied beginnings of her pulsating delirium.

"You're killing me," she sobbed weakly as the last of her tremors faded, but still his mouth sought out her sweet taste, his tongue drinking in the last of her moistness, his lips kissing and soothing her essence into his mouth.

Her body was slick with sweat as he slid up her slender frame and entered her at last. His passion was thick, hot, pulsating with blood, alive to all sensation. He filled her to overflowing. Deeper, deeper he drove, striving to take her with him on this exquisite journey of pleasure.

Maggie's back arched, and a low guttural sound escaped her throat in response to the power of his thrust. She lay helpless beneath him as he worked her body into a frenzy of tormented need, sharpening every nerve ending with delight. Again and again and still again, she reached the peak of ecstasy, each time higher, more rapturous, only to find he refused to allow her to ease back into contentment but demanded her to strive for still another. Maggie was nearly delirious as he moved against her, barely able to respond to his movements, lost in a world of enchantment.

Her head twisted back and forth as she fought to hold back what was coming, for she doubted she had the power to withstand the last. "Nay," she whimpered as she tried to crawl out from beneath him. "I cannot," she cried, but he insisted and pulled her back. "I'll not survive," she pleaded, her words broken and breathless as he gave no quarter but demanded all.

"You will," he breathed heavily against her mouth. "Let it come, Maggie, let it!" he demanded as he took her mouth, his tongue thick and insistent, absorbing her cries, stealing her breath, as his body threatened to take her very life.

Maggie groaned as the sensation began, her need to breathe forgotten as she clung to his damp, hot body, answering his powerful thrust, digging her nails into the flesh of his back, pounding her fists, urging him on, demanding of him with almost depraved excitement until she was rendered mad with the lust he instilled.

She cried out. Her body stiffened as her hips rose to take all he would give. Lights flashed behind her closed eyes, and the spasmodic throbbings lurched forward to take her in their grip, nearly splitting her in two with the force of their pulsating strength, lifting her to a plain where only ecstasy existed, holding until the final shaft of blinding pleasure-pain clutched her tightly within its fold.

Endless breathless moments passed where Maggie felt herself suspended in time. She thought she might have died, but no, the sweet sensations came to ease her gracefully into bliss, growing sweeter and more delightful as each echoing aftershock gathered her more securely within a leisurely cocoon of enchantment.

The room was silent now, except for the heavy breathing of its occupants. Matthew groaned at the effort to lift his head and smiled as he gazed down into her glistening eyes. His tongue licked at the moisture above her lip, and he opened his mouth. But whatever he was about to say was brought to a sudden halt by the soft knocking at Maggie's door.

Maggie gasped, instantly aware of the danger of being found out. In a flash, she jerked him so hard that his relaxed body went flying off the side of the bed and landed with a crash to the floor.

"Maggie, are you all right? Is something amiss?"

Maggie's heart pounded furiously as she scrambled over the edge of the bed and leaped onto Matthew's unsuspecting form. He was laughing so hard that his shaking nearly toppled her, but she clung to him, straddling his hips as she leaned forward and clamped her hand securely over his mouth.

"Mrs. Forrest?" Maggie asked, praying that the breathless fear she suffered made her voice sound sleepy.

"Yes, my dear. Is everything all right?"

"Indeed, Mrs. Forrest," Maggie returned while shooting daggers at the man who snorted merrily beneath her.

"I thought I heard sounds of crying."

Maggie leaned harder against his mouth as strangled sounds of laughter escaped through her fingers. "I was dreaming, 'tis all. I'm fine now." Maggie prayed that the woman would believe her feeble excuse and tensed, knowing she was sure to ask about the sudden crashing sound. Mary Forrest would have had to be deaf not to have heard her son hit the floor, and Maggie sighed with relief when no mention of it was made.

Mary Forrest grinned when she heard the clear sounds of a man's laughter beyond the door and instantly knew the cause of the very odd noises within. "Very well, dear. I'll see you in the morning."

"Good night, Mrs. Forrest," Maggie called. She sighed with relief as she heard the woman making her way back to her bed.

Assured that his laughter was at last under control, Maggie released Matthew's mouth. He eyed his assailant with a lecherous grin. Her damp hair was tossed wildly about her shoulders, her lips were swollen from his kisses, and her breasts swayed temptingly above his mouth as she leaned forward with relief at what she obviously considered a close call. "Mayhap the next time we make love I'll hold on. You're a mite stronger than you appear," he teased.

"If you don't lower your voice, there'll be no next time," Maggie warned.

"Yes, mistress," Matthew answered obediently. "Do you think we could get up now?"

"Oh," Maggie said, forgetting for the moment that they were on the floor.

Matthew tried to sit, but the temptation of swaying breasts above his face was more than he could ignore. His mouth took the tip of one as his thumb caressed the tip of the other. Gently he suckled, enjoying for a moment the taste and texture of her skin. Suddenly his strong arms swung her onto the bed. An instant later he joined her there with a not too gentle dive. His merriment was still evident.

"Stop laughing, you dolt. Do you want your mother to ask me to leave?"

"She cannot," he reasoned correctly. "Tomorrow you will be my wife, and as such you will have every right to remain."

"Matthew, please," she begged as she covered his mouth again. "Lower your voice. I'd not have her hear."

"'Tis too late, I fear." He chuckled softly. "No doubt she knows well enough what we were about."

"Oh no," Maggie groaned, pressing her face into his shoulder. "I'll not be able to face her again. Do you really think she heard us?"

"Darling Maggie," Matthew soothed as he cuddled her in his arms. "You need not fret. My mother is not a young girl to blush at the hint of lovemaking. She's lived on a farm all her life and knows well the workings of both humans and animals. She and my father have been married nigh on thirty-five years. Do you imagine I was an immaculate conception?"

"Matthew, be serious," Maggie returned, and before she could continue he interrupted with a long, searching kiss, his hands showing clear signs of his need to put conversation behind them.

"Is this serious enough?"

"Oh, aye," Maggie sighed as his mouth nuzzled the hollow of her throat and his hands searched for a means to appease his never-ending need for his lady.

"I swear I never imagined I'd spend my wedding day racing over the countryside." Matthew grinned as he snatched Maggie's slender form from Red's back and cuddled her close in his arms. "I have greater plans involving your delicious rump than watching it bounce upon a horse."

"We could always go back." Maggie laughed. "Mayhap you could then show me exactly what you mean."

Matthew groaned as he envisioned the mob of people that no doubt filled the farmhouse at that very moment. He knew they'd not find a moment to themselves should they return, and Matthew did not want to share this woman.

"I do not look forward to a day and night spent conversing with others."

"You were the one to insist on a speedy marriage ceremony, were you not? We could have spent the morning abed had I not been nearly dragged from its warmth by some madman intent on making me an honest woman." Maggie pouted beautifully and then shrugged. "We could have waited a day or two, but would you have it? Nay. Why, 'twas all I could do to decently cover this skinny body before you had me standing before the parson."

"I'd not chance a change of mind," Matthew grinned smugly. "After last night, I swore I'd not wait another day to make you mine." He laughed tenderly as his mouth came to nuzzle her neck. "I'd not have you believe me easy, mistress."

Maggie laughed. "Sir, it matters not our quick trip to the altar, for you are surely the easiest man I know." She shot him a daring look from beneath thick lashes and continued cockily, "Why, I could have you anywhere, anytime I choose."

"Could you?" Matthew grinned.

"Indeed," Maggie announced confidently.

"Now?"

"Where?" she asked as her gaze moved over the autumn-brown earth of the countryside, finding no likely private spot.

"Here," he returned.

"What? Here on the horse?" Maggie giggled, her eyes alight with pleasure and daring.

"You said anywhere, anytime," he taunted. "The horse will not object, at least not overmuch." He grinned as his gaze dared her to make good her words. "Was it simply an idle threat?"

"Your mother expects us back soon. You haven't forgotten she's invited the neighbors for a wedding supper."

"Ah," Matthew sighed. "'Tis as I thought. All talk and no action, Mrs. Forrest."

Maggie grinned and took his dare. She reached beneath her skirts, and, after some tugging, grunting, and adjusting her bottom, her hand came away with her drawers. Instantly they disappeared into her skirt pocket. She held tightly to his shoulders as she twisted and turned to face him, not an easy accomplishment considering the space allowed and the length of her legs.

Her bottom was bare against the saddle, her skirts adjusted and smoothed around her, her brandy-gold eyes daring him to disallow what she was about. "You'd best cover us with your cloak, sir, for I'd not have an innocent passerby be unnecessarily shocked," she advised as her fingers sought out the buttons of his pants.

To afford some privacy, Matthew brought the horse to a nearby grove of evergreens as Maggie's mouth ran over his jaw, her hands trying to release his building passion from his clothes as she whispered, "I fear we lack enough space."

Matthew sighed with pleasure as her fingers managed at last, and he lifted her and impaled her on his stiff manhood.

Matthew's eyes closed with pleasure, and Maggie cried out, her breath hissing between her teeth. Her head was flung back as he slid within her moist warmth, his body causing feelings so intense that they robbed her of her senses.

"We'll make do, I'll wager," he groaned as his lips sought out the deliciousness of her mouth, his words almost indistinguishable as he spoke against her lips, "for space is the last of our needs."

═══ *Twenty-Six* ═══

MATTHEW SCOWLED. HIS SMILE of delight at the first sight of Maggie disappeared as he watched his wife waddle from the inn toward Hannah's old cabin, her arms filled with swaddling and bunting cloth, tiny blankets, embroidered and lace-trimmed dresses, plus a small wooden tub.

With a curse, he dropped the pail, half filled with freshly caught fish, at his feet and moved quickly to her side, relieving her of her burden. "Madam," he muttered, his displeasure apparent, "I have told you repeatedly you are not to lift such weight. What must I do to ensure your obedience in this matter?"

"As you can clearly see for yourself," Maggie returned, her jaw lifting at a stubborn angle, "baby clothes are not heavy."

"Nay, not when lifted one at a time. Maggie," he warned, "I'll not repeat myself again on this subject. Do you understand?"

"Indeed," she snapped in an instant temper as she followed him inside the newly whitewashed cabin that was to be used for the coming birthing. Her added weight and the heat of the day combined to make her somewhat irritable, but it was his annoying overprotection and insistence on treating her as if she were no more than a simpleton that galled her most. Suddenly it was too much to bear, and she lashed out. "You'd see me cart one legging at a time to the cabin. At that rate, the babe will reach his first birthday before I am ready for his birth."

Matthew's chuckle at what he perceived to be a nonsensical remark was clearly the wrong response, and he stared in astonishment as the door slammed behind her suddenly running figure. Matthew cursed and lunged after her. In his haste, he nearly knocked the door from its hinges as it crashed into the wall.

Maggie realized she was acting irrationally. There were times when no one was more astonished by her actions than she. Still, no matter how she might try, she couldn't seem to help the sudden and often childish changes in mood. She was tired. Tired of carrying an extra twenty pounds. Tired of walking like a duck. And, most of all, she was tired of his concern. Don't do this, don't do that. She couldn't stand anymore. She wanted to be treated like a woman again, not some piece of fluff that would evaporate in a stiff wind. She wanted him to see her as he once had, as a woman, not simply the mother of his child.

Blinded by tears, she ran from the cabin, but she had barely managed ten feet when strong arms swung her up against his chest. Matthew carried his weeping wife back inside.

It was obvious from his pained and confused expression that he had little experience with women in the last stages of pregnancy, and he was momentarily at a loss regarding the sobbing lady in his arms. All too often a word or a look from him might send her into a tantrum, leaving him astounded by her bizarre change of character. Daily he grew more perplexed, while she became more of a shrew, neither realizing that nothing but time and patience would remedy the situation. Suddenly a terrifying thought occurred to him, and he asked with no little concern, "Do you ail, Maggie? Is it the babe?"

"The babe, the babe, the babe," she ranted, trying to push herself out of his firm embrace. "I'm sick to death of hearing you on it." She sniffed loudly and, realizing she could not break free, wiped her teary eyes on the sleeve of her shirt and continued on with her righteous self-pity. "You care more for the babe than for me."

Matthew smiled, wisely refraining from laughing out loud at her outrageous comment, for there was nothing on earth he loved more than this woman. He nuzzled his face in her hair and breathed in her sweet, clean scent. He gave a silent curse as the devastating aroma jolted his senses and brought to mind vivid pictures that were best kept at bay. He trembled and felt his body instantly come alive as a raging need almost overtook his common sense. Determinedly he pushed his longing aside and groaned, "Maggie, my love, if I could but love you less."

"Ha!" She laughed humorlessly as her angry, glistening eyes rose to meet his. "Your words are pretty, sir, but you need not pretend. I know the truth well enough."

"Do you?" he asked gently. "And what is it you know?"

"I know that since I've grown round with your child you no longer want me." She glared at him, ignoring his shocked expression. "Dare you deny it?"

Matthew looked at her with no little surprise. "I thought we could not without chancing injury!"

"Does that mean you must never touch me?"

"Maggie," he groaned, pulling her closer, "to touch you is to want you. Even now your nearness tears at my control. God, how I suffer."

It took her a long moment to digest this information, so convinced had she been of his indifference. Suddenly her eyes grew round with surprise. "Do you?" she asked almost joyfully, obviously thrilled.

"Madam, you are sitting on my lap. Has it been so long that you have forgotten the signs?"

Maggie laughed as she saw the truth in his words, for the

evidence of his need pressed against her leg. Her spirits soared; she was ecstatic. For the first time in months, she felt like a woman, the object of his desire.

Matthew suddenly groaned, knowing he couldn't resist her glowing beauty. Without a thought to the pain he was sure to suffer at this lapse of control, his lips came to caress her mouth, his fingers lifting her heavy breast.

Maggie's eyes half closed with her own need. Between breathless, heart-stopping kisses, she dared to ask boldly, "Why is it, then, that you've done nothing to ease your suffering?"

Matthew pulled back and eyed her suspiciously, for, of late, he could never be sure what she might do or say next. "What is it you suggest?"

Maggie shook her head, her cheeks coloring to a vivid red. Dare she tell him her most private thoughts? Would he think her wanton if he knew?

"Tell me, Maggie."

There was no hope for it. She would never find release if he had no inkling of how she felt. Finally she sighed. "Matthew, there is more to the act of love than the actual coupling."

Astounded, Matthew could only grin quite stupidly. He had never imagined she too felt this horrible emptiness, this endless, aching longing. He managed a teasing grin. "Have you a suggestion?"

Seeing that he was intensely interested in this conversation, Maggie gave Matthew a deliciously wicked smile and slid from his lap. As she made her way toward the door, she remarked, "I suggest we ease each other's suffering with other available means." She locked the door and turned to face him. Her heart pounded with her daring as she slowly moved toward him. Her shaking fingers quickly undid the buttons of her shirt, stopping only when her heavy breasts swayed free, and shirt and chemise lay discarded at her feet. She stood directly before his chair.

Matthew groaned as she leaned close to him, her fingers

272

easily disposing of his shirt's fastenings, her breasts swaying heavily, temptingly, before his mouth.

Matthew couldn't seem to get a full breath. His heart hammered wildly in his chest. His body felt ready to burst as his mind raced ahead, contemplating the many ways they could love each other. Why had he held himself from her? Was she right? Did he find her less desirable now that she was to have his child? He knew he did not. If anything, she grew more desirable daily. It was simply his fear and ignorance of her condition that had caused him to thwart both their needs.

Maggie smiled and reached for the fastenings of his trousers, her task causing her to drift slightly away from him as his mouth tried to nuzzle the silken flesh of her breast. Suddenly he growled and caught her to him. "Madam, I've a need to sample these delicious morsels. I advise you not to linger overlong."

"Nay, sir." She smiled invitingly. "You must have patience."

Matthew stood abruptly. He tore the shirt from his back and tugged himself free of his pants and boots. In an instant he was sitting again with Maggie positioned between his legs. A few moments later she matched him in his state of undress. Gently he guided her to his lap, his hand reaching for her breast, his mouth hungering for the sweetness of her. He murmured, "I've done with patience."

Matthew sighed as he enclosed his sleeping wife comfortably within the circle of his arms. She had been right, of course. There were many ways a man and woman could make love, and he cursed his own foolishness for the weeks of needless suffering they had both endured. In the future he would know better. It took some getting used to, this husband business.

He smiled as he realized the bedding would have to be changed again, for Maggie was anxious to set the cabin aright, readying it for the coming birth of the baby. This afternoon they had put the bed to an entirely different but most satisfying use.

Matthew sighed again. In his lifetime he had never known such utter contentment, such happiness. Peace had been signed in Paris the September past, and the British had quit American soil, leaving Maggie with no fear of returning home.

Matthew, unable to deny her her slightest wish, had brought Maggie back to the inn. Hannah had helped with Maggie's last delivery, and he knew his wife would feel more at ease in her capable hands.

Since their arrival, it had grown increasingly clear that neither relished the thought of remaining innkeepers. They were farmers at heart, finding untold pleasure in the feel and smell of the rich earth. Together they decided that Hannah and Elijah should have the inn, while Maggie's family's farmlands would be set aside for their second child.

Maggie stirred sleepily in Matthew's arms, her rounded belly pressed close to his own. Matthew suddenly laughed as the baby kicked out, apparently annoyed by the pressure.

Maggie opened her eyes, her expression puzzled as she looked up into her husband's smiling face.

"It appears the babe is already showing signs of jealousy. Apparently he objects to my loving my wife," Matthew offered as a means of explaining his laughter.

"Too bad," she murmured sleepily, a smile teasing the corners of her mouth as her tongue slid across his collarbone and her lips paused to nuzzle the pulse in his strong neck. "He'll just have to find a wife of his own."

Maggie turned to her side, frowning as she unconsciously tried to throw off the uncomfortable sensation. She pressed her back hard against Matthew, and as his soothing warm hands came to caress the ache, she slid back into sleep. Later a soft, sleepy moan escaped her lips, and she moved yet again.

In the light of the early morning, Matthew glanced at his

time piece and nodded his head. Twenty minutes, exactly. All night long he had lain awake, too excited to sleep as she had periodically tossed about. Each time she had stirred, he had been tempted to awaken her so they might share this time together, but he had not, knowing she would need all her strength to withstand what lay ahead.

Careful not to disturb her, Matthew eased himself from the bed. He would fetch her a pot of tea. His hands shook as he fastened his trousers, and he cursed his sudden need for a drink. It mattered not that it was barely dawn. The enormity of what was about to happen nearly staggered him, and he longed to hide himself in a bottle so as not to witness what he knew he must. But he'd not take the coward's way out. She'd need him today, and she'd need him with all his wits about him.

By the time Matthew returned with a steaming pot of tea, thick slices of ham, and fresh bread and butter, Maggie was sitting up, her back resting comfortably for the moment against fluffed pillows. She smiled as he carried the tray toward her. "Oh, what luxury!" she exclaimed. "Breakfast in bed." Maggie smiled as she raised her gaze to his. "To what do I owe this honor?"

"Take advantage, madam," Matthew advised, "for 'tis not often a wife, and a farmer's wife at that, is so indulged."

"I didn't sleep well last night," she remarked. She motioned for him to join her on the bed. "I suspect my time is near."

Matthew nodded. "I know. Your discomfort comes every twenty minutes."

Maggie glanced up with some concern. "Did I disturb your sleep?"

"Worry not about my sleep, darling," he answered as he poured some heavy cream into her tea. "I shall have plenty of time to sleep later." He eyed her seriously. "How do you fare?" And then, at long last, he asked the one question that had been plaguing him for months. "You will be all right?"

She smiled reassuringly, hoping to ease the helpless terror

275

that suddenly showed in her gentle giant's eyes. "I shall be fine, have no doubt. Joseph's birth was not so difficult. In truth, none is easy. Still, the worst of it lasts but a short time and is soon forgotten."

"If anything should ever happen to you . . ."

"You will take care of the baby," she insisted gently, "and perhaps one day find another to love."

Matthew suddenly found himself dangerously close to disgracing himself with tears. His throat closed up, and he couldn't swallow or speak. He shook his head dumbly. In his heart, he knew he'd never love another. Suddenly a horrifying thought occurred to him. "You don't think something will happen?"

Maggie laughed and then grimaced as another dull ache seized her back. A moment later she laughed again. "Of course something will happen, silly. You don't suppose I intend to spend the rest of my life looking like a whale, do you? We will have our baby today." Maggie giggled as she gazed at her husband. Never had she known a man so big, so confident, so virile, and, judging by the sickly gray hue of his skin, so ready to faint. Gently she rested her hand on his arm. "And if his father grows any more nervous, it may be that he'll have greater need of this bed than I."

Maggie hissed between clamped teeth, her eyes squeezed shut, her hands knotted into fists as the pain came again. It tore at her back and stiffened her body with its blinding force. Beads of perspiration dotted her skin and had already soaked through her second nightdress. She threw off the light sheet, desperate for a breath of fresh air. A fire burned in the grate, and the July sun glared pitilessly down on the tiny cabin. It was all Maggie could do to breathe.

"Sally, please, open the windows."

At Sally's nod, Matthew instantly flung open all the windows. A few moments later he managed to fasten a thick branch, heavy with leaves and broken from a maple out back, to one of the cabin's rafters. By pulling at an attached rope, he created a delicious breeze, which brought Maggie untold relief.

Maggie began to tremble. She shook so that her words were garbled and unintelligible.

"Are you cold?"

"Yes." She shivered. And then a second later, "No. I don't know why I'm shaking."

"Talk to me, Matthew," she pleaded as her teeth rattled in her head. Her words were jerky and disjointed. There wasn't a part of her that didn't tremble, and the bed fairly shook with the force of it. "Tell me a story." Maggie needed something to take her mind from her pain, and she knew it would also ease his terror to direct his thoughts elsewhere.

For a moment he was at a loss for words. Finally, he grinned as he began to relate a happening he had heard of during one of his many spying expeditions.

"Somewhere in Connecticut there lives a lady and her young daughter, known to sympathize with the rebel cause. The lady often entertained British officers with the purpose of finding any useful information that could be forwarded to Washington. As it happened, one of the king's men had grown enamored of this lady, and she managed to obtain much vital information by entertaining him in her bedroom.

"On one occasion, she was speaking to one of Washington's men when the officer came for a visit. The rebel hid, and it seems the officer was in the midst of, to put it delicately, relieving his baser instincts, when from beneath the bed came a sneeze. Mayhap the officer would never have noticed, but the lady began to laugh. At the sound of her hilarity, the man in hiding, having no notion of the officer's depth of concentration, thought his position found out and spoke out, 'You're under arrest, sir.'

"Whether because of the officer's intense preoccupation or the fact that the quilt muffled his words, no one will ever know, but the officer apparently thought the sound came from his partner. Instantly he believed the woman to be the possessor of some supernatural powers. To add to his conviction, the bed began to shake violently. In reality, the man beneath the bed was caught by the buttons of his shirt and was trying desperately to extricate himself so that he might be about his duty. Now the bed was literally lifting from the floor with his efforts.

"The officer was terrified and leaped from the bed. With his clothes in his hands, he ran naked from the house into the waiting arms of Washington's forces. The woman, obviously reading his fear and knowing well enough his thoughts, lay helplessly laughing at all that was happening around her."

Maggie found herself laughing at his story. Now and then she had asked him to repeat parts, as the pain left her exhausted and she sometimes slid into sleep between them. But amazingly, concentrating lessened the intense pain. "In truth?" she asked as her teeth clamped over her lip and another pain came.

"I've no knowledge of its truth, Maggie, merely of its being told as such."

Maggie's trembling eased, and her smile turned into a grimace of pain as yet another cramp came. Matthew was at her side again, rubbing her back, trying to soothe away her ache. The pain was splitting her back in two. Would the baby never come? It was growing dark outside. It had been hours. Ten hours at least, she estimated. Ten hours of almost endless pains, now barely a minute apart, and still the baby showed no sign of entering this world.

But no, she was wrong. Something was happening. The pain spread now, no longer centered in her back but reaching out tentacles of agony, grabbing at her abdomen and turning it harder than a tree trunk. She felt ready to burst. Had the baby grown confused and forgotten how to escape her body? Was he trying to exit through her belly? She felt a pressure and a need to push that couldn't be controlled. Maggie gasped and gave a guttural groan as the need blocked out all else. Her head twisted back and forth over the damp pillow, and she tried uselessly to stop what was sure to be. She didn't want this. She changed her mind. "I cannot," she groaned. "Wait! Stop! Help me, please. I'm not going to make it!"

Matthew was instantly terrified, and his words came angrily to hide his fears. "You're going to make it, Maggie, damn you. Jesus, do you think I've waited all day just to see you give up now?"

"Go to hell," she growled as she glared into her husband's determined face. "I know what I can . . . Oh! It's coming again!"

"Let it come, Maggie, don't fight it."

"I'm too tired," she gasped. "I can't do it anymore."

Matthew was beside himself with panic. Never having witnessed a birth before, he knew nothing of the wild speech of a woman in the last moments of delivery, and he took her words to heart. He was terrified as he grabbed at her shoulders and gave her a hard shake. "Do it! Do you hear me? I said do it!"

"Get the hell out of here." Maggie glared as the pressure eased, only to start again. "Get out!" She didn't care that she had obviously hurt him. At that moment she couldn't stand the sight of him. She hated him. She hated them all. All they could do was stand there and watch her suffer. Not one of them could do a damned thing. But when she felt him start to rise from the bed, she clutched at his shirt and screamed, "No! Don't go!"

The veins stood out in her neck, and her face turned cherry red as she bore down. Matthew held her upper body close to him, willing her the strength she needed.

Maggie gasped for air and pushed again. She could feel her body widening. It was coming. She wanted to cry out with relief, but she hadn't the time before the urge to push was again upon her. It was almost over.

Her eyes glistened with tears of joy as Hannah remarked nonchalantly, "By the looks of his face, I'd say you have a son."

Maggie clung to Matthew's shoulders and laughed as she pushed again.

Matthew watched his wife with awe. He couldn't believe it. She was laughing. Between her straining and groaning, and what he imagined to be agonizing pain, she was laughing!

With a new surge of strength, Maggie pushed again, and the baby eased itself gently from her body. It was covered with blood and horribly wrinkled, the tiniest creature he had ever seen. But it was so beautiful that he couldn't hold back his tears. It was a boy! Matthew thought his heart would burst with joy at hearing his high-pitched cry fill the cabin.

"Maggie, you did it!" He was so amazed that he couldn't do anything but stare at her, his eyes wet and beaming with pride.

"Of course I did it, silly. Did you think I wouldn't?" But Maggie's lighthearted words were suddenly replaced by a deep gasp. Another pain ripped at her, and the pressure to push came upon her yet again.

"Hannah!" she called out as the woman finished tying off the cord and handed the tiny baby to Sally for her to clean. "Hannah, something is wrong!"

Hannah's eyes's narrowed with suspicion, and her hand moved to Maggie's still extended abdomen. She felt the hard contraction and grinned. "Nothin' wrong here, child. Your man done you proud. Two for the work a one."

Maggie laughed as understanding set in. But Matthew was totally confused. "What is it? What's wrong?"

She was pushing again, but this time, with less than half the effort, another tiny head appeared.

Matthew was stunned. All three women laughed as a baby girl came squalling into the world. He was going to faint. He couldn't take it. It was too much to ask of any man.

Maggie looked with pride at her husband and grinned. "Mayhap you should lie beside me, darling. You don't look at all well."

He turned away, sitting on the side of the bed with his head in his hands, and his back to the women. Suddenly Sally was standing before him, pushing a tankard half filled with rum into his numb fingers and lifting the vessel to his face. "Come on, drink it. I have other babies to attend to."

Matthew gasped as he swallowed the brew in one gulp. It cleared the fuzziness from his brain, and he felt immeasurably better. But he was suddenly embarrassed, and the sly smiles the women were giving him as they went about their chores didn't help. Hannah was taking something that looked like a huge piece of liver out of Maggie, and Matthew couldn't control his low groan as a wave of dizziness overcame him. Then she was cleaning his wife and staunching the flow of blood with thickly folded cloth. Sally was busy with the second baby, and Maggie was exclaiming over the beauty of the first, whom she now held in her arms.

For a moment he felt useless and totally mortified to have displayed such weakness. Sheepishly, he glanced at Hannah, who was now humming. "You ain't got no need to feel bad, Mr. Forrest. My Elijah midwifed me when James came, and after he was all through he fainted dead away at my feet." She grinned knowingly. "You'll get used to it. Next time it will be easier."

Matthew looked aghast, his eyes huge with horror. "Next time!" And all three women laughed as he groaned, "Jesus, I can't go through this again."

═══ Twenty-Seven ═══

Maggie grinned as she watched her husband. Matthew's eyes glowed with pride, and his hands were clasped behind his back as he moved almost cockily between the two cradles, each holding a sleeping baby. It had been more than two months since their birth, but time had obviously not begun to dim the thrill of fatherhood. "Mighty proud of yourself, I'd say."

Matthew shot a glance at his wife, who was sitting in a small chair near the fireplace. She was putting the last touches on yet another tiny dress, while a teasing grin played at the corners of her delicious mouth.

Matthew moved to sit opposite her, drinking in the sight of her loveliness. "I'd say I had every right, madam."

"Perhaps," she granted, and then she smiled as she glanced up from her sewing. "Still, your swagger daily grows more similar to a prize-winning rooster's. Indeed, one might fear the throwing out of your back with your chest so puffed."

Matthew laughed. "Well, I did have a hand in it."

"No doubt." Maggie chuckled, her eyes aglow with a decidedly wicked light. "But as time passes, memory fails, and I seem to forget exactly how you were involved."

Matthew gave her a long, steady look, his body instantly throbbing with a desire only she could arouse. His voice held a husky note as he recognized her deliberate taunt. "Do you? Mayhap I could refresh your memory."

Maggie looked him straight in the eye, her cheeks flushing with the promise of passion. The air seemed to crackle between them as she boldly answered his veiled suggestion. "Would you?"

"Come here, madam, and we'll see if we cannot put this memory of yours to right."

Matthew's eyes glowed with pleasure as he watched his wife put aside her sewing and rise to her feet.

It was evening, and Maggie, in the privacy of their rooms, had long since discarded her mobcap. Her thick hair fell loosely in soft waves about her face and shoulders, a silky veil of fire reaching to her waist. Her skin was creamy white, having lost the light tan of summer, while her form was nothing less than outstanding. In the short time since the babies were born, she had regained her former slimness, and, while her breasts had always been large, now that she nursed they were enormous.

"I'm at your service, sir." The twinkle of anticipation belied her long, weary, dramatic sigh. "Do your worst."

Matthew laughed at her magnanimous attitude as he came to his feet. "You portray the sacrificing virgin with a flair, madam."

"Indeed?" Maggie couldn't prevent her lips from twisting into a grin. "'Tis been a very long time since I've had cause to worry on that score."

Matthew gave a wicked leer. "Much to my pleasure, I'm sure." His mouth lowered to graze the white column of her throat, and she shivered with longing, her voice already thick and husky.

"And mine."

Slowly, his fingers worked the fastenings of her blouse until her breasts fell free. He couldn't pull his gaze away, mesmerized by the loveliness displayed before him. "You are so beautiful."

He had watched her nurse the babies countless times, his

love and pride knowing no bounds. Yet he couldn't deny the tiny stab of jealousy that they should have what he could no longer claim. With a twinge of guilt he had often fantasized about the taste of their nourishment, for there was nothing about her he didn't ache to know. Matthew lowered his mouth and licked away the moisture his gentle handling had brought to the tip.

"Maggie," he groaned. He instantly tore his mouth from her lest he give in to this sinful impulse. He nuzzled his cheek upon her soft flesh. His body trembled with desire, his mind plagued with guilt that he should dare to want what was not his to take. Determinedly, he pushed aside the urge to suckle.

But Maggie seemed to know his most secret thoughts and gently reassured him. "You need not fear, Matthew. The babies have already taken what they will. More will come when needed."

"But . . ." His eyes, wide with astonishment, came level with hers, and he groaned as her hips moved suggestively against him. He felt the return of a paralyzing ache that grew in seconds to a throbbing, living pain, hewn razor sharp over the last two months of celibacy.

Maggie's eyes dared him to retain his control. "You take nothing from them and only add to my pleasure. Please."

Matthew felt no need to resist her gentle plea as her hand offered her breast to his mouth. With a groan, he swooped down and greedily took her sweetness into him.

Maggie felt her knees buckle with the pleasure that filled her body. Instantly she was lifted high in his arms, and seconds later she found herself through the connecting doors, lying across the feather mattress. His mouth never left the softness of her flesh as he eased her out of her remaining clothes.

"I'd not hurt you, Maggie, but I fear I've waited too long to remember the gentle art."

Maggie laughed with delight, her hands cupping his face

so that her tongue could slide across his parted lips. "Worry not about gentleness, Matthew. You will not hurt me."

"That's it! I'm going to find a wet nurse. One more interruption like this will be the end of me." Matthew eyed his baby son, Michael, suspiciously. "I swear they know. I can just hear him telling Mary, 'Come on, he's trying to get at her again.'"

Maggie laughed at his outrageous comments as the baby snuggled close to her breast, almost choking as he drank greedily from his mother. "I'll not allow another to feed these two, Matthew."

"Madam, I ask not that you totally give it up, only that you occasionally allow another to care for them, thereby giving this poor husband of yours a turn at your affections. At this rate they may never know another sibling."

Maggie smiled as he closed her and the baby in his arms, and she shivered as his hand cupped her unoccupied breast. Perhaps he was right, Maggie reasoned. She could use a break now and then. Taking care of two babies was tiring. Many nights she fell exhausted into bed, her one and only prayer, "Please, God, let them sleep." Matthew was right too about the interruptions they suffered at the most inopportune moments. Of late, she had been hesitant to begin an intimate encounter for fear of having to stop midway, and she had no wish to see that part of their marriage suffer.

"I'll ask Hannah tomorrow, Matthew. Mayhap she knows of someone."

Matthew sighed and snuggled closer to his wife. At birth the babies had shared the weight of a half-stone, and it had been many months before their mother and father could rest easy with the surety of their survival. Now, as he watched the chubby bundle suckle in his wife's arms, Matthew couldn't prevent a smile from curving his lips. "Do you think they are ready to go home? It would not cause them injury to travel?"

"Are you anxious to return to the farm?"

"Aye, Maggie. There is much to be done to secure the house against the coming winter. My father is old, and I'd not see the chore fall to him again."

"I see no reason to delay. The babies grow stronger and healthier every day. Would the end of the week suit?"

Maggie snuggled deeper into the warmth of the soft mattress and groaned as the high-pitched cry dragged her unwillingly from sleep. "Will they never sleep the night through?" she muttered as she stumbled through the dark doorway and into the tiny nursery.

Maggie sighed with longing. Perhaps tomorrow they would find a wet nurse and she'd be able to sleep. It was more difficult than they had first imagined, since the woman would have to move with them to Matthew's farm. So far, they had found no one willing to make such a journey.

A menacing shadow passed silently along the wall, but Maggie, in her sleepy state, felt no premonition of fear. She leaned over her daughter and gently rubbed her back. Knowing it was too soon to feed them again, she soothed, "Do you have a bubble, sweetheart?"

Out of the dark, an arm reached around her, and Maggie would have smiled but for the pressure given. Suddenly her heart thudded with alarm, for she knew in an instant it was not Matthew who held her.

Maggie opened her mouth to scream and found to her horror a sickly sweet scented cloth clamped tightly over her nose and mouth. She began to choke, but each gasping breath she took only brought in more of the scent and caused her to sink closer to oblivion.

Maggie never struggled. In truth, she didn't even have the time to think. In a matter of seconds she was unconscious.

Strong arms slung her limp form over a thickly muscled shoulder, and regardless of the cold autumn night, she was taken from the inn clad only in her thin nightshift.

* * *

Matthew stirred as the babies' cries grew steadily in strength. Sleepily, he reached a hand toward his wife, only to find her side of the bed empty. Puzzled, he raised his head and glanced toward the dark nursery. He had never known the babies to wail so. Maggie had always seen to their care at their first cries.

Matthew groaned and rolled from the bed, a frown creasing his brow as the crying grew louder still. What the hell was going on? he wondered. What was Maggie about that the little ones should cry so?

He stubbed his toe on a rocking chair, and a curse cut into the cries that were clearly becoming hysterical. Who the hell had moved it away from the wall? And where was Maggie?

He felt the first inkling of dread at finding the room empty but for the two squalling babies. But then he reasoned that she must have gone downstairs for something.

Matthew called out, receiving only silence for an answer. He made the stairs in two leaps. A quick examination of the first floor only made his heart lurch with fear. The kitchen door was ajar.

In his bare feet, Matthew raced outside, oblivious to the thin layer of newly fallen snow. Where in God's name had she gone? Again and again he called out, hearing only the echoing of his own voice for an answer. Panic set in. His mind was a jumble of crazed thoughts. He imagined she had run away but instantly realized the absurdity of that notion. Maybe she had need of the outhouse, although he couldn't imagine why she wouldn't have used the chamber pot at that time of night. He imagined her dead or injured. Perhaps she had fallen and couldn't call out for help. With great dread, he forced himself to search the area carefully. Had there been some trouble? If so, why hadn't she awakened him? Grasping at straws, he headed for Hannah's old cabin, praying all the way that he would find her there. But Matthew knew what he would find long before he entered the small darkened structure. Still, he called out and searched every corner of the cabin.

He was clearly in a panic now. For a long moment he found himself taking huge breaths, trying to clear his mind, desperate to think what to do next. He returned to the inn to find Hannah and Elijah, each holding an infant, helplessly trying to soothe their cries.

Matthew returned to his room, dressing faster than he ever had in his life. Almost flying down the stairs, he was outside before James, who pointed out in the newly fallen snow the clear sign of a carriage's recent visit.

Matthew studied the trail of narrow wheels as it moved from the inn's back door to the Post Road. He gave a round of violent curses. In his heart he knew Maggie had been taken, and his greatest fear was being unable to find her amid the many trails that covered the road.

But Matthew was wrong in his expectations. It was still the middle of the night, and most folks were abed. The road was marked with but one set of wheels.

Matthew and James armed themselves and saddled their horses. In ten minutes they were already some miles from the inn, racing down the road, following the trail in the snow toward New York.

Matthew wanted to cry out his rage. It was starting to snow again. If they didn't come to the end of the trail within minutes, there'd be no trail at all. Matthew pushed his horse to its limit, heedless of the hazard the snow caused the horse's footing. He had to find her. Please, God, he had to find her! His hands were frozen. But he barely noticed the chills that wracked his body.

Matthew pulled his horse to a sudden stop, almost losing his seat as he did so. They were at a crossroads. His curses filled the silent night as he furiously searched for a continuation of the trail. More than one vehicle had passed that way in the last hour.

It was James who found it some one hundred feet beyond the junction, and the two were off again, racing against time and nature.

Mile after mile was quickly swallowed by racing hooves. Neither Matthew nor James gave his mount a moment's rest. Maggie was somewhere at the end of this trail, and no doubt her life depended on their reaching her in all haste.

The horses were lathered, and their misty breath showed clearly in the biting cold night. The two men pulled to an abrupt stop as the sight of a three-story house loomed up ahead. The trail of carriage wheels had turned into its long drive, and even now a dark, closed carriage stood ominously silent before the wide doors of the white building.

Despite the cold, sweat ran down Matthew's back, and he prayed they had not blundered and followed the wrong vehicle. Silently, they dismounted and tethered the animals to a hitching post just behind the house.

They made their way to the house. Instead of approaching the door, they moved to a ground-floor window and peered inside. Matthew gasped as he took in the sight of a dozen or so nearly naked women sitting in a comfortable-looking parlor.

It was clear this was a bawdy house. The question was, why would someone have taken Maggie to such a place? If the man's intent was to assault his wife, why take her so far away to do it? Surely the madam would not permit a woman to be brought struggling from the street. How was she to make a profit if men brought their own inside?

What the hell was going on?

Suddenly Matthew pulled back from the window. Peggy! So this was where she had gone to set up business. But what did she have to do with Maggie? Matthew knew that Caleb and Peggy had once been lovers. At the time he had not cared, for in his own mind the man's obvious disinterest in his wife had merely furthered his own cause.

Matthew looked into James's puzzled face. Neither could understand what was happening, until James gave a sudden gasp. Matthew looked back into the room and was equally astonished. Peggy had walked toward a man who was sitting with his back to the window. She smiled as his hand reached familiarly into her low bodice and lifted a plump breast free of the bright red material.

But it wasn't until she sat at the man's side and reached to caress between his legs that the man turned and Matthew and James saw his profile.

Caleb! Sweet Jesus! Caleb was alive! Who, then, had they found in the ashes?

Caleb leaned toward Peggy and whispered something. Peggy laughed and called out a moment later. At her call, a giant black man entered the room. A word or two passed among the three, and Caleb was lifted in the man's arms and brought to the stairs. They disappeared as the black man began to climb the steps.

Maggie stirred and moaned as she slowly regained consciousness. She was chilled, and her body shivered uncontrollably. How had it gotten so cold? Had Matthew not stoked the fire before they retired? Suddenly she gasped. The babies! They'd need extra covering in this temperature. But as she tried to rise, she grew confused. Something was holding her back. Maggie tugged but could not bring her arms closer to her body.

Suddenly wide awake, Maggie opened her eyes and found herself in a strange room. Her hands and feet were tied to the corners of a four-poster bed. Something was wound around her mouth, and she couldn't speak. She lifted her head and looked down at her naked body. What in God's name had happened? Where was she?

Suddenly a low sound of laughter made her head turn to her side. She almost sighed with relief, for now she knew she was sleeping. What a god-awful dream! Next to her sat Caleb. Beside him was a vaguely familiar woman. Maggie watched with some amazement as the woman lowered her head and took Caleb's hardened member deep into her mouth.

Why should she dream such a thing? But as Maggie continued to stare, she became slowly aware that this was *not* a dream. Her eyes widened with astonishment, and she gave a soft sound of protest. It couldn't be! But it was. Caleb was alive. He was here! Now! Laughing as a woman made love to him on the same bed on which she lay. His eyes never left her, and he grinned obscenely as his hands moved over Maggie's naked body. A gloating look was in his eyes.

Maggie closed her eyes and shuddered with disgust, but Caleb's evil laugh brought her gaze back to the couple.

"Thought I was dead, did you?" He laughed again. "Nay, 'twas that stupid bastard Jack you found in the ashes. I trust you did not shed too many tears, my love." Caleb's fingers pinched at her sensitive breasts before trailing idly to the junction of her thighs. Finding no obstacle to prevent his entry, he thrust his fingers into her soft flesh, uncaring of the fact that she was obviously dry and his touch brought discomfort. "You cannot imagine how much I hate you, how much I've always hated you. You ruined my life, and I've waited a long time for the chance to return the favor."

He chuckled gleefully. "You, my dear, if you survive this night, will serve our best customers. This will be your first lesson on how to please a man. From past experience, I'd say you'll need many."

Maggie moaned as his fingers violated her body, but her horror and disgust only seemed to bring him greater joy.

"Stop, Peggy," he ordered as he pulled the redheaded woman from him. "Your mouth feels too good tonight, and I wouldn't want my beautiful wife to see the end of this so soon." He grinned evilly, "Nay, I'd see her pleasure lasts as long as ours."

"Move over here, Peg," he directed. He wiggled his hand between Maggie's thighs and then laughed as her eyes grew round with terror, for she instinctively knew what was to come. "That's it," he remarked as the whore positioned herself between Maggie's immobile legs.

Maggie's scream of horror was muffled against the rags tied around her mouth. Caleb laughed with pure joy as Peggy began to caress her most secret of places.

Maggie trembled under the woman's light touch. This was a nightmare, worse than anything she could ever have imagined. She had never, not even in the midst of Samuel's assault, felt such revulsion.

With a great deal of effort, she forced her nausea aside. Maggie dared not allow the sensation, for she had no doubt that these two would watch her choke to death rather than release her gag.

For an instant the thought of death beckoned alluringly, but Maggie's anger quickly squashed the notion. To be sure, she'd find release from this horror in death, but suddenly it was not release she sought. It was revenge she wanted. She almost laughed as wild pictures of Caleb's approaching death danced in her mind's eye. This dirt deserved not a moment's pity, and she prayed only to live long enough to see his end.

Maggie soon realized, with no little amazement, that if she concentrated hard enough, she could not feel their cruel caresses and taunting pinches. Like the animals they were, they could use her body, but her mind would be forever free. She wasn't there, not in the true sense. She was with Matthew and her babies. She was laughing at something, she couldn't remember what, but the feeling of happiness persisted.

Maggie's senses appeared dull, but in truth they had never been so acute. She could hear things she had never before noticed, like the ticking of some faraway clock and the gentle patter of heavy snow as it hit the window pane. Their breathing sounded loud and harsh, and the musky scent of sweating bodies and sex was nearly overpowering. Her anger and hopes for revenge dissolved into nothingness. She would have smiled had the gag allowed. She was going mad, of this she was sure, but she cared not.

"Jeremiah!" Caleb called out, suddenly filled with disgust. His anger was provoked when his wife showed no reaction to his lover's sensual advances. "Come here and see if you can get this bitch to show a glimmer of life." With a long, weary sigh, he continued, "Jesus, I've forgotten just how dull and dreary she could be."

The large black man came from the shadows and into the shaft of light that illuminated the bed. Maggie closed her eyes, refusing to acknowledge what was about to happen, when a sharp slap to her face made her instantly aware of her new situation.

Caleb laughed as he watched her eyes fill with terror. Maggie moaned with fear as the man stripped the clothes from his body, and she couldn't control the shudder that raced up her spine.

This giant wasn't about to let her ignore his presence. Every time Maggie closed her eyes, he slapped her again. Helplessly, Maggie groaned as her eyes were drawn to his naked body. Her eyes grew round with horror. The man was diseased! His already stiff organ was covered with open sores. If she survived this, she too would be riddled with them.

She closed her eyes again and received still another slap. She didn't care. He could beat her to death. She wouldn't watch. Maggie moaned as another slap left her seeing stars. Still another caught her nose, and blood squirted everywhere.

Maggie was in serious trouble now. Not only was she about to be raped, but she couldn't breathe, for blood filled her nose. It ran over her cheeks and soaked her hair.

It was one thing to wish death upon oneself but quite another to face the gruesome promise headon. Maggie fought with the last of her strength to save herself. The wooden posts creaked at her straining. But the ropes at her wrists and ankles refused to give as she fought her desperate battle for freedom. The ropes tore at her skin, splitting the delicate layers until bare flesh showed raw. In her struggles, small vessels broke, and blood, rich in color and warm against her cold skin, began to seep down her arms and dribble on the white sheets.

She couldn't go on much longer. Already a dark, misty cloud was forming around the edge of her consciousness, causing everything to appear in slow motion. Maggie watched as Caleb's lips parted in a grin. His hands slid over her body, and his low, evil laughter filled the room as the cold fingers of death beckoned her ever closer.

The black man was above her now. Maggie knew her mind was playing tricks on her, but she couldn't find it within herself to care. The man's face grew oddly distorted, as if she were watching the scene through a defective mirror. His lips thickened grotesquely until they seemed to cover most of his face, and Maggie wondered if she was not dreaming after all.

His punishing shaft stood hard, oozing and menacing, while an evil smile showed several missing teeth as he positioned himself above her. Maggie closed her eyes, praying for a quick end. Her low cry of horror came from deep within her soul, a cry she heard echo again and again in her brain until it became one endless moan of terror. He fell upon her.

Matthew and James entered the house by way of the darkened kitchen and stealthily made their way up the back stairs. Now and then a woman could be heard laughing from beyond closed doors, but neither man gave a thought to being discovered. No one but Caleb would question their presence there.

One of the many doors that lined the second-floor hall opened, and a small blonde stepped out. "Jesus, ain't you a piece?" came a soft, breathless exclamation. "You wouldn't be looking for me, would you?"

Matthew stopped dead, his heart pounding furiously against his ribs, his hand resting casually on the revolver at his hip. He had a time of it, but finally managed a smile. "In truth, I was looking for Peggy."

"Aw, Peggy ain't so much." She eyed him lustfully, her gaze lingering at the junction of his thighs. Suddenly her hand reached out and caressed him, her voice low and throaty as she leaned close. "I could show you a good time. I'd even take your friend with you, if you want."

Matthew almost gagged at the suffocating mixture of stale perfume and body odor. Her breath was disgusting, and he fought against a shiver. But the blonde felt the slight motion and laughed, taking it for desire.

He could have given her a story, made up some excuse, but that would have taken time, and right now he had not a moment to spare. Maggie was somewhere in this house, and he didn't dare look for her at his leisure.

The blonde never knew what hit her. She was standing and fondling what she supposed to be a prospective client, when suddenly fireworks exploded inside her head. The last thing she remembered before all went black were the pretty lights.

Matthew allowed James to drag the whore into the room from whence she had come, while he continued down the long corridor. Matthew eased open door after door, sometimes to find the room empty but more often to find a couple too intent on what they were doing to notice the intrusion.

Matthew began to panic as he and James found themselves at the stairs leading to the third floor. They had checked every room, and Maggie was nowhere to be found.

Silently they mounted the steps. Matthew prayed he'd find her in time.

They were halfway down the third-floor hall when the muffled sounds of heart-rending screams broke the eerie silence. Matthew's blood ran cold to the marrow of his bones. He knew it was Maggie, but in his terror he couldn't decide where the sound had come from. James darted ahead.

Guns drawn, they crashed into the room, smashing the door into the wall with the force of their entry. Three faces turned in shock. A glance at the two men left no one in doubt that their last moments on earth were clearly at hand.

Matthew's fury was directed at the huge man who was about to abuse his wife. Instinctively, his hand tightened around his pistol, and when the man fell upon Maggie, most of his face was no more.

Maggie lay still, covered with blood and oddly shaped pieces of soft gray matter, but blessedly knowing naught of the carnage that surrounded her. She had succumbed to her terror and slid mercifully into unconsciousness.

Caleb knew his end had come. The woman at his side was already dead, but he cared not. The warm blood seeping from her lifeless body brought not a flicker of concern. He began to plead for his life. He raised his hands before him, as if to ward off the next shot, and seemed about to speak when a small, neat hole formed just above his collarbone, instantly cutting off anything he might have said.

Dumbly, he looked down, intent on finding the cause of his suddenly garbled speech and the fiery pain, but, as he did, he found to his amazement that his jaw had just as suddenly disappeared. A black hand holding a gun blocked out all else from his mind. James's lips curled away from gleaming white teeth. The gruesome smile alone would have frozen the heart of the bravest man, and Caleb would have screamed with terror had he seen it. But he did not, for his eyes were already beginning to close. In a dazed fog, he slumped at Maggie's side and listened to the last words he would hear before God's judgment: "For my friend, Mr. Caleb, sa'."

=== Twenty-Eight ===

MATTHEW SMILED, HIS LONG sigh of pleasure bittersweet, as he listened to the sounds of laughter. How long had it been since she had relaxed in his presence and laughed so easily?

Pushing aside the foliage, he led the horses toward the sound. He spied his two dark-haired toddlers moving as fast as their unsteady, chubby legs would allow toward an excited Fluffy. Their high-pitched screams of delight, accompanied by Maggie's soft, gentle laughter, should have been a balm to his soul, but it had been many months since he had felt the luxury of contentment.

It had been a little more than six months since the filth she was once married to had died, and even though Matthew rarely allowed an hour to pass when he didn't give thanks for her safety, he was thoroughly frustrated. Since her rescue, Maggie had been his wife in name only, and he could not ease the tension between them.

But Matthew was determined that today would see the end of his dilemma. He understood her trauma, but the longer he waited for her recuperation, the more she withdrew into a frozen shell. Night after endless night, they were left in the tormenting throes of their own private hells. Restless and shaken, they lay side by side, neither daring to acknowledge awareness of the other. Yet each knew the other could not sleep.

Maggie gave a stiff smile as her husband came into view. "Have you finished for the day?"

Matthew nodded as he tethered the horses and came to sit at her side. "I've left the men to finish up." His eyes darkened with concern and his gaze tenderly caressed her strained features. He dared to add, "It's been some time since we were alone. I thought we might ride and picnic this afternoon."

A pulse pounded in her throat, and Maggie felt a wave of excitement engulf her, but as always the excitement turned instantly to dread. Her gaze moved to her children as she spoke. "What about the babies?"

"Katie will be along presently to take them back. She will feed and bed them tonight."

"No!" Maggie gasped, her dread accelerating to fear, for she had no doubt what her husband was about. "They will fuss. They need me there."

Matthew put his hand over her nervously fidgeting fingers. "Nay, Maggie, I need you more."

Maggie nearly groaned aloud. Her eyes looked like those of a cornered animal, and she felt petrified with fear. She couldn't be alone with him. He would want to make love with her, and she'd die if she were ever touched again. She shuddered uncontrollably. She couldn't bear the thought of it.

Maggie rose to her feet, ready to take flight. She'd not stay and await her final humiliation. That part of marriage was finished for her. Caleb had seen to that. Never again would she be a plaything for a man. Not even for the man she loved above all else. She still loved Matthew, but love wasn't enough, not anymore. Too many memories persisted, too much horror.

They had spoken of this before. Maggie had hinted that if Matthew desired another to slake his passions, she'd not object. To her surprise, he had not taken to her suggestion. He had become very angry indeed, protesting that he wanted no other but her, and storming from their room.

Matthew moved quickly to stand at her side. His steely arm came instantly around her and prevented her from leaping away as Katie arrived in the little clearing and began to bundle up the children.

A moment later they stood alone. Maggie felt a panic that nearly left her paralyzed. Her voice was shaking as she pleaded desperately, "Matthew, please. Do not do this. I'm not ready."

He sighed softly as he took her stiff form against him. "It must be thus. You will never be ready on your own. The horror grows as each day passes."

"No! I cannot," she nearly screeched as his hand moved familiarly to her rump. She broke free and darted for her horse. In a flash, she swung herself up onto Red's back and left a dumbfounded Matthew to watch in helpless frustration. But a moment later a light of determination came to his eyes, and he too mounted his horse and gave chase.

Maggie, heedless of the lack of proper riding attire, bent low over the animal's head as she galloped wildly over the countryside. Skirts flying, she cared not that most of her leg was exposed to any who might happen by. Her one and only thought was to escape. But Maggie had not reckoned with the determination of her husband to see things set right between them.

Her heart pounded with terror, almost choking her with its force as she heard the sounds of racing hooves behind her. Desperately, she urged Red on. Maggie did not think of her actions or the eventual consequences should she succeed in escaping him. She thought only of that moment and her desperate need to leave him behind. Recklessly, despite the obvious danger to Red, she gave the horse full rein.

Maggie was destined not to get her wish, for Matthew was just as relentless. He pushed his horse harder, faster, knowing he was gaining on her, knowing today would see the end of their estrangement.

Maggie turned Red to the left as they cleared the brush

and came to the water's edge. With nothing to impede their progress, Maggie urged her horse faster, faster, down the almost endless stretch of rocky sand.

Strong arms lifted her easily from her saddle, but Maggie screamed and fought like one gone mad as she tried to jump free of Matthew's hold.

Matthew pulled his horse to a stop and quickly dismounted, dragging a struggling Maggie with him. He took her by the shoulders and shook her until she thought her head might snap from her shoulders. "Stop fighting me, damn it! Why won't you listen? Why won't you give us a chance?"

Maggie reached out and clawed at his face. Matthew cursed and instantly released her as the smarting pain brought tears to his eyes.

Maggie only knew she must take the chance and flee. On her feet now, she lunged back into the foliage, creating a zigzag trail, praying she'd lose him. She ran as fast as her legs could carry her. Branches slapped at her unprotected face and scratched her arms. Twigs tore her skirt, ripping away chunks of material as she tried to elude him. But Maggie gave no thought to scratches and torn clothing. She had to get away. Indeed, she believed her life depended on it.

Maggie veered toward the water again, and just as it came into sight she found herself suddenly lying flat on her face. At first she thought she had simply tripped over something and fallen. It took a full moment for her to realize she had been tackled, for the heavy weight on her back could not be rationalized at first.

Matthew's breath was heavy and harsh to her ears. She screamed as all the old terrors returned full force with the sound. Suddenly she was back with Caleb, tied helplessly to the posts of a bed, knowing she would be forced once again to endure his evil actions.

Matthew flipped her easily to her back. His hand muffled her tormented screams and forced her eyes to his face. His voice was still breathless as he spoke. "'Tis I, Maggie. Do you know me?"

It took a few moments before Maggie's eyes lost their glazed look, and she finally gave a silent nod. Her chest heaved as she gasped for her next breath, desperately trying to come to grips with her fears. "Let me up, Matthew."

Matthew smiled down at his wife's lovely, if frightened, face. "Nay, love. 'Tis time to put this thing to right."

Maggie stiffened again, her eyes wild with fright. "Matthew, please! I cannot. I'll not be able to bear it should you take me by force."

Matthew gazed down at his wife and felt an unmistakable stirring in his loins. She was beautiful in her dishevelment. Her hair framed her flushed face in wild glory, her eyes flashed golden fire in her fear, and her chest heaved with her rapid breathing. He questioned his ability to hold to his control.

But when he spoke at last, he knew he'd not give in to his mad desire. Not this time. "I'll not take you by force, darling. We've been through much, you and I, perhaps too much, but we will fight this, and together we will win."

"I'm afraid," she said, her voice breaking as tears filled her eyes.

"I know, darling, but we must conquer this fear. If not, we shall never again know the love we once shared."

"Find it with another, then, damn it. Leave me be."

Matthew chuckled at her simplistic answer. "Maggie, there is no other for me but you. I love you and only you." He lowered his mouth to caress her cheek. "Trust me, Maggie. Trust me to love you. Trust me to make it right."

Maggie's lips were tight and unyield' as his mouth brushed tender kisses upon them. Her body grew stiffer than ever. She'd not give in to his disgusting lust. If he meant to take her, he'd have to do it without her consent, for she'd never give in, never!

Maggie was forcing her mind away. She'd not be a party to this lechery. She wanted none of it.

Matthew could feel her withdrawal and increased the pressure of his mouth. "Maggie," he murmured gently, "I love you, remember, I love you."

Maggie fought against the sound of his voice, for it was doing things to her insides, things she had believed she could never feel again, should never feel again.

Suddenly tears began to stream from her eyes, and huge, wracking sobs tore at her chest and throat. With a groan, Matthew rolled to his side and gently pulled her into his arms. For the first time in months, she was really crying, and he knew she needed that release above all else. The pain she held within was eating at her like a cancer, squeezing her love to death, until she knew naught but pain, suffering, and fear.

He held her gently, waiting patiently for the tears to stop of their own accord. He'd not rush her, not now when she might never have more need of his patience and understanding.

Maggie's tears went on and on, until she thought they might never stop. When at last they did, they seemed to leave a great emptiness in their wake. It was only Matthew's tender words and warm caresses that brought a soothing balm to her aching spirit.

An hour passed, and Maggie, exhausted from the upheaval, dozed in the comforting security of his arms. His dark eyes were tenderly exploring her face when she awoke, and Maggie felt embarrassed at her loss of control.

Gently she disengaged herself from his arms and sat, while her fingers fidgeted with her skirt. She was clearly nervous to be alone in his company.

"I'm sorry," she murmured, not looking at him as she spoke. "I've been acting so horridly. You've every right to be angry."

Matthew gently tugged her back to his side. "Maggie, you've no need to apologize. I can only imagine the horrors that burden you so. Let me help you."

"Do you think you can make them go away if we make love?"

"Nay, my love. Only time will accomplish that feat. But I can soothe, I can make you happy again."

"But I am happy, Matthew. I have the children. They fill my life with joy."

Matthew couldn't prevent the flicker of sadness in his eyes at the absence of his name on her tongue. But he pushed aside his own needs determinedly and concentrated his attention on hers. "There is more, Maggie, than children. Much more."

His lips sought out hers, and he almost shouted with joy as he felt her soften in his arms. It was a beginning, to be sure. If she was not yet an equal participant in the kiss, at least she was not fighting him.

Maggie sighed as his mouth moved from hers to nuzzle the skin of her cheek and jaw. His tongue flicked out and tasted the sensitive flesh beneath her ear, and Matthew felt her suddenly stiffen. "Slow, Maggie," he whispered. "I promise to take it slow, and if you truly cannot bear it we will stop." He groaned softly at his own words, for he knew not from where he would gather the strength to do so.

She relaxed again, enjoying the feel of his mouth as it caressed her throat. She moaned softly as he returned to take her mouth again.

He lifted his mouth from hers, his gaze intent on her softened features as he opened the bodice of her dress. Matthew couldn't suppress his gasp as her full breasts tumbled free of her garments and filled his hands to overflowing.

A look of alarm flickered in her eyes, and she almost pulled back. "'Tis Matthew, Maggie. I'll never hurt you," he assured her, holding himself rigidly still until he felt her relax again.

Matthew's tongue slid erotically around the tips of her breasts, slowly, achingly slowly until her body began to throb with a need she could have sworn had died. Gently he eased her out of her clothing, never hesitating until she lay naked before him, never easing his loving assault on her mouth and breasts until Maggie, despite her fears, felt her heart melting beneath the magic of his mouth.

With the tenderest of smiles, Maggie sat up again. This time she did not avert her gaze from his but reveled in the knowledge that her love had brought fire again to his dark eyes, a fire she no longer feared. On her knees, she reached for the fastenings of his shirt. Matthew was instantly facing her, his hands helping her to dispose of his clothing.

He took her in his arms and pressed her cool body close to his heated form. His eyes half closed, and he sighed with a pleasure that knew no bounds. Suddenly his mouth was on hers, cautiously exploring. He knew that a hurried and careless action on his part could bring her beautiful responses to an abrupt end.

His hands slid down her back, while his lips gave extra care to her soft, giving mouth. She was breathless and dizzy by the time he released her lips and lowered his mouth to suckle at her breast. Her arms came around his neck, lest she wobble and fall out of his light embrace. She held him to her as she felt her body responding to his lovemaking. Suddenly she knew she needed more than kisses.

Maggie sighed as he laid her upon his shirt, and she greedily received the homage he paid to her breasts. By the time he had slid between her legs, she was wild for him, but his gentle probing suddenly and abruptly eradicated every trace of passion he had so diligently stirred to life.

Her body tensed as he entered her, and once again she found herself back in the room with Caleb and his evil comrades. "No!" she cried as she desperately tried to free herself. But Matthew was not lost in his passion. He had purposely and firmly kept his head. Quickly he took her hands in his and raised them over her head.

Being held prisoner in his arms only increased Maggie's

agitation, and she fought with new determination to be free. "Maggie," Matthew soothed her as he held her firmly in place and gently caressed her face with his free hand and lips. "Maggie, my love, it's Matthew. Can you hear me?"

Slowly the veil of terror cleared from her eyes, and she began to relax beneath him. "Do you know I love you?"

Maggie nodded her head, but her wary look would not dissipate. Even yet she was afraid. *He is your husband, Maggie. You have suffered no cruelty at his hands. You can trust him,* she told herself.

Matthew began to move his body against hers. Still, he did not release her hands, for he was not unconscious of the fact that she held herself stiff and unyielding beneath him.

"Let go, Maggie," he coaxed as he continued his movement and brought his mouth to hers again. "Let go of your fears. Give them to me."

Maggie groaned as his tender words and the motion of his hips and mouth erased the last of her terror. Suddenly, and without thought, she was answering the movement of his hips as her mouth greedily sucked his tongue.

"Matthew!" she cried out as his movements grew more forceful and frenzied. He released her hands and groaned as she cupped his hips as if to guide him closer, the pressure of her hands leaving him no doubt of her need.

Matthew's tongue delved deep into her mouth, imitating the movement of his hips, and Maggie could only groan as the aching pressure of ever-growing need mounted until she knew nothing but the taste and feel of this one loving man.

The lovers lay helplessly gasping for air, their bodies slick with sweat, cooling in the early-evening breeze, replete in the aftermath of fiery love.

Matthew smiled as he rolled away from her and gathered her nearly limp body to rest on him. It was some time before Maggie gained the strength to raise her head and look down at her husband's satisfied expression.

"Gloating, are we?" She chuckled softly as she brushed her hips against his.

"Woman," he sighed as he closed his eyes, his body closer to exhaustion than he could ever remember, "I'd say I've every right to gloat. You gave me the hardest battle I've ever fought." He sighed with exaggerated satisfaction. "Ah, but the prize . . ."

Maggie laughed. "I take it the prize was worth the effort?"

Matthew's eyes were aglow with love. "What do you think?"

Maggie laughed as she leaned back and rested her head on her propped-up elbow. Idly she traced a pattern in the hairs of his chest. "I think I love you too much."

"Do you?"

"Do I what?" she asked coyly.

"Love me, damn it."

Maggie laughed at his frustration. "Do you need to constantly hear the words, Matthew? Do not my actions prove it louder than if I screamed it from a mountaintop?"

"I need both."

Maggie smiled and whispered gently, lowering her mouth and teasing his face with fluttery soft kisses. "I love you," she said, and then finished by mimicking his own "damn it."

"Madam," he grunted as he pulled her down to lie flat against him again, "you are a wretch."

Maggie giggled. "Such extravagant praise, sir, will surely turn my head.

"Oh, Matthew, look," she exclaimed as the setting sun lit up the sky and left a dark glow of shimmering pink on the still waters of the Sound, bathing the two of them in magenta fire.

Matthew's soft chuckle was muffled as he nuzzled her throat. "It happened again."

Maggie, confused at first, soon joined his laughter as she remembered the time it had suddenly stopped storming when they had made love and they had joked about their ability to harness nature. "'Tis no surprise to me."

Matthew gazed down at his precious wife, waiting for her to go on. "From the first moment I saw you, I knew you had the power to make me see red."

About the Author

PATRICIA PELLICANE lives on Long Island, New York, with her husband and their six children. She loves to read, particularly about America's Revolutionary War. *Desire's Rebel* is her fifth novel. Readers can write to her at Post Office Box 2250, North Babylon, N.Y. 11703.